To My Family

New Beginnings

Anne Marie Busch

iUniverse, Inc.
New York Bloomington

New Beginnings

Copyright © 2009 by Anne Marie Busch

All rights reserved. No part of this book may be used or reproduced by any means, graphic, electronic, or mechanical, including photocopying, recording, taping or by any information storage retrieval system without the written permission of the publisher except in the case of brief quotations embodied in critical articles and reviews.

This is a work of fiction. All of the characters, names, incidents, organizations, and dialogue in this novel are either the products of the author's imagination or are used fictitiously.

iUniverse books may be ordered through booksellers or by contacting:

iUniverse
1663 Liberty Drive
Bloomington, IN 47403
www.iuniverse.com
1-800-Authors (1-800-288-4677)

Because of the dynamic nature of the Internet, any Web addresses or links contained in this book may have changed since publication and may no longer be valid. The views expressed in this work are solely those of the author and do not necessarily reflect the views of the publisher, and the publisher hereby disclaims any responsibility for them.

ISBN: 978-1-4401-5109-5 (sc)
ISBN: 978-1-4401-5110-1 (ebk)

Printed in the United States of America

iUniverse rev. date: 7/29/2009

Chapter One

A CELEBRATION

John Stanton had a house full of guests. His son Scott had finally graduated from Becktown-Devonwood High School, and today was the celebration of his achievement. John's large two story house was full of guests. They were in the great room, with it's high ceiling, fireplace and paintings. They were in the dining room and kitchen. Most of them were outside, including about two dozen of Scott's friends who were lounging and fooling around by the pool.

John would have been much happier with a party that was intimate, with just family and close friends. But this party had much more than that. There were many people there that he barely knew, and others that he didn't even like. Most of these people were invited by his wife, Darlene, and he knew from experience that it was best not to argue about it. Darlene had made all the plans and sent out all the invitations. She wanted to make a good impression to the right people, and John was forced to deal with the consequences. This was the catered party that she wanted. At least someone was happy. John was not.

A bit claustrophobic, John wanted to get away from the crowds, but was stuck playing the good host, opening wine bottles and running other little errands that Darlene had found for him when she was not happy with the caterers. He was introduced to various important people and was very uncomfortable because he hated to make small talk, especially with people that he did not necessarily like very much. He longed for a free moment, and wanted to get away to re-group and nurse a small headache that was beginning to form in his brain.

John finally managed to somehow slalom through the well-wishers and escape to his bedroom up the stairs. He closed the door and looked at himself in the large rectangular mirror. He checked his appearance to see if anything was out of place. Upon close inspection, he noticed that a few gray hairs had appeared on the sides of head by the sideburn area, but it was not enough to notice in his full head of short, wavy, light brown hair. He figured that it was just a another consequence of three years of marriage to Darlene, who at times could make life a bit difficult.

He took off his linen sport coat and placed it on the floral designed king sized bed and breathed a sigh of relief. He turned to peek out of the curtain and looked into his large backyard full of guests. He watched the teenagers jumping into the pool, and the people milling about. He was happy to be away from everyone, and hoped that no one noticed that he was missing. He felt a little naughty hiding out in his bedroom, but at that moment, he did not care. He was finally free … for however long that freedom would last.

He reached into a dresser drawer next to the bed and took out a framed picture, and sat on the floor. As he looked at the picture, he stroked it lovingly and kissed it.

"You should have been here Jen," he said wistfully as he gazed at the picture of his first wife, Jenny and their two children that was taken twelve years before, "you would have been so proud of him."

It was times like these that he missed her the most. Jennifer Channing Stanton was his first love. They met in high school and married while in college. She gave birth to his two children. First, there was the birth of Scott, eighteen years ago. Two years later, they were blessed with the arrival of their daughter, Margaret. They were together for eleven wonderful years. Then, suddenly she was gone. Breast Cancer had taken her away.

He shook his head to try to break out of the melancholic feeling that was starting to develop. Whenever he thought about that time in his life, the painful feeling of loss always came back. Even eight years later, the pain was almost too much to bear. But, even though life was Jenny had been cut so terribly short, if he had the choice, he would have done it again.

He heard his name being called from down the hall. He wiped a small tear from his right eye and stood up onto his feet, quickly putting his tan sport coat on over his light blue buttoned down shirt. He managed to hide the picture of Jennifer back into its sanctuary before the door was opened. He returned to his place in front of the mirror and combed his hair.

A few seconds later, Darlene appeared at the door in a sleek black dress.

"John, you have guests downstairs who are wondering where you are," she said, acting as if the guests were forming a search party to find him. She was visibly annoyed at him, and tapped her feet as if she was a principal scolding a naughty child that was sent to her office.

"I'll be right down, Darlene." John said.

New Beginnings

"This is so embarrassing," she scolded. "The least you could do was to stay and help me out down there. This party is for your son's graduation. We have a houseful of guests and you're hibernating in the bedroom. What will people think?"

"Don't exaggerate, Darlene. I've only been here for five minutes," he groaned, as he watched her face and neck turn red as her temper rose. He hoped that this would not lead to another of her famous explosions.

"I'll never understand you, John, I've invited some very important people down there. The least that you can do is pretend to be a good host," she said with a mocking tone. "I'm doing this all for you."

"That's laughable," he said sarcastically, knowing that his reply would have the desired effect.

"How could you say that to me?" She asked, through clenched, unnaturally white teeth. She glared at him furiously.

"You are more concerned about yourself, and you know it."

"Excuse me?"

"I think that you know what I mean, Darlene. This party may be for Scott, but it's all about you and your image. What was wrong with having a party that was just with the family and good friends?"

"Maybe that is not enough for me."

"This is not about you, Darlene."

"What's new? It's never about me. It's always about Jenny and her parents, and your precious children. I will never be good enough."

"Darlene, come on. We've been through this hundreds of times. Jenny is gone," he explained.

"Said the man who constantly looks at that damned picture."

John did not now how to reply, and Darlene realized that what she suspected was true. This was not the first time he had done this. As he searched for the right words to say, Darlene decided to break the silence.

"I'm going to go back downstairs. I expect you to do the same," she demanded. Then she spun around, whipping her long blond hair, and walked off in a huff.

John returned downstairs. He didn't want her to get started, and have another excuse for unpleasant behavior. This was Scott's celebration, and John didn't want anything to ruin the day. He decided to try and play the good husband and party host to the best of his ability.

John returned to his post, and was introduced to a few off the small town dignitaries that Darlene pushed upon him. He shook hands with the mayor, the chief of police and their wives, both of whom were polite and seemed to be enjoying themselves. He mingled and made small talk until Darlene dragged him over to say hello to her work colleagues.

As he shook hands and played the good host, his thoughts drifted back to the picture of Jenny and the kids. How he longed for her. He was desperate for the affection that was so abundant in his first marriage, but was so lacking in his second. He needed emotional support from his wife and was starved for true companionship. Darlene was incapable of both.

After being sent towards the kitchen to open another special bottle of wine, which in Darlene's words was "only for the important guests and not for the bartender to pour out willy-nilly", John was met by his son, Scott.

"What did she do, read you the riot act?" The tall, blond haired young man asked, with a bit of concern in his steel blue gray eyes.

"What else is new?" John said as he shrugged his shoulders.

"Doesn't she ever cut you a break?" Scott asked.

"Scott, it's fine ... don't worry about it." John said to his confidante as he patted him on the shoulder. As they conversed, they walked into the kitchen.

As John started to open the bottle of wine, Scott leaned his body against the kitchen counter. It was a rather large kitchen, with stainless steel appliances and light brown cabinets. The newly renovated marble counters were covered with food and the kitchen itself was busy with caterers rushing by.

"Dad, do you know even half the people that are here today?" Scott asked with a bit of that humor that John had grown so dependant upon.

"Nope." He said as he opened the cork on the bottle.

"I didn't think so."

It was at that moment that John's sixteen year old daughter Maggie approached the two of them in the kitchen. She had a look of disgust on her flushed, heart-shaped face. This expression was very familiar.

"What is it, sweetheart?" John asked.

"Dad, she's driving me crazy." Maggie said, then she proceeded to name off a laundry list of Darlene's faults for the day.

"I'm sorry, Maggie, but you know how she gets when she has a party. It's a lot of work and stress. She does not handle anxiety well."

"But does she have to treat all of us like garbage? Especially you?" Maggie asked. "You bend over backwards all the time, and for what?"

"Maggie, I can handle it."

"Dad, you have to say something to her. Stick up for yourself." Scott insisted.

"I will." He lied.

"You won't ... I know you. You never stick up for yourself. You just let her walk all over you." Maggie pointed out.

"Maggie ... come on ... let's just try to enjoy what's left of this party." He begged.

He patted her on the back to try to comfort her, but it was of no use. Maggie was determined to have her say. When Maggie was determined, there was no stopping her.

"Dad, I can't take another summer with Darlene. I want to go Gram and Gramps house this summer."

"What?" he asked as he looked up at the guilt in her piercing blue eyes.

"I want to go home with them today. I can't stand Darlene anymore."

"Maggie ... Don't do this to me." John begged. "Can we discuss this later?"

"Dad ... they are here now. I know that if I don't leave with them now, I will be stuck here all summer."

"Would that be so bad?"

"Dad, you know that I love you. I'm sorry if it seems like I am deserting you, but as far as Darlene goes ... I'm sorry Dad. I need to get away from her!"

"What did your grandparents say?"

"They are all for it, as long as you agree with it. Please Dad, save me."

"How long do you want to stay?" He asked as he held his head in his hands.

"Until August, at least. I have to be back before soccer practice begins."

He wished that she had not confronted him in the kitchen while he had a house full of guests, but it was part of her plan. She knew that she was putting him on the spot, but she was determined to have her way. She wanted to get away from the house, even if it meant that she would be away from her father, brother and friends, especially her best friend Lizzy, who lived next door.

John thought about his predicament. Jenny's parents loved Maggie very much and there was no one in this world he trusted more than them when it came to looking after his children, other than his own mother. He knew that Maggie needed some space away from Darlene, but the prospect of spending the summer without seeing Maggie's cherubic face every day was heart-breaking.

"There you are." Darlene said with a stern expression as she walked into the kitchen and saw the covert Stanton gathering. "Can you all stop hiding in the kitchen please? We have company."

"We are not hiding, Darlene." John explained.

"John, did you open up that bottle of merlot?"

"Yes." John sighed, exhausted at being barked at once again. John handed her the bottle, and she turned to Scott.

"Scott, you should be out there with your guests. This is a party for you, you know."

"I know."

"Well ... get out there!" She ordered. Scott rolled his eyes and stormed out of the kitchen.

"I don't understand you people!" Darlene said, "I go through all this trouble and for what?"

"Darlene ... please ... don't blow this out of proportion. We are not hiding in the kitchen. We just wanted a private area where we could talk."

"About what?"

"Darlene ... that is between Maggie and myself."

"So, it's none of my business?" Darlene asked, a bit insulted. "Does my opinion even matter to you people? Maybe it would be better if I just left."

"Darlene...don't get upset." John begged. "I'll come wherever you want, okay?"

"Then meet me in the great room. A couple of more guests have arrived that I want you to welcome."

"Fine." He said as she left the room, special bottle in hand. When she left, the air seemed to return to the area.

"Daddy..." Maggie pleaded with her best imploring eyes.

"Maggie, I know what you are going to say."

"Please Daddy. Let me go. I need a break from the drama."

John walked into the great room, and he shook hands with two of the people that he liked least, George Cooper and his wife Patricia. George Cooper was a high-priced lawyer with a very inflated opinion about himself. He was one of those men that thought that he was too big and important for the small town that they lived in. He oozed pomposity with his expensive country club clothing and jewelry. His wife was his perfect match.

He looked around at the decorations and complimented a giddy Darlene on her talent for interior design.

"It looks like you have finally gotten the hang of this decorating thing, Darlene." George said in a condescending way as Darlene poured he and his wife a glass of the special wine. Darlene took his critique as praise and offered to give him a tour of the newly renovated kitchen, which she had supervised. John noticed that her face lit up when she talked to George, as if she was ecstatic that he was impressed by her talents. John rolled his eyes as he saw his wife jump through hoops for the egotist.

As George and Darlene withdrew to the kitchen, John was left to make uncomfortable conversation with Patricia and her children, Trent and Frank, who seemed bored with the whole occasion.

"We're taking Trent on a cruise to the Mediterranean." Patricia bragged.

"Is that so?" John said, feigning interest.

"Yes. Next month. Graduation present." Patricia said through her plastic face. That face had seen more upgrades than a laptop computer. "George's law firm is doing so well this year. A lot of divorces, you know. People just can't seem to stay married anymore."

She continued to babble on, and John searched around the room for something to save him. He finally set his eyes upon Jenny's parents who were sitting on the couch talking to his mother, and saw his escape hatch. "Can you excuse me for a second, Patricia?"

Jenny's parents, Anne and Robert Channing, were sitting and talking to his mother, Rita Stanton. His mother had taken a plane from Florida with John's sister Marilyn for the important occasion, and he really did not have two seconds to spend with them since the party started.

When John walked over to talk to the small group, Rita noticed that he had a pained expression on his face as a result of a recent altercation with his wife, which was overheard by those close to the kitchen. Even though John tried to pretend that all was well, his mother could see that it was not.

"Did you take an Advil for that headache, Johnny?" His mother asked, knowing from experience when her son had a headache.

"How did you know?"

"I'm your mother, Johnny. I can see when you are in pain."

"It's just the crowd, Mom."

"Johnny, why do you put up with that woman?"

"Mom, please, don't start," he begged.

"I just never will understand what you saw in her."

"I know, Mom, I know. You have mentioned that several times."

"Rita, we really should stay out of it." Anne whispered. Anne was always cool headed and sensible. Unlike Rita, she always hated confrontations.

"Anne, I am fed up with that woman. Jenny would have never treated John like that. You know that."

"I know, dear, but Jenny is not here." Anne reasoned, "Darlene is his wife now. We cannot interfere."

"I don't like it, John. You deserve better."

"Mom ... please. Don't make a scene." John begged his mother as he put his hand beside his aching head. The sweat started to bead up around his temples as he was afraid that his mother was getting a little restless. He looked around to see if Darlene had returned from the kitchen to witness the scene, but she was nowhere to be found.

"Mom, what are you doing?" John's sister, Marilyn said in a hushed tone as she handed her mother another glass of red wine that she had retrieved from the bartender.

"I'm just pointing out to your brother that he should stick up for himself. Your father would not have put up with it."

"I'm not Dad." he reminded her, speaking of his father who had died fifteen years ago from a sudden heart attack. He was a primary doctor and active in the Becktown Community, and John sometimes felt that his father's shoes were very big to fill.

"Johnny, I'm not trying to insult you. I know you are different than your father. I just hate to see you suffer."

"Mom, stay out of it." Marilyn insisted.

"I just can't wait to leave this place tomorrow. That woman would drive anyone to drink." Rita said, as she took a gulp of wine.

As Rita drank her wine, John called his sister over a few steps to ask a question.

"Marilyn, how many of those has she had?" John asked in a whisper.

"A couple ... not too many."

"Just watch her. I don't want a scene tonight." He said, then he turned and walked back in the direction of the kitchen to find his wife, and a couple of Advils for his head. Once John returned to the kitchen, Rita turned to Anne to ask a question.

Are you still saying the novena?" Rita said under her breath.

"Every day." Anne replied in a whisper.

"Me too. Unfortunately, the Iron Maiden is still here."

"God must have a plan." Anne explained.

Rita Stanton was good at making scenes. She was not the type to keep quiet when she saw something that she thought was not right. In this case, she saw that her son was hurting, and she didn't like it. Her boisterous attitude was heightened, on occasion, if she had imbibed a couple of glasses of wine. She was not a heavy drinker, but when she did have a few too many, she often said or did things that she should not. John hoped that this was not going to be one of those occasions.

Thankfully, Rita held her tongue and never did make he scene that John had dreaded. John was thankful for that. Even though he did see her make comments now and then to her captive audience in the great room, he was satisfied that she did not yell them out.

Once back in the kitchen, John thought again about Maggie's request. Then, he thought about Robert and Anne Channing. Robert and Anne were wonderful people. They were the kind of people that would give you the shirts off their back. They were invaluable to he and Jenny in their first years of marriage, and even though Jenny had been gone for ten years, he still considered them as second parents.

He searched for the bottle of pain pills, and found them. After taking a couple of Advils to stem the tide of his headache, he turned to find Anne suddenly standing before him. He was a little startled, because he did not hear her approach.

"Johnny, you look like you have something on your mind." Anne said.

"I talked to Maggie."

"Oh ..." Anne said with a bit of guilt as she put her hand on his shoulder, knowing what that conversation had been.

"Do you really want her to stay with you for a month?"

"Johnny, only if you agree. But, of course we will take her. We love to have Maggie around. She is no trouble at all."

"But, a month?" John asked, "that's a long time."

"It doesn't have to be a month, Johnny. I think that she just needs a couple of weeks. You know, to get away." Anne said sweetly.

"I think that I can live without seeing her for a couple of weeks. I don't know what I'm going to do without her, though." He sighed.

He knew that once Maggie was gone, Scott would be spending the summer working as a lifeguard at the local lake and going out with his friends at night. John would be left with Darlene, and she never seemed to be home. But, even when she was home, he felt more alone than anything else. However, he could not let Maggie suffer just because he needed her companionship. After much soul searching, he decided that he would let her go.

After toasts, well wishes, graduation cake and gifts, the guests had finally started to disperse, one by one. All that was left was a large mess, that thankfully, was being handled by the catering company. Robert and Anne prepared themselves to leave, which meant that Maggie would leave as well.

When the time came, Maggie tearfully said goodbye to her father. As he hugged her, he realized how much she resembled Jenny. She had long, wavy brown hair that reached midway down the back of her well trimmed figure. She had Jenny's mannerisms as well. It was almost uncanny. She was no longer the little girl who he used to push on the swing in the backyard in the little house that he shared with Jenny. Maggie was a young woman now.

He embraced Anne, and she told him that she missed him.

"Johnny, you should come by more often. We miss you."

"I know, Mom." he replied.

"I still consider you my son, you know. Even though Jenny is gone and you are with Darlene now. You are still welcome in my home. Both of you."

"I know. I will try," he replied.

He knew that he could never bring Darlene to Robert and Anne's house. She had a very difficult time dealing with the fact that he had a previous life where he was so contented. For some reason, she had serious reservations about anything that had to do with Jenny. Whenever he and the children visited Robert and Anne, Darlene never wanted to join them.

He shook Robert's hand and Robert patted him on the back. Then, Scott said goodbye to his grandparents and thanked them. John gazed at Maggie and gave her another hug.

"I'm going to miss you, beautiful. These few weeks are not going to be the same without you."

"Come visit me, Daddy. On the weekend."

"I'll try to get there soon." He replied. "Have a good time, sweetheart. Call me once in a while, won't you?"

"I will, Daddy." she said as she kissed him on the cheek.

With that, she was out the door. Immediately, he regretted letting her go. However, it was for the best. He only wanted Maggie to be happy, and she was more content to stay with her grandparents. He just wished that he was not going to miss her so much.

After the guests were gone and John said good night to his mother and sister in the guest room, John showered and changed for bed. He walked into his bedroom intent on making love to his wife, but was spurned like so many other times before.

"John, I'm tired," was all that she could say.

The next day, John and his mother, sister and son attended Sunday Mass at St. Joseph's, John's local Catholic parish. Darlene did not partake, which was no surprise. Darlene was never much for organized religion, and often scoffed at John's faithfulness, calling it a waste of time. These views did not endear her to her mother and sister-in-law, but she never really wanted their approval, and did not care.

After the mass, John drove his mother and sister to the airport, where they said their final goodbyes. When he returned home, he walked into an empty house. Scott was working at the lake, and Darlene was nowhere to be found, probably out with her friends. He reveled in the peace of these quiet moments. He grabbed a Coors from the refrigerator, walked into the family room and turned on the television. He sat down, use the remote to switch to a Yankee game, and relaxed.

Chapter Two

A TYPICAL DAY

John had his own pediatric practice in the middle of the town of Devonwood, NJ. Devonwood was a quiet town with several small shopping centers and medical centers and one main road that connected it to all the other larger towns and highways. It was a beautiful town with large wooded areas and several lakes, and because of those lakes, it used to be a popular vacation destination for weary people from New York City. Years later, Devonwood was a thriving community with people of all types and incomes, with houses big and small. There were several elementary schools, a middle school and a high school that was shared with it's neighboring town, Becktown.

On a typical day, John arrived at nine in the morning. and left at five in the evening, with lunch at around noon, depending on which way the wind blew at times. He had two employees. Janice was his nurse and his first employee and he has known her for ten years. She was there when he proudly opened his doors for the first time and has been there through good times and bad, and was one of his closest friends.

Nadine, the receptionist, was hired three years after the office doors were opened. Once the business was full of activity, there were not enough hours in the day to handle all the paperwork. John needed an extra hand to help out, and Nadine answered the call. Nadine has been there for five years, and he could not imagine running the office without her.

This day was like any other in the summer. Most of the appointments scheduled were for sports physicals or check ups. There was an infant coming in at eleven o'clock for shots. Pretty basic stuff. There were appointments up until closing time, and it was going to be a long day.

Even his lunch was booked up. Patricia Cooper was coming in to solicit a donation for the football program in town. John hated when Darlene's friends came in to ask for things. There was a certain air about these women.

They were all so artificial. Patricia Cooper was one of the worst. Of all the appointments in the day, this is the one that he dreaded the most.

At nine o'clock, Pete McNally was in examination room one. Pete was thirteen and was there for a physical examination for football. In examination room two was eighteen month old Sammy Braskin. He was there for a check up and immunizations. More shots were required in exam room three, where six month old Theresa Bryant waited for her immunizations. It was going to be an interesting morning, with a lot of tears.

The morning progressed in pretty much the same way. There were screaming babies from top to bottom on this day, with adolescent check ups in between. Mondays were always packed, since he did not keep weekend hours. When lunchtime finally came, he had barely touched his sandwich when Nadine's voice came over the intercom.

"Dr. Stanton, Mrs. Cooper is here to see you."

"I'll be right out, Nadine, thank you." He replied.

He stood up, adjusted his tie and coat, and prepared to meet Mrs. Cooper. He glanced back at his sandwich, and folded it back up, placing it back in the bag. Hopefully, this would be a short meeting and he'd be able to eat.

He walked out into the waiting room and put out his hand.

"Nice to see you again, Patricia." He lied.

"Hello John, how are you?" Patricia asked.

She asked it in a way that really didn't expect a reply. She was a tall and very glamorous woman, with blond hair that obviously came from a bottle. She had tanned skin that was due to a tanning machine, and John could swear that her eyes looked different than the last time he saw her. She probably had some kind of plastic surgery or botox to take care of that, John guessed. There was really nothing real about Patricia Cooper. She reminded him of a mannequin or a Barbie doll.

He watched her saunter into the direction of his office, and he glanced back at Nadine and Janice while rolling his eyes.

"Would either of you like to stay and take this meeting?" He begged. Both of them giggled quietly.

"I'm sorry Dr. Stanton, we are going to lunch." Janice replied with a sly smile.

"Okay …"John sighed, "I hope to see you both in an hour … if I survive."

With that, John began the long walk down the hall.

The meeting was more of the same. A donation was needed for the football team, as expected. Soon, the conversation was again about her wonderful son Trent, who was the same age as Scott. Trent had graduated at the top of the class and had been accepted at an Ivy league school, which Patricia was sure to point out.

As she gushed on about how Trent wanted to be a lawyer "just like his father", John found his attention wandering off. He always remembered Trent as the spoiled child that used to come into the examination room, jump on the scale and touch everything. John also recalled how his son, Scott had told him stories about how Trent behaved at school. Trent went through girls like they were possessions. When used, Trent just threw them away for a never model. This son that she was gushing about was in fact, a fiend.

"Perfect lawyer material", he laughed to himself.

Although, he was looking in her direction, and she could not tell that he was staring into space, he was daydreaming and constantly had to re-focus. He glanced at the clock and it was nearly twelve-thirty. He prayed for something to save him from this meeting. He tried to think of some kind of way to excuse himself. As if on cue, the phone rang.

"It's my personal line," he said, trying not to look too relieved.

"My goodness ... look at the time! I better get going, then!" She squealed.

He stood up, shook her hand quickly and picked up the phone receiver.

As she left, he reached inside his lunch bag again, trying to retrieve his lunch with one hand, while holding the phone to his ear with the other.

"Hello?" He asked.

"John, did you remember to pick up the dry-cleaning?" Darlene asked.

"I haven't been able to get out the office yet, your friend Patricia just left."

"I need it for tonight. I just found out that I have to show a house at five o'clock."

"Darlene, I have appointments throughout the day. I cannot be home until at least five-thirty."

"Can't you just cancel them?"

"Of course I can't do that, Darlene, you know that."

"Forget it. I don't know why I ask you to do these things for me. I can never count on you," she said. He could tell that she was infuriated.

"Darlene, you know that Mondays are always booked up. Can't you just wear something else?"

"John, I'll pick it up, okay?" She yelled.

"Okay," he answered.

"Don't wait up for me tonight. I'm going out after the showing with Brad and Tanya."

"Whatever," he sighed.

As he hung up the phone he was in a state of shock. What just happened? He felt like he had just been hit by a truck. Unfortunately, he had that feeling more and more as the months had passed. Darlene was not the person that he married. She was so distant, and at times seemed disgusted at the sight of him. Even his choice of career was not good enough for her anymore. Suddenly her job as a real estate agent was the all-consuming important thing in her life.

He looked at his sandwich, and he had lost his appetite. He threw the lunch in the trash can beside the desk, leaned back in his chair and closed his eyes wishing to be transported to another time and place.

Eventually, he heard the front door open, and two chattering women walked into the office. He heard footsteps down the hall and there was a knock on his door.

"Come in, it's open," he said as Janice peeked in.

"We're back, Johnny," she said. Then she noticed the exasperated look on his face. She knew that this face was not the result of a visit from the famous Mrs. Cooper. This look was definitely a result of a argument with his wife.

"What did she do now?" Janice asked with concern.

"It's nothing," he replied. He did not want to hear another one of Janice's lectures about Darlene.

"When are you going to give up, John, it's not working"

"It's not that bad," he lied.

"John, in the last two years you have been the most unhappy person that I know. When are you going to wake up?"

John did not have a response, he just shrugged his shoulders. She raised her eyebrows and decided that she would leave him along with his thoughts.

At around six o'clock, John came home to an empty house. Maggie was at the Channing home and Scott was out with his friends Pal and Ben, leaving a note on the hallway table as usual. His sizable house could often be a lonely place, and this was one of those nights. He decided to take his mind off of his loneliness go for a quick swim in the pool.

Once inside and refreshed, he walked into the kitchen and searched for something to eat. The kitchen was spotless because the maid had been there earlier in the day and everything smelled sterile. He opened the refrigerator and as he searched for sustenance, he grabbed a raw baby carrot out of Darlene's forbidden salad stash. As usual, there were no leftovers to heat up in the microwave. Once again, dinner was in a box in the freezer.

He grabbed a box of frozen lasagna, opened it, and placed the tray into the microwave. As the lasagna heated up, he grabbed a Coors out of the refrigerator and opened it. The first gulp is always the best. He felt like swimming in it, after the day that he experienced. Even after lunch break, the appointments were back to back with no real break in between.

When dinner was done heating up, he grabbed a fork, a napkin, the beer and the dinner and brought it into the family room. He turned on the television, found a baseball game, and sat on the couch. He started to eat his dinner, and noticed that the lasagna did not taste like it should. He thought that it more or less resembled cardboard with tasteless cheese and bland sauce. But it was low fat, which was the way that Darlene wanted it, because it kept John in shape. She often told him that nobody wants an out of shape doctor.

He found himself longing for Jenny's lasagna. In the beginning of their marriage, Jenny's lasagna was nothing to write home about, but she tried so hard to please him. At it's worst, with it's undercooked noodles and burnt cheese, it was still better than this tasteless lasagna in the box. As the years passed Jenny perfected her lasagna, and it was his favorite dish.

He started to think about Jenny again and wished that she was still around. The more unhappy he felt with Darlene, the more he thought of her. She would be cuddling with him, watching the Yankees. He missed her voice, her wit and her patience. She was a great cook, a wonderful mother, and a selfless lover. She was the love of his life and he ached for her.

The game was over, and Darlene still wasn't home. Maggie had called at around eight o'clock to say hello. Scott had called at around nine-thirty and told him that he'd be home around eleven. Everyone was accounted for, except for his wife.

He wondered if he should even attempt to sleep in his own bed that night. Usually, when there was a confrontation, he was ejected from the master bedroom and banished to the guest room. It was beginning to turn into his personal bedroom. It was easier on his ego anyway. Lately, she had been spurning his attempts to make love with every excuse in the book. It had been so long since their last encounter, that he felt more like a priest.

When the game was over and he turned off the television. He cleaned up whatever mess he had made, and he yawned and looked at the clock to see that it was ten-thirty. He was so tired, that he thought that he could not wait any longer for her to come home. The continuation of the argument would have to wait. He walked up the stairs, and walked into the familiar surroundings of the guest room.

Chapter Three

A NEW FACE

By August, Scott was prepared attend Brick State, a college in upstate, New York in a town called Madison Hill. On the day of his departure, the small family gathered to send him off. Anne and Robert were there as well, which made things a little bit tense, since Darlene as usual did not make them feel welcome. After hugs, kisses and best wishes, John and Scott left on their three hour journey to Scott's new life.

Once there, the two men unpacked the car and were assisted in setting up Scott's dorm room with the help of Scott's roommate and another student named Tom, who was a sophomore. Tom was there to show the new guys the ropes. After several hours, they were finished and were all were exhausted and hungry.

John offered to take them all out for dinner to celebrate their new life. Since Tom seemed to know his way around, they took his advice as he recommended a place that was close to John's hotel. He suggested a Bar/Restaurant called Huntington's, which was a place where college aged adults usually hung out on the weekends.

After a short drive, the four men walked into Huntington's. It was located close to the college and it was the was a very lively place. It reminded John of a TGIF's, as it was extremely crowded and noisy. It was not a place that John would have picked, but it had an atmosphere that the three young men could appreciate.

John tried to be cheerful, but his lean, thirty-eight year old body ached from the move. The boxes and other items that Scott brought on the trip were coming back to haunt him. Along with the body aches, John felt the early stages of a headache. Loud crowded places always affected him in this way. The surroundings were busy, bordering on chaotic.

Somehow, they were able to find a table, and they were seated in the bar section, which was the loudest part of the restaurant. John could not wait until the dinner was over so that he could deposit the young men back to their dormitory. All he could think about was the thought of the inviting king sized bed in the hotel room, where he would find peace and a much needed quiet.

"Dad, how are you doing over there?" Scott asked. Scott knew his father very well and always knew when his father was not enjoying himself.

"Yeah, you should loosen up, Dr. Stanton." Tom suggested. Tom was having a wonderful time, of course.

"I'm sorry, guys, I've just got this headache that is bothering me," John explained. He did not go on to suggest that the headache was caused by their choice of restaurant.

When the waitress arrived, Tom said hello and called her by name.

"Hey Wendy, I didn't know that you were working tonight," Tom commented.

As Tom conversed with the waitress, John was barely listening to the conversation. Instead, he looked down at the menu to see what was available to eat.

"I'm filling in for Denise … she's away for a few days, and I could use the extra cash. Do you guys know what you want to drink?"

Tom mentioned that his friend had a splitting headache and asked her if she had an aspirin. John overheard it, and looked up to tell her that it wasn't necessary. It was then that their eyes met. Immediately, his heart skipped a beat. He was stunned because she was amazingly beautiful. He was instantly attracted to her.

He stumbled through his words, and she patiently waited for him to gather up his thoughts and say what he wanted. She smiled at him with a flirty smile which he picked up immediately. He wondered if everyone at the table noticed how she was looking at him, but they were more interested in their menus.

He asked what kind of beer was available, and from memory, she listed what was on tap and in bottles. As she spoke, he tried with all of his powers of inner strength to keep from scanning her physical appearance. She was perfect, as far as he was concerned.

He managed to make up his mind, and order one of the ales available on tap. The young men barked out orders for sodas. After writing down the drink order, Wendy promised that she would be right back. As she turned and walked away, John watched her intently as she glided away. Or so he thought. He could barely breathe and tried to shake off the attraction. How old could she possibly be? He was almost embarrassed about how he felt, and he wondered if anyone had noticed that he was staring at her.

"Isn't she hot?" Tom asked the younger men at the table, not even considering that the old guy felt the same way. They all agreed, "I don't think that she's dating anyone, but she doesn't play around either. She's a mystery."

"What do you mean?" Scott asked, and John pretended not to be too interested, but his attention was focused.

"I've heard that in all the time she has been here, she has never gone home with anyone." Tom whispered, "God knows, many guys have tried. She's like a brick wall. Probably the last virgin left on campus."

"That's ridiculous." John said in defense of young girls everywhere. "There have to be virgins around."

"Not virgins who look like that." Tom pointed out, "You went to college, didn't you, Dr. Stanton?"

"Yes." John replied ... obviously. He wasn't born with the doctor title.

The conversation was suddenly interrupted when Wendy came back with the drink order. She placed the drinks on the table and looked directly at John.

"I have something for you," she told him.

John became nervous for a second, wondering what she was doing. Then she asked him to put out his hand, which he did. She put two Advils in his hand, and said that they were from her secret stash. As she placed the pills in her hand, she did it in a way that brushed his hand softly.

"Thank you," he said as he looked at her smiling face.

"Any time," she said suggestively.

John blushed a little bit. He felt as if there was a mutual attraction, but then thought that he must be crazy. All this was unnoticed by the three young men at the table. They were only interested in the menus that they held in their hands.

"Do you see anything that you like?" She asked.

"Uh ... Excuse me?" He replied.

"On the menu, silly," she giggled.

There was a stoned silence because John was not sure what to say next, as his heart pounded out of his chest. That silence was soon broken by the three young men who ordered their food in machine gun fashion. As she wrote down their order, John was trying to keep his composure. He was trying to breathe deeply and re-group.

"Did she just hit on me?" He thought to himself. "Am I seeing things or delusional?"

"And what about you, handsome, do you see anything that you want?" she asked.

Another innuendo? He stumbled with words again, and nervously looked through the menu. In all this time, he never looked in the menu.

"Dad, you never looked in the menu?" Scott laughed.

"Oh great," John thought, now she knows I'm his Dad and she's probably doing the math right now ... eighteen plus blank equals...Then, he felt guilty. "Why am I even worried about this?"

Finally, he got his nerves together and managed to order a bacon cheeseburger. It had been the most arduous task that he had completed in the past few weeks. As she walked away, John felt like a total idiot.

"She must think that I'm an imbecile," he thought. He was embarrassed by his behavior. He felt like a inexperienced teenager.

The young men started to babble on about other subjects. The conversation ranged from classes and teachers and things that were important to young men their age. As they talked, John scanned the crowd to catch another glimpse of Wendy, as if he could not wait to see her again.

"Earth to Dad," Scott said.

John snapped out of his trance, then realized that Scott had asked him a question. He gathered his thoughts in his best fatherly manner and managed to make a quick answer that actually made sense. Once the question was answered, the young men started to babble again and John's mind was back in outer space.

Before he knew it, she was back again to ask for another round. This time he noticed how beautiful her face was. She had deep brown eyes and short black wavy hair that fell into her face a bit. She had a smile that was warm and comforting. He could not help but to stare at her. Then, his gaze worked its way downward.

"Do you need something?" she asked with a quizzical look.

"Hmm ... what?" he asked, a little embarrassed that she probably caught him gazing at her breasts.

"Another beer, perhaps?" she asked.

He looked down and noticed that his beer glass was empty. He did not remember drinking it, but he did not remember much about the past ten minutes.

"Sure," he replied. "I'll have the same."

As she left, he was mortified, "now she thinks I am a pervert," he thought.

He suddenly wanted to apologize. Maybe not. He didn't know what to do. He definitely wanted to get out of the booth. He felt claustrophobic with the noise in the crowded room, the knick knacks on the wall, the TV screens everywhere, each broadcasting a different sporting event. The room started to spin.

"Guys, I'll be back in a couple of minutes. I have to take a break," he explained.

"The men's room is on the other side of the bar," Tom said.

Tom seemed to have a lot of knowledge of the place. John had to wonder how Tom knew so much about the restaurant and it's ins and outs, including the gossip. He was suspicious because Tom had not yet reached the legal drinking age.

John stood up and managed to work his way through the crowd and towards the men's room. He instead took a detour and headed towards the front door for a breath of fresh air. Once outside, he breathed in the fresh air, until he noticed a few young adults having a smoke on a bench. There was a young couple making out on another bench, which was the last thing that he wanted to see. But, aside from the smoke and tonsil hockey lesson, it was pretty quiet out there. He was able to relax a bit and pull himself together. After a self-imposed pep talk, he began to walk back into the hellhole.

It was then that he bumped into Wendy, who was walking out.

"Hello handsome," she said.

At first he looked behind him, then he realized that she was talking to him.

"Are you talking to me?" he asked.

"I was looking for you."

"You were?"

"Yes, your appetizers are on the table and your son didn't know where you were. I told him that I saw you go outside," she explained. "I could tell that you were a little out of sorts in there ... this place can get a bit overwhelming ... Tonight especially. It's pretty busy because of all the new students moving in."

"Do you always spy on your customers?" he teased. It was amazing that he could flirt so well, since he was so out of practice. He was proud of himself.

"Only the handsome ones," she teased back.

He smiled again, but this time he did not blush like a teenager. This time, he felt something different stir inside of him. It was something that had not been present for some time. He felt a warmness about her, and was a comforting feeling. He felt at ease enough to go a step further and apologize for his earlier indiscretion.

"Listen, about before, I'm sorry that I was glaring at you," he said, in a earnest manner. "I really have no excuse."

"You're cute," she said, as she patted his arm as if he were a puppy. "It's not the first time anyone has looked at me like that, but it's the first time anyone has apologized to me for it"

"Well, it was inappropriate ... and I'm sorry."

"I accept. I appreciate that you are being such a gentleman," she said, "Although, it was nice to have a real man look at me for a change. There can be a lot of jerks here, and you can just imagine what it's like."

"So, you're not offended."

"Not in the least."

They exchanged smiles and there was an awkward silence afterwards. In order to break the silence, Wendy mentioned that he should go back to the table before his food got cold, and he agreed. As they walked towards the door, she was almost run over by a drunken frat boy barging through the door. John managed to grab her just in time before she was trampled. As he held her in his strong arms, they glanced at each other and smiled.

"Thank you," she said.

"Any time," he replied.

After going their separate ways, John returned to the table and realized that the appetizer was almost empty. The three ravenous young men had attacked the super nachos as if it was their least meal on earth. They did not have to wait too long for the dinners to arrive, however, and John was happy to see Wendy's smiling face once again.

After the four men finished their dinner, it was time for John to return the young men to their dormitory. Wendy wished the new students good luck, and she and John once again exchanged smiles.

"I hope to see all of you again," she said, while she glared directly into John's eyes. He felt a tingle as their eyes met. There was definitely a mutual attraction, and they both felt it. He could not believe that he was feeling this way.

"It was nice to meet you, Wendy," he said as he shook her hand.

"Same here, John."

John dropped off the young men at the dorm and said goodnight to his son. It was clear that the night was still young for the college men, and Scott asked him rather half-heartedly if he would like to stay and hang out with them. Realizing that Scott had just made the offer to be polite, John mentioned that he was exhausted from the move and would rather return to the hotel. He and Scott planned to meet for breakfast early the next day before he left for the journey home.

As he approached the hotel, he caught a glimpse of Huntington's out of the corner of his eye. It had been at least an hour since he had been there, but curiosity made him he wonder if Wendy was still working. Against his better judgment, he made the fateful decision to pull into the parking lot and find out.

Chapter Four

CURIOSITY

Once in the parking lot, he sat there for a second, conflicted about whether he should get out of the car or go straight to the hotel and forget about it. He just wanted to get another look at her. After a bit of soul searching, he took a deep breath and decided to go back inside the restaurant.

He walked into the restaurant, which was more crowded than before and it was filled with people who were visibly drunk, and who had gathered by the bar. The place was a bit louder than before, if possible. There was a karaoke set up on a makeshift stage, and an inebriated, extremely large man was singing a Barry White song.

He searched the premises for about ten minutes, but there were so many people that he was unable to see her. He deduced that she probably had left for the night. A bit disappointed, he decided to sit down at the bar and have one drink before heading over to the hotel. After being bounced around a bit by people bumping into him by accident, he miraculously found a barstool. Dejected, he sat down and ordered a beer.

As he drank his beer, he looked up at one of the flat screen televisions that was airing a female boxing match, and wondered what in the world he was doing there. Suddenly, there was a tap on his shoulder, and a feminine voice came from beside him.

"Is anyone sitting here?" the woman seemed to yell.

He turned to offer the empty seat and he saw that it was Wendy. She had just turned in her uniform and was off of work.

"Hi handsome …" she said with a warm smile.

"Hi," he said, a bit stunned that he actually saw her again.

"I didn't expect to see you back here," she said as she touched his arm. He could barely hear what she was saying, because it was so loud in the room.

"Did you tuck the little kids into their dorms?"

"I brought them back, but I think that they'll be up for a while," he yelled.

As he spoke, she leaned in closely to hear what he was saying. Her face was so close that her hair brushed against his lips and her sweet scent overwhelmed him. She nodded to react to his last statement, but conversation was challenging, since the bar noise was so deafening. The music and banter overtook the moment, and the two of them glimpsed at each other as if to say "I can't hear you."

She had an idea, and asked him if he wanted to talk in another area of the restaurant that was quieter. He ordered her a drink and paid the tab. The two of them escaped to a booth that was away from the boozing and carousing crowd, and was in a closed section of the restaurant. It was dark, but at least they were able to hear each other. She lit a candle so that they could see each other's face, and they sat down.

Suddenly, the virtual quiet made conversation uncomfortable. "Now what do I do?" he thought. He was quite nervous, and didn't know what to say. They sat silent for what was only about a minute, but seemed like an eternity. Then she asked him about his son, and the ice was broken.

"Scott is my oldest child. I also have a daughter named Maggie. She just turned 16 last April."

"You and your wife must be very proud of them," she said.

"My wife ... actually, my current wife is not their mother. She's my second wife," he said as he cleared his throat. "My first wife died a while ago."

"Oh ... I'm very sorry," she said

"Her name was Jennifer ... Jenny, for short. We were high school sweethearts. Got married when we were nineteen. She was my first love. Actually, sometimes I think she was my only love."

"You were very young, huh?"

"Yeah, when I think about it now, it is amazing how young we were. I see my son, Scott and I can't imagine him being married in a year. Especially Scott."

"I guess that you knew what you wanted."

"Oh, definitely. I had no doubts at all. She was the love of my life," he said as he took another swig from his bottle. "We dated for five years before we got married. All through high school."

She was easy to talk to. He was able to talk to her about things that he never talked about with a stranger. John told him about his family. He told her that after they married, they lived with her parents in Becktown as he went to med school and residency training as a doctor. While they lived with her parents, she had both of the children. Finally, when he was a full fledged pediatrician and they finally were able to buy their own small home in Devonwood.

"Within a year, she found out that she had breast cancer. It was just a routine checkup. Less than a year later, she was gone."

"I'm so sorry," she said as she placed her hand on his.

She could tell that it was difficult for him to tell the story. He told her about the devastation that he experienced when she was suddenly gone at the age of thirty, and how hard it was to raise his two children by himself. He said that it took him a long time to recover.

"If I didn't have her parents to help me out, I don't know what I would have done. They were incredible. They were always there for me."

"John, I'm sorry if telling me this has brought up painful moments."

"No, it's alright. I've been thinking a lot of Jenny lately, with Scott's graduation and all that. At the graduation party, I was sitting on the floor in my bedroom staring at a picture of her, talking to it. Do you think that it sounds weird?"

"Not at all."

"I just miss her, I guess."

"That's understandable."

"Darlene wouldn't understand it."

"Who is Darlene?"

"She's my second wife."

"She doesn't understand?"

"No. Darlene flinches at even the mention of Jenny's name."

"But, Jenny is your children's mother."

"I know. Let's just say that I wasn't paying much attention to anything while I was courting her. I must have had some kind of tunnel vision. Everyone tried to tell me, but I didn't listen."

"I don't know what you mean." she said.

John shifted his position in his side of the booth and took a deep breath. Explaining his reasons for marrying Darlene was not an easy task. Most people did not understand why he went through with the marriage, and considering how it all was falling apart, he had a hard time defending his decision to turn his children's world upside down.

"Darlene and I met four years ago. I needed a bigger house and Darlene was the real estate agent that sold me the house. At the time, we really connected, and within a year we were engaged and married at the courthouse."

"That was fast."

"That's what everyone else was trying to tell me. Everyone else was trying to tell me that it was a mistake, especially the children."

"Why didn't you listen to them?"

"It had been many years since Jenny's death. I wanted to move on. I was lonely. She made my life exciting."

"Not anymore?"

"No. It's a disaster. I thought I found a mother figure for my kids, but they can't stand her. What's worse, I think that the feeling is mutual."

"What about you?"

"Well, it was great in the beginning, but downhill ever since."

"So, you're not happy?"

"No. I'm very unhappy. But, trust me. It's not a pick up line."

"I didn't think that it was."

Suddenly, he was embarrassed that he had gone on so long and divulged so much personal information. He felt as if he were burdening her.

"I'm sorry. I shouldn't be talking about this. I'm just rambling on," he said.

"Don't be sorry," she said.

"Enough about me. I haven't given you a chance to tell me about yourself," he said, causing her to roll her eyes.

"Well, there isn't much to tell," she explained.

"Tell me. I'm sick about talking about myself."

He took a deep breath, and exhaled with relief. He was happy to get off the subject of the sad life of John Stanton. Although, he was glad to have a listener who seemed so interested in his troubles.

"Okay … well I'm an only child. I grew up I a small town called Upland that is about an hour south from where we are sitting right now."

"Was it a happy childhood?"

"Yes … very happy. I'm part of a huge family. I have relatives all over the country. Once in a while, we get together for a family reunion. They all come back home and we have a great big party."

"Sounds like fun."

"It is."

"Are you close with your parents?"

"You could say that. Although I kind of screwed up a few years ago. There was this guy …"

"There's always a guy," he said as he rolled his eyes and the two shared a laugh.

"Yeah … well … he was my boyfriend in high school, and we dated for a couple of years. Then when he was a junior in college, he got an apartment and I got it in my head that I was going to leave town with him. You know, live with him while he went to college? This college, as a matter of fact."

"Sounds like a problem."

"Big problem. My parents were not happy at all. They forbid me to do it, and told me that it was a big mistake. But, I was twenty. I thought I knew everything. So, I did it anyway."

"So, what happened?"

"They were right. It didn't take long before we broke up. He had some girls on the side, do you know what I mean?"

"I've heard about it."

"So we broke up. Suddenly, I was homeless."

"Did you go back home?"

"No way. I was too humiliated."

"Then what did you do?"

"I already had this job, and Denise was looking for a roommate. It was almost like fate stepped in."

"Can't you go home again?"

"I could. I mean, every time I go home to visit, my mother tells me that the door is always open. But I like living on my own."

"Whatever happened to Mr. Right?"

"Don't know ... Don't care. After he graduated, we lost touch."

John took another swig of beer, and noticed that he was empty. He asked Wendy if she wanted another round, and she said yes. He stood up and promised to be back shortly. He walked from the virtually quiet area that he had shared with Wendy and into the still unbelievably noisy and crazy atmosphere. He waited for a chance to order another round of drinks, but he was unable to squeeze himself into the crowd. After several attempts and what seemed like a lifetime, he just gave up and started to return to the table. He saw that she was already standing and close to the front door. He wondered what was wrong.

"What's the matter?"

"Nothing now ... I thought that you were not coming back."

"I was trying to get us a couple of drinks, but I couldn't squeeze my way in there. I could try again."

"No, that's okay. I know how this place can get," she said. "I would really like to get out of here. Would you like to sit outside? There's a little area."

"I remember."

They left together, but walked past the tables that he had seen before. She led him around the side of the building, and into the parking lot. They finally stopped at the edge of the parking lot and sat on a stone wall. Once there, it was finally quiet enough so that he was actually able to hear her voice without distortion.

"This is my favorite spot," she sighed, "I usually go here when I have a break. It reminds me of my parent's home in Upland."

"Why is that?"

"You can't see it now, but there is a little stream right over there," she said as she pointed in that direction. "There is a stream next to my parent's house."

"Do you miss being home?"

"Sometimes. It's a lot easier there than it is here. But, I'm twenty-five."

"What does that have to do with it?"

"I'm a little old to be living with Mom and Dad ... no offense."

"None taken."

"But, at least when you lived with Jenny's parents, you were working towards your future and taking care of your family."

"I know."

"At least you knew what you wanted when you were twenty-five."

"It sounds like you don't."

"I don't know what I want. I'm just living life day by day right now. Maybe I will figure it out," she sighed.

She briefly looked back on all the bad choices that she had made, and how it affected her life. Knowing that the past could not be changed, she shrugged her shoulders.

"Do you like this job?" He asked.

"Sometimes I like it. Most of the time, I don't. But it's a job, and it pays pretty well."

"Did you ever want to do anything else?"

"I don't know," she said. "I never really thought about it. When I was growing up, all I wanted to do was to get married, have a bunch of kids and settle down."

"You wanted to have lots of babies?" He mused.

"Lots of babies," she laughed. "Not as many as my grandmother though. She had eight."

"Eight? Wow."

"Yeah, I don't know how she did it."

"Jenny and I wanted to have a big family too," he reminisced.

"What about Darlene?"

"No ... She doesn't want to have any kids. Never did."

"Why not?" she asked curiously.

"She just doesn't. It was another little thing that I did not think about before the marriage. I want to have more kids and she doesn't. Surprise!"

"So, you can't talk her out of it?"

"Nope ...Her career is her baby," he shrugged, "besides, at this point it would be a miracle if she conceived a child."

"She can't conceive?"

"No, it's more like there is nothing going on ... in that area. No ... you know."

"Sex?"

"Just call me Father John." He joked sheepishly.

"You're joking."

"Wish I wasn't. I can't tell you when the last time was. I should have marked in on my calendar as a national holiday."

"That's unbelievable!" She gasped. "She doesn't know how lucky she is. If you were my husband, I wouldn't be able to keep my hands off of you."

Open mouth, insert foot. After she made that comment, their mutual attraction returned, and conversation was once again difficult. She realized that she might have stepped over the line, and she apologized.

"Sorry ... sometimes I don't think before I speak. I shouldn't have said that. I've got a big mouth."

"It's okay. I don't mind," he said as he grew more curious about her.

"I just don't understand people sometimes. They just don't know what they have. It annoys me. I would give anything to have a good husband to come home to. It's such a waste."

The magnetism still lingered as she gazed up at him and was drawn to him. He was such a fantastic guy. It was so unfair. Why was it that all the wonderful men were either married or gay? They seemed to move closer to one another without effort, and it might have led to a kiss if she did not back off suddenly.

"John ... do you know what time it is?"

He looked at his watch and was surprised to find that it was after eleven.

"Oh great," she said.

"What is it?"

"I missed the eleven o'clock bus," she gasped as she started to pace. "I can't believe how late it is. Where did the time go? The next bus doesn't come for another hour."

In a moment of chivalry, but more of a desire to have the evening continue a little bit longer, John offered to drive her home.

Chapter Five

NOT A USUAL NIGHT

After about a ten minute drive, John's car pulled up into the parking lot of Wendy's small two story apartment building. He turned off the car, not knowing what to do next. Finally, Wendy broke the silence.

"Thank you so much. I would have been out there for another hour waiting for that bus, and I hate to walk home at night."

"No problem," he replied.

"So …"

"So."

"Would you like to come in for a drink?" She asked a bit nervously. This was a bit of a leap, since she was terribly afraid of being rejected.

There was a sudden silence between them as John tried to figure out what to do. The silence was so uncomfortable that she backed off a bit.

"But, I guess that you probably have to get going."

"No, I can stay for one drink," he said, suddenly finding the courage out of nowhere.

"It's just that we get along so well, and I don't know if I will ever see you again."

"Just because I'm going in there doesn't mean that … you know."

"Of course not," she said. "We're just going to continue the conversation that we started in the restaurant. I know."

He agreed to come up for one small drink, knowing full well where this all might lead. Somehow, he tried to convince himself that it was all very innocent. Although, it was quite obvious that they were greatly attracted to one another. They walked into the apartment, and she threw her keys onto a small table in the hallway.

They walked into the diminutive kitchen, past the small round table with two chairs, and she grabbed two bottles of beer out of the well worn refrigerator. As she turned around, she noticed that he was glancing at the cow theme in the kitchen. There were a couple of square pictures of grazing cows on the wall and a pot holder that looked like a cow's head.

"Denise likes cows." She explained as a reply to his curious expression. She leaned against the sink in order to block his view of the small collection of dirty dishes in the sink.

"I can see that."

"All I have is beer," she said as she handed a bottle to him.

"That's fine."

"Can you excuse me for a minute? I just want to change. I've got all this restaurant gook on me. I'll be back in a second," she said as she pointed out a ketchup stain on her green polo-styled shirt.

"Sure ... go ahead," he said.

"Make yourself comfortable." She said nervously as she left quickly.

She bolted into the bedroom and straightened up, just in case. God knows if anything was going to happen that night, but if it did, she did not want her bedroom to look like a pigsty. Then she threw off her work clothes, threw them in the hamper, and tried to look for something else to wear as she rifled through her drawers.

He gulped a little beer as he waited for her to return. He looked around the tiny kitchen, and then walked into the small living room. There as a small stereo on top of a shelving system that had a collection of CDs stacked haphazardly upon it. He searched through the collection and realized that none of the artists were anything that he recognized. There was no Billy Joel or Beatles in the stack, but rather names like "Bounding Fury" and "Scenic Roads". He wondered if Maggie had ever heard of them.

There were candles and floral arrangements all around. There was a bookcase with a few dozen romantic paperback novels, a hardcover dictionary and a leather bound Bible. There were a few family pictures on the shelves as well. One was a picture of Wendy and an older couple that he assumed was her parents. She had on a blue cap and gown, and John assumed that it was from her high school graduation. They looked like they were about his age, which made him think a bit.

After perusing his surroundings, he sat on the couch, adjusting the throw pillows in an attempt to make himself more comfortable. He put down his beer and straightened up the gossip magazines that were thrown upon the coffee table, and used the remote control to turn on the medium sized television that stood on a faux wood television stand.

As he switched through channels, he unexpectedly became very uneasy about the situation he had gotten himself into. The longer he waited, the more he wanted to disappear. The cautious and sensible person was starting to return and his conscience accosted him.

"What are you doing here? You're a married man. You should leave before it gets too far!" His conscience said to him. He tried to excuse himself by telling his conscience that nothing would happen. It was all very innocent. They were just going to talk and that was all.

Finally she returned, and it was not a moment too soon. He stood up and noticed that she had changed into something a bit more comfortable. It was not anything that was seductive, just a buttoned down red shirt and a pair of jeans. However, he was so attracted to her at that moment, that she could have been wearing a burlap bag and he would have found it appealing.

"Well, I'm back ..."

"Yes you are ..." He said, with a little bit of anxiety. He took another gulp of beer to calm his nerves, and she did the same, and then they put the bottles on the square glass coffee table as they sat back down.

They made some small conversation about the décor of the apartment, which was obviously an attempt to kill time. She did not take credit for any of the furnishings in the place, explaining that everything except the personal pictures belonged to Denise. All of the small talk was of no use, because it did not get their minds off of each other.

Then suddenly, she courageously leaned over and kissed him, then pulled away.

"I'm sorry, I just couldn't help myself," she apologized as she looked at his shocked face, "I wanted to do that all night."

"Don't be sorry." he replied, as he felt his heart start to race.

"I've wanted to kiss you ever since I first saw you sitting at the table, stammering and stumbling while trying to make your order."

"That's me, Mr. Smooth," he said with a bit of embarrassment.

"I thought that you were so adorable. I just wanted to kiss you right there."

"I couldn't speak when I saw you," he said, "You are so beautiful, Wendy. You took my breath away."

The two kissed again, and this time John took the lead. They found themselves wrapped up in each other, kissing on the couch and their passion made things move very quickly. John forgot about everything but her. With her consent, he lifted and carried her into the bedroom where they made love.

After the lovemaking, she drifted off to sleep in his arms. As she slept, John's mind began to race. He was torn between elation and guilt. He was happy because he finally shared a mutual attraction with a wonderful woman.

He was alive again. He truly connected with her, and he wished so much that he had met her four years ago, before Darlene.

Then he thought about Darlene. Even though he and Darlene were in such a bad marriage, he still felt remorseful about what he had just done. He had never once considered breaking his vows, even though he was so unhappy. He never cheated ... ever. He felt like he had been weak. He believed that he should have resisted the temptation.

But even though he had just met Wendy, he felt more of a connection to her then he ever had with Darlene. It was almost like it was in the beginning with Jenny. She was so much like Jenny. Her mannerisms were the same. The smile was similar. She was so easy to talk to. Maybe they could have talked all night if it wasn't for that first kiss. When that happened, the build up from the entire night was too intense. He could not resist her and wanted be with her.

He wondered what he should do. How should he handle this? Should he leave? What kind of man would that make him? He decided that he did not want to leave that night. He did not want to use her, then leave her because he was too fond of her. But, would this only be a one night stand? What happens now? With all of this inner angst, it was a miracle that he finally drifted off to sleep.

When he awoke, he realized that it was not a dream. Although, he was in an empty bed, he knew that he was not alone. He could smell that bacon was being cooked in the kitchen, and there was coffee being brewed. He sat up, found his boxers and t-shirt and put them on. He stumbled out into the direction of the kitchen.

Once in the kitchen, he saw her wearing his blue button down shirt from the night before. He wondered if she had anything on underneath it, and tilted his head to try and find out. As he watched her move, he saw a flash of skin and realized that the cupboard was bare. She was so alluring, and the passion started to stir inside of him again.

He walked over closer, and was tempted to embrace her. But then he thought it would be a bit presumptuous, so he sat down at the small table in the corner. He watched her as she moved from the stove to the refrigerator and back. She seemed to glide. She was so graceful. She must have felt the heat from his gaze, because she turned around.

"Hello handsome," she said sensually. "Would you like some coffee?"

"Hello beautiful," he replied, "I would love some coffee."

"I'm glad that you are still here," she said as she poured coffee in a cup and put it on the table. "Do you take cream in your coffee?"

He nodded as she poured milk into his coffee cup, then he started to speak.

"Where else would I be?" he asked,

"Some guys would just leave."

"I'm not the kind of guy who normally does this kind of thing," he replied, "I'm probably not like other guys you know."

"I know. I can tell," she noticed. "I've never done this before, either. You are the first guy I've ever brought home."

The two paused, perhaps thinking about the situation that they were in. Neither of them had ever been involved in a one night stand, and did not know the protocol. It was new territory.

"I see you've found my missing shirt," he flirted, steering the conversation in a more playful direction.

"Would you like it back?" she teased with a smile as she moved closer to him.

She started to unbutton the shirt, revealing the prize that was inside. Instantly, like he was on autopilot, he started to kiss her neck and work his way down as she straddled his legs. Then his lips worked it's way up to meet her passionate kiss. Another rendezvous was a certainty until something interrupted their excitement.

"Wendy, I think that there's something burning," he pointed out as he turned to look in the direction of the stove.

"The eggs!" she exclaimed. She practically leapt off of his lap. As she scrambled to save breakfast, his cell phone rang.

He checked the phone number on the display, and then he realized that he had totally forgotten about his planned breakfast with Scott that morning. He was scheduled to pick Scott up at nine, and when he checked his watch, he realized that it was eight-thirty.

"Uh oh," he said as he excused himself and walked into the living room to have a quick conversation. When he came back into the kitchen, he had some bad news for his new lover.

"Wendy, I'm sorry, but I have to leave."

"What's wrong?"

"I completely forgot that I was meeting my son for breakfast."

She was very understanding, but he could tell that she was disappointed.

He ran into the bedroom and raced to find everything that belonged to him. He tried to dress while tripping and fumbling. He did no want to be late and cause any kind of suspicion on Scott's part.

"Wendy, I'm so sorry," he apologized when he returned to the kitchen, "You probably think I'm a terrible person," he stated.

"That's not true, John ... I really don't."

"I feel awful. The last thing that I wanted to do was to leave you like this. I don't want to leave at all. But, I totally forgot that I was meeting my son for breakfast. I just got so caught up in … you know."

"I know … so did I."

"This is not me, you know … I'm not like this," he tried to explain.

She nodded her head, trying to be as understanding as humanly possible. Then she said something that surprised him.

"John, you don't have to worry about me."

He was confused, but then she explained that she did not expect anything from him. She knew that he was married, and that this probably was a one night stand.

"John, I don't expect anything. I know that you live three hours away."

"I don't like it, though," he replied.

Some other man in this situation might have been relieved to have been let off the hook, but he was not. He felt like he used her. It was a horrible feeling. He had never been intimate with anyone besides his two wives. Faithful until the end. Well, until now. This was a new experience for him, and it was a difficult situation. He was also struggling with his new found feelings for Wendy, and was unsure if he wanted this night to be only a one night stand.

"You're a wonderful man. I don't take just anyone home, you know," she said as she walked over closer to him and stroked his shoulder.

"You're giving me too much credit. I feel like a total idiot. I want to see you again before I leave for home," he promised with all sincerity.

"You don't have to do that … it will just make it harder. It would be better if you did not come back."

"No, Wendy. I am not going to do that. I want to come back," he said.

He asked her for a piece of paper, and she found an envelope on the coffee table. He wrote a number on it, then he gave the envelope to her. "This is my cell phone number. If I cannot come back today, I want you to call me."

She said that she would call, but even he did not believe that she would.

"I promise that I will come back here. Believe me."

"Okay … I believe you," she said, believing that he would not.

He leaned in, grabbed her in his arms and kissed her. After they kissed and said goodbye, she did not believe that she'd ever see him again.

He raced out the door and into his car. A few seconds later, he drove away. She watched as the car disappeared down the road.

He returned to his unused hotel room, showered and quickly changed. It was at that moment that he realized that he had left his blue shirt on her body. He thought that it could not be in a better place.

By some miracle, he managed to pick up his son on time, and the two traveled to a local diner for breakfast. During the breakfast, John's mind was obviously somewhere else. He could hear his son talking, but it was more like a humming noise in the background.

In the foreground, his mind kept drifting back to the night before. He recalled her face and he could still feel her warmth of her body against his own. He longed for her touch. He could still see her wrapped in his shirt, and the wondrous gift that he attempted to unwrap earlier that morning.

Scott noticed that his father's attention was not quite there.

"Dad…"

"Hmmm…what?"

"Where are you?"

"I'm right here … what did you say again?"

"Dad, you just had a dopey smile on your face, are you all right?"

"What do you mean? I'm fine."

"No there's something different about you…What's going on? You were the same way at the restaurant."

"I have no idea what you are talking about. There's nothing going on."

John managed to come up with some explanations that Scott seemed to accept, saying that he did not get a good night's sleep and was dreading the long ride home. From the look on Scott's face, he probably thought that something was up, but pushed it no further.

Back at the dorm, John said goodbye to his eldest child. He was a little down-hearted and was going to miss seeing him every day. But, he knew that he son was beginning a new and exciting time in his life, and he was happy for him. He told Scott how proud he was of him and they both had tears in their eyes as the exchanged their final goodbyes.

John returned to the hotel and checked out of his room. As he pulled out of the parking lot, he caught a glimpse of Huntington's. Immediately, his thoughts drifted back to the night before and his promise earlier that morning. His long drive home would have to wait.

When he arrived at Wendy's apartment, he knocked on her door, but there was no answer. It had been a couple of hours since he had left her and he was afraid that she might not be home. Undaunted, he decided to knock again. Frustrated, he was just about to leave when the door opened. She was there. She was showered and dressed, but was wearing his blue shirt.

"I forgot my shirt," he said with a quiver. He could barely contain his overwhelming desire to have her. He felt like he was just about to come out of his skin.

"I found it," she replied.

Without speaking another word, they leapt upon each other hungrily. He gathered her in his arms and kick the door closed behind them. He carried her into the bedroom where they made love frantically until they were exhausted.

As the two lovers lay there in each other's arms, they shared a closeness that John had longed for, and a satisfaction that he had needed for quite some time. She felt the same connection. They both knew that this was not just another one-night stand. It was something more than that. It was magical. They knew that they had discovered feelings for each other that were hard to suppress.

"I know that it's hard to believe, given the circumstances, but I am usually not the type to cheat on my wife," John said after long contemplation, "I'm usually a very faithful guy. I never cheated on Jenny. The thought never crossed my mind."

"I know," she said as she kissed his shoulder and stroked his chest.

"But, this is not just another one night stand, Wendy. Do you know what I mean?" he said as he turned to face her.

"I know exactly what you mean."

"We have a connection, you and I. I'm so comfortable here with you."

"And I feel the same way. It's like we've known each other for a very long time."

"I wish things could be different." John sighed with regret as he turned onto his back again, "I wish that I could stay here. I'm happy to be here with you."

"I wish you could stay too," she said, with a tear in her eye. He did not notice because she hid it well.

He felt like he was falling in love with Wendy, and he almost told her, but stopped himself. It was such a ridiculous thought since he only knew her for less than a day, but if felt so real to him. She was perfect for him. This was a fact that he had to admit to himself.

He considered that this feeling of love may have occurred because she was so much like Jenny. He wondered if he had been fantasizing about Jenny while he was with Wendy. He contemplated it, but realized that he had not. He truly did have feelings for Wendy, and it surprised him that he was falling so hard and fast for her.

He did not want to leave. He tried in his mind to concoct excuses not to go, but he knew that he had responsibilities at home. Maggie expected him to be home later that night and he had patients that depended on him who had appointments on Monday. He really had no choice but to prepare to leave his new lover behind, however painful that might be for both of them.

The fact that Darlene did not cross his mind with regards to whether or not to stay was a true indication of how his love for her had withered on the vine. He had no desire to see her at all.

After a couple of hours, John finally admitted to himself that unfortunately it was time to leave. He wished that he could stay forever, but reality had come, and he had to go back to his unfulfilling life. He asked Wendy for her phone number, and promised to keep in touch.

She told him that she understood if he could not. "I'll never forget you," she said as he prepared to leave. They faced each other, and as she touched his cheek softly, "I will be dreaming of you."

"Sweetheart, this is not the end. I will keep in touch. Please believe me." he promised, "I will find a way to see you soon."

They shared a goodbye embrace, and they kissed again. He was a moment away from confessing his new found love when she interrupted his progress.

"You have to go." she said, as if she knew that he was about to say something that he might later regret.

His declaration of love would have to wait. He walked out the door, then turned to look at his blue shirt on her wonderful body.

"God, that looks good on you," he sighed, almost forgetting about the trip ahead of him. He started to gaze at her again. "You may as well keep it. It looks better on you."

"I was hoping you'd say that," she replied with a smile. "I'll treasure it."

"I treasure you," he said, then he leaned in and kissed her again, then quickly let go to avoid getting sucked into the black hole that was her apartment.

"Okay, I'm really going now," he said as he backed away.

"Goodbye John," she said as she blew him a kiss and he smiled and winked. Then, he finally turned and walked down to the sidewalk and towards the parking lot. As far as she knew, he walked out of her life.

Chapter Six

BACK TO REALITY

Several months passed, during which, John dealt with mundane life as it was. But, at least he would escape a few times a week, having conversations with Wendy. As soon as he heard her sweet voice, he was brought back to that warm August evening and day after, when he was enveloped in her embrace. He longed to see her again, touch her lovely face and kiss her inviting lips.

He bought a throw away cell phone that he kept only at the office. It was a phone that he would buy minutes for, then use when needed. This way, there were no bills with phone numbers to explain away to Darlene.

He called her after hours when the women of the office were gone, or sometimes he would break down and call her during lunch. The more he talked to her, the more he wanted to see her again. He was madly in love with her.

One Tuesday in September, Wendy called him after five, to thank him for a bouquet of flowers that he sent her. He sent the flowers "With love", and even though he was sure that he loved her, he wanted to tell her in person.

"Wendy, I have to see you. I'm going crazy over here."

"I want to see you too."

"I wish that you lived closer to me."

"So do I," she said, "Maybe I can come down there to see you."

"No, you don't have to do that."

"Why not? Are you afraid that someone will see us together?"

"Well, I can't say that it hasn't crossed my mind, sweetheart. But the main reason that I don't want you to drive down here is because it's too far. If anyone should make the trip, it should be me."

"Always the gentleman, aren't you?"

"Well, it all depends on the situation, Wendy."

"What do you mean by that?"

"The next time I am with you, I can't guarantee that I will be such a gentleman."

"You've got a naughty mind, Dr. Stanton."

"And you are constantly on it," he flirted, "I just can't wait to make love to you again, Wendy. I miss you."

"What if we met halfway? We can meet somewhere in the middle. I'll borrow Denise's car and drive down the Thruway for an hour and a half. You can drive an hour and a half to meet me. We can spend a few hours together."

"Sweetheart, when I see you, I am going to need more than a few hours."

"Then, why don't you stay overnight?"

"I wish I could, but I can't promise anything."

"Well ... I'll tell you what. I'll find a motel that is in the middle. I will stay overnight, and you stay as long as you can."

"Who knows, maybe it could be overnight."

"We'll cross that bridge when we get to it."

Finally, they agreed to meet at the Pinewood Holiday Inn which was about an hour and a half drive for each of them. The reunion was planned for mid-October. He had no idea how he was going to manage it, but he was determined to see her. Somehow he was confident that he would find some way to be with her again.

Then suddenly without warning, he tried to call her in early October and her phone number had been disconnected, and there was no forwarding number. Her cell phone number was no longer in service. Nearly two months after they started their long distance affair, he was not able to reach her. All of a sudden, they went from regular tête-à-tête to nothing at all. As a last resort, he went so far as to call Huntington's to try to catch her at work. He was informed that she no longer worked there.

On that Saturday in mid-October, John still left the house, using golf as an excuse, and traveled all the way up to Pinewood and checked into the Holiday Inn, which was still reserved under her name and under her credit card. He walked into the empty room, and waited for her to arrive. As he waited, he was extremely troubled and wondered what might have happened to her. He had briefly entertained the idea of driving up to Brick State to see if she was there, but he did not want to leave the room just in case she did arrive. She did not. After waiting five hours, he paid the bill in cash, and returned home helpless and miserable.

He was so miserable on that night and the days that followed, that Maggie became very concerned about him. She knew that he was not usually very content with his life, but for a few months, he did look very happy.

Unfortunately, that good mood had taken a sudden and worrisome turn. She constantly asked him what was wrong, thinking that he had some kind of fatal medical condition. He found himself defending himself, and assuring her that he was not on borrowed time.

By Thanksgiving, he was happy to finally have an excuse to drive up to Brick State. Scott had offered to save his father the long trip and take a bus home for Thanksgiving, but John would have none of it. He insisted that he would take the three hour trip to pick up his son. No one could understand his reasoning, especially not Darlene, who thought that he was being ridiculous.

John was the only one who knew why he wanted to take such a long trip, but he could not tell anyone. It was the first opportunity he would have to see Wendy. Once in town, he drove directly to her apartment. He knocked on her door and hoped that he would finally see her. The door opened and there stood an older woman with a perplexed look on her face.

"Can I help you?" she asked.

"Hello ma'am. I am looking for Wendy Burke. Is she home?" he asked as he tried to look inside the apartment. There were a few children running around in the background, and the furniture looked different than the last time he had been there.

"Wendy who? There is no Wendy here," she replied as she tried to block his view. He realized that he was invading her privacy and backed off.

"I know that she lived here in August," he explained.

"I've lived here since October, I don't know anyone named Wendy, I'm sorry."

"I'm sorry I bothered you" he said as she closed he door abruptly.

John intended to stop into Huntington's to see if anyone knew how to get in touch with her. Unfortunately, the place was closed.

"Looks like I'm batting a thousand" he said out loud.

After striking out twice, he had no idea where to look next. He started to accept the fact that maybe she did not want to be found.

After his little excursion, he drove to the dormitory and met his son in the dorm lobby. The two men hugged, and John asked his son how he was doing.

"Dad, I'm great," Scott replied. "How are you doing? You don't look so good."

"I'm fine," he lied. He could not explain why he was so melancholic, but the misery was written all over his face.

"What did she do now?" Scott asked, assuming that his father's mood was the result of something that Darlene had said or done.

"For once, it's not Darlene," John explained with dejection.

"Then what is it?" Scott asked, a bit concerned.

"Don't worry about it, Scott. I'll be fine."

John changed the subject to try to get his mind off of Wendy. He asked Scott about college, and it opened the flood gates. Scott told him about friends, classes and some vague details about some parties. Scott's excitement about school made the trip go quickly, but John still had his mind on something else.

"Scott, do you guys still go to that place, you know, the one that we went to after I drove you to college in August?"

"What ... Huntington's?"

"Yeah, that place."

"We go there once in a while ... Why?"

"Just wondering."

"Well, I don't go there to get drunk, if that's what you are thinking."

"Why would I think that, Scott? You're under age."

"Oh yeah." Scott said, then he moved the conversation into another direction. "Dad, I forgot to tell you...that waitress was asking about you! You know, that hot waitress?"

"What hot waitress?"

"You know, the one that was flirting with you. What was her name?"

"Wendy." John answered almost immediately, then had to back off a little bit, "At least I think that it was her name."

John felt his face turn red from the fear of revealing his dark secret.

"Wendy. That's right. I guess that you do remember her." Scott mentioned, "She's hard to forget, isn't she?"

"Well, I can't really remember her face so much."

"But, I'm sure that you remember the body, huh Dad?"

"Not really, Scott. It's just the name. Like Wendy from Peter Pan." John said feigning complete amnesia about the face, eyes and body of a woman that he could never forget.

"Wendy from Peter Pan? Dad, what made you say that?" Scott asked with a mocking tone in his voice.

"I don't know, Scott. It just stuck in my head. You don't hear that kind of name often."

Scott laughed, as if hearing the Peter Pan reference was the funniest thing that he had heard in years. As he cackled, John suffered in silence. John decided to stop interrogating his son for more information. He tried to calm himself, and his mouth became very dry.

"She left, you know."

"Who?"

"Wendy. You know, the one from Peter Pan?" Scott chuckled.

"She did? When did that happen?"

"You seem really fascinated, Dad."

"You brought it up." John quickly answered, defending himself. "I'm only interested because you're interested."

"Okay Dad, relax ..." Scott said, sensing something different in the tone of his father's voice. He was unexpectedly defensive, and that was not his usual demeanor. John realized that he was acting out of character, and calmed himself down.

"I'm sorry, Scott. I've been in a really bad mood lately. I don't mean to snap at you ... Go on."

"Dad, what's going on? Is it your health?"

"No Scott, I'm fine. You can finish your story. When did you say that this young woman left the restaurant?"

"She quit the restaurant in October, all of the sudden," he said. "There are a lot of rumors going around, but you know how that stuff can get."

"What kind of rumors?" John asked, afraid to hear the answer.

"Dad, there are so many rumors about everybody. I never believe half the stuff I hear. So, it doesn't make any sense for me to repeat it."

"Oh."

"But she was asking about you." Scott said, expecting to hear some kind of reaction from his father.

John did not show him that he was intrigued, and decided to change the subject. Unfortunately, John left himself hanging, with no way of finding out what Scott had heard. John didn't want to look too disappointed, so he was forced to give up.

Chapter Seven

REVELATIONS

For Christmas break, Scott took the bus down from college. John had no need to drive to Brick State to pick him up and would have been happy if he never saw the Brick State campus again. When John picked Scott up at the bus station, Scott informed him that his girlfriend was going to visit for a few days after Christmas. John was surprised because he had no idea that his son had a serious girlfriend.

"Are you serious about this girl?" John quizzed.

"Serious enough to have her meet my father." Scott said.

John was dumb-struck. He really did not know what to say.

"Dad, don't worry about it. Once you see her, you will love her."

When Scott informed the rest of the family, Darlene, surprisingly, was very excited to meet Scott's girlfriend. Her responses had become so predictable, recently, that her sudden charity was a bit refreshing and much appreciated by her husband. For once, she was acting like the mother figure that he had always wanted for his children.

Christmas came and went with what was expected to be another stress filled family gathering. Whenever Jenny's parents came over, it was always an excuse for Darlene to exhibit bad behavior, but this time she was very pleasant. The family was stunned, and wondered what had come over her.

After Christmas dinner was over and the company had left, he escaped to his office. Once in the office, he laid down upon his old beat up couch that was in his first home with Jenny. He could not help but feel sorry for himself as he drank his glass of wine. He was so despondent because he still missed Wendy.

There was a knock on his door, and Darlene was there at the door. She had been drinking wine all afternoon and was feeling a little tipsy and took a sudden interest in her husband. She looked down at his sorrowful appearance and felt pity on him.

"Are you coming up?" she asked as she walked into the room.

John seemed a bit surprised by the request, as she hadn't propositioned him for nearly a year. This suggestion had come several months late.

"Up for what?"

"You know," she said as she sat next to him on the couch and affectionately massaged his leg up to the inner thigh.

"Do I? Did I win the lottery or something?" he said sarcastically.

"John, come on. Do you want me to beg?"

"That would be a switch, wouldn't it?" he said as he stared blankly across the room, trying not to make eye contact, as he drank another sip from his wine glass. His coldness caused her to stop her advances and she stood up with disgust.

"Suit yourself, then," she said, with anger. "But remember, John. I came to you this time."

"I guess that I'm just tired, then!" he barked back.

She walked in a huff towards the door, and left the room.

The next morning, John apologized to Darlene for his behavior, but he was not forgiven. It was the first time he had denied her, and she was humiliated.

The following Saturday, Scott's girlfriend was expected. She had taken a bus, and Scott took the family car to pick her up at the bus station. John and Maggie anxiously awaited the arrival of the Scott's girlfriend, and hoped that he had picked someone who was well suited for him.

When they arrived, John, Darlene and Maggie were waiting in the great room on the couch. When they walked into the door, Scott's girlfriend took off her coat and revealed that she had a little baby bump, which shocked the family. Moreover, the young woman someone that John had met before. It was Wendy!

As Darlene started to wail about the impossible situation, John was weak in the knees had to sit down. His mouth gaped open as his wife lost her mind. John was speechless and the room was spinning. Wendy ... here? She's Scott's girlfriend? Pregnant? How could she be pregnant?

"Dad, I can explain," Scott begged, as his attention was centered on his father's agony.

John held his head as Darlene yelled and screamed about how Scott had ruined his life, asking him how he could be so stupid. He could not get his thoughts together, as Darlene's babbling voice pounded in his head. John had so many questions that he wanted to ask the young couple, especially Wendy.

He wanted to speak, but he could not get a word in edgewise. John finally opened his mouth to stop the madness.

"Darlene, would you please just shut up!" he bellowed, which caused her to finally close her mouth. When she gave him a horrified look, he said "I can't think," in a calmer tone.

"Who do you think you are? How dare you talk to me like that!" Darlene shrieked.

"Darlene, please. I need you to relax. I will handle this."

"Like you handle everything else?" she asked in a shrill voice that seemed to go right through him. His head was starting to pound.

"Darlene. Just be quiet!" he yelled.

"I'm not going to stand there and let you treat me like that," she announced, obviously offended. She stormed to the hall closet, grabbed her coat and stormed out of the door, slamming it so hard that it made the decorations on the Christmas tree sway. John did not attempt to stop her from leaving.

John sighed with a bit of relief. He wanted her away from the situation anyway. This matter was between him, his son, and Wendy. He turned back to face them, and looked into Wendy's lovely face. He could tell that she was nervous.

"Dad, we need to talk to you alone," Scott said to John, "can we talk in your office?" John could hear his son's voice, and nodded, but his gaze remained on Wendy.

"Okay," he said.

The three excused themselves from a stunned Maggie, who sat down in the couch while still in shock. John did not want Maggie to hear the conversation anyway, however exciting the news may have been.

Once in the office with the young couple and the doors closed, John still could not keep his eyes off of Wendy. He could not believe that she was actually standing in his home office. After all this time, he was happy that he could finally see her. Unfortunately, it was not the reunion that he had dreamed about. As he looked at her abdomen, he wondered how far along she was. She was still so beautiful, even more so than before, as the pregnancy added to her loveliness. He felt guilty for feeling this way, and tried to stop himself, since she was apparently his son's girlfriend.

John sat in his desk chair and the couple sat on the couch. Scott took a deep breath and started to speak. John's gaze kept finding it's way back to Wendy.

"Dad, I know what you're thinking," Scott began.

"Trust me Scott, you really don't."

"Yes, I really do Dad."

"I don't understand ... what do you mean?" John asked, finally taking his eyes off of Wendy and turning to his son, curious about what the clarification might be.

"She's not my girlfriend, Dad." Scott explained, "and the baby is not mine."

John was relieved temporarily, then confused once more.

"Excuse me?" John inquired, "then who…"

"I think that you probably know the answer to that question, Dad." Scott responded, "She's nineteen weeks pregnant. Probably conceived sometime in August. Does this ring a bell?"

Suddenly it all came together, and John's breathing temporarily stopped. John realized that he was the father, and furthermore, Scott knew about his affair in August. He put his hand over his mouth, probably out of panic, but then he was able to recover long enough to speak.

"Wendy, is this true?" John asked as he looked into her eyes.

"I'm sorry!" She said as tears started to roll down her cheek. "He just found out somehow, and he confronted me. I was not going to tell you. I swear. I didn't want to ruin your life."

As he heard her speak, he sat there silently, unable to speak. He could not believe what he was hearing. The reason she left and went into hiding was because she was pregnant with his child.

"Dad, I did not want you to be in the dark and I thought that you needed to know." Scott explained as he stood up from the couch, "The reason that I said that she was my girlfriend was to try and find a way to get her in the door. I'm sorry I lied to you."

Scott stood up from the couch, walked over to his father and patted him on the shoulder. Then he walked towards the office door.

"I guess that you guys need to talk, so I'll leave you alone. The rest is up to you now." Scott said as he walked out the door.

John watched as Scott left, realizing that he had a lot of explaining to do to his children. He wondered if they could ever forgive him.

Meanwhile, Scott walked into the great room and met up with his sister, who was still sitting on the couch with a befuddled look on her face.

"What's going on?" Maggie asked with concern.

"Dad's in love." Scott said with a smile, then he headed for the kitchen.

"Excuse me?" she said as leapt off the couch and chased after him.

Once alone, John looked back over at Wendy, who was sitting on the couch with her head down and tears rolling down her cheeks. He said nothing, then sat down next to her and hugged her tightly. Afterwards, he cradled her face in his hands and finally gave her the kiss that he had been waiting to give her for the last four months.

"Where have you been?" he asked with concern, "I tried to contact you … I was going out of my mind."

"I didn't know what to do, so I moved," she said, "I guess I was scared"

"Scared of what?"

"Well, I've never been pregnant before, for one. I thought that you would be mad at me."

"How could I be mad at you? It's not like you were alone in the conception of this baby."

"I didn't think that you would believe me. It seemed like such an obvious set up."

"I would have believed you."

"But, I didn't want to complicate your life. You're a married man, John."

"Nobody knows that fact more than I do, sweetheart, but I am married in name only."

"My heart told me that, but my head told me otherwise." she said.

"You still should have told me. I thought that we connected that night, and then for the next month…then all of the sudden you were nowhere to be found."

"I wanted to tell you so badly. I was so close to calling you. I looked at your number every day, but I just couldn't do it. I'm so sorry"

"Didn't you know how I felt about you? Didn't you understand that I wanted you to be part of my life?"

"I thought that if I told you that I was pregnant, you would think that I was trying to trap you."

"I wouldn't have thought that."

"Why not? What reason do you have to trust me? I'm just some waitress."

"Don't say that about yourself. You are so much more that that."

"Anyone would think that. They would just say that I was trying to trap you because you're a doctor."

"Wendy, stop. I know that this wasn't planned. I don't care what other people think." he assured her.

He placed his hand on her abdomen, which had a small, but noticeable baby bulge, "I need you in my life. My life will be more complicated, yes, but I could not live without you. The baby is icing on the cake."

They kissed again more passionately, and as they embraced they heard a commotion in the great room. After that, they heard a hurried knock on the door. Scott had returned to warn him that Darlene had just pulled back into the driveway. It seemed to be as if she just went for a drive around the block. She probably wanted to come back for round two, and John wished to shield

Wendy from her anger. When he opened the door, Scott was there to help to hurry Wendy out.

"Scott, I want you to bring Wendy upstairs to my room," he said. Then after a quick smirk from Scott, he corrected himself. "I mean, the guest room. I'll stay in the office tonight."

John did not know what to do next. Scott convinced him that his plan was the best for now, since John was still in shock and needed to recover before making any major decisions. He didn't need to do or say anything stupid.

As Maggie and Scott escorted Wendy up the stairs, John waited for Hurricane Darlene to walk in the door. The evening's festivities were not over yet.

"Where are they?" Darlene demanded as she hung her coat into the hallway closet. She was primed and ready for a confrontation, and John was not going to let it happen.

"She's going to stay in the guest room tonight."

"Over my dead body!" she barked.

"Don't tempt me," John thought. Instead he calmly said, "Darlene, relax."

"I can't believe you John. You're Mr. Catholic. Do you approve of this?"

"Scott is staying in his own room. They will not be together."

"That tramp is not going to stay in my house!" she demanded as she pointed in the direction of the stairs, loud enough for people to hear in China.

"This is my house, Darlene," he reminded her. "As long as this is my house, Scott's girlfriend can stay."

"You're a goddamned hypocrite!" She yelled in an wounding way, "you can sleep in the office tonight."

"Tell me something that I don't already know," he voiced sarcastically.

Darlene stormed away after berating her husband for his stupidity, raced up the stairs, almost knocking over Scott, and slammed the bedroom door. The sound of the door echoed throughout the house. Scott walked down the stairs to greet his mentally exhausted father, and put his hand on his shoulder.

"Dad, can we have a new Mom?" he kidded.

"That's enough out of you," John scolded lightheartedly.

Scott was the cause of all of this, but he had also given him a future, and for this John was truly grateful. John put his hand on Scott's shoulder, smiled and invited him back into the office to have a heart to heart.

"I guess that I have some explaining to do." John said.

"Not really," Scott joked, "I know about the birds and the bees."

"You're a very funny guy," John said, "you know what I mean. Is Maggie still up?"

"She went to bed when Cruella started to go into her song and dance routine. Didn't want to see you get yelled at … again."

"I don't blame her. Does she know the whole story?'

"I just told her that you were in love and left it at that."

"So, now she's more confused than ever."

"Pretty much."

The two men sat down and John started to wonder what he was going to say next. How do you explain something like this to your son?

"Scott, I don't know where to begin."

"Dad, I know when it happened," Scott said, "It was that night when you first brought me to school. You hooked up that night, right?"

"How did you find out?"

"Well, word got around that some old dude brought the hot waitress home that night."

"Old dude?" John asked, "Thirty-eight is not old, Scott."

"If you think so, Dad," Scott joked.

"I know so."

"Well, obviously some things still work."

"Scott…" John sighed, as the teasing was getting annoying. "Please … just get back to the story. Okay?"

"Okay, I'm sorry." Scott relented.

"So, you were saying?"

"At first, I didn't catch on at all. Although I did notice the way that you were checking her out that night."

"You did?" he asked. He was surprised to hear this because he thought that he hid his desire so well.

"Dad, you were such a dork. You were totally stuttering. It was pretty pathetic."

"Go on …" John insisted. He did not wish to hear about his faults.

"At first, no one knew who this mystery guy might be. No one had ever seen him before. Then Tom put two and two together. He works there, you know."

"Works where?"

"Huntington's," Scott explained, "Tom was talking to another waitress who had worked that night, and she told him that she thought that the guy who took Wendy home was the same guy that he had dinner with earlier that night. That's when Tom told me that he thought that my Dad took home the hot chick from Huntington's"

"What did you say?"

"I told him that he was full of crap," Scott said confidently.

"So you didn't believe him?"

"No way. You're so…you know…a choir boy" he explained, "You're not the kind of guy who goes to bars to pick up girls. You're not smooth enough."

"And you know what smooth is …" John asked.

"Well, I know more than you do," Scott said.

Then he had to know something.

"How did you pick her up, anyway?"

"I didn't plan on it, Scott, it just happened."

"But, you did go back to the bar, Dad. So, you must have been thinking about it."

"I went back to the bar, yes. But, I did not plan on having an affair. I just wanted to talk to her. We talked for hours. Then it got late and I drove her home. Then …"

John paused, because he realized that he was talking to his son about an extramarital affair that he had experienced. Suddenly, he felt like Hugh Hefner.

"Well, you see the results."

"Yeah, I do. Nice work."

"You still didn't tell me what made you finally believe it."

"Tom just convinced me. All the evidence pointed to you."

"Sorry about that."

"Dad, I'm not here to judge."

"I'm not a very good example of a dedicated family man."

"Are you kidding me? After what you've put up with for the past three years? You did your best to keep the family together. You had to break down eventually. You are human after all."

"Why didn't you say something to me?"

"What am I going to do, ground you?" Scott asked, "besides, I was kind of happy for you. Of course, I was hoping that this meant the end of Cruella as my wicked stepmother."

"It doesn't mean that it was right, Scott."

"Dad, you thought about yourself, for once. You've spent three years trying to be nice to the Wicked Witch with no results. If you were willing to get it on with someone else, that had to mean something, didn't it?"

"I still broke my vows, Scott."

"Vows that were taken in a courthouse, Dad. Not in the church. It was more of a contract than anything else."

"I still promised to be faithful, Scott. I didn't keep that promise."

"Dad, she made it impossible to love her. She made you miserable. Why don't you cut yourself a break?"

The conversation had veered of into a direction that John did not want to continue, and Scott sensed it by the look on his father's face. Scott decided to steer back into the right path.

"Maybe you were supposed to meet Wendy. Did you ever think of that?"

"I think about that a lot," John admitted. "You know. We did keep in touch with each other for a month in a half, then in October…nothing."

"I know. I used to see her once in a while, and that's when she'd asked about you. I even told you about that, remember? That's another reason why I thought that the rumor was true," Scott said. "Then after Thanksgiving, I heard a rumor that she left the bar because she was pregnant. That blew my mind."

"I can just imagine."

"I realized that this baby was probably yours, so I tried to find out where she went. I finally found out that she was at her parent's house. Tom found out the number, and I called. She was scared to tell you about the baby, Dad, and it took me a while to convince her that you would want to know about it.

"You were right," John agreed.

"I know." Scott said, "I hope that I didn't give you a heart attack when I came here and said that she was my girlfriend … and she was pregnant to top it off."

"I was a bit in shock, Scott, I didn't know what to do at that point."

"Sorry Dad. I was just trying to get her in the door."

"Don't be sorry Scott, you did me a favor. I appreciate all that you have done. You have changed my life."

The two men stood up and hugged.

"Thank you so much Scott."

"I love you Dad." Scott said.

"Love you too." John replied.

Scott yawned and proclaimed that he was tired, joking that he was going to retire to his nice warm bed, after which he said that he hoped that his father had a good night's sleep on the old beat up couch in the cold office.

"You could always sleep in the guest room. I'm sure that it's nice and warm in there," Scott teased.

"Very funny," John said, and he told his son to get out of there. It was going to be a long day on Sunday.

John laid down on the couch that he once shared with Jenny and thoughts were racing through his head. He was going to be a father again! It was an amazing development. How was he going to explain it to Darlene? That was something he was not looking forward to doing.

He awoke to the feeling of his forehead being stroked by Wendy and her soft kisses to his face. He thought that it was a wonderful way to wake up, and it was something that he could get used to.

"Hello you," he said with a smile, "did you get lost?"

"I'm not lost now." she said.

"And I'm found," he joked. She kissed him again, softly, and stroked his face. He sat up, yawned and he patted on his lap for her to sit down. She sat down gingerly as if she felt that she would break his legs. Then he kissed her again.

"I'm sorry that you got banished to your office," she lamented.

"I don't think I could have slept in the master bedroom anyway ... after what Darlene said, and how she treated you," he replied.

"Scott prepared me for what her reaction might be," Wendy said, "I'm so sorry that I am the cause of such heartbreak."

"Heartbreak? Sweetheart, The heartbreak happened when I couldn't find you," he said, while sincerely into her eyes.

"I'm sorry about that," she said as her eyes started to tear up from the guilt.

"This is not the first time that I have been ejected from the bedroom. I told you that already."

"There's plenty of room in the guestroom," she teased.

"The offer is tempting sweetheart, but you know I have to say no."

"I know." she said.

"Even though I desperately want to show you how much you've been missed," he said suggestively.

She giggled in reply. The two of them knew that it was impossible, but it was a fun thought. He stroked her curved abdomen again and sighed.

"How do you feel?" he asked.

"Fat," she replied lightheartedly.

"You're stunning," he corrected her.

"I bet you say that to all the pregnant women that you see." she joked.

"Are you taking care of yourself with a doctor and all that?"

"Yes, Doctor Stanton...vitamins and milk and all that good stuff," she said diligently. "My mother is making sure of that."

"Do you know what we are having?"

"Didn't ask ... I want to be surprised."

"Well, you are full of surprises," he observed.

"I aim to please."

"I know," he said playfully.

He embraced and kissed her again. This time, he slid her off his lap and onto her back, and the embrace became more intense. He kissed her neck and worked his way down to her stomach, where he stopped and kissed where the baby was. Then he worked his way back up until they were facing each other.

"I wish that I could make love to you right now," he whispered with frustration in his voice.

"Me too," she sighed.

"I swore to myself that if I ever saw you again, that I would never let you go," he said. "Now that you're here, I'd like you to stay in town. I do not want to let you out of my sight."

"How can we do that?"

"I will figure something out. I want to be with you. Will you wait for me? It won't be that long. I promise."

"John, I would wait for you forever."

They agreed that it was too risky or her to stay in the room any longer, so they decided that their rendezvous in the office would have to be cut short. They kissed, and she managed to return to the guest room undetected.

John knew that this plan of Scott's would not last forever. In less than a month, Scott was scheduled return to college and their cover would be blown. John wanted Wendy to stay with him, and not return to her parent's house. Darlene would have to be told the truth as soon as possible. John just didn't know how to do it.

Chapter Eight

SOME TIME ALONE

It had been another one of those hectic Mondays at the office. Runny noses, ear infections, cough and sneezes were everywhere to be found. To top it off, they had to stay open a extra half hour because Mrs. Bennett was running late. John finally managed to crawl in the door at seven o'clock, exhausted and in need of a hot shower.

During the day, he received a scathing call from Darlene telling him that she was going to stay a week at her mother's house in Delaware…again. She had reached her limit, and needed some time away to think things through. No doubt, she was prepared to hang out all their dirty laundry for everyone in her family to dissect and mull over.

This was not the first time she had escaped to the sanctuary of one of her mother's homes to complain about her husband, his children, her marriage, and whatever was the big problem of the moment. It would most likely not be the last time, most likely, since the big secret had yet to be revealed. John figured that when that time arrived, she would probably escape to the house in Florida.

"That will be an exciting day," he thought to himself as he shook his head.

He knew that he could not keep this secret for long. He could not expect Scott to put up with the abusive treatment from Darlene for much longer. No matter how much Scott has tried to convince him that everything was fine, John would have to stand up and face the music, and let the chips fall were the may. Even though it was a day that he was dreading, afterwards, he would finally be free to be with Wendy.

John found two notes on the hallway table. One was from Maggie.

"Dad, I'm sleeping over Bridget's house. I already got permission from Cruella before she left. See you tomorrow. Love you, Maggie."

The second one read as follows:
"Dad, I went to a party with Pal and Ben. Have fun (smiley face). I have my phone if you need me (not). Scott."

It took a moment before John realized what Scott meant when he wrote have fun with a smiley face next to it. It was the first time that he would be alone with Wendy, and his son thought that he would take advantage of the situation. Although, it seemed like a golden opportunity, John had many reservations.

He did not have reservations about Wendy. He was in love with her. He knew that as soon as he saw her beautiful face, when she walked in the door and shocked the family. He wanted to be with her, there was no doubt about that. John had a problem with was the where and when. Even though his love for Darlene had diminished entirely, he still did not feel that it was appropriate to be with Wendy in the house that he and Darlene shared.

He smelled something cooking in the kitchen. Now, that was something that he was not used to experiencing. Darlene used to cook in the early days of their marriage, and she was a very good cook. But, that was only in the beginning. Lately, with the kids on the go and Darlene barely around due to her career, his home cooked meal was usually in a box in the freezer.

He walked into the kitchen and found Wendy at the table reading a magazine. There was something in a pot on the stove and it smelled terrific.
"So, you cook more than eggs?" he asked as he walked over to the table.
She glanced up at him, smiled and answered him. "Yes, John, I cook."
"What's for dinner?"
"I just made Meatballs and Gravy. Nothing exciting."
"Trust me, anything homemade is exciting. It smells terrific."
"Thanks."
"How long do I have? I'd like to shower before I eat. It's been a busy day."
"Not too long. All I have to do is cook the pasta. I was just waiting for you to come home."

With that, he promised that he would be right back. He ran upstairs, showered, put on something comfortable and returned to the kitchen. By the time he sat down, the table was set and the food was on the table. Everything looked great. He felt as if he were in a dream.

He didn't realize how hungry he was. The food was delicious. It was the best Meatballs and Pasta that he had ever eaten. Maybe it was the combination of the food and the company across the table from him that made the dinner so perfect.

"That was delicious, Wendy. Thank you," he said.

"You're welcome."

"You didn't have to go to so much trouble, though. I didn't expect you to cook for me."

"Well, actually…I was nervous, and I always cook when I'm nervous. It's kind of a thing with me," she said as she started to clear off the table. He stood up to help her with the dishes.

"Nervous about what?" he asked lightheartedly.

"Well, your wife, for one."

"Yeah, she scares me too," he laughed. He was actually joking about it.

"Seriously, John," she admonished, "I really shouldn't be here. I'm the other woman. This is her home. Your kids think that there's some kind of naughty thing that we're trying to get away with tonight. You should have heard Scott's tone of voice when he left today."

"Well, I think that Scott thinks that he set it all up."

"Don't you feel a little bit funny about it?"

"Yes, I do."

"I mean, I know we couldn't do anything anyway. My condition and all."

"Well, technically…we could," John countered. "Jenny and I made love right up until about a week before Scott was born."

"You did?" she asked with surprise and a little excitement at the same time.

"Yes, we did."

"Oh," she answered, "and that was okay?"

"Yeah, we just had to be a little creative," he recalled with a smile on his face. Then he returned to the original subject, after clearing his throat. "But, I know what you mean. I couldn't do it here, either. Not in this house while Darlene lives here."

"Because this is her house."

"Because this is the house that we share as a married couple, even though there's nothing really between us anymore."

"That's how I feel. I should not be here. It's too hard. I should really go back to my parent's house."

He stopped, and gently grabbed her hand, turning her towards him so that they were face to face.

"Wendy, listen to me. I know that I have no right to tell you what to do. But, let me be very clear about this. I want you to stay. I don't want to lose you again."

"But, I've screwed up your life. I've messed up Scott's life. If it wasn't for the baby…"

"My life was a mess before I met you. I told you how unhappy I was back in August, remember? If I was a happily married man, I would have never gone back to the bar to find you. I would have gone straight to the hotel," he explained, "I knew what I wanted that night, and I know what I want now. I want you."

"But…"

He put his finger softly over her lips to stop her from speaking and then he continued.

"I love you Wendy. I'm in love with you," he confessed. "I want to spend the rest of my life with you. I didn't realize that until I lost you. Then, when I saw you again…I knew that I couldn't live without you."

"John…"

"You don't have to say anything now, just think about it," he interjected. "I know that it's all very fast and we barely know each other."

"True…" she pondered.

"I just wanted you to know how I feel," he clarified.

She looked at the earnestness on his face, and smiled. He looked so adorable.

"John, it's impossible not to love you. Don't you know that?" she said, "Of course I love you!"

"Thank God for that!" he sighed, as he held her face in his hands. He leaned in and kissed her, then they embraced while kissing. John pulled away to stop the forward progress.

"I better stop now, or I will not be able to stop."

"Good idea," she agreed.

"I'll finish up here. Why don't you go relax"

"You don't have to."

"It's my house. It's the least I can do. Put your feet up or something. Doctor's orders."

He convinced her to take his advice, and she left the room without further argument. He was happy that she left, because he was finding it very hard to be near her without wanting her more. This was going to be a long night.

After he put the dishes in the dishwasher and finished cleaning the kitchen, he decided to join her in the family room to watch television. To his surprise, she was not there. She was not in the great room either. He checked his watch and noticed that it was only seven-thirty. He wondered where she went. He decided to go upstairs and check the guest room, which was dangerous territory for a man who has just taken a vow of celibacy.

He knocked on the door softly, waiting for a reply.

"Yes?" Wendy replied.

"Wendy, are you okay in there? Can I come in?"

"The door is open," she replied sweetly.

He opened the door and saw her laying there in a sleek three quarter flannel nightshirt, reading a book, and looking gorgeous. He silently prayed for strength.

"Oh God, Wendy, you're killing me."

"What?" she teased as she feigned ignorance.

"You know what. You're trying to torture me."

"I am doing nothing of the sort. I was tired, I changed into my nightgown and I'm reading a book on the bed."

"Couldn't you have worn some footed pajamas or something like that?"

"I don't have any footed pajamas."

"I really wish that you had a pair."

"John, would you really rather see me in footed pajamas?"

"Just for a week or two. It would have to have some stupid snowman design. If you wore some of that green facial mask stuff on your face, it would also help."

"With the cucumbers on my eyes?"

"Yeah, and the curlers. Lots of curlers. This way, your whole body is covered. No legs exposed."

"Don't you like what I am wearing?"

"Of course I like it. I love it. I love it so much that I have to leave," he said, trying to make a graceful exit before he passed out from the stress. "So, good night."

"John, you don't have to leave."

"Oh, yes I do," he insisted.

"Come over here, John"

"I'm really trying to practice what I preach over here."

"Just because we sleep in the same bed, it doesn't mean that we have to make love."

"It does in my book."

"Come on John, you're a big boy. You can handle it."

"Wendy, trust me. If I get in that bed with you, I will be a big boy. I can guarantee that."

"Just for a couple of minutes?" she begged, "I just want to cuddle a little bit. I've waited so long to lay in your arms again. You can't deny me, John."

"Wendy, please ... have mercy on me ... I'm begging you."

"John, come over here."

Against his better judgment, John took the bait. As he crept over, she slid under the covers and flipped over his side, patting on the bed. She giggled playfully and he grumbled under his breath. This was going to be the longest five to ten minutes of his life.

"You are actually keeping your clothes on?" she teased, commenting on the fact that he crawled into bed wearing a Yankees t-shirt and blue jeans.

"Absolutely," he replied, "it's the only chance I've got. No funny stuff, lady."

Once under the covers, he lay there still as he could be. She leaned over and cuddled him with her hand and head on his chest. She teased him a little bit in the beginning, lifting his shirt to slide her hand under it and onto his stomach, causing him to react swiftly.

"No, no, no. I'm warning you. I'll be out of here in two seconds."

She giggled and apologized, then did it again.

"Wendy…I swear…"

"Sorry."

He tried to think horrible thoughts in order to keep his excitement down. Car crashes, horror movies, and tax audits spun around in his mind, but he could not hold them in. It was not easy to keep thinking the horrible thoughts, because the heat of her soft body made his heart beat faster, and his desire for her grew. He was relieved that he remained fully dressed, because if he felt any her softer skin touching his, it would have certainly been over.

"My God, she smells so good," he thought. It was intoxicating! He closed his eyes again, thinking "horrible things, horrible things!"

She did not tease him any further. She truly did want to cuddle, and that was all. Any further advance from her would have started an avalanche, and she knew that. She wanted to be fair about it and try not to torture him too much. Happy just to be in his loving arms, she closed her eyes, and drifted off to sleep.

At the first sign that she had fallen asleep, he managed to squirm out of her grasp. He had already set such a horrible example for his children, as far as he was concerned, and he did not want to continue the trend. The last thing that he wanted was for Scott to find him sleeping in her bed.

Once out of the guest room, he breathed a sigh of relief. He had passed the test this time. He would not be able to resist her for long. He would have to find a way to have her all to himself, but it just had to be in another place.

Chapter Nine
A SURPRISE AT THE OFFICE

The next day at the office, John was just finishing up a checkup for a six-month old boy named Randy. Randy had just gotten his shots, and started to wail. He was so loud that it was difficult for John to have a simple conversation with his mother. As Randy screamed, John wrote out a prescription for vitamin drops.

"He's doing really well, Mrs. Gonzalez." John assured her, as she dressed her son. "Randy is growing like a weed. He has really caught up to where he should be at this point."

"He's a fighter," she said, "as you can tell"

"He certainly has strong lungs," John joked as he handed her the prescription. I will see you in three months for his nine-month check-up. You can make the appointment with Nadine at the desk.

"Okay, thank you," Mrs. Gonzalez said as he carried poor Randy out of the examination room. John said goodbye to Randy, but Randy wanted no part of him.

As Mrs. Gonzalez left the room, John walked down the hall in the other direction, walked into his office and closed the door. He looked at his watch. It was lunchtime, and he wondered what he should do for the next hour.

"Dr. Stanton," Nadine's voice said over the intercom, "There is a Mrs. Johnson to see you. She says that she brought you lunch."

"Who the hell is Mrs. Johnson?" he thought to himself. He scanned the internal memory bank of his brain as if he were going through his personal files. Mr. Johnson…Mrs. Johnson…who the hell is Mrs. Johnson? He assumed that it must be another one of Darlene's friends come to beg him for some kind of donation for baseball, soccer or whatever.

"I'll be right out," he groaned as he straightened his clothing with his free hand.

He walked into the waiting room, expecting to pretend to know whomever this woman was. But when he saw her, recognized Mrs. Johnson immediately. He smiled as he gazed into Wendy's lovely face. He tried to contain his joy at her presence, but it was hard to contain.

"Mrs. Johnson..." he teased as he held out his hand to greet her.

"Doctor..." she replied, shaking his hand. The feel of her touch sent shivers up his spine.

"Nadine, I would like you to meet Mrs. Johnson. She's a close family friend."

"Very close," Wendy said with a wry smile. She turned to shake Nadine's hand, and they exchanged niceties. Janice walked into the room as well, and noticed a smile on John's face that was hard to ignore.

"And this is Janice," John explained, as Wendy shook her hand and said, "Nice to meet you."

There was a bit of an uncomfortable silence as John tried to restrain the goofy look on his face. His mind was telling him to keep cool because they will know that something was going on. The rest of him was telling him to jump Wendy.

Finally, the silence was broken by Nadine.

"Doctor Stanton, we're going to go to lunch now."

"Sure, go ahead," he permitted almost immediately.

"I'll lock the door on the way out," Nadine said, while observing that John kept his gaze on Mrs. Johnson, and was not really listening.

She glanced at Janice as if to say "What's going on over there?"

John had not smiled that much in years. Nadine whispered to Janice that they could probably take a three-hour lunch and he would not notice. Unfortunately for all, John had an appointment with another adolescent at one o'clock.

"Right this way, Mrs. Johnson," John said, leading her down the hall and into his office. Once inside with the door closed and locked behind them, he grabbed the bag from her hand and put it on the desk. He took off her black winter coat and hung it up on the hook. Then he put his arms around her and kissed her passionately. When he released her, she almost lost her balance.

"Nice to see you too," she giggled.

"Interesting name...John...son," he observed.

"Or daughter," she implied. "Do you think that they suspect us?"

"I don't really care about that right now," he said as he kissed her again, leading to another romantic embrace.

Once the clinch was released, he did comprehend where he was and that this was not the time or place for an afternoon delight. Nadine and Janice were due back at a quarter to one. Usually though, they would race into the office at five to one.

"So what's in the bag?" he asked as he peeked inside. He could tell by the scent in the room that the food was Chinese.

"Well, there is Orange chicken for you," she said.

"How did you know?"

"A little bird told me," she confessed.

"Which one?"

"Maggie."

"It's a conspiracy," he sighed. He took the lunch out of the bag and a wonderful smell filled the room. "You're going to spoil me."

"You deserve to be spoiled. You've been a very good boy."

"Too good, if you ask me," he replied, "I would like to be extremely bad right now."

"So would I, John..." she cooed.

"But making love on a desk full of papers is not your idea of a good time?" he joked.

"Don't tempt me." she replied, "But if that happened your food would get cold."

"I wouldn't want to do that," he teased, letting the subject be changed. "I guess that you are not having any of this."

"No, Orange Chicken would do horrible things to me in my condition, although I normally would love to have it. Mine is not spicy, I'm afraid. I'm having Chicken with Chinese Vegetables."

"Good Choice."

"I thought that you'd approve," she said as he pulled out his desk chair for her to sit in. He kissed her on the head, while giving her a gentle massage on her shoulder, which gave her more pleasure than it usually would, and she admitted it. "Wow, you could do that for an hour."

"There are plenty of things that I would like to do to you for an hour, but we only have forty minutes," he joked with a hint of dismay.

"And we are in your office."

"That too," he said, as he said down across from her and opened up his lunch.

Lunch hour seemed to pass too quickly, and before he knew it, he could hear the front door of the waiting room being unlocked. Nadine and Janice had returned from lunch. They were early, for once in their lives. John thought that possibly they were early for a reason? Trying to catch him in the act, perhaps.

He could hear footsteps down the hall, and he quickly unlocked the door carefully so that she did not notice that it was once locked. As he returned to the chair, he could hear a knock on the door.

"Doctor Stanton?" Janice asked.

"Come in, Janice," John replied.

Janice opened the door and curiously peered in. She saw the two of them sitting innocently across from each other at his desk finishing their lunch.

"I just wanted you to know that we were back."

"Thank you, Janice," he replied.

Janice was able to make a quick inspection of the two of them before she closed the door. She didn't see anything out of place and there were no buttons unfastened. John still had on his doctor whites with his tie neatly nestled in place. She almost seemed disappointed. She walked back to give Nadine the discouraging news that Dr. Clean had been a good boy.

"Maybe I should go before your patient arrives, and some parent sees a strange woman in your office," Wendy suggested.

"Wouldn't that be scandalous," he replied seemingly in a dream state. Breaking out of his trance, he realized that time was getting away from him. The patient would arrive shortly, and it was back to reality for him.

As he stood up to help her get out of her chair. She was a little slow getting up, and she felt a kick inside her as she rose. She paused for a second. "Woh..." she moaned.

"What is it?" He asked with concern.

"I think that your little one is kicking."

He asked if he could feel it, and she placed his hand on the area where the last kick occurred. They waited about a minute and it happened again.

"There he goes," John exclaimed excitedly in a low voice, "or she."

He crouched down and kissed her abdomen, rubbing it gently, then putting his ear against it. The baby kicked again and John giggled like a child.

"It's a miracle, isn't it?"

"Yes it is," she said with a smile, then he stood up and kissed Wendy's face.

"You're a miracle," he gushed. "You make me so happy."

"Hey happy boy, don't you have to go back to work?" she asked with a sly smile. The last thing she wanted was Janice to walk in on this tender moment.

"You're right," he agreed. "I guess that I will see you later in the real world."

"Yeah, I better go. Scott is supposed to meet me in front of the CVS at one o'clock."

"I was wondering how you got here," he said as he walked over to retrieve her jacket, then helped her put it on.

"He's the master planner."

"He's got it all figured out, I guess." John said as he opened his door and the two of them walked into the hallway and towards the waiting room. It was time for them to begin acting again.

"Nice to see you again, Mrs. Johnson," he said as he shook her hand. "I will send you a check for the donation as soon as I can."

"Thank you, Dr. Stanton," she replied. He walked her to the front door, opened it, and held it open as she passed by. Once outside, she glanced back at him and he winked back, knowing that they shared their own little secret. She walked away and he watched her with a smile, which was hopefully undetected by his clerk.

"Baseball." he said as he passed Nadine and Janice in the waiting room.

He really did not care if she believed him or not. As John practically floated back to his office, Janice turned to Nadine and raised her eyebrows suspiciously.

"Baseball, my foot … did you see his goofy smile?" she said.

"He did look a bit suspicious."

"Whatever it is…Good for him!" Janice declared.

John had a smile on his face for the rest of the day. By four-thirty, his docket of appointments was clear, and he prepared to leave a little early for some extra time with his new love. He told Janice and Nadine that they could leave a little early that day. Once Nadine left, however, John found himself cornered in his office.

"What's going on," Janice pried.

"What do you mean?" John said, pretending not to know of what she was speaking.

"Johnny, you know what I am talking about. I saw that goofy look on your face. You've been smiling all day since that meeting with Mrs. Johnson. What's going on between the two of you?"

"There's nothing going on," he lied while trying to keep a straight face.

"Johnny," she said sternly.

"Janice …"

"Johnny, I thought we were close."

"We are close. You're my best friend."

"I've known you for ten years. I know when you are lying to me. What's going on?"

"There's nothing," he said, rather unconvincingly.

New Beginnings

"John, if you don't tell me what is going on, I'll call Fred at the station, tell him to get his ass over here, use his handcuffs and attach you to that chair until you tell me the truth."

"Janice…"

"John, don't mess with me."

He could see the determined look on her face and knew that he wasn't going to be able to leave until he divulged his secret. He took a deep breath, and stood up from his office chair, and checked the office door.

"The front door is locked, if you're wondering. Nadine left already." Janice assured him as she waited to hear the news. She watched as John turned back and returned to his chair as Janice pulled up a chair of her own.

"Well?" she asked, "do I have to call my husband?"

"No, you don't have to call Fred. I'll tell you. I was going to tell you anyway, but I wanted to wait."

"Why wait?"

"It's a hell of a story."

"Tell me, John. The suspense is killing me."

"Janice…I'm in love!" he said excitedly as if it was an unknown revelation.

"I can see that, John," Janice sighed as she rolled her eyes. "But is there something going on?"

"Well, yeah."

"So, you're having an affair with Mrs. Johnson?"

"Her name isn't Mrs. Johnson. Her name is Wendy Burke. Mrs. Johnson was just a cover name."

"John, that's not important. Are you having an affair?"

"Technically…yes."

"Technically?"

From then, he told her about their story. The overnight affair, the loss of contact and the reunion. He also told her that the baby that she was carrying was his.

"Oh my God, John," she gasped as she covered her mouth. "I don't want to rain on your parade, but are you sure it's yours?"

"I trust her, Janice. She wouldn't lie to me. I know that the baby is mine."

"How do you know?"

"I just know. There's more to the story. If you knew all of it, you would understand."

"Does Darlene know?"

"Not yet, but she will know soon."

"She will have your balls on a plate, you know."

"I know that. I don't care."

65

"So this is the end of Darlene?"

"Janice, I love Wendy. I want to spend the rest of my life with her. I'm not going to let her go."

Chapter Ten

THE CAT IS OUT OF THE BAG

Eventually, Darlene came home from her mother's house and there was a definite chill in the air. Darlene tried to be civil, however, seemingly accepting the impossible situation of her stepson. The good will did not last more than a day. Soon she was back to her old ways, and John could not take it anymore. He could longer let his son take the heat for something that he had done. Once he had her alone, he decided that the secret had to be revealed.

"Darlene, Scott is not the father of the child," John blurted out. The words seemed to leave his lips before he had the chance to catch them.

This was it. Darlene was taken aback and she was off stride. So much for the current direction of her anger.

"Well, that's stupid," she mocked. "Now, he is dating a woman who is carrying another man's child?"

"He's not dating her. They are just friends."

Now Darlene was really confused.

"Well, why would he come here and say that he was the father and that she was his girlfriend? Why go through all that? Was it just a joke?"

"No joke, Darlene. He was protecting someone."

"Who could he possibly protect, and why would I care who this father was? I probably don't even know the idiot."

There was a pause in the conversation as John knew that the truth was about to leave his lips. He knew that the following minute, day, week, and month was about to become a circus. However, he could not keep the secret any longer.

"The child is mine, Darlene."

"What?" Darlene asked quizzically as if she had just heard a lie.

"It's my baby."

"John, this is no time to joke," she said in a skeptical fashion.

"I'm not joking, Darlene, it's the truth," he convinced her.

"How? What ... I don't understand," she stammered.

Darlene's jaw dropped as if she had been frozen in time. She had to sit down.

"We met when I dropped Scott off at college."

"This is impossible, John. Why are you doing this? Why are you lying to me?"

"Darlene, I am telling the truth."

"John, you don't have affairs. I've never seen you look at another woman."

"I did this time."

From the look in his eyes, she knew that it was true. It was all coming back to her. There were glances between John and Wendy at the table just the night before. She had seen it, but tried to convince herself that she was over-reacting. John had never been the type to even look at another woman, and was definitely not the type of guy to cheat, or so she thought. He was still pining for his dead wife, for God's sake!

"This is unbelievable! I can't believe it!"

"I'm sorry, Darlene."

"And she's pregnant, John? Are you sure that the baby is yours? She may be trying to blackmail you."

"It's mine."

"How do you know?"

"I just know. She wouldn't lie to me."

"And you know her so well, right?"

"I'm in love with her, Darlene."

Now, suddenly he was in love with someone else? It was unbelievable! Darlene's temper started to flare as if someone had turned on her inner furnace. How dare he do this to her? She hung around in this lousy marriage for this humiliation?

"Are you trying to tell me that after one night…you are in love with a waitress? Are you kidding me?."

He could hear the fury in her voice as she said the word waitress as if it were a dirty word. Mount Darlene was about to blow, and John braced himself for the explosion. Darlene stood up from her chair and started to pace. Then she lunged towards John and slapped his face.

"You've ruined us, John!" she shrieked, "how am I going to face my colleagues again?"

"Is that all that is important to you?" he asked, surprised that she was only worried about how it looked to the outside world.

"That's all I have left, John. That is important to me."

"So the marriage means nothing to you?"

"Ask yourself that question, John, you're the one who screwed around. The marriage wasn't on your mind that night," she commented.

"Darlene, I wasn't looking to fall in love. It just happened."

"Mr. Noble. You're such a joke. What would your sainted wife think of you now?" she said, suddenly fighting dirty.

"Darlene, don't go there" he said as he walked from the kitchen and into the great room. He wasn't trying to escape the argument, but he wanted a little space. She followed close behind and continued to squawk.

"No really, John, what would Jenny think if you cheated on her?"

"I was happy with Jenny." he said as he turned around to face her. He looked directly in her eyes. "I would never have cheated on her."

She asked for it.

"You son of a..." she tried to strike again, and he caught her arm.

"Enough, Darlene," he said.

"Enough is right. I've had enough of this whole miserable marriage. I don't know why I put up with you for so long."

"We both know that this marriage has been over for months, maybe even a year," John pointed out. "We've been unhappy for a very long time. We don't even sleep in the same bed. We barely spend time together anymore and when we are together, we argue."

"Maybe I wanted a little bit more. I spent a lot of time making us look respectable with the right people. Meanwhile, you're slumming around with this whore waitress."

"Don't call her that, Darlene."

"She slept with a married man, John, what else would I call her?" she sneered. "You probably have been sleeping with her in my own house. You had a lot of free time when I was away at my mother's house. Did you have fun, John? Even with your children in the house? You all must have had a great time laughing at me."

"I was not with her in this house, Darlene. Whatever I have done, I would not do that."

"Well, maybe your body was not with her, but your mind was unfaithful. I saw how you looked at her last night. You never looked at me like that. You never really loved me."

"That's not true, Darlene. When I married you, I was in love with you. I would not have married you if I didn't love you."

"And now you're not?"

"Can you honestly say that you still love me?"

"No," Darlene said solemnly, "I don't love you anymore."

Well, that was something that he had known already, but it was a poignant statement to hear. The love was gone, and the marriage was over. After those words, there was nothing left to say. The cat was out of the bag, and it was time for them to make some decisions. As he left her sitting on the couch in the great room, he knew that she could think of various ways to destroy him. Hopefully, that would not be the case. He could feel her wheels turning but he did not care. As long as he could be free and able to start a new life with Wendy, nothing else mattered.

As he attempted to make his exit, Darlene turned around and called his name.

"John, I want her out of this house."

"Darlene, she lives two hours away, I can't just drive her home tonight."

"John, this is your problem, not mine. I will make her life miserable. You know that. It is my right."

"Darlene…"

"John, I want her out of my house!" she screamed as her voice cracked, while holding back tears.

"Okay, Darlene. I'll figure out something."

To solve his problem, John turned to the people who had always been there for him. About an hour later, he was knocking on Robert and Anne's door with Wendy at his side and explanations at the ready.

"Mom and Dad, you had better sit down," John suggested to a very confused Mr. and Mrs. Channing.

After the story was told, a shocked Anne looked at her husband, and both were speechless.

"John, I don't know what to say. I'm surprised," Anne said.

"Are you disappointed in me?"

"Not disappointed, John. Never disappointed. Just surprised."

"You have to admit that this is a bit out of character for you," Robert added.

"Dad, I can't believe it myself. I happened so quickly. It was like I was struck by lightening. Do you know what I mean?"

"I understand it completely," Robert said as he gazed over at his wife and held her hand.

"I need a favor. Wendy needs a place to stay for a few days until the weekend when I drive her up to her parents house."

"Of course, John. We'd love to have her."

When John returned from the Channing household, Darlene called him into the living room.

"Did you ever love me, John?"

"You know I did. I tried very hard to make this marriage work. You shut me out."

"There were always three of us, John. It was you, me and Jenny. I never had a chance," she said, finally showing a little vulnerability.

"That's not true, Darlene. I loved you very much. You just never tried very hard to love me back."

"Maybe I thought it was a losing battle because I could never measure up to your sainted wife."

There was another pause, because John realized that it was useless to try to convince her that he once loved her. Her mind was made up. John decided to turn the subject into something more productive. He asked her to join her as they both sat on the couch.

"I think that we both know obviously where this is headed. Neither one of us is happy."

"Divorce." She replied.

"Unfortunately. God knows that you've hinted at it long enough."

"Are you trying to be funny now?" she snapped. She was not going to take the blame for any of this.

"I'm sorry … okay?" he sighed, "we just have to figure this thing out. What do you want?"

"What do I want?"

"I'll give you whatever you want. I'll call my lawyer and we can work out a settlement."

"Just like that?"

"Not just like that, Darlene. I want to be fair. "

"Better late than never, right?" she mocked.

"Just think about it. Whatever you want."

"You're willing to throw your life away for her?" she asked, "you're in love with her that much?"

"Yes, Darlene. I am."

The next day, when John was on lunch break, Darlene called to inform him of the price that he would have to pay for his betrayal.

"I want the house." Darlene said.

"The house?"

"Yes, the house. I want the house and everything in it."

"Darlene, this is my children's home. I can't just give it to you."

"You said that I could have anything I wanted John. I thought about it, and I want the house." she demanded.

"But, they have friends here. We have the tree in the back."

"You can take the tree. I don't want the damn tree, John. You can take your children's things. All I want is the house and the furniture."

John was silent. Somehow, this demand never crossed his mind. He expected her to ask for half of his assets and various other things, but the not the house that he bought for his children. They loved the house.

"How badly do you want the divorce, John? I could drag this thing out for years and your new, precious child will be born a bastard. All I am asking is for the house. That's all I want."

"I have to talk to Scott and Maggie about it."

"You do that."

Darlene seemed to relish seeing him in his bewilderment. She had found the perfect way to hurt him where it did the most damage. If he was going to humiliate her, she wanted him to suffer as well. Let this eat at him for a while as he figured out how to break the news to his precious children.

She considered dragging out the divorce in the court system, but she wanted to be free of the constraints of marriage. She was sick of the whole routine. She wanted to be free of his children and his first wife's parents. She was most looking forward to being free of Jenny Stanton, and was happy to pass on that burden to Wendy.

"My mother is going back to her winter house in Florida and I am going to spend a week with her. I want to get away from this whole mess," she explained. "You have one week to tell your precious children and your little girlfriend about my offer. If you agree, you have one month to get your belongings out, then I will want my house."

"What if I do not agree?"

"Then I'll see you in court, and your bastard will be born to an unwed mother."

As he hung up the phone, John knew that he had a heart wrenching decision to make. His first instinct was to call Wendy and tell her of his predicament.

"I don't know what to do," he sighed, "my children love that house. It has been their home for four years. We have the tree in the back for Jenny ... I don't know what to tell them."

"John, you should let them choose."

"But, what about the baby? I wanted to marry you before the baby was born."

"He or she will still have your name, John. Nothing is going to change that. If your children want to keep the house, you have to fight for them."

With Wendy's help. he decided that he would let his children choose his path.

Chapter Eleven

SACRIFICE

John sat down with his son and daughter in the great room. It was always their favorite room in the house. It was where their Christmas tree still stood in front of the large window, waiting to be undressed, and it had a large fireplace where the stockings were hung, even though there was no-one who still believed that Santa Claus existed. It was more a decoration, than anything else.

"Guys, I have some news."

"What is it?" Maggie asked, "is it about last night?"

"So you heard?"

"I think that they heard it in Russia, Dad" Scott commented, causing his father to raise his eyebrows.

"So, you and Darlene are breaking up?" Maggie asked.

"Yes."

"That's great!' Scott exclaimed glad that he was getting a new mom after all.

"Well, it's not all great," John explained.

"How is this not fantastic? Cruella is out of here!"

"There are conditions."

"What conditions?" Maggie asked as if she knew what they were.

"She wants the house."

"Our house?" Maggie fretted.

"Yes." he said, intently watching his daughter's reaction, "but I discussed this with Wendy, and if you don't want to give it up, I will fight her in court."

"I knew that she would want the house." Scott said. "It's like a status symbol for her ... not a home."

John could see the distress on Maggie's face. Of his two children, Maggie was the one who loved the house the most.

"Maggie, are you all right?" he asked.

"What about Mom's tree and garden?" Maggie asked with concern.

"It will have to be moved once we find a new home."

"Can we do that?"

"Sure, we can do that. But we won't have to if you don't want to leave."

"But, then you'll be chained to that wench for at least another year," Scott remarked.

"Don't worry about me ... I can wait if you do not want to give up the house."

"Dad, you could lose the house anyway, no matter what we say today," Scott said, "you could fight for a year and she probably will still get the house."

"I know," he said. "But, I am willing to fight for the two of you. You are the most important people in my life. Don't ever forget that."

"Daddy..."

"Yes, Maggie."

"I've seen you so unhappy for so long. If this house stops you from being happy one more day, I don't want it."

"Maggie, are you sure?"

"I just want to see you smile, Daddy. Wendy makes you happy."

"I agree Dad. Let Darlene take the house. If it means that she will be out of our life forever, it is worth it."

The three Stantons made their decision and afterwards, they hugged in front of their beloved fireplace.

"I love you guys," John said as they embraced his children.

After they embraced, John called Darlene and told her of their decision. They agreed to move out of the house in a month, and she would allow him to have the quick divorce so that he could marry Wendy as soon as possible. As he hung up the phone, the next thing he wanted to do was to see Wendy, and he left the house, promising to return.

As the children waited for their father to return, Maggie looked at the tree and fireplace wistfully.

"I'm going to miss this house," she said.

"So am I," Scott sighed.

"Do you think that Dad will get another one with a fireplace?"

"I'm sure that he can."

"I'm going to miss living next to Lizzy," she said, with a little bit of dejection. "She's not going to be happy that we're moving." Maggie knew that Lizzy had a crush on Scott and would be devastated.

New Beginnings

"She can come to visit," Scott said, oblivious to the potential heartbreak of the girl who loved him.

"Do you think that we'll still be in town?"

"I'm sure that Dad will find some place close. He'll want to be close to work and stuff like that."

"It sure will be interesting at school when this all comes out," Maggie said.

Once John returned with Wendy, the small family discussed their next moves. Scott would have to be back at college in January, so he did not have much time to help with the picking of a new home. They planned to move quickly, considering that Darlene had only given them a month.

"I assume that we are not going to use Talbot Realty." Scott joked.

The next day, the lawyers were called and the uncontested divorce papers were filed. John admitted his affair and the divorce was filed as his fault for the adultery. He agreed to give her the house and the furniture, and anything else that she wanted within those walls and on the property, except for the memorial garden, which she was happy to give up. Leaving his four hundred thousand dollar house seemed like a raw deal to his own lawyer, but John was just happy to reach some kind of agreement, so that his new life could begin as soon as possible.

That night, Wendy threw a quick dinner together, and the she, John and his children sat and ate in the dining room. It was so natural that it almost like she was already the mother of her new family. They worked together to clean up after the dinner, washed the dishes and put them away. John commented that he had never seen his children be so willing to lend a hand.

"Maybe they are trying to get on your good side," he joked.

"If anyone has to do any brown-nosing, it should be me," she commented. "I'm the one that is turning their whole world upside down."

"For the better, Wendy…only for the better," John said as he kissed her softly on the lips. She sighed and tried to convince herself that he was right.

Afterwards, Wendy relaxed on the couch in the family room in front of the television. She was a bit exhausted from the day. There were so many emotions in the house earlier in the day, and she still felt accountable for what the children had given up for their father's happiness. Although John insisted that Darlene would have asked for the house regardless of the reasons for a split, Wendy still thought that she was responsible.

As Wendy recuperated, John's children left the house to be with their friends. Maggie wanted to break the news of the move to her next door neighbor, Lizzy. There was a sleepover planned, it would probably be filled with plenty of tears. Scott intended to have a good time with his friends Pal and Ben, and God knows what they had in mind. John decided not to worry about it.

After his children left the house, John had one thing on his mind. He found Wendy half asleep on the couch and when he sat down beside her, her eyes opened wider, especially considering the seductive way that he looked at her.

"What are you up to?" she asked suspiciously.

"The children have left the building," he said

"Oh really?" she replied, knowing what he was thinking.

"So, it's just you and me ... and the little one, of course," he said as he leaned in and felt her tummy. He leaned in and kissed her, and then she pulled away slowly to tease him.

"John ... what about what you said about being together in this house? You know ... not in Darlene's house?" she said with a tinge of sarcasm.

"Well, it seems that I found a loophole,"

"Loophole, huh?" she teased.

"Yeah. It just so happens that the house does not become hers until a month from now. So technically, the house is still mine."

"Is that so?"

"It's true ... and she'll be at her mother's house for the next week."

"That's very true ..." she said, feigning surprise at the news.

"So ..."

"So?"

"No more excuses."

"Who me?"

"You're just going to give in."

"Really?"

"Really," he insisted. He leaned in and kissed her again, and this time, she did not pull away.

They kissed passionately on the couch, then he led her up the stairs and into the guest room. Wendy was still more comfortable there than in the master bedroom and John did not argue. John didn't care where he and Wendy made love. It could have happened in the car ... or the roof for that matter ... just as long as he finally had the opportunity to show her how much he loved her.

After they made love, they both drifted off to satisfied slumber. During the night, John was suddenly awoken to Wendy's plea to wake up. He was startled, and immediately thought that something was wrong with the baby.

"What is it?"

"You have to get out."

"What? Why?"

"Scott's home."

"So?"

"Please, John...Go!" she begged as she pushed him towards the edge of the bed.

"She's serious...she's really kicking me out of bed!" he thought as he teetered on the edge of falling over onto the floor. He finally realized that he would have to go.

"Okay...Okay...I'll go." he said as he barely kept his balance, then crawled out of bed. The room was dark, and he fumbled to find something to wear so that his son did not catch him running through the hall in his birthday suit. He managed throw on his t-shirt and jockey shorts, than walked back to kiss her goodnight.

"Go! Go! Hurry!" she whispered, as if being caught would mean certain doom.

"I'm going!" he explained with a bit of a giggle.

Although, it was not his choice to leave the bed at that moment, he couldn't help but chuckle as he left the room. He was still in a daze, however, being a victim of such an abrupt interruption of his dreams. In addition, he realized that it was very cold in the hallway compared to the warmth of her body. He felt a chill and looked for a place to lay his head for the next six hours.

He turned around and Scott was standing there, staring at him holding his pants and socks.

"Dad..."

"Scott..."

"Did she kick you out?" Scott chuckled, noticing his father's disheveled appearance.

"What do you think?" John replied, a little startled by the sudden appearance of his son.

"She does realize that I know how babies are made, doesn't she?"

"Very funny."

"Did you at least...you know...Have fun?"

"Scott, that's none of your business," John replied. He started walking in the direction of the master bedroom, then turned around. "See you in the morning."

"Good Night, Casanova," Scott mused as he opened the door to his room. He walked in and closed the door behind him.

Scott was obviously not fooled, and he knew what his father was trying to conceal. The deception did not work, but it really did not bother John. He contemplated returning to the coziness of the guest room, and the comfort of sleeping next to Wendy's wonderful figure. Unfortunately, he could not return because then he would have to admit that he failed in their covert operation.

Instead, he tapped on Scott's door, and asked him to pretend that he didn't know about the liaison. Scott was in stunned disbelief, but agreed to go along with the subterfuge.

"She shouldn't worry so much about what I think. I'm just happy that you're happy."

"She still feels a little bit funny. I am still married, and you guys are my children."

"Yeah, but Darlene is not our mother. Far from it."

"I know that this sounds ridiculous, considering Wendy's current condition, but I think that she's worried about how it all looks."

"Dad, I'm happy about it."

"Maybe it's not about you so much. I think that she really cares about what Maggie thinks about it all, and what kind of example she is setting."

"I don't think that I'll ever figure out what makes women tick, Dad."

"Scott, trust me. You never will."

Chapter Twelve

THE MEETING

The next day, John and Wendy took the two hour long drive to her parent's house. Wendy had planned to spend at least the next month there, maybe more. This way, Wendy had time to get her things together while John and the rest of the family found a new home.

By the time they pulled into the driveway, John's face looked a little pale.

"John, are you alright?"

"I'm fine. Just a little nervous."

"Nervous? Why?"

"In your condition, you have to ask why?"

"John, don't worry about it. They will love you. Just like I love you."

"I wish that I had your optimism," he said as he turned off the car.

"John," she said as she held his hand and looked in his eyes, "my parents know how happy I am. They know that I am deeply in love with a wonderful man. They could not be more satisfied. Everything will turn out great. Trust me."

"Okay," he said as he lifted her hand to his lips and kissed it.

"And even if they hate you and it all falls apart in there, I will still marry you," she said with a mischievous smile.

"Thank you," he laughed.

"But, we don't have to worry about that because they will love you."

Her words were very comforting, and after a deep cleansing breath, he had the courage to walk in the door. As soon as they walked in, they were met by Wendy's parents, and John's heart started beating rapidly, and his body started to shake. He felt like a teenager again.

"Mom and Dad, this is John."

After introductions, the women remained in the kitchen as John and Joe walked into the den to have their little talk.

As they walked into the room, John was looked around at the plaques on the wall related to Joe's career as a policeman. There was a Yankees banner, a framed picture of the Super Bowl Champion Giants team, and a 1994 Stanley Cup Champion Rangers cap on top of the television set. John nervously sat down on an old loveseat that was against the paneled wall, and was close to the brown easy chair that Joe nestled in. When John sat down, he sank into the loveseat and he looked up to the imposing man beside him, as Joe turned off the television.

"So…you're the married man who knocked up my daughter?" the very robust and intimidating Joseph Burke said with authority.

"Yes, I am, Mr. Burke."

"What do you have to say for yourself?"

"I'm sorry that it happened that way. I'm not sorry that I fell in love with her. But, I'm sorry that it wasn't the usual way."

"Right. Marriage first, then baby."

"Yes. Marriage first," John gulped.

"I hear that you have a daughter of your own, John, wouldn't you want her to be married before conceiving a baby?"

"Of course."

"So, you see my predicament, here?"

"I definitely see it."

"And you're still married. To top it off."

"I know. But, we have filed for divorce, and my current wife and I have agreed to a settlement."

"Just like that."

"Well…it's not just like that, sir, my marriage had been crumbling for a while. We do not love each other anymore."

"How do I know that five years down the line, my daughter will not be in the same situation? We take our marriages very seriously around here, John."

"Mr. Burke, I put a lot of effort into trying to save my marriage, but my effort was not reciprocated. I take marriage very seriously. I know that it's hard to believe, given the circumstances."

"It's very hard to believe, John. You had an affair with my daughter while you were still married to your current wife. You left my daughter pregnant and alone."

"I did not know about the baby, Mr. Burke."

"But, you left her in a horrible position. She had to choose whether to raise this child alone or to break up a marriage."

"I'm very sorry about that." John said sheepishly. "But, she disappeared on me. I did not know where she was. If I knew anything about this, I would have told her that I wanted to be with her. I wanted to be with her since the first moment I set eyes on her."

Joe stood up and started to walk around his den. He touched the mouth of a musical fish plaque and turned around to once again face the man who had an affair with his daughter.

"You know, Wendy is my only daughter. My only child, for that matter. When she came home in that condition, I really wanted to use my contacts, find you and wring your neck."

"I completely understand."

"Do you?"

"If I was in the same situation, I would have felt the same way."

"But, Wendy begged me to leave it alone because she said that she loved you. She loved you so much that she was willing to give up her happiness so that you did not get hurt."

"I realize that, Mr. Burke." he said, "but, I would not have been happy without her. It hurt more that I couldn't find her. I love her very much."

"Do you know how lucky you are?"

"Yes, I do. Wendy is an amazing woman."

"She's the best," Joe said as he pointed directly at John.

"I know," John agreed, "that is why I can't live without her."

Meanwhile, in the kitchen, Wendy worried about John. She knew that her father would not be easy on John. Her mother saw the worry on her face and tried to reassure her that everything would be all right.

"Don't worry, Wendy."

"They've been in there a while."

"Your father just wants to make sure that John is who you say he is."

"He's everything and more, Mom. I'm so happy that his son, Scott found me. I made such a terrible mistake running away like I did."

"You did what you thought was the right thing to do. You were trying to protect him."

"But, he was so unhappy. I almost sacrificed both of our happiness."

"Love can make you do foolish things, sometimes."

"I can't imagine my life without him. I love him so much."

As John prepared to drive home and did not want to leave her. They stood by the car, and she played with his shirt as they said goodbye.

"I don't know if I can do it." he said with a bit of sadness as he ran his hand up and down her arm.

"It'll go quickly." she replied.

"No, it will be painfully slow."

"Yeah, you're probably right." she laughed.

"I'm going to miss your beautiful smile."
"I'll miss you too."
"Maybe I can get up here in a week or two."
"I don't expect it, John."
"But, I want to see you. I need to see you."
"Okay, John."

He hugged her tightly, and she started to get emotional. Then the lovers kissed and embraced again, exchanging declarations of love. Eventually, the time had come for him to leave, and then he got into his car and drove away. As he drove away, he knew that he still needed to earn the trust of her parents, especially her father.

A few weeks later, he returned again for another Sunday with the Wendy. This time, he brought Maggie and Scott along to introduce Maggie to Wendy's mother and father. Scott had been there before and was invited to come back if he ever needed a home cooked meal, since he was only an hour away at school. John could sense that Sarah had grown fond of him, and Joe was beginning to trust him. He found himself comfortable within the bosom of their family unit, and it was a feeling that was quite appealing.

Chapter Thirteen

GOODBYE TO THE PAST

John, Scott and Maggie found it easier than expected to find a home across town in Devonwood that filled all of their needs. It was close enough to the high school, and John's office. It was a two level home with four bedrooms, a kitchen, dining room and two bathrooms. It was a cozy older home, and it needed a lot of work, but they loved it. As Maggie had pointed out, as it reminded her of her grandparent's home. She said that the outside reminded her of the Walton house.

It was smaller than their current home, had no great room but rather a family room with a fireplace. There were no high ceilings in this home and no big windows. There was a large yard in the back with an old rusted swing set, and although there was no pool, they did not care. What they did care about was that this large yard had a perfect area for Jenny's memorial.

"I think that I like it better than the other house," Maggie commented, and Scott agreed.

The decision had been made. Unfortunately, since the closing was set for mid-February, they had to find some place to live for two weeks until the closing. Needing a place he and Maggie to live, John once again he turned to a familiar place.

On the final night in the house, John and Maggie found themselves packed and ready to say goodbye to their beloved home. Maggie and Scott's rooms were empty, and the office was empty as well. John made sure that nothing of sentimental value was left behind. The memorial garden for Jenny would be moved as well, when the weather allowed the tree to be moved without damage.

John searched the house, room to room to see if he could find anything that he could have left behind. After doing so, he went looking for Maggie. He knew where she would be.

He walked into the snowy backyard and past the covered pool, and into the area of the Memorial garden. Maggie was sitting on the bench, wiping a tear from her eye. She must have heard his footsteps crunching in the snow, because she started to speak without looking at him.

"Do you think that the tree will be all right?" she said as the cold air made her words animate.

"The tree will be fine. It'll stay here until late March, and then we'll bring it over to the new house."

"I still can't believe that we have to leave. Why can't Darlene leave?"

"Everything will be alright, Maggie. Don't worry. The tree will be fine"

"You know that she's probably going to sell the house, Daddy."

"I really don't think so."

"You'll see"

"Maggie, we will be fine. Don't worry about this house anymore."

"You're right. I'm sorry Daddy." she said, touching the tree and turning around. Maggie turned around and hugged her father. "I really do love the new house."

Father and daughter said goodbye to the tree, and walked hand in hand into the big house.

"Did you talk to Scott?" Maggie asked.

"Scott is back in the college routine. He wishes that he was here to say goodbye to the house."

"What about Wendy?"

"She'll be staying at her parents house until the wedding."

"I thought that you said that you didn't want her out of your sight."

"It's just until mid-March. She has to pack and take care of other things."

"Once Wendy is with us for good, it'll be nice to have a woman to talk to for a change. I never could talk to Darlene."

"That makes two of us."

He took another look around at his soon-to-be-former home and breathed a nostalgic sigh. Then he called to Maggie.

"So Mags, are you ready to go?"

"As ready as I am going to be." she said.

The two of them walked to the front door and turned around.

"Goodbye house." Maggie said.

From there, they drove to Robert and Anne Channing's home, which would be the home of John and Maggie until the closing of the new home. Once again, Robert and Anne Channing opened their home to John and Maggie. During the visit, Anne had a confession to make.

"John, your mother and secretly hoped that this day would come. For the past two years, we have been saying daily novenas that you and Darlene would split up."

"What?"

"I'm sorry dear. We really did try to like Darlene, but she made it impossible."

"But to say a novena?"

"It was only after the first year was over. You do know that she changed, and she did treat you horribly."

"I'm aware of that."

"We wanted you to find someone else, but of course you would not listen to us. You were determined to make it work, no matter what."

"So you're telling me that you and my Mom prayed that my marriage would fall apart?"

"I wouldn't exactly put it like that, John. We prayed that you would find contentment in your life. We knew that Darlene was not capable of making you happy. We just prayed that you would find someone else."

"Incredible," he said with astonishment.

"Well, It worked, didn't it?" Anne asked sheepishly. "You're happy, aren't you?"

He could tell that she felt a little bit guilty for her actions, but since everything worked out to his benefit, he was not angry. Whether or not he believed in the power of novenas, the result was everything that he had dreamed about. He had once again found lightening in a bottle. He had found another soul mate.

Things were not working out so well on the divorce front, however. Ever since Darlene had been back from Florida and living in the same house as John and the kids, she found many things for him to be involved in, and many requests regarding the divorce itself. One night, it was a dinner party that she expected him to attend. The next, it was something else. She explained that she just needed his support, and then she would let him free of the marriage with no other strings attached.

On the night that he finally moved out, he once again agreed to go to dinner with Darlene and her work colleagues from Talbot Realty to celebrate the big sale of a two million dollar home in the new section of Devonwood. The house that was sold was in a development called Burlington Rise, which was a exclusive community, with a country club which included a eighteen hole golf course. Darlene had taken the lead on this sale, and the agency made a hefty commission. John agreed to attend the dinner as the last official act as her husband.

The evening was certainly pleasant as it was nice to spend some time with Darlene without having a heated discussion regarding the divorce, or other things that complicated their life together. She acted like she did when they were first married. She was smiling, laughing and having a very good time and it was easy to remember what originally attracted him to her. She was nothing like the wife he had been living with for the past two years. It was refreshing to see her in this light, and he hoped that this would lead to a better relationship once the divorce was finalized.

When the evening was over, he drove her home and as they sat in the driveway, she asked him to come in for a second.

"I have something for you. Can you wait a couple of seconds before you leave? It's upstairs in the bedroom."

"I can come up and get it." he volunteered, trying to make the visit to his soon to be former home as short as possible.

"No, I'll get it," she said sweetly. "Just wait in the living room."

As he waited, he took one last look at his beautiful home. He had a melancholic feeling in his heart as he gazed at the fireplace. He was going to miss the home that he once loved.

"John, can you come up here for a second?" he heard Darlene's voice call out to him, "I'm having a little trouble."

He turned and ran up the stairs and opened the bedroom door. Once inside the room, he noticed that she was dressed in a diamond colored silk nightgown, with a matching robe. She was stunning.

"Darlene…what are you doing?" he asked.

"I remember that this always was your favorite nightgown," she said as she walked over towards him. When close to him, she stroked the front of his jacket with her long, French manicured fingernails.

"It was," he said.

"Remember that first night when I wore it? You couldn't keep your hands off of me." She said as she unbuttoned his top coat and suit jacket. She slid her hands inside of his suit jacket and was able to slide the suit jacket and top coat off of his shoulders and onto the floor.

"I remember, Darlene," he said.

Darlene put her arms around his neck and kissed him, and he responded as if going through the motions. The passion was not there. She noticed his resistance, but continued to press on.

"I miss you, John," she said as she stroked his face and smiled, looking longingly into his eyes. "I miss what we used to have."

John really did not know how to reply as she began to loosen his tie and unbutton his shirt, exposing the nape of his neck. She was so bold that it astounded him. Where was all this coming from?

"Make love to me." she said, trying to pull him back into her web. She kissed his neck as she tried to encourage him to react in a way that pleased her, but he did not respond the way she desired.

"No, Darlene." he said as he released himself from her grip. He backed away from her grasp.

"John, it's okay. We are still married, and this may be our last time together. Let's make love one last time. Wendy will never know."

"That's not the point, Darlene. I would know."

"I know that you are still attracted to me, John. You can't deny that."

"Darlene, I do not love you anymore. I love Wendy. I will not make love to you. I'm sorry."

"So, you really don't want me anymore, do you?" She said, with humiliation.

"I'm sorry, Darlene. I know that it's not what you want to hear." he said.

He lifted his jacket up off the floor, but did not notice that his cellular phone had dropped out of his pocket and slipped underneath the dresser. As he walked out the bedroom door, he left without it.

"Well, I hope that this is all worth it!" she yelled out after him as she heard him walk down the stairs and though the front door.

Several minutes later, as Darlene sulked on the bed, she heard the unfamiliar ring of John's cell phone. She looked underneath the dresser and found the phone, looking at the display. The phone call was from Wendy.

"Hello Wendy." Darlene said with a smile to the stunned woman on the other end, "John is indisposed right now, would you like me to leave a message?"

Chapter Fourteen

PERMISSION

The next day, when John called Wendy, she did not want to speak with him.

"I'm sorry, John. Wendy does not want to talk to you." her mother explained.

"Why? What is wrong?"

"I don't know, John."

"Tell him to ask his wife!" he heard Wendy call out from other side of the line.

"What did she say?" asked John.

"She said to ask your wife."

"Ask my wife? What does that mean?" John asked, puzzled by the request.

"John, I don't know. Maybe you should ask Darlene."

His quest found him back at his old house, looking for answers from Darlene. He pulled up to her driveway and noticed that Darlene's car was there and also there was a brand new black Mercedes.

He knocked on the door and there was no answer. He checked the spot where the spare key was usually stored, found it, and opened the locked door. As he called out to Darlene, he noticed that the stereo was playing Mozart. There were a couple of half empty wine glasses on the coffee table and a tie and jacket on the floor.

He continued to call out to Darlene as he walked up the stairs, but he still didn't hear a reply. He walked to the bedroom and knocked on the door.

"Darlene, are you in there?" he asked.

Still no reply. He opened the door and looked inside. The sheets on the bed were untidy, but there was no one inside the room. He did, however, find his cellular phone on her dresser. From that moment, everything started to make sense. He heard the shower running, and decided to wait at the edge of the bed to find out who would emerge from the bathroom, so that he could get some answers.

The first person that walked out of the bathroom with a towel around his waist was George Cooper. He was startled to see John sitting there, but was arrogant enough to not be concerned about it.

"Hello John."

"George..."

At that moment, Darlene walked out dressed in a towel, and she was surprised to see John standing there.

"John, what are you doing here?"

"Question is, darling, what are you doing?"

"That's none of your business, John. You gave up that right." she said as she passed him and fixed her hair in the mirror.

"George, can I speak to my wife in private, please?" John requested.

George picked up his clothes from the floor, and excused himself from the room. Once George had left, John stood up and walked over to Darlene, spinning her around.

"I guess that you don't miss me so much after all," he said sarcastically.

"Jealous?"

"Not in the least. I just want some answers."

"I don't have to explain anything to you."

"I could care less about you and George, Darlene. I just want to know what you said to Wendy."

"I don't know what you're talking about."

"You had my cell phone. I know that you said something to her."

"She called, and I told her that you were not available."

"So you made her think that we were sleeping together, didn't you?"

"I can't control what your little girlfriend thinks, John," she said, "if she has a complex, that's her problem."

"So that's why." he said, realizing what had happened to make Wendy so distant.

"What's wrong, John. Is she mad at you?" Darlene mocked, mimicking sorrow.

"Darlene. Give me the divorce."

"You are getting a divorce."

"I want a quick divorce, Darlene. I'm sure you don't want Patricia to find out what's going on over here. If you make this quick and painless, I will keep your secret."

"That's blackmail!" she accused.

"You're right," John said. "So how about it?"

"Fine." Darlene agreed.

With that, the fun and games would finally end.

On the weekend, John drove up to see Wendy to try to explain the situation. He had attempted to do it via the telephone, but she still would not talk to him. He decided that he would try to see her and explain in person, even if he had to get down and crawl on his knees.

Once there, he said hello to her mother, then walked into her father's den to talk to him first because he wanted to explain the whole situation. Luckily, he found a sympathetic ear.

"Please talk to her," he begged, but her father would not intervene.

"That's up to you, John. My daughter is a twenty-five year old woman. She can make her own decisions at this point."

"But, she will not listen to me. She will not let me in the door."

"John, that's your problem. Wendy is bullheaded sometimes. You may as well know it now."

"Mr. Burke, I want to ask her to marry me today. I would like to have your blessing."

Joe paused for what seemed like an eternity, then gave his answer.

"You have it."

"That's it?"

"Well John, do I wish that all of this had been done the traditional way? Of course I do. I would have preferred it you were not a married man. I wish that you and my daughter had gotten married first before expecting a child. But we can't have that can we?"

"I guess not," John said sheepishly.

"I will trust Wendy's judgment on this, but I really do think that you love her. It is very important to me that she is married before the baby is born. I am very happy that you are taking responsibility for your actions, and you want to marry her. I hope that the two of you can work it out. "

"I hope so, too, I love her very much."

"I'm glad to hear it. Like I said, you are a very lucky man, John. I hope you know that."

"I know how lucky I am. I won't let you down. "

"From your mouth to God's ears," Joe said as he looked up and pointed to heaven.

"Thank you, Mr. Burke," John said as he stood up to shake Joe's hand.

"Call me Joe," he corrected him.

"Joe."

"John, lets have a cold one before you crawl upstairs and beg," Joe joked as he patted John on the back and the two of them returned to the kitchen. He grabbed a couple of cold Budweiser long necks from the refrigerator and handed one to his future son in law. They opened their drinks and Joe made a toast.

"To you and Wendy, for your happiness," Joe said as he lifted his bottle.

"Cheers to that!" John said as he tapped Joe's bottle with his own.

"May you have a long and happy marriage."

After the toast, John left to find Wendy. Sarah directed him to the bedroom where Wendy locked herself inside, waiting for him to leave. John camped out by the door and kept knocking, hoping that she would eventually let him in.

"Wendy, I will stay out here all day if I have to."

"John, please go away."

"Wendy, you're a pregnant woman. I know that you will have to go to the bathroom eventually," he joked, "you can't stay in there forever. I'll just camp out here and wait."

"John, can't you take a hint?" she asked.

"Wendy, I have to admit something. I'm very dense."

"Don't joke about this, John."

"Wendy, if you just let me explain, this will all be water under the bridge."

She did not reply. He found himself on his knees, begging for forgiveness for something that he did not do. Then, he decided to go ahead and do what he came to do.

"Wendy, I'm on my knees," he explained, then he went further as he took a small white box out of his pocket. "I have this little box that I have to give you. I'm opening the box, Wendy."

He heard a little stirring in the room and he knew that he had gotten her interest peaked. Then he continued.

"Wendy, I love you more every day. I want to spend the rest of my life with you. Will you…"

"Wait John!" she demanded as she unlocked the door as quickly as possible and opened it to find him on his knees in front of her.

"Hello beautiful," he said as he looked into her blotchy face. She had been crying.

"Hi handsome." she sniffed.

He remained on his knees and gazed into her puffy red eyes.

"I didn't sleep with Darlene. I know that she tried to make you believe that I did," he said with all sincerity.

"I know that now. I can tell by the look on your face. I'm sorry that I shut you out."

"Don't do that anymore, Wendy. You have to know that I will never want anyone else ever again. All I want is you."

"I promise, John," she said, "I will always try to hear you out from now on."

"Okay," he replied.

Then her attention was focused elsewhere. "You said something about a box?"

"You mean this box?" he asked as he opened the box and revealed a sparkling engagement ring in a gold setting which took her breath away.

"John...it's beautiful!" she gasped, then she looked into his eyes and prepared to hear the words that she always dreamed about.

"Wendy, I love you more every day. I want to spend the rest of my life with you. Will you marry me?"

"Of course I will marry you."

She knelt down to meet his embrace, then the couple shared a long, sensuous kiss. He then slipped the ring onto the finger on her left hand and she gazed at it.

"I'm so happy, John. I love you so much. I'm so lucky that you found me."

"I'm the lucky one, sweetheart. You have changed my life."

After lunch, the discussion turned to the wedding. It was planned for March, after John's divorce was finalized. He still had to have the second marriage annulled, even though it had been a civil ceremony. But, when the time came, he would have the paperwork ready so that it would not take very long.

The wedding was going to be performed at Holy Trinity church in March, which was the Burke's parish. It was also very convenient for Scott, since it was only an hour away from the college. Joe and Sarah offered to have a small reception afterwards at their home, and wanted to handle everything, which was much appreciated. Before John left for home, went with Wendy to meet the priest, and set the date.

The next month would be a busy one for the Burke family. Wendy planned to stay at her parent's home until the wedding to help with the preparations. John hated to leave her again, because he already missed her terribly. But, with his current living conditions, and the uncertainty of when the new house would be ready, he decided that it was probably for the best.

Chapter Fifteen

THE GOOD LIFE

John and Wendy Stanton were finally married at Holy Trinity Church, on the first Saturday after St. Patrick's Day. Thankfully, after a cold and snowy winter, the day was quite warm and beautiful. It was as if God was smiling down on them.

Scott was John's best man and had come down from college for the occasion. Maggie was the maid of honor, and looked beautiful in her three-quarter length pink dress. When John first saw Wendy appear with her father to walk down the aisle, he was speechless. She was stunning in her gorgeous maternity wedding dress with long lace sleeves. She looked like a princess. He felt like the luckiest man on the earth.

The reception that was held at Joe and Sarah's house was very small, but filled with friends and relatives, including Anne and Robert Channing. John's mother and sister came up from Florida for the occasion and stayed with Anne and Robert. Rita made sure that was there, because she would not have missed it for the world. She could not wait to meet the woman that was the answer to her prayers.

Another very important guest at the wedding was Maureen Burke, also known as Grandma Mo. She was Joe's mother and grandmother to Wendy. She was eighty-two years old and in a wheelchair because of a recently broken hip. She had recently moved in with Joe's sister, Meaghan Peale, who also lived in Upland. Aside from the fact that Maureen could not walk easily, she still had her wits about her. She was feisty and liable to say anything.

When the moment finally came for John to introduce his mother to his new wife, Rita was more affectionate to Wendy than she had ever been to Darlene. She greeted her by flinging her arms around her, and hugging her tightly. The hug was so complete that it shifted Wendy's veil off kilter, and it was quickly readjusted by John's sister Marilyn.

"Young lady, you are the answer to my prayers." Rita said.

Wendy was a little embarrassed to be complimented in such a way, but she had a declaration of her own.

"If anyone is the answer to someone's prayers, it's your son." Wendy corrected her, "I've been praying for him all my life."

"I like how you think." Rita said with a wink and a smile as she touched her face. She could tell that Wendy was her kind of girl.

The families mingled together, and enjoyed the food and company of one another. All were very happy that John and Wendy had found each other, and were obviously very content. As John and Wendy danced together to a love song that was playing on the stereo, Rita watched them and smiled. Then she turned to Anne and raised her glass.

"To John and Wendy's happiness," she said as she winked at her co-conspirator.

"Cheers!" Anne replied.

The toast was overheard by Grandma Mo, who had her own response.

"I'll drink to that."

The three women smiled and tapped their wine glasses together.

When it was time to throw the bridal bouquet, there were really not a lot of options. Maggie was the only available unmarried woman in the room, so Wendy handed the bouquet to her. As Maggie held the bouquet in her arms, she imagined herself as a bride and smiled.

As Maggie stood there, she caught the eye of Grandma Mo, and she grabbed Wendy's arm as she walked past.

"Wendy, I'd like to ask you a question."

"Yes, Gram. Anything."

"This daughter of John's, she's a very sweet and pretty girl. Is she attached?"

"No, I don't think so."

"Very interesting," Grandma Mo said.

The look on Grandma Mo's face was a familiar one. Wendy had seen this look before, usually directed at herself. Her grandmother was morphing into matchmaker mode.

"Gram, what are you up to?"

"I'm just thinking ... do you know who she would be perfect for?"

"I can read your mind. I know exactly what you are thinking."

"It would be my best work yet. Two in one shot."

"Gram, you just met her and you're setting her up already?"

"Why not? They are both unattached. Look at her. Wouldn't they make beautiful babies?"

New Beginnings

"Grandma, please. I beg you. Turn off the matchmaker switch. Just for today."

"Okay," Grandma Mo frowned, showing a bit of disappointment. Her wheels were turning, and she didn't want to stop their forward motion. She had a new mission. However, since it was Wendy's wedding, she agreed to postpone her quest until the right time.

Later on during the reception, John and Wendy informed Anne and Robert that there was a plan to transplant Jenny's tree to the new house within a week. Maggie had already picked out the spot in the backyard for the memorial, and they planned to have a small ceremony where they would toast the memory of Jenny.

They also had another request. John explained that since he always wanted Anne and Robert to be part of his life and the lives of his wife and children. With that in mind, he asked them to be the godparents of the new baby.

Anne and Robert were thrilled to accept.

A week later, after Wendy and John had settled into their new home, Jenny's tree was planted in the backyard in the spot that Maggie had chosen. The Stantons and Channings made a toast to their lost loved one.

Afterwards, after the families dined together, Wendy had a present for Maggie.

"This is for you and Scott, but I didn't want to wait until May to give it to you. I talked to Scott and he understands."

"What is it?" she asked as she held the flat, rectangular gift that was wrapped in blue paper.

"Open it," John insisted.

Maggie looked at Robert and Anne, who egged her on, as they were just as curious to find out what was in the wrapping. She ripped open the package and found that it was a large, framed picture of Jenny and her two children. It was an exact copy of the photo that John kept hidden in his dresser drawer.

"I want you to know that the memory of your mother will always be welcomed in our home." she said.

"Oh Wendy, it's so wonderful!" Maggie sighed. "Thank you so much!"

"I'd like you to hang this anywhere that you want."

"Even if it is in the living room?"

"Absolutely. Wherever you want. Your mother is a very important part of our family."

Maggie found a spot in the living room that was next to the entranceway between the living room and kitchen, and John hung it with care. The picture of Jenny and her children was finally given the status that it deserved. It was no longer hidden in a dresser drawer.

Chapter Sixteen

A NEW LIFE

Wendy Stanton was sick of being pregnant. For seven months, she had gone through shock, sorrow, guilt and then finally happiness. In the beginning of her life together with John, she would wake up like the good wife and fix him breakfast and coffee, then pat him on the bottom and send him off to work. All through the pregnancy, she tried to be as cheerful as possible. She would look in the mirror at her protruding belly and would laugh it off.

Eight months into the pregnancy, Wendy had just about had enough. Her back and legs hurt, and her ankles were swollen. Her breasts were heavy and sensitive. She could not go three minutes without having to go to the bathroom, and could not see her feet. By the eighth month, she did not even roll over when his alarm went off. By the time that John walked in the door after a day of sick and screaming children, sometimes he was lucky if he got dinner at all before she crawled back into bed.

She was depressed. She was over-tired and under-sexed. The former having everything to do with the latter. She just did not have the energy to do anything anymore.

John understood what was going on, however, because he had seen it before. Jenny had become very melancholic in the last stage of pregnancy, and he knew the signs. He was just happy that this time around he would have the opportunity be available to his young wife.

When he came home to find Wendy sitting on the couch and crying silently, he did his best to comfort her. He sat down next to her, looked into her watery eyes and told her that she was beautiful, but she did not believe him.

"You're just saying that."
"It's true, Wendy."

"John, I've gained forty pounds. My belly is out to here. I can't even see my feet. Forget about putting on shoes. My ankles are swollen. I live in the bathroom. I'm tired and ugly. I should have my own zip code. I'm my own state."

"I wish you wouldn't say those horrible things about my wife," he joked.

"John, don't laugh at me. I'm serious."

"I'm not laughing at you. You're just so cute."

"I'm a whale. No wonder you don't want to have sex with me anymore."

"Sweetheart, stop. That's not true."

"But it is true. I'm a mess," she wept, slumping over onto her side. She was a pitiful sight.

He moved onto the floor and onto his knees to see eye to eye with her as he stroked her aching back.

"Wendy, the reason that we haven't made love lately is because every time I go up to bed, you are out like a light. I want to make love to you. I want you more than anything."

"Really?" she sniffed. "Even though I look like a cow?"

"Even if you looked like cow, and by the way, you don't. You're beautiful."

"Further proof that love is blind."

"Wendy, give yourself a break."

"I'm sorry that I'm complaining so much."

"You have every right to complain. Do you know what you should do? You should punch me in the face because I'm the one that did this to you."

"I would never do that, John," she said reacting to what she thought was a ridiculous request.

"Wendy, that's what I'm here for. I understand, I can't begin to know what you are going through, but I am here for you when you need me."

"You much think that I'm an awful wimp. I bet Jenny wasn't like this."

"Jenny was a mess the first time," he said, correcting her. "Unfortunately, I probably was not very helpful at that time because of college, and everything else. I tried to be supportive, but I'm sure that it wasn't enough."

"How did she deal with it?"

"She had the support of her parents when I wasn't around. They were irreplaceable."

"I didn't think that it would be so hard."

"I know it's hard. But, you're in the final stretch, sweetheart. You're almost there. It's my job to do everything I can to help drag you across the finish line."

He touched her face, gently wiped the tears from her eyes and kissed her. She smiled and he could see that his words finally sunk in. Another crisis had been averted, and he knew that it was not the first or last. He helped her to a sitting position, and then helped her stand onto her wobbly feet.

He made dinner, and as they ate, he promised her a foot and back massage. After a little TLC, he planned on taking care of the rest of her problem by showing her how much he wanted her.

"If you can stay awake." he teased.

After dinner, he delivered on his promise, massaging her from head to toe. It was something that she definitely needed, and it was greatly appreciated. During the process, she let him know when the baby was shifting and he watched in awe as her stomach moved. It reminded him of rolling waves in the middle of the ocean, and he placed his hand on the area where he was moving.

"It's miraculous, isn't it?" he said as he kissed her protruding stomach, and ran his hand across where the baby moved.

"Yes it is." she said with a smile, forgetting her earlier misery.

He moved up until they were face to face, and continued to give her a pep talk.

"You know, all this sacrifice; the back pain, the swollen ankles, the weight gain. It's all going to be worth it once you hold that little sweetheart in your arms and he is looking up at you."

"I know."

"Right now, you probably don't think that it is worth it, but having a baby is the greatest thing in the world."

"But what if I don't know what I'm doing?"

"You'll know. You learn as you go. You're going to be a great mother, Wendy."

"Do you think so?"

"Of course I do. Any child would be extremely lucky to have you have you as his mother. You're a patient, loving and beautiful woman. I love you very much, and I'm so happy to have you as my wife."

"I love you too, John."

The couple kissed tenderly, then he returned to the massage. When he was finished, he intended to become reacquainted with her. But, when he asked her how she felt, there was no answer. She had fallen asleep. The time to get reacquainted would have to wait.

About a week later, John informed Wendy that he had invited her parents to stay with them about a week before the baby was due. He wanted someone to be around to take care of her during the day, and this way she would also have company to take care of her loneliness. It also helped to have someone around just in case the baby decided to make an early appearance into the world.

It was a well thought out plan, but it was not to be, because the baby had different ideas. About two weeks before the due date, Wendy thought that she was in labor. It turned out to be a false alarm, but it was a trial run for what was to come.

Two days later, Maggie came home from school at three o'clock to find Wendy in labor on the kitchen floor, unable to reach the phone. Her water had broken.

"Wendy! Are you alright?"

"I think that this is it, Maggie."

"How long have you been feeling the pains?" Maggie said as she rushed to pick up the phone and started to dial her father's office.

"I've been having pain on and off since this morning, but it didn't get really bad until the past half hour. I tried to get to the phone, but it hurts too much to get up."

Maggie called John, and after discussing it, they decided that it would be best if Maggie called an ambulance to take her to the hospital, and he would meet them there. Maggie was a little nervous, but John encouraged her the best that he could, telling her that everything would be all right.

Once at the hospital, events happened very quickly. John met them at the door of the emergency room, and Wendy was put into a wheelchair immediately. From there, John and Wendy disappeared to the delivery room.

Maggie sat in the waiting room alone, but later was met by her grandparents, Anne and Robert. Together, all three sat and waited for the news.

After about a couple of hours of labor, John emerged from the delivery room with the news they had all been waiting for.

"It's a girl!" he beamed, and he was embraced by his family.

Afterwards, Maggie, Anne and Robert were able to come into Wendy's room and found her holding her little cherub, as John looked on, beaming with pride.

"Anne and Robert, say hello to your godchild. Allison Jennifer Stanton."

Chapter Seventeen

THE CHRISTENING

The day of the Christening was a beautiful June day. Family and Friends gathered at John's parish, St. Joseph's to welcome little Allison to the Roman Catholic family. Family members were all there to help celebrate. Joe and Sarah Burke were there, as were Jenny's parents, Robert and Anne Channing. Some members of Wendy's family had driven three hours for the occasion. There were aunts and uncles, and one cousin.

The one cousin was Michael Burke, who was Wendy's favorite cousin. Wendy and Mike were very close while growing up, because they were the same age, even though they lived an hour away from each other. They kept in touch while she was away in Madison Hill and he was away at law school. Even though they did not see each other that much anymore, they still remained close.

When Maggie first saw him walk into the church and say hello to some of Wendy's other relatives, her chin practically dropped to the floor.

"Who is that?" she asked Wendy, enthralled with the presence what she considered to be a six foot two inch Adonis.

"That is my cousin, Mike. I told you about him, didn't I?"

"Yes, you told me that you had a favorite cousin named Michael. You did not tell me that he was so…"

"Good looking?"

"God, yes."

"I guess that's not the first thing that I think of when I am talking about him. I don't suffer the same symptoms as ever other girl."

"Every other girl?"

"Maggie, there have been quite a few. Nobody who has really been serious, though. He's not the type."

"Oh…"

"Would you like me to introduce you?"

"Definitely." she replied, excitedly.

As if he could feel the heat of Maggie's stare burning through him, he glanced in her direction and started to walk over. Maggie held her breath as he approached and gave Wendy a big hug.

"Hi sweetie," Wendy said.

"Hi Wendy." he replied

"Mike, I would like you to meet someone. This is Maggie, my step-daughter."

"Hello Maggie," he said as he held out her hand and looked at her with those deep brown eyes.

Maggie almost could not speak when introduced to Michael. He was so handsome in his dark blue pinstriped suit with a white shirt and light blue tie. He smelled so good. She was mesmerized.

After a couple of seconds, however, she managed to recover long enough to speak.

"Nice to meet you … I'm Maggie."

"I know." he said with a smile.

"Right … she already told you … sorry about that," she said as she stared at his wavy and perfected styled hair.

He laughed at the situation, which was a little embarrassing to her, "It's nice to meet you Maggie."

She continued to hold on to his hand, and held it until Wendy whispered in her ear.

"Maggie, he needs his hand back."

"Oh … sorry," Maggie said. She felt her face turn red with embarrassment, and she felt a little warm. As Wendy introduced Mike to John and Scott, she was able to re-group before she passed out.

He was wonderful.

After the church ceremony, the family returned to Wendy and John's house for the christening party. Wendy and Maggie were managing the party like they have worked together for years. They both loved to cook and were terrific hosts. John and Scott spent most of the time making conversation with the men in the living room.

In the midst of the preparations, Maggie took time out to gawk at the new man in her life, and unfortunately her brother noticed her ogling.

"Why don't you take a picture?"

"What?"

"You're staring at him. You've got hearts in your eyes."

"I do not."

"Yes, you do … it's so obvious."

"Scott, I do not have hearts in my eyes. You're exaggerating, as usual."

"Lizzy…come over here," Scott called out. Lizzy was in another section of the kitchen, and was more than happy to come to Scott's call.

"Yes, Scott … What is it?" she asked sweetly.

"Doesn't Maggie have hearts in her eyes today?"

"Definitely," Lizzy replied, not one to disagree with Scott very often.

"Jeez Lizzy, I thought that at least you would back me up," Maggie commented to her blond haired friend.

"I'm just calling it like I see it." Lizzy stated

"Oh, I forgot … you're the expert about hearts in the eyes."

Lizzy got the point. Luckily, Scott did not.

Wendy walked over and immediately became involved in the conversation as she took the vegetable platter out of the refrigerator.

"What is this about hearts and eyes?" she asked.

"Do you ever watch the Warner Brothers cartoons with Pepé Le Pew?" Scott asked as he grabbed a pig in a blanket off the plate that Maggie had been setting up, and popped it into his mouth.

"Yes, I remember it."

"Well, when Pepé was in love, he got hearts in his eyes," Scott explained. "It's the same kind of look that I saw my father have in the restaurant when he saw you."

"Really?"

"Absolutely," he insisted.

Hearing that made Wendy smile, and she almost drifted off into the world of John, but stopped herself because there was too much to do.

"Anyway, right now, Maggie has that same look," Scott said.

"Who's the lucky guy?" Wendy asked.

"Scott, stop. You're embarrassing me."

"She's been watching your cousin Mike all day," he said with a knowing look on his face.

"My Michael?" Wendy asked, feigning surprise. She had noticed Maggie's attention span since she had first met Michael, and she thought that it was a cute little infatuation.

"Yes, Michael," Scott said with a smirk, admiring his sister's red face.

"I think that I'm going to bring out the pigs in the blanket," Maggie said as she grabbed the completed tray, and hurried out of the kitchen. Wendy looked at both Lizzy and Scott, and raised an eyebrow.

"She's in love," Lizzy announced.

Maggie walked into the dining room, where the older women were sitting and talking. As she placed the tray on the table, their attention was upon her.

"Maureen, you have met my granddaughter, haven't you?" Anne asked.

"We met at the wedding," Grandma Mo said, "you're a very pretty little thing. What is your name again?"

"My name is Margaret. Maggie for short."

"Do you have a boyfriend, Maggie?"

"Uh ...no, I don't ... have a boyfriend at this moment," she said with a confused look, as Wendy brought in the vegetable tray and became interested in the conversation.

"You know, you'd be perfect for my Michael. He's a lawyer, you know." she said as she tapped Maggie on the arm as if she were letting her in on a secret.

Then she did something unexpected. She looked around, found him standing in the living room, and called to him.

"Michael dear, come over here," she yelled out, causing Michael to turn around as he heard his name called.

"Yeah, Grandma Mo?" Mike replied as he walked towards the congregation of women.

"Gram...what are you doing?" Wendy whispered, trying to spare Maggie from any predictable embarrassment.

"Trust me, Wendy, I know what I'm doing," Grandma Mo assured her.

Wendy knew that once Grandma Mo had a mission, there was nothing that could stop her. By the time Mike had reached the group of women, he found himself greatly overmatched.

"What is it Gram?" he asked, as the rest of the women watched him walk over.

"Maggie is a beautiful girl, isn't she?" she asked pointedly as the rest of the women waited for his answer.

"Uh ... yeah ...she is ...very beautiful," he said as he smiled in her direction and winked to the uncomfortable teenager.

Although she appreciated his vote of confidence, Maggie felt like crawling underneath the couch at that moment. It was so horrifying, but it would soon become worse, because Grandma Mo was just getting started.

"See, Michael? This is the perfect type of girl for you. She's a smart, beautiful young woman. Look at that body. She's got perfect childbearing hips."

"Oh God..." Wendy said weakly. Her past was coming back to haunt her, and was now haunting poor Maggie.

"Mother...Stop...you're embarrassing her!" Aunt Meaghan beseeched.

"Am I wrong?" she asked, turning to Maggie's maternal grandmother, Anne, who was speechless. "Look at her! She's got the perfect build to have children. She could have at least five of them with no effort at all. Those breasts could feed an army!"

"Mother, I can't believe you said that!" Aunt Meaghan gasped.

"Well, am I wrong? Look at her! She's perfect mother material."

Over the quiet gasps of the collected women, including Mike's mother Jeanette, Maggie could hear Scott chuckling in the next room. He was having a grand old time listening to the conversation. She darted a blistering look in his direction. She felt her face burning from heat of the embarrassment, and sweat was pooling under her arms. She must have been as red as a tomato. She wanted run out of the room and escape, but she knew that Grandma Mo meant well, in her own misguided way.

Michael was flabbergasted as he stood there with eyes wide open. He knew that Grandma Mo had said all those things as a compliment to the poor girl. He had seen her say the same kinds of things to other young women in his family, including Wendy. Gram meant well, but as he watched Maggie squirm, he felt sorry for her.

Wendy was mortified, and relieved that John had not witnessed the spectacle, although Anne was there front and center. This was such an unbearable situation for everyone involved, especially Maggie. She needed to find a way to get her out of this predicament. Finally, she found a way to save her.

"Maggie, I think I heard Allie crying upstairs. Could you check it out?"

"Absolutely." Maggie said with much relief.

As Maggie left, Mike watched her and wished he could get away as well. He tried to slink away, but Grandma Mo would not let him off the hook so easily.

"Michael...where do you think you're going? I'm not done with you yet."

"I'm still here, Gram." he sulked as he sauntered back.

"How old are you now?"

"Twenty-six," he replied. "Here it comes …" he said to himself.

"See, that's almost criminal. You should be married by now."

"Mom … men don't get married at an early age anymore," Aunt Jeanette said, trying to defend her son, although she felt the same way. She would have loved to have him already settled down, and a responsible adult.

"That's ridiculous," Grandma Mo stated, then she turned to Anne again, "He is quite a catch, don't you think?"

"He's very attractive," Anne agreed. It was Michael's turn to turn fire engine red as he felt like someone who was being auctioned off.

"He's a lawyer. He would provide very well for a family." Grandma Mo bragged proudly, "he's been looking for a job in New York City."

Mike looked up to the heavens for some help from above. He felt a little sweat under his collar, and loosened his tie, as he now was the subject of his grandmother's fantasy.

"Oh really?" Anne commented with interest.

"Yes, it's true. Isn't it Michael?"

Mike managed to nod his head with a forced smile, as he silently prayed for God to take him.

"Now, if we could get our two grandchildren together, wouldn't they make the most beautiful children?"

"Gram, I'm begging you," Mike said, pleading for mercy.

"Gram...she's only seventeen years old," Wendy reasoned.

"So what? I had my first child when I was eighteen, and my husband was twenty. It's better to have children at an early age, when your body bounces back easier. I had eight children!"

"Eight children?" Anne gasped.

"Yes, eight! And I was lucky that I started that early. If you ask me, people wait too long these days. You don't want to be fifty years old and chasing after a toddler," she said as she looked directly at her grandson.

"Mother...please," Aunt Jeanette begged.

"You're not getting any younger, Michael. You have to find the right girl and settle down."

"Yes, Gram ... I know," he agreed, wishing that she would just stop.

"If you ask me, you don't have to look very far," Grandma Mo said.

"Okay Mother, I think that you've tortured my son long enough," Jeanette said, sparing her son from any more suffering at the hands of her well meaning mother. "Michael you better go before she starts sending out wedding invitations."

"Thank you," Michael said with relief, as he backed away from the interrogation.

As he escaped from the all woman prison, he found the nearest cooler, grabbed a beer, opened it and took several large gulps. Afterwards, he breathed a huge sigh of relief. While trying to avoid the hen convention, he turned towards the kitchen and almost bumped directly into Maggie who had returned with the baby. The two tried to pass each other, but when she moved right, he moved in the same direction and vice-versa.

"Would you like to dance?" he joked.

"So, we are married already?" she giggled in reply.

"Practically."

"I see that you finally got out of the hen house."

"Finally...and I have the scars to prove it. You were the lucky one. At least Wendy was able to get you out of there."

"Well, the damage had already been done," she said, sheepishly. She was still embarrassed to talk about it and could barely look him in the eyes.

"You must know that she means well. I know that it's hard to believe, but everything she said in there was intended to be a compliment."

"I guess so."

"It's true. If she tells a woman that she had child bearing hips it is the highest praise she can give you."

"I guess that I should be grateful, then."

"Just don't get her back on the subject."

"I wouldn't want to do that."

At that moment, Wendy came over to grab the baby. She was horrified with what her grandmother had said, and felt that she needed to apologize.

"Maggie, I'm so sorry."

"It's okay, Wendy, Michael explained that it was a compliment."

Mike excused himself from the heart to heart between the two women, and Maggie followed him with her eyes until he turned the corner. Once Wendy regained Maggie's attention, she had her own stories about the famous Grandma Mo.

"She used to do that to me all the time…especially at Christmas." Wendy explained.

"What did you do?"

"I always got really embarrassed. One time, There was a family party and there was this guy there. He was the neighbor's son. She started with the child bearing hips routine and I was completely mortified. I hid in my room until she left."

"I can certainly understand why you did that."

"She's a matchmaker at heart. She can't help herself. She wants everyone to marry, start a family and have a few children. You know, keep the Burke family tree growing."

"So, I guess that you're off the hook now." Maggie said.

Wendy smiled and snuggled little Allison.

"Unfortunately, sweetie…you're on it."

"Terrific."

At the end of the party, all of Wendy's relatives decided to leave a the same time. Maggie walked outside to bid everyone farewell, and while doing so, leaned in to kiss Grandma Mo on the cheek as she sat in the back seat of the car. It was then that the old lady grabbed her hand.

"You are a sweet, sweet girl." Maureen said as she touched the young woman's cheek.

"Thank you." Maggie replied.

Then Grandma Mo asked her to lean over closer so that she could tell her a secret.

"I know that he will fall in love with you. By next year, he will be yours." she whispered. "I promise. Okay?"

"Okay," Maggie said as she smiled and nodded. It was a wonderful thought, but she assumed that Grandma Mo's imagination was hard at work again.

As Maggie pulled away, she saw the intensity in Grandma Mo's face. The old woman was serious.

"Michael, come over here." she said, as Maggie backed away a bit to let him lean in. Maureen gave her grandson a big kiss and a hug, then whispered in his ear.

"Take care of our Maggie." she whispered.

"Of course." he promised, then he turned to look at Maggie, who once again had turned several shades of red.

He did not want to argue with his Grandma Mo, but even though Maggie was very attractive, he was not interested. Even though he had to admit that she was a sweet girl with many wonderful attributes, she was seventeen years old and a junior in high school. Imagine how that would scandalize his life? It would certainly be fodder for the gossip mongers to wag their tongues about around the water cooler.

She was not at all what he was looking for in a companion. She was nothing like the women that he preferred. It was much easier to continue his dalliances with experienced women who did not expect much from him with regards to a relationship.

Besides, even if he considered taking his grandmother's advice, he knew that he would never get the approval of anyone else. As he thought about it, he laughed at the prospect. Wendy would certainly kill him, because she knew of his unrestrained past. If she did not succeed in wringing his neck, her husband John would be more than happy to finish the job.

Chapter Eighteen

THE GUEST

Mike was able to find a job at a law firm in Hoboken, but as he was searching for a place to live, Wendy talked him into staying the guest room downstairs. After resisting the offer at first, he finally agreed to stay for the summer so that he would have the time to find a home that he could buy, without having to rent.

In exchange, he offered to help them paint and do some needed repairs in their newly purchased home, which was an older home and needed a little sprucing up. Mike had a some experience in that department, working side jobs as a painter and handyman while he was in high school and college. It seemed like the perfect trade off, as they were thankful to have his help and expertise.

On a Thursday afternoon in late June, Mike arrived, with suitcases in hand, ready to start his new life.

"Well, here it is," Wendy said. "Home sweet home."

She opened the door to the small room downstairs, which revealed a twin bed, closet, and dresser with a small television upon it.

"I can't thank you enough Wendy," he said. "You have really done me a favor."

"Anything for my favorite cousin."

"It's perfect. It's all I need."

"Great."

He tossed his suitcase on the bed, then turned around to face his cousin. There was something different about the way she looked. She was luminous.

"By the way, you look very good."

"Really? Can you notice?" she said proudly with a twirl, "I've lost twenty pounds already."

"Twenty pounds? That's a lot in a month"

"Most of it was the baby and what came with her. I still have about twenty pounds to go."

"What have you been doing?"

"Walking, mostly. Some Yoga," she said, "and I'm watching what I eat."

"When do you go out?"

"Three times a week. Usually after John comes home. Why?"

"I was just wondering if you wanted company."

"What, do you want to be my personal trainer?"

"Do you need a personal trainer?"

"It couldn't hurt."

"Then you're on. But, there's one problem."

"What's that?"

"I work out in the morning. Before I go to work. That would probably be at around five or six o' clock in the morning."

"I guess that I could do that. But, not every day. I still need my sleep. Allie still gets up during the night."

"Then we're on. he said as he stuck out his hand and they shared a handshake. Then they laughed and hugged instead. As they hugged, Wendy heard a little noise coming from the nursery.

"Speak of the angel. You have to excuse me, the boss is calling," she explained.

"I hear."

"I'll be right back," she said, heeding the call of her baby daughter.

Before she left, she let him know that there was food in the refrigerator if he was hungry. He had not thought that he was hungry, but when he looked at his watch, he realized that it had been eight hours since he last ate. Maybe a sandwich would be sufficient to quell the recently discovered hunger pang. He walked into the kitchen, opened up the refrigerator, found some ham, cheese and wheat bread, and made himself a sandwich. Unpacking could wait, for now.

At first, he felt a little funny. It was not like being in his parent's kitchen, where he could grab anything he wanted. There were bottles of beer in the refrigerator, but he did not take one, opting for a soda instead. Then he felt guilty about taking take the soda, since it could have been Maggie's. He needed to find out what the ground rules were, then he would become more comfortable.

Wendy walked back into the kitchen with Allie in her arms and was happy to see that Mike looked content sitting at the table eating his sandwich. The soda sat on the table, unopened.

"I'm surprised that you didn't have a beer," she commented.

"I felt a little weird about that."

"Why?"

"I figured that the beer was John's. I didn't want to take one if it was his."

"Mike...don't be silly. We have plenty. Right now, you're my guest. If you don't want that soda, go get a beer."

"If you insist," he said as he grabbed the soda can and returned it to it's home in the refrigerator. He grabbed a bottle of beer, opened it and brought it to the table where he took a swig.

"Better?" she asked.

"Much better," he replied. "Are you going to have one?"

"No...I'm breast feeding. I'm not going to have one of those for a while."

"Oh...sorry...I should have known that."

At that moment, the front door opened and Maggie came in the door, home from school. She knew that Michael was moving in that day and she was so nervous to see him again. It was surprising how nervous she had become.

The whole day at school, she dreamed about what she would say when she saw him. She practiced her delivery of "Nice to see you again." in a low, sultry voice. But, as she opened the front door, she suddenly lost her voice and her nerve. She decided that it was best to take the safest route up the stairs to her room.

"Coward!" she said to herself as she looked in the mirror, "Are you going to stay up here forever?"

Well, maybe not forever, but at least for the next few minutes. She knew that Wendy had heard her come through the front door. It was not long before she heard the sound of Wendy's footsteps coming up the stairs. Maggie was relieved to hear her pass her door headed for the nursery. The relief did not last, because after the baby was placed in the crib, the next stop was Maggie's door.

She heard three light taps on the door. Wendy was always very polite when it came to disturbing Maggie's privacy, It was quite different than the way that Darlene used to practically barge down the door as it she was part of a S.W.A.T. team. It was such a noticeable change, and one of many wonderful things that came with Wendy as she joined their family. Even though she was her father's new wife, and her step-mother, Wendy was more like the big sister that she never had. She was someone that Maggie had begun to count on for advice, and a trusted friend.

"Maggie, are you in there?"

"It's open," Maggie said, opening a textbook and trying to look busy when Wendy opened the door. She noticed that Maggie had a textbook open, and apologized.

"I'm sorry that I bothered you," she said. "I just heard the door and then I didn't see you. I thought that you would come into the kitchen and say hello."

"I should be down in a little bit," Maggie said. "I've just got this big test tomorrow. Final Exam in History."

Even though it was a quickly thought out excuse, it was the truth. However, Maggie did not need to study the whole evening long. History was one of her strongest subjects.

"Ugh. I don't miss that," Wendy gasped. "I'll leave you alone, then. Should I bring up dinner? It should be ready at around six."

Another new perk in the new Wendy Regime. There were homemade meals that she did not want to miss. Darlene never made homemade meals, and never even pretended to know how to cook, especially after the first year. Even if she cooked for the family, she certainly would not have delivered it to Maggie's room. Maggie considered the offer, but thought that it would be too cowardly to accept.

"Thanks, but I think that by six, I will definitely need to come out for some air. I'll come downstairs."

"Okay sweetie," Wendy said with a smile.

As Wendy closed the door, Maggie felt a tinge of guilt come over her. Wendy was so excited to have her favorite cousin living there with them. Maggie felt as if she were acting like a spoiled little step-daughter, hiding out in her room and avoiding the family. She was not going to be able to stay up there forever. Dinner would come ... eventually.

At five-thirty, Wendy heard John walk in the door, and into the kitchen to find her. She had just finished making hamburger patties and placed them in the refrigerator on a plate, covered in Saran Wrap. A cookout was planned for dinner on that night, and Wendy had prepared salads and other good things to eat. He found her by the sink, preparing a green salad for the feast.

"Hey beautiful," he said, then gave her a tender kiss. He hugged her from behind, as her hands were busy.

"Hi sweetheart."

"So, did Mike get in okay?"

"Yes. He's on the back deck with Scott. I asked them to start the grill."

"Where's Maggie?"

"She's upstairs studying for a final exam."

"Oh," he said with a smile, remembering those days.

He was proud to hear that she was hard at work. She was always a honor student, and he was not surprised that she had been studying since walking in the door. Then his attention turned to his youngest daughter, Allie, who was awake and lying in the play yard in the living-room within the sight of her mother.

John walked over to the playpen and talked to his six week old cherub.

"Hello Allie. How's my beautiful girl?" he asked. He lifted her out of the playpen, and kissed and cuddled her gently.

Wendy walked in to see her husband snuggling their newborn, and felt such a feeling of euphoria in her heart. This is the life that she always wanted and thought that she would never have. A year ago, she would have never imagined that she would be this happy.

"You are not spoiling our daughter, are you?" she teased.

"Always," he replied.

"She's lucky to have such a loving Daddy."

"I'm the lucky one."

"Well, since she's in good hands, I should go upstairs and get Maggie."

"We'll get her. Won't we Allie?" he said as he nuzzled Allison and she inadvertently smacked his face. He walked up the stairs with the baby, and Wendy returned to the kitchen.

At around a quarter to six, Maggie heard a knock on her door. She had not spent one moment studying for the test. All of her time was focused on what she was going to say or do during dinner. Although, she did pick up her textbook to make it look good.

"Maggie?" Her father asked, "can we come in?"

"It's open, Daddy".

John opened the door to see his daughter allegedly hard at work, with the History book open.

"We just came to tell you that dinner will be ready in fifteen minutes. I'm going to be putting the burgers on soon."

"Okay Daddy, I'll be right down," Maggie assured him.

"Okay, sweetheart," John said to his oldest daughter, then turned to his youngest. "Say goodbye, Allie," he said as he moved Allie's arm to pretend that she was waving.

"Goodbye, Allie!" Maggie said, as she waved back.

With that, John left with Allie and returned downstairs where John took his place as the family griller.

There was no avoiding it. She could not hide in the bedroom any longer. She had to go downstairs and deal with her newly developed infatuation. She took a deep breath, opened her door, walked down the hall and then the stairs. She found Wendy in the kitchen, ready to set the dining room table. She did not see Mike, since he was still outside with the men. She helped set and bring the side dishes to the table, then tried to keep her composure as she waited for the men to come inside.

When the men walked in, they were talking about the house and what needed to be done.

"I can start with the bedrooms tomorrow. I don't start at the office until Monday. I have all day tomorrow," Mike said to John. "Scott, you're going to be around, right?"

"Sure…" I can help you out," Scott replied.

The men were talking as John placed the grilled meat in the middle of the table. Mike sat across from Maggie, and she finally was able to see his face. He seemed more handsome than before in his t-shirt and blue jeans, and suddenly her heart was beating a little faster, and she became very nervous.

He looked at her and smiled. "Nice to see you again, Maggie," he said in a friendly way, like one relative would say to the other.

"Nice…" she said as her voice started to give out. She cleared the frog out of her throat and made another attempt. "Nice to see you too."

"I heard that you were hard at work up there."

"Yeah…" she lied nervously. "History"

"She does very well in History" John said, bragging a bit. "In fact, she's a terrific student all around."

"Really?" Mike said with a smile, seemingly interested.

Maggie was a bit embarrassed by the conversation about her, and John noticed how uncomfortable he was making his daughter.

"But…I'm embarrassing her, so I'll be quiet."

Mike smiled at Maggie, and she rolled her eyes as if to say, "There he goes again." Maggie's face felt hot, and she hoped that her face was not red.

"Anyway…are you sure that you want to start tomorrow? I feel a little funny that I'll be at work and I will not be able to help out," John said, continuing the conversation from before. "I do have all the supplies, though. It's all in the garage."

"Great," Mike replied. "So, Scott and I can start in the morning."

Scott's stomach dropped when he heard the word morning, but tried to look as if the word did not bother him.

"I can help too," Wendy volunteered.

"No thanks, Wendy. I've seen you paint," Mike commented.

"I was fifteen years old then," Wendy said, defending her honor, "and I really did not want to do the job. I wanted you to do it."

"Oh, so that's what happened?" Mike asked.

"Yes, I did a horrible job painting the shed in my parent's backyard because I wanted you to do it for me."

"So, the truth comes out."

"It worked, didn't it?"

"Yes it did. I finished the whole thing!" he laughed.

"And that's exactly what I wanted."

The two shared a laugh, which gratified John. He loved to see her enjoy herself. She was radiant.

Suddenly, Maggie had a wonderful idea of her own.

"I can help," she chirped.

"You…can help?" Scott chuckled, thinking the idea hilarious.

"Yes, Scott. I can help too," she said with a cold stare directed at her brother.

"When have you ever painted?"

"I…paint," she insisted.

"When?"

"Maggie, I think it's great that you want to help, but we will be painting while you are at school tomorrow." Mike explained.

"I can help after school." she said.

She was quite determined, and nobody attempted to talk her out of it, although Scott was not impressed with her ambition. He knew that she just wanted to get Mike's attention, and wanted an excuse to be near him. However, he was amused by the spectacle.

The next day, Maggie could not wait to come home and be Mike's little helper. The Final Exam in History was but a blur. She knew every answer and was positive that she had gotten an A+. All of that did not matter, however. All that mattered was that she was spending the rest of the day with Mike.

Well, that's what she thought. By the time she arrived at home, the men were done for the day. Mike and Scott were sitting on the couch relaxing, eating popcorn and watching a baseball game on ESPN.

"What happened?" she asked, with stunned disappointment.

"We're done for the day," Scott said. "We painted the master bedroom, my bedroom and the guest room. I think that it's enough for one day."

"But, I was going to help."

"You'll get your chance," Scott said, snidely.

"We're going to paint your room tomorrow," Mike assured her. His tone of voice was much more agreeable to her ears.

"By the way, the baby will be in your room tonight," Scott informed her.

"The baby? Why?"

"Since we painted the master bedroom, we thought it would be best if the baby slept in a room that hasn't been painted yet," Mike explained. "So, we moved her crib into your room."

"Oh, I understand now," she said with sweetness in her voice. The tone of her voice was quite different than it had been with her brother, and Scott noticed the difference.

She somehow squeezed herself in between the two exhausted men, which was fine with her. Scott was not too thrilled, because there was a perfectly fine chair in the corner that she could have rested in.

"Maggie, what the heck?" Scott complained.

"What?" Maggie asked innocently.

"It's a little tight, don't you think?"

"There's a chair over there," she pointed out helpfully as she grabbed a handful of popcorn that was in a bowl on the coffee table.

"Thanks for all your help," Scott said sarcastically.

Scott ceded defeat and stood up to take his place in the chair while Maggie cemented her spot on the couch next to Mike. Even though there was more room to relax in, she still remained close to him.

Mike was amused by the little territorial fight, and snickered to himself. It reminded him of when he was younger and how he used to have arguments with his sister. They would fight over who wanted to sit in the front seat, or which television show to watch. Since she was the oldest, and five years older, she usually won. He always fought like a tiger, though, and never gave up.

He was also impressed with Maggie's moxie. She was a cute little ingénue who had the determination to get what she wanted. Mike was surprised how quickly Scott gave in, and he was sure that if the roles had been reversed, Maggie would not have been so accommodating.

"I'm going to take a shower," Scott sighed, as he stood up from his chair.

Maggie had thrown a wrench into the male bonding session, and it was senseless to argue about it. Besides, the Yankees were losing the game and he no longer wanted to watch.

"Thanks for helping, man," Mike said as he stood up and shook Scott's hand.

"Hey, don't thank me…I should be thanking you. I would have been doing this job, anyway," Scott pointed out, "your being here is a blessing."

"Sure is," Maggie added.

She counted her blessings for a different reason, and Scott glanced at her with raised eyebrows as if to say "I know why you just said that."

"Well, I'm glad I can help," Mike said.

During the night, Allison woke up two or three times during the night, screaming for attention. Wendy tried her best to grab Allie before she would wake Maggie up, but it was never quick enough. Every time, Maggie's sleep was disturbed. Maggie had a horrible night's sleep.

Maggie finally managed to put a few hours of sleep together, but the next thing she knew, she was being awakened by an older brother who took great joy in interrupting her slumber.

"Wake up sleepyhead," Scott said as he messed her hair.

Maggie must have had several bags under her eyes, and when she turned around, he was startled by her appearance.

"Yikes, Mags. You look like hell!"

"Thank you very much. What time is it?"

"Seven."

"Seven o' clock? What are you, crazy?"

"I'm sorry, my darling sister, but your boyfriend wants to get an early start on this room."

"Oh God...where is he? He can't see me like this!" She said in a panic as she sat up and pulled the covers up to her neck.

"Calm down, Barbie...he's in the kitchen eating breakfast."

"I've got to take a shower."

"What's the point? You're just going to get paint on yourself. Take one later."

"That's why you're the guy and I'm the girl. You're disgusting."

She crawled out of bed, grabbed a robe and clothes and checked the hallway. The coast was clear. She darted into the bathroom and took her shower.

"Good morning!" Maggie said in her best cheerful voice as she met her fellow painters in the kitchen. She was dressed in an old white t-shirt shirt and faded blue jean cut off shorts, but was fully decked out in makeup and perfectly styled hair.

"Are you dressed for a date, or are you dressed for work?" Scott teased.

"What?" she said, feigning ignorance. "These are my old clothes."

"You're going to need a hat, Maggie," John suggested, "and it would probably be a good idea to put your hair in a ponytail."

Maggie seemed to agree on the outside, but she was disappointed because she had spent so much time getting her hair just right. Now it was going to be put up in a ponytail and hidden underneath a baseball cap. She could hear Scott cackling with delight, and she gave him a dirty look.

"Do you want a coffee, sweetheart?" Wendy asked.

"Yes, thank you," Maggie replied.

As Wendy poured a coffee for Maggie, she had an apology that came with it.

"I'm sorry about Allie last night. She must have known that she was in a different room. It must have made her uncomfortable."

"That's all right ... I'll live," Maggie yawned.

"You look like crap," Scott pointed out.

"Scott, cut it out," John scolded. "Leave your sister alone. She had a rough night."

"What happened?" Mike asked.

"Allie woke up at least three times last night," Wendy explained, "so, Maggie woke up three times last night."

"I'm fine." Maggie insisted.

"Are you sure?" Mike asked Maggie with a concerned look on his face. "If you need to rest, we really can handle the job."

"No, I want to help." she said sweetly, "Besides, it is my room."

"Then it's settled." Mike replied with a smile. She smiled back. Mike probably didn't notice the hearts in her eyes, but they were there. Scott saw the hearts and he rolled his eyes.

Midway through the day, Maggie had started to fade. She spent an awful lot of time sanding, and later doing trim. Her arms felt as if the were ready to fall off. During lunch break, she rested her head on the kitchen table before anyone else came in.

"You know, the men would understand it if you took a break, Maggie. You look like you are about to fall apart." Wendy said as she walked into the kitchen.

"I'm fine."

"You don't look fine."

"I can handle it."

"Do me a favor. Just take a little nap in my bedroom to take the edge off."

"Wendy, if I close my eyes for two seconds, I will not wake up until tomorrow."

"Doesn't that tell you something?"

"It tells me that I need some chocolate."

The women could hear the men coming closer to the kitchen and Maggie quickly picked up her heavy head and pretended to look wide awake.

"Now that's a pitiful sight," Scott commented with a laugh, as the first man to enter the room.

"Shut up, Scott," Maggie said as she stood up to help Wendy take out the cold cuts.

"Give her a break," John requested, as he walked towards Maggie and gave her a quick massage by her aching shoulders. "Are you okay, sweetie?"

"Why does everyone keep asking me that?"

"Because you look like you're about to drop," Scott said.

"Scott!" both Wendy and John said in unison.

Mike was the last to walk into the room and noticed the commotion.

"Torturing your sister again?" Mike asked.

"That's my job," Scott said with pride. Then he excused himself to make a cell phone call in his bedroom.

"Mike, there's Ham, Cheese and Turkey...Wheat and Rye bread," Wendy said as Mike walked over to the counter where the rest of them stood.

John finished rubbing Maggie's shoulder and kissed her on the head for comfort, she thanked him. In the background they all heard Allison's call.

"I'll get her," John offered.

"I'll join you," Wendy said, "it's time for me to feed her."

Mike noticed that while Maggie was making herself a sandwich, she would pause and then rotate her shoulder and grimace as if something was wrong.

"Are you okay?" he asked her.

"To tell you the truth, my arms and shoulder are killing me."

"Where about?"

"Right in the middle of the upper part of my back, and the muscles over here," she pointed out as she massaged her own muscle, "it's like a rock."

"I can try to work it out, if you let me."

"I don't mind," she said with a little smirk on her face. He did not see it as she was facing the other way attempting to make herself a sandwich. As he massaged her shoulder, she made him a sandwich as well.

"Is this where it hurts?" he asked as his worked his gentle fingers in between her neck and her right shoulder.

"That's one of the spots," she replied, thinking of so many other ones. He worked his way down from her shoulder and to her right shoulder blade area. As he worked on that area, there was a little pain, and she flinched.

"Does that hurt?"

"It's just really sore."

"You really should take it easy for the rest of the day."

"It's okay. I'll be all right," she said. Nothing was going to stop her on that day.

As he rubbed her back, several times she closed her eyes and let the pleasure of his touch overwhelm her. His hands were strong and warm, and her imagination ran wild. The massage continued until they heard footsteps coming down the stairs, then Mike stopped as if he was doing something wrong, and walked over to the side of her.

"Here," she said, giving him his sandwich.

"Thank you," he said.

"Thank you too," she replied as she rolled her shoulder again. "I think it helped".

"Good," he said as he walked back to the table and sat down, then she sat next to him.

She was content to feel that they had shared something intimate, however silly that might have seemed to everyone else. On the other hand, he felt like he crossed the line a bit. Why else would he stop when he heard the footsteps?

After lunch, the group continued to paint the living room, which was the last project of the day. Everything was spackled and sanded, and all that had to be finished was the painting. The ceiling was done, and all the small family needed to do was to work together and paint the walls, then and the project would finally be done.

However, two hours later, the work ethic of the group started to wane. Scott excused himself to use the phone in his room, again. Then John and Wendy started to flirt, then kiss each other in the kitchen, later disappearing altogether from the area.

"Where did everyone go?" Mike asked, noticing that after a few minutes, Maggie was his lone assistant.

"I don't know," Maggie said, slowing down to a crawl, barely able to lift her arm.

"Why don't you take a break?" he said as he looked at her with concern.

"I'm alright," she lied.

"Maggie, you've been painting the same section for the last ten minutes."

"Has it been ten minutes?"

"Yes," He laughed as he walked over and took her roller from her hands.

"What are you doing?"

"I'm relieving you of your duties. I can finish up. There's only your section, and that area over there and it's done."

"But, I want to help you."

"It's almost done. Why don't you just sit on the couch and relax," he said as he pointed in the direction of the couch.

She stared at it, and it looked so inviting. Maybe a couple of minutes would do her some good, she thought. He did insist, after all.

"I'm just going to sit over here on the couch and put my feet up for just a couple of minutes." she said as she walked over and sat on the couch, which was covered in a gray painting tarp with dried multi-colored paint specks all over it. It felt so good to sit down and put her feet up. Predictably, she fell asleep two seconds later.

As she slept, she fell into a deep sleep that turned into a dream. She dreamed that Mike put down his roller, and walked over to her. He looked deeply into her eyes and stroked her face, as she stood up from the couch. He leaned in to kiss her softly on the lips, and then…

"Maggie…" she heard Mike say, softly as she felt him touch her shoulder.

At first, his voice was in her dream. Then when she opened her eyes, it was a reality.

"Did I fall asleep?" she asked as she rubbed her eyes. Her heart was still beating rapidly from the dynamic dream.

"About two seconds after you laid down on the couch," he laughed.

"I'm sorry."

"Don't be...I told you to take a break. Besides, it's done."

"We're done?"

"Yeah...I wanted to show somebody, but nobody else is around."

She sat up on the couch and looked around at the newly painted living-room.

"It looks great."

"Doesn't it?" he said as he sat down next to her. "Thanks for your help. Especially after your rough night."

"I'm just glad it's over," she sighed with relief.

"So am I," He responded. "But, I better get up off this couch before I get lazy. I should clean up."

"I'll help you," she groaned. He did not protest.

As the two cleaned up the mess, Mike turned around and accidentally bumped into Maggie with his roller, thus rolling paint onto her shirt.

"Oops," he said. The two of them looked down at the damage done to the front of her shirt. "I'm really sorry," he said with a chuckle.

This mistake was soon countered with a retaliation that was not so innocent. Mischievously, she took her paintbrush and marked his cheek, which surprised him.

"Oops," she said. "Sorry about that."

"You little stinker!" he said playfully.

He rolled his paint roller down the entire front of her shirt, and she evened the score by painting an x on the front of his shirt.

"That's it!" he said, intent on painting her some more, but she escaped by running out of the living room.

He chased the giggling Maggie through the kitchen and out the back door onto the deck. She was faster than he expected. She ran down the stairs of the deck and into the backyard, trying to avoid his paint roller, and he struggled to keep up. Finally, she stopped and held out her paintbrush as if she were a fencer and she warned him not to come any closer, or she would give him her "mark."

He took the challenge. He lunged and painted her bare leg, and she assaulted him on the arm. He decorated her arm and she highlighted him on the other arm. Finally, he just tossed his roller off to the side.

"That's it," he announced, as grabbed and picked her up, slung her body easily over his right shoulder, and carried her back into the house.

121

He carried her back up the deck stairs, through the back door and kitchen and he gently dropped her back onto the living room floor where they both sat down, exhausted. He took off his paint-covered shirt to reveal his muscular form, as Maggie looked on.

She leaned in towards him, and she revealed that she still did have her paintbrush, as she took the final blow of the paint fight by painting his bare chest.

"I give up ... you win," he laughed, raising the imaginary white flag.

"Good," she sighed, still panting from running.

"Maggie...come here," he asked, motioning with his finger for her to come closer.

Intrigued, she moved in closer. When she was within striking distance, he touched his hand to his painted chest, reached over and smeared it onto her face, tipping her over onto her back. She was left his hand print on her face.

She laid there on her back and surrendered to exhaustion, as he did the same. The war was finally over.

"What happened?" A surprised, and newly showered Wendy said, as she walked down the stairs followed by a squeaky clean John. They saw Mike and Maggie covered in paint and lying separately on the tarp covered floor.

"We're finished," Mike announced, breathing heavily.

"I can see that," John commented.

Chapter Nineteen

SUMMER FUN

"Good morning Mrs. Stanton." Nadine said as she greeted Wendy when she arrived for Allison's two-month checkup in mid-July.

"Good morning, Nadine." Wendy replied. Nadine practically leaped out from behind the desk to greet the infant.

"Look at her! She looks just like you ...She's so beautiful." Nadine proclaimed as she noticed Allison in a little pink dress and sun hat.

"Thank you." Wendy replied.

She was happy to see a friendly face for a change. All too often she was subject to the disapproving stares from judgmental people who knew John and Darlene, and the gossip mongers were hard at work. Wendy was subject to whispers at Church, the grocery store and anywhere else she tried to live a normal life. She tried to ignore it, but it was hard to do.

Janice walked down the hall and joined in the adoration.

"Good morning, Mrs. Stanton."

"Good morning, Janice. Nice to see you." Wendy said, then she mentioned something that had been bothering her. "You know ladies, nobody loves hearing the name "Mrs. Stanton" more that I do ... but ... I really would like you both to call me Wendy."

"Well, it's official ... things have definitely changed around here." Nadine said.

"What do you mean?"

"It was always formal with Darlene. She treated us like the help."

"That's a shame"

"Sure was."

"Well, things are different now."

"Thank God for that!"

The door to John's office opened, and a woman walked down the hall, passed the three fawning women and turned around.

"So you're the new Mrs. Stanton?" she asked. Janice and Nadine paused and looked at each other as if they were waiting for something terrible to happen.

"Yes, I am."

"How does it feel to be a home-wrecker?"

"Excuse me?" Wendy asked, surprised at the sudden attack on her character.

"That's enough, Mrs. Davis," Janice said.

"I've just told your husband that I will no longer bring my children to this office. He has you to thank for that."

"Georgia ... you've had your say ... Now you can leave." John said, from behind them. He had approached quietly and had heard what Georgia Davis had said.

"You will regret this, John. I never thought you were the type of man who gave into a mid life crisis."

"Regret has not even crossed my mind, Georgia. You know your way out ... don't you?"

Georgia stormed out, and Janice turned to John with word of wisdom.

"We don't need people like her in here. He elitism contaminates the place. Now we have to get it fumigated."

"I'm sorry that you had to hear that, Wendy," John apologized.

"How many patients have you lost?"

"Nobody that is worth keeping, I tell you that much." Janice interjected. Then she excused herself, saying that she was going to prepare Allie's examination room. Nadine excused herself as well, disappearing behind the desk.

Janice's attempt at reassurance did not make Wendy feel any better.

"How many have you lost?"

"All of Darlene's friends. Georgia was the last."

"I'm sorry."

"Don't be. It just infuriates me how she talked to you. She has no right to demean you like that."

"It doesn't bother me, John. Don't worry about it."

"It bothers me," he said, showing concern for his new wife. He was visibly frustrated.

"John ... relax ... I'm fine, okay?" she said as she stroked the side of his pensive face. "Now, say hello to your daughter."

John changed his outlook and looked down at his baby daughter. His face lit up when he saw her in her baby car seat.

"There's my little sweetheart!" she said as she cooed back. He unfastened her restraints and lifted her out of the chair. He lifted her in the air and kissed her little stomach, which made her giggle.

"She loves her Daddy," Wendy pointed out.

"But will she love me in a half hour after I've given her the shots?" He said as he snuggled Allie, than started to walk towards the examination room.

"Only time will tell …" Wendy joked as she grabbed the car seat and diaper bag, and followed her loved ones.

Allie's examination went very well. She was the perfect weight and height, and everything was either average or above average. John was very happy with the results. As for the shots, the unhappy person was Allie, of whom John cuddled and apologized. Wendy finally had to breastfeed Allie to calm her. When the baby finally relaxed enough to fall asleep, her parents were finally able to return to his office and eat lunch.

During lunch, John seemed a bit pensive and drifted off a bit. It was enough for his young wife to mention something.

"John … is there something wrong?"

"I'm sorry, sweetheart."

"What is it?"

"It's just what happened before. I can't let it go. Why do people have to do that?"

"Maybe she's unhappy and wishes that other people felt the same way."

"It's just so unfair."

"Don't worry about it Johnny, I'm fine."

"Johnny?"

"Oh, I'm sorry. Does it bother you when I call you that?"

"It's the first time I've heard you call me that. My mom and Jenny's parents call me Johnny, and so does Janice. Jenny used to call me Johnny, too."

"Would you rather that I didn't do that?"

"No … I like it. It makes me feel young."

"You are young."

"Tell that to my legs after a long day."

"I'll tell it to your whole body, if you want me to."

"I wish you could right now, but I have appointments up until four-thirty."

"You look really stressed."

"I am really stressed."

"Well, maybe I can take care of that later."

"I'll pencil you in for an appointment," he joked.

After lunch, Wendy and Allie left and John was again back to business as usual. He would have loved to leave with them and take the rest of the day

Anne Marie Busch

off. Nothing would have been better than to spend a quiet summer afternoon with two of his favorite girls, maybe even three if Maggie was around. Sometimes having your own business makes life difficult, and today was one of those days.

At around five o'clock, Wendy walked back into the waiting room and was greeted by Nadine again. This time, she was dressed in a raincoat.

"Mrs. ... Wendy ... back already?"

"Yes. Is the doctor still in?"

"He's in his office ... it's not raining is it?"

"Nope," Wendy replied, then she saw Janice walk in.

"Wendy ... what are you up to?"

"A little stress relief. Can you ladies ..."

"We can leave immediately," Janice chuckled.

"Wait a second. I have an idea," Nadine said, "She picked up the phone and buzzed John. "Doctor Stanton, there is a mother here who would like to see you in your office. Should I send her in? Okay ..."

"What did he say?"

"He was cursing like a sailor."

"Perfect," Wendy said.

The ladies giggled, gathered their belongings and left, locking the door behind them. Wendy turned off the light to the waiting room and walked down the hall and knocked on the office door.

"Come in ... it's open," John said, as he straightened his white jacket and adjusted his tie.

"Dr. Stanton, I'd like to speak with you." Wendy said as she walked in the door, closed it behind her and locked it.

"Wendy ... what are you doing here? Did you forget something? Where's the baby?"

"The baby is with her big sister," she said.

"Then, what is the matter?"

"Nothing is the matter," she explained. "I just have a gift for you."

"What kind of gift?" he asked.

"This kind," she said as she opened the rain jacket to reveal a red satin negligee with black trim. She slid the jacket down her arms and let it fall onto the floor.

"Oh ... sweetheart!" he gasped as he looked at her wonderful form. He was thunderstruck.

"Do you like it?" she said suggestively.

"You could say that. You look amazing."

"Thank you, Dr. Stanton."

He was right. The workouts with Mike had been paying off. Wendy had lost more weight and had become more toned than before. Her body looked wonderful in it's red wrapping.

John stood up from his seated position and pushed in his chair. He started to walks towards her.

"Mrs. Stanton, if I didn't know any better, I'd think that you were trying to seduce me," he said as he approached her and put his arms around her waist as she put her arms around his neck. He leaned down and started to kiss the space right below her collarbone.

"Is it working?" she asked.

"You certainly have the undivided attention of every inch of me."

Chapter Twenty

THE BEACH HOUSE

John and his extended family rented a four bedroom beachfront house for a week in late July, down at the Jersey Shore. This house had been reserved every year by the Channings since Jenny was young, and it was their yearly ritual. The Channings were there earlier in the week, but left on Thursday. Mike was invited to join them, but he could not come down until the end of the week, so he arrived late Friday afternoon after work.

He was able to meet John and Wendy on the beach at around five. They had a small beach setup with a blanket and Allie in a playpen under a large umbrella, several chairs and a cooler.

He asked where everyone else was, and Wendy told him that Scott met a friend, and Maggie was talking a long walk on the beach. He sat down in a beach chair and relaxed, relieved that the work week was finally over.

"Would you like a beer?" John asked.

"Absolutely. I think that you've read my mind," Mike replied.

John discreetly poured a can of beer in a blue party cup and handed it to a thirsty Mike as he thanked him. The two men talked about the traffic on the Garden State Parkway, and other small talk. It was quite evident that the two men enjoyed each other's company, as Mike had become a good friend to John.

They played golf together several times, most recently on the previous weekend, and Wendy was happy that her favorite cousin and her new husband had become buddies. The experiment had worked out well.

Eventually, John returned to reading his book, and Mike set up a chair next to Wendy and looked out onto the horizon. It was a beautiful day. As he relaxed and breathed in the warm salty air, his attention was set upon a beautiful and shapely woman who was walking by the waves. She was so perfect, and he was so intrigued by her presence that he couldn't keep his eyes off of her. She was stunning.

He watched as her long, brown, wavy hair was tossed around by the ocean breeze. His instinct was to approach her, and as he pondered the thought of talking to this wonderful woman, Wendy interrupted his fantasies.

"There she is," Wendy said to Mike.

"There who is?" Mike replied, noticing that she was talking about the mystery woman who had become his infatuation.

"Maggie. She's right over there."

"That's not Maggie," he laughed in a lowered voice that John could not hear.

The whole idea was ridiculous. That woman was definitely not Maggie. She was talking about somebody else.

"That is Maggie, Mike. Don't you remember what she looks like?"

"Of course I know what she looks like. That is not little Maggie. It can't be."

"What do you mean, it can't be her?"

"I think that I would notice it if Maggie looked like that," Mike said, while glancing back at John to make sure that he did not hear the conversation. Oblivious to the discussion about his daughter, John was completely engrossed in the book that he was reading.

"Well, I have news for you, my dear cousin. You have been either in a daze or blind, because Maggie does look like that. That woman over there with the black one piece bathing suit and the long, brown hair is Maggie Stanton!" she said as she pointed towards her.

"You're crazy," he said as he shook his head in utter disbelief, as he squinted his eyes.

"John," Wendy called out, trying to get her husband's attention.

"Don't asked John," Mike whispered, embarrassed that now the father had to be brought into the conversation.

"John, sweetheart…isn't that Maggie over there?" Wendy asked, attempting to get a second opinion.

John looked up from the book that he was reading, looked out at the mystery woman and nodded his head. "That's her."

"See? I told you," Wendy said triumphantly.

Mike could not believe it. This perfect woman that he was lusting for was actually sweet, innocent little Maggie. Suddenly, he felt a little sick.

Maggie started to walk towards them, and as she moved closer, he realized that Wendy and John were right. He was speechless. He felt like stabbing his eyes out. How could he think such impure thoughts about Maggie?

She walked directly towards John intent on asking him a question, and Mike put his sunglasses back on and watched her intently, pretending to look somewhere else.

"Holy Crap!" Mike thought to himself. Her tanned body looked magnificent, and all her curves were in the right places. Had he been so blind for the past month?

"Dad…"

"Hmm?" John replied, still reading his book.

"Have you seen Scott?"

"He went off with some girl named Susan …"

"Sally," Wendy corrected him.

"Sally."

"Did he say when he was coming back?" Maggie asked, concerned about something.

"What's wrong, honey?" John asked as he put down his book and looked up at her.

"He's supposed to be my partner in the volleyball game."

"Oh," John said, then he turned to Wendy to see if she knew anything. "Wendy, did he say when he would be back?"

"Maggie, I think he forgot about the game. He said something about going to the arcade," Wendy said.

"I can't believe he dumped me like that," Maggie said with frustration. "Dad…can you play?"

"No way, Maggie…really…I'm not into it. The last time I played beach Volleyball, I did something to my back."

"Come on, Dad."

"Maggie…I really don't think…" he said, then he realized that there was a sacrificial lamb who was sitting in a chair to Wendy's right, chugging beer from a red Solo cup, "Why don't you ask Mike? He's in shape."

The three Stantons looked in Mike's direction as he quickly looked away so that they would not notice him staring at Maggie's wonderful form.

"What?" he asked as if he had been caught doing something mischievous.

Maggie could not believe that she had not noticed Mike sitting there. She had been so focused on her anger at Scott, that when her attention was diverted in Mike's direction, she was stunned to see him. When she saw him, she had her own moment of silence when she saw him dressed only in bathing trunks. He was so handsome, and his body was absolutely outstanding.

"Mike…I'm sorry…I didn't see you," Maggie said, wanting to kick herself for not noticing that he was there. It was too late for her to check and see if she looked presentable.

"Hello Maggie…" he said, fairly uneasily.

"Do you play beach volleyball?" she asked.

"I haven't done it in a while…but, yes."

"I need a partner. Would you play with me?"

Play with me. That was a dangerous request under the circumstances. He tried to ignore the double entandre and reply correctly.

"Maggie…I don't know. I haven't played in so long, I don't know how good I would be. I can't make any promises."

"Don't worry about that. I'm not looking for an all star. Basically, I just need a good body…I mean, another person. Do you want to help me out? Please?"

He thought about it, and although he assumed that it would probably be a humiliating experience, he did not want to let her down.

"Sure, why not."

"Great! Come with me," she said

He finished the last few gulps of his beverage, then stood up from his beach chair. Maggie already had a head start.

"Good Luck!" Wendy snickered to her workout partner, "you're going to need it."

"Thanks," he said, needing to run a little bit to catch up.

With that, Mike was recruited to play in a two on two beach Volleyball game with Maggie, which they lost pretty badly. They did not play horribly, but they were seriously overmatched by another team who had much more experience playing as a team. The match left the two of them covered in sand and sweat.

"Sorry Maggie," Mike said mournfully, as they started to walk back to their home on the beach.

"It's okay. I had fun, and that's all I wanted. We didn't lose that badly."

"True…" he said with a bit of irony, "if you don't think that twenty-five to seven is a blowout."

"Well, I guess it was pretty bad, wasn't it?" she laughed.

"Pretty horrible, actually," he laughed back.

When they finished laughing at themselves, Mike stopped and looked at the ocean, longingly, determined to jump in. He asked her if she wanted to join him.

"No, I don't really want to go in."

"Why? You don't want to mess up your hair?"

"No. That's not the reason. I went in before. Why do you think that my hair is all wiry?"

"Your hair is not wiry."

"Yes it is. You can't even get your hands through it…see?" she said, demonstrating her troubles.

As he watched her play with her hair, he could see the sweat beading up on her body, and knew that he had to do something to change the direction of his forbidden attraction to her. Mike decided not to think about the offer to run his hands through her hair and tried to change the subject.

"Come on, Maggie. It's hot out here."

"I'm not going in," she insisted.

"Yes, you are," he said, playfully.

"No…I'm not."

"Yes…you are," he said as he grabbed her hand and dragged her towards the waves. At first, she went with him willingly, because she thought that it was a fun idea. But, as they were just about to hit the waves, she pulled back.

"I'm not going to go in," she said, with a nervous laugh.

He flashed a devilish look in her direction, then lifted her into his arms. He carried her into the cold waves, then dropped her into the water. Before she surfaced, he dove in himself.

When she finally faced him again, she splashed him.

"You're an evil man," she kidded.

"You looked hot…overheated…you know what I mean."

She stood there with wet hair in her face and suddenly she looked like a teenager again. Thankfully, she did not look as alluring as she had before. He breathed a sigh of relief.

When the two bathers returned to the Stanton camp on the beach, they noticed that John was packing up for the day.

"What time is it?" Maggie asked, as she toweled off her soaking wet body, and Mike tried not to stare.

"It's six o'clock." John said as he looked at his watch. "Wendy went back to the house to bathe Allie and start with dinner. I'm guessing that we'll be ready to eat at around seven-thirty."

"Wow, I can't believe that it's that late, already," Maggie commented. It was such a beautiful day, and the whole clan had been on the beach for many hours.

"You guys can hang out a little bit longer," John said, "I just want to get back, take a shower … you know. Can you get the rest of the chairs and the blanket?"

"Sure." Mike said.

"So, I'll see you for dinner in an hour and a half?"

"Okay, Dad," Maggie agreed.

John returned to the house, rolling a beach cart behind him, filled with chairs, the cooler and play yard. Maggie and Mike were left alone to relax on the beach. They laid next to each other on the blanket and stared out at the waves.

"It really is a beautiful, isn't it?" she asked as she watched the waves hit the beach. Her question caused him to turn and look at her face.

"Yes it is," he replied, looking only at her.

At seven-thirty, they were showered and ready for dinner. The five of them dined together, as Scott had returned to feed his face before disappearing again.

After dinner was over and everything was cleaned up, it was close to nine. The baby was asleep in her crib, and Wendy and John gave themselves that special look, and started to slow dance to the music in the background. Maggie had grown accustomed to that little routine, and knew that it was time to make herself scarce.

"Uh oh." she said to Mike, out of earshot of her father and stepmother.

"What?" he said.

"They're at it again," she snickered.

"Oh," Mike said, finally realizing what was going on.

"Ever since the wedding, it's been …"

"All systems go?"

"You could say that," she whispered.

"Does it bother you?"

"No. Not at all. Look how happy he is," she said with a smile, as she and Mike watched Wendy and John slow dance.

"Maybe we should ourselves scarce?"

"Definitely," Maggie said.

The two stood up from the couch and prepared to make their escape.

"Wendy, Maggie and I are going to go for a little walk," Mike announced, "We should be back in about, what? … an hour?"

"Maybe two. I want to show him around. We're going to go to the boardwalk and arcade," Maggie added. "We'll be back at around eleven."

Maggie and Mike walked on the beach and stopped for about a half hour to sit on the cold sand and look out into the waves. They watched as couples passed by walking hand in hand by the shoreline. It did not become uncomfortable until one of the couples stopped and started to kiss passionately in front of the moonlight. It was then that Mike became a little uncomfortable and asked Maggie if she would like to leave the beach and go to the boardwalk.

Once on the boardwalk, they came across an ice cream stand. He saw another opportunity to treat her like a teenager, and he immediately took up the task.

"Come on…I'll treat you to some ice cream," he said as they continued to walk towards the stand.

"No thanks."

"You don't like ice-cream?"

"Of course I like ice-cream, silly. I just don't think that I should have any. It'll go right to my thighs."

"What thighs?"

"Oh, I've got thighs," she insisted, lifting up her denim skort to reveal more than he needed to see. He tried not to look too long.

"Maggie…you're on vacation. You've got the perfect body. I think that you can afford to have one little ice cream cone."

She laughed out loud. Now he was really being too nice.

"Perfect body? What are you, blind?"

"Perfect body. It's true. Have you looked at yourself in the mirror lately?"

"I try to avoid the mirror as much as possible, thank you very much. I could lose at least ten pounds or more."

"You're nuts."

"It's true."

"Maggie, do you want to be like one of those bony models?"

"No, I think that would be a bit unrealistic. But, I do need to lose some weight."

"You do not. You are fine the way you are."

"Thank you, Cousin Michael. I appreciate the pep talk. I'm fine just the way I am … I get it," she said as if he were a doting uncle talking to his wallflower niece.

"I'm not saying it because you are my cousin."

"Then, why are you saying it?"

"I am saying it because it's true. No guys really like being with a skinny little scrawny thing," he said, as the two of them approached the creamery door and stopped. "Like a friend of mine once said, it's like going to bed with a bicycle."

"I've never heard that one before," she chuckled.

"It's true. I've experienced it."

"Is that so?"

"Never mind. The point is you should be proud of your…curves," he said, a bit uncomfortably. He decided to the conversation in another direction. "So, are you going to have some ice-cream or am I going to eat alone?"

She paused, and the more she thought about it, the more she wanted some ice cream. Besides, he was very persuasive. One little cone was not going to hurt anyone.

"All right," she said, giving in to the temptation. They walked up to the window, and a tanned, rotund woman with a white hat asked what they wanted to order. He ordered a strawberry shake, and then turned to see what she had decided.

"I'll have a banana split, please."

They found a table in a little area used by the ice cream shop for people to sit down and eat their treats. Halfway through dessert, Maggie was laboring. Her eyes had definitely been bigger than her stomach. She knew that ordering a banana split was a big mistake, but it had been so long since she had eaten one that she just could not resist it when she saw it on the menu. Mike was already done drinking his small strawberry shake, and was amused to see her suffering with her dessert.

"Do you need a little help there?"

"Please. There is no way that I am going to finish this," she said, appreciating his assistance. As they shared the dessert, his curiosity got the best of him.

"Tell me something…are you happy that your father married my cousin?" he asked her.

"Why do you ask that?"

"I don't know … there's a big age difference between them. She's closer to your age, isn't she?"

"Yes, she's a lot younger than he is, but my Dad is really happy. Last year at this time, he was so miserable. There was like this little cloud of gloom over his head all of the time," she said, lifting her hands up as if to demonstrate the imaginary cloud above her head. "Now he's always smiling. Scott and I call it the goofy smile. We have Wendy to thank for that."

"How do you and Wendy get along?"

"Great! I really love her. Although, she's more like a big sister to me than a step-mother."

"I'm glad that the two of you get along well. She looks very happy."

"She is very happy. I know it. She and Dad are inseparable."

"I'm happy for her. She's waited a long time for the right guy."

"She's got him. Trust me."

"I'm glad," he said, as he pushed the plate away. He pushed it towards her, and she shook her head. She had eaten too much already.

She then curiously shifted her attention towards Michael.

"What about you?" she asked pointedly.

"What about me?"

"Why haven't you found the right girl?"

"You sound like Grandma Mo."

"Sorry."

"Don't be. It's just not an easy question to answer."
"Tell me something. How old were you. When you ..."
"When I what?"
"You know…"
"Oh that? You don't really want to know about that, do you?"
"I'm just curious."
"I shouldn't tell you that. Your father would kill me."
"Why not? I'm a big girl. Come on…You weren't eleven were you?"
"No, not eleven." he laughed.
"So how old?" she asked, her curiosity peaked.
"Do you promise not to spread it around?"
"I promise," she whispered, practically splitting from the enthusiasm of hearing the secret.

He leaned in across the table to tell the big secret.
"I was sixteen."
"Sixteen?" she gasped, "you're kidding me! How old was she?"
"She was eighteen. She was the local teacher."
"Teacher?"
"No, no…Not that kind of teacher. She was eighteen, remember? Although, she was very experienced. She liked to break in beginners. It made her feel important, I guess."
"Did you like her?"
"I liked her that night," he laughed, causing her to roll her eyes.
"I can't believe you just said that," she said.
"Well, it's true," he reasoned, and then he felt a little guilty telling her about it. She looked a little embarrassed.
"Why are you asking me these questions, anyway?" he asked.
"I don't know. I guess that I am just wondering."
"About what?"
"I'm almost eighteen and I haven't…you know."
"And the problem is?"
"Well, other girls are more experienced."
"So what? Are you worried that they are more popular with the guys?"
"Well, they are…"
"Why do you think that is?" he snickered, "but, that's probably the only reason that they are so popular."

Then, he got serious. Suddenly, the thought of Maggie's lovely assets being pawed by some grungy teenager made him sick to his stomach.
"Maggie, do me a favor, don't let anyone talk you into anything that you're not ready for."
"Now, you sound like my father."

"If that's the case, I must be doing something right."

"Thanks," she said with a tinge of sarcasm.

"Maggie...don't worry about it. When you find the right guy, you will know, and it will happen. Hopefully, it's after you get married, of course."

"You're joking, right?"

"Well, don't use my life story as a blueprint. I may have a lot of experience, but I've never had a serious girlfriend. Who knows if that will ever happen."

"Why not? Haven't you ever been in love?"

"Other than Jeanine Bunting in the second grade? No."

"Why not?"

"I don't know."

"I don't think that I could ever make love to someone if I wasn't in love."

"What can I tell you? I haven't been able to find the perfect woman. But, I don't exactly believe in living like a monk."

"So you just sleep around?"

"That's a pretty crude way to put it."

"Well how else would you describe it? You have mindless sex with women that you don't care about. You take the easy way out."

"Wow, you think that you have me all figured out, don't you?" he said.

"I think that you are scared."

"Scared of what?"

"Commitment. Maybe you're afraid that you will fall in love, and then you'll get hurt."

"Are you psychoanalyzing me now?"

"No, I just think that you are selling yourself short. You should let yourself fall in love."

"It's easier said than done, Maggie. You just don't fall in love overnight. It's not like high school. No offense."

"Maybe you're just looking in the wrong place."

"Maybe you're right," he said defensively.

He felt a little uncomfortable, and shifted in his chair as if he was being interrogated. This was turning out to be a conversation that he would usually have with his mother or father. He wanted to put an end the whole conversation.

"Judge, can I get off the witness stand now?"

"Yes. I'm sorry. I got a little carried away," she replied, although there were still so many things that she wanted to find out.

"You should be a lawyer."

"No, I wouldn't want to be a lawyer."

"Why not? you are very good at cross examination. But, you're probably right. You probably aren't a very good bullshit artist."

"I'm going to go to school to be a nurse."

"That's more like it. I can see that."

There was a sudden silence, and they noticed that the ice cream shop was closing up for the night. Mike looked at his watch and realized that it was approaching eleven. They walked on the boardwalk back to the beach house and after they walked into the door, then turned to say good night to one another.

"Do you like sunrises?" she asked.

"Of course. If the sun wouldn't rise, we wouldn't have the day," he joked.

"Mike, you know what I mean. Did you ever watch the sunrise?"

"I have, on occasion. Usually after a long night before I go to bed. What about you?"

"All the time. When I was little, we used to come down here during the summer, and my Mom and I used to watch the sunrise. I still do it. Especially when I'm down here. "

"I'm more of a sunset type of guy."

"Really?" she said skeptically.

"Why. Don't you like sunsets?" he asked.

"I think that they are kind of depressing."

"Why is that?"

"Because it represents an ending."

"It's the ending to the day, but it is a beginning of the night. Plus, they are sometimes more beautiful to look at."

"True."

"So, don't write off sunsets just yet."

"All right, I'll take your word for it. But you should give my sunrises a chance too. In fact, I'll be up tomorrow watching it. Do you want to join me? I used to be able to get my Dad to come out, but for some reason he wants to sleep in."

"I wonder why," he said lightheartedly.

"Come on. Just tomorrow and I won't bother you on Sunday."

"Do I have to get out of bed?" he teased.

"Obviously. But, I'm only going to the back porch. The view is perfect there."

"What time will this be?" he asked, afraid to hear the answer.

"Around five-forty-five, but I'm going out there before five-thirty, when the colors start."

"I don't want to make any promises, but I'll try."

"Great! So I'll see you tomorrow morning. Good night, Mike., she said as she skipped up the stairs to her adopted room for the week.

"Good night, Maggie," he replied.

No sooner did he close his eyes for the night than they were opened again six hours later. He had been awakened by her soft voice whispering for him to wake up. It was five-thirty, and the sunset was just a half hour away.

"Is it that time already?" he asked, wishing that he had two to four more hours to sleep.

"Come on, you're going to miss it!" she said as she grabbed his hand and started to tug at it.

"Wait, Maggie, let me at least get dressed first," he pleaded, not wanting her to see him undressed.

Suddenly, she was embarrassed and apologized, but was also intrigued. She told him that she would wait for him on the swing on the back deck and excused herself. After she left the room, he stumbled around, found a pair of denim shorts and t-shirt and threw them on. He went into the bathroom, splashed water on his face and took care of other business. He looked at himself in the mirror and asked himself why he was up so early. When he opened the door, he found out. Maggie was standing there, anxiously waiting for him.

"You're going to miss it."

"I'm ready, I'm ready," he said.

She grabbed his hand and led him through the door and onto the swing, where she threw a blanket over the two of them. It was a little chilly that morning, and she was prepared. She held his hand again as she waited for the sun to peek it's head out of the watery horizon. Finally, the sun started to appear.

"Isn't it beautiful?" she said as she commented on the beauty of the orange and yellow sky with a tint of blue. She leaned her head on his shoulder, but heard no response to her question. She turned to notice that he had fallen back to sleep.

"Mike... Mike!" she said, trying to awaken him.

"Huh?" he asked, suddenly jolted back from the dead, "sorry. Did I miss it?" he yawned.

"No, it's just starting," she said, holding his hand tighter, "isn't it beautiful?"

"Yes it is, Maggie."

Saturday came and went and before they knew it, Sunday had arrived and the van was packed and ready to go home. Maggie looked at the loaded van and did not look forward to being stuffed in the back seat.

On the ride down to the shore, she had taken a ride with Scott, but since he was spending the rest of the day with Sally and returning later on that evening, he did not want his younger sister tagging along. She was disappointed, but did not blame him for ditching her. There was another option.

"Maggie, would you like to ride with me?" Mike asked from the drivers side of his car, after noticing the look on her face.

She almost jumped out of her sandals, as she spun around to beg her father.

"Dad, can I?"

"I don't see why not. We're all going to the same place," John reasoned.

She never loved her father more than at that moment as she kissed his cheek, thanked him and pranced to the passenger side of Mike's used, but well maintained blue Volkswagen Jetta. She threw on a pair of sunglasses, and sat down before her father could change his mind.

"See you back at the ranch," Mike said as he started the car, waved and pulled the car out of the driveway.

The last thing that John saw was Maggie's beaming smile and her enthusiastic wave as Mike's car sped down the road.

Once they were on the highway, Mike suggested that Maggie search through his CD collection to find something that she liked. As she looked, she noticed that most of the music was classic or hard rock. Led Zeppelin, Van Halen, Guns N'Roses and Velvet Revolver were a couple of the choices that she was left with, but none of them tickled her fancy at the moment.

"This collection looks like a combination of Scott's and my Dad's. See, there's the Beatles." she commented.

"Is that bad?"

"I didn't say that."

"Who do you like, Britney Spears?"

"No, of course not. I don't like pop music," she said.

"Rap?"

"God, no."

"Country?"

"That's Wendy's favorite."

"I know. She used to torture me with that."

"It's not that bad. I like the contemporary stuff."

"What else do you like?"

"I like soft rock…and classic rock. Hard rock is not so bad, but I don't like the real Heavy Metal. I also like classical. That was one thing that I learned from Darlene. Darlene played it constantly, and I grew to like it."

"Classical, huh?" he said with a quizzical look. "Reminds me of Warner Brothers cartoons."

"See, you're more cultured than you think."

She continued to look, then noticed a CD that was different from the rest.

"Elvis Presley?" she asked with surprise.

"Well, he is the King."

"Interesting," she replied, "you are a surprise a minute, Mr. Burke." she said as she slid the Elvis CD into the car stereo, "but, I do like Elvis."

"You have good taste." he said.

"I know." she replied.

As Jailhouse Rock played on the stereo, Maggie leaned back, closed her eyes and smiled. It had been a very informative trip. Little by little, she was learning more about the man sitting next to her. She knew that there was no place in this world that she would rather be, and it was a wonderful thing.

Chapter Twenty-One

THE HERO

By August, life had started to get back to normal. Scott had driven his car to college for his sophomore year. Maggie was a senior in high school and had been practicing with the girls soccer team. She practiced daily, and then John would normally pick her up at the end of practice.

"Mike, can you do me a favor?" Wendy asked as she walked from the kitchen into the living room with Allie in her arms.

"What is it?"

"John just called. He can't get away to pick up Maggie at soccer practice. I would do it, but I still have to feed Allie, and give her a bath. Can you pick her up?"

"Sure, no problem."

"Thank you so much, Mike, I really appreciate it. I have so much to do before John and I go to dinner tonight."

Wendy gave Mike directions, then he jumped into his car and drove to the high school. He parked and then walked around the football field where he could see the young men practicing, and it reminded him of ten years ago, when he had been on a similar team in his home town. He managed to get the attention of a student who was running around the track that surrounded the football field and ask him the location of the soccer field. The young man directed him to an adjacent field, which was within walking distance.

Finally, he found the girl's soccer team, and saw Maggie involved in passing and shooting drills and watched from a hill in the distance, but close enough to recognize her. He was very impressed with her skill, as on one occasion, she kicked the ball past the goalie and into the far right corner of the goal. As she ran back, she noticed that he was there. Suddenly became nervous, forgot what she was doing and accidentally stepped on the ball, turned her ankle, and fell like a stone onto the ground.

She cursed to herself and tried to stand up. Unfortunately, her ankle was throbbing. The whole team gathered around her as the coach came over to check her injury, and Mike walked over to find out what was wrong. She was so embarrassed by her fall and injury, and felt like a klutz. Her coach informed her that it was not broken, but probably was a first or second degree sprain. The coach gave her ice, and advised her to go to the doctor. She told him that she had a doctor at home.

Maggie attempted to walk, while leaning on Michael, but she found it too painful. He decided to run back and retrieve his car, and drive it closer to her location. When he returned, her friends had helped her across the field, but she still had a long way to go.

"This is silly Maggie. I can just carry you."

"No, really, it's all right," she tried to convince him. She wanted to save herself from the mortification of being carried off the field, however tempting the offer might have been. Her friends continued to help her walk across the field, and Mike felt helpless because she would not let him help.

Finally, when she stopped again, he decided to take charge. He asked the young women to excuse him, he lifted her into his arms, and after doing so they exchanged glances.

"I hope you don't mind," he said

"I don't mind at all," she replied. She was speechless. He had lifted her so quickly and easily that she was literally swept off her feet. As he carried her, she put her arms around his neck and felt warm and comforted in his strong arms.

"I guess you'll be all right, then," one of her teammates said, as Maggie beamed.

Once home, John informed her that she had a first degree sprain, which would take a few days until she could walk without pain. He told her to ice her ankle for fifteen minutes, then off for fifteen minutes.

"And try to stay off of the ankle as much as you can," John suggested. "No soccer for a few days."

With that comment, Maggie tilted her head back with disgust.

"I can't believe this is happening. I'm such an idiot."

"Maggie, don't worry about it. You'll be back on the field soon," John said.

"John, we should forget about going out tonight," Wendy suggested.

"Maybe you're right," John agreed.

"Oh, come on. Don't do that. I'll feel really bad," Maggie said.

"But, you can't take care of the baby if you're hurt, sweetheart," Wendy explained.

Maggie turned her attention to the other man in the room.

"Mike can help me."

"Mike?" Wendy laughed

"What? You don't think I can do it?" Mike asked.

"No, I don't." Wendy joked. "I bet that you've never changed a diaper in your entire life."

"I've changed many…a diaper in my time."

"Oh really?" Wendy asked suspiciously.

"Really," he replied.

"So, it's settled. You two can still go on your date," Maggie urged, trying not to reveal her ulterior motives.

"Maggie…are you sure?" John asked.

"Daddy, I'm fine. I want you to go. I…we can handle it"

"Allie is in the crib already, John. She has been fed and changed. She probably won't even wake up until the morning," Wendy reasoned.

"Yeah Dad, she'll probably sleep all night."

"Are you sure?" he asked Maggie.

"Very sure, Daddy, If I need anything, Mike is here."

"Yeah. I'll be here," Mike assured him. "I'm not going anywhere tonight."

"Alright…we'll go," John finally agreed to his daughter's delight.

Wendy and John finally left for their first dinner alone in a restaurant since the baby had been born. No sooner did they leave the premises, then Allie started to bellow.

"I thought that Wendy said that Allie will sleep all night," Mike commented.

"Maybe she sensed that her parents aren't home," Maggie suggested. "I'll go check on her."

Maggie was in obvious pain as she tried to hop on one foot up the stairs. Mike decided to follow her, then assist her up the stairs. When they walked into the baby's room, there was a definite foul smell in the air. Allison was screaming at the top of her lungs and looking for a diaper change.

"So, are you going to handle this?" Mike asked.

"I thought that you said that you've changed plenty of diapers."

"You believed me?"

"I knew it!" Maggie said, "it figures."

"Why would I know how to change a diaper, anyway?"

Maggie sighed and hobbled over to Allie's crib. She tried to pick her up, and found it difficult to keep her balance on her injured foot.

"Mike, you're going to have to pick her up and put her on the changing table. I can't put any weight on this foot."

"Okay," he said as he lifted up Allison and got a good whiff of the package that she had waiting for them. "My God…what is in there?"

"Nothing good, I can tell you that," Maggie replied as she hopped over to the changing table, ready to change her sister. Mike laid Allie down, and Maggie began to undress her. She felt a little wobbly on her feet.

"Mike ... I need you to hold me steady."

"Okay," he said as he held either side of her hips for stability. "Oh man, that smells horrible."

"Looks even worse ... would you like to take over?"

"You must be hallucinating," he replied.

"Some help you are."

"Hey, I'm helping you," he reasoned. "What else can I do? You're the one with the childbearing hips."

"Very funny."

"and the ..."

"Don't say it."

"Breasts that would feed an army."

"You're very lucky that I have a baby in front of me, funny guy. How would you like a dirty diaper in your face?"

She enjoyed the attention and the game that they were playing. He seemed to enjoy himself as well as he tapped her on either side of her hips and continued to tease her.

"You know, Gram was right. You do have wonderful child bearing hips, I can tell by the way that they feel."

"Here."

"What?"

She handed him the dirty diaper and told him to put it in the diaper bin.

"Thank you so much."

"My pleasure."

When he finished his task, she had another job for him.

"Your turn."

"Excuse me?"

"I took off the diaper, and cleaned her. Now I want you to put a new one on her."

"You're kidding."

"You have to learn how to do it, Mike. Considering your track record, you are going to father a lot of children in the future."

"You are very funny ... you must be getting your jokes from my cousin."

"The diapers are in the cabinet."

"You cannot be serious."

"I'm deadly serious. Here, I'll get it for you, Mr. Perfect." she said as she retrieved, then handed him a diaper.

"What do I do?" he asked as he looked down at Allie with a frightened look on his face. Allie reacted by shoving a fist in her mouth and cooing.

"You better put that thing on her before she pees on the table," Maggie said.

That got his attention, and he stood there in front of the table holding the new diaper and looking it over, not knowing the next step. Maggie sighed, then told him of the next step.

"Open the diaper, pick up her legs and put the diaper under her butt," she said.

He did as she asked, then looked for further instructions. Maggie continued to school him in the fine arts of diaper changing.

"Mike, the diaper goes the other way, the tags go in the back. Now you've got it … now take the front part and put it over the front. Then take the adhesive tape and attach it to the front part … that's right. Good boy."

"Not too bad for a small hipped playboy."

"Not bad at all. Now you can put the pajamas on her," she said as she patted him on the shoulder, then leaned on the table for support.

Maggie helped Mike manage to put the pajamas back on Allie without breaking her arms and legs, which was his biggest fear. She was so tiny compared to his large hands. He could not get over it. Afterwards, he lifted Allie and brought her back to the crib, placing her inside. Allie looked up at him with contentment.

"She's a cutie," He whispered to Maggie as the two of them hovered over the crib. They watched as Allison slowly closed her eyes and fell back asleep.

As they turned to sneak away, Maggie accidentally stepped down on her bad ankle. She did not scream, although the throbbing pain was intense. He could see the pained expression on her face, as her eyes glazed over.

"What happened?" he whispered.

"I stepped down on my bad foot … I'm such a jerk"

"Do you want me to bring you downstairs?"

"Could you, please?"

"No problem."

With that he lifted her again, with no trouble at all, and carried her down the stairs. He brought her to the living room and carefully positioned her down onto the couch. He propped her foot up onto a pillow at the end of the couch, and positioned the ice pack gently onto her ankle, asking if it felt all right. Once that was done, he sat down next to her.

"Tell me something," she asked as she propped herself up on to her elbows.

"Uh oh. Should I get a lawyer?" he asked, feeling a new interrogation developing.

"Why don't you bring any girls home?"

"I'm actually between girlfriends right now. Besides, I've been forbidden to bring women home."

"Why is that?"

"I don't think that Wendy wants you corrupted by my wicked ways."

"I don't think that you're wicked," she said.

"Thank you for your vote of confidence," he replied.

It was that moment that as she slid her head back and rested onto his lap and he felt a sudden tingle up his leg.

The feeling came upon him like a bolt of lightening, and it was quite surprising. His first instinct was to jump away off of the couch and take a cold shower, but he could not do that because she was comfortably resting and he did not want to disturb her. At least one of them was relaxed. He was trapped there, breathing slowly to try to reduce his blood pressure, and thinking of horrible things to get his mind off any arousing thoughts in his head.

Finally, she drifted off to sleep and he was able to slide out from under her head. He placed a pillow under her head and disappeared into the bathroom to look at his guilt ridden self in the mirror.

"What are you doing?" he asked himself. Then he looked down, trying to calm down his stimulated body. "Not now!" he pleaded.

His body was not convinced, and was still ready for combat. It was going to take a cold shower to take care of the problem. As he showered, he wondered if this was going to be a regular occurrence. Hopefully, it was just a fluke. Either way, this was going to be a long couple of months. He needed to find his own place ... and fast.

Finding a place was easier said than done, however. Even though he now made a decent salary in the firm, he still did not have enough saved to be able to buy a condominium, which was his goal. He briefly had the idea of finding an apartment, but most of the places that he looked at required a year lease, and he did not want to stay in an apartment for that long. He decided to stick with his original plan and wait until he could a place of his own.

Chapter Twenty-Two

THE PLAN

John and Wendy left early in the morning one Saturday in early September to take the two hour trip to visit Joe and Sarah. They had planned to sleep over and return the next day. Normally Maggie would have accompanied them, but she had a soccer game that day, and did not want to miss it. Mike volunteered to drive her to the school, where she would grab the team bus to the game, then after the game was over she had planned to go to a friends house, then sleep over. Mike was asked to pick her up the next morning.

At around eight in the evening, Mike received a frantic call from Lizzy that Maggie had gotten herself in trouble.

"What's wrong?" he asked.

"Maggie is drunk and she's in the room with Josh. I don't know what she's going to do!" Lizzy said in frantic tone.

"Where are you?" he asked. Lizzy gave him the directions, and within a second, he was out the door.

He walked in on a scene of carnage that he had experienced on a regular basis almost ten years ago, when he was about her age. The interior of the home was filled with beer bottles, cigarette smoke and drunken teenagers. There were pizza boxes and chip bags strewn all about. He felt like he was reliving his past, and it was unnerving, especially considering who he had come to rescue.

He searched for Lizzy and finally saw her in the crowd. She had a look of concern on her face.

"She's in the last room upstairs. I keep knocking on the door, but she keeps telling me to go away!" the frantic girl said.

"Show me where," he insisted.

She led him up the stairs and down the hallway to what must have been the master bedroom. He pounded on the door.

"Maggie!" he yelled. "Maggie, come out of there!"

A couple of moments later, Maggie opened the door. Her clothes and hair were a bit disheveled, but she was still fully clothed, thank God.

"Michael!" she said with surprise, "what are you doing here?"

"Maybe I should ask you the same question," he scolded, but not too harshly. He was just happy to see her unharmed.

"What are you, my protector, now?" she mocked, unconvinced of his fatherly tone.

"I'm taking you home," Mike said, not wanting to debate the fact. His forceful manner met with resistance from the other man in the room.

"Hey man, this is my house. Get your own date," Josh protested, while swaying noticeably.

"I would back off, if I were you, buddy," Mike fired back.

The tone in his voice told Josh that he had better leave it alone. He could tell from Mike's cold stare that if he tried to take her back, he would have ended up with a fist through his face.

"Come on sweetheart, you can't stay here," Mike said as he reached out his hand and she grabbed it. As he led her down the hall and they descended the stairs, Maggie leaned on his strong arm.

"You're very strong," she said, with a tipsy voice as he led her our the door.

Once outside, and away from the crowd, Maggie got a little lightheaded and started to wobble a bit, having to stop.

"Wait …" she said, "I'm a little woozy."

"I got you," he replied as he put his arm around her for support. As they walked to the car, they could hear Lizzy's voice from behind them.

"Don't forget about me!" she exclaimed, as she ran past them. She found his car and sat in the back as Mike left Maggie in a standing position next to the car.

"Are you alright?' he asked softly.

"I am now," she replied, then she leaned forward, threw her arms around his neck and kissed him fully on the lips.

It was a long embrace and she held him so tightly. He wanted it to stop, but he did not pull away, because he did not want to embarrass her in front of her whistling friends that were hanging around outside. He let her have her moment, and it was not such a terrible thing after all. It felt almost like it was the natural thing to do, and at least it answered a couple of questions that his body wanted to know.

She finally let go of her clutch and smiled.

"You're a really great kisser," she cooed.

"Thank you," he said with a bit of amusement. "Now, come on and sit in the front seat, like a good girl."

"I'm a very good girl," she said.

"I know," he agreed.

He opened the door and made sure that she made it into the front seat without falling to the ground, then he reached over and put on her seat belt, which made her smile at him dreamily. As they drove away, they could hear the sound of police sirens approaching the party location. She was lucky that he had arrived in time. He had saved her from disaster.

After dropping Lizzy off, Mike drove Maggie home, once she told him that the sleep over was off. Once inside, Mike followed her up the stairs, so as to protect her from falling down them. As she climbed the stairs, he followed and watched her intently. First, he was wondering if she would fall down the stairs, but he also watched her with the interest of a man.

He thought about the kiss by the car, and he liked the way that it felt to kiss her. Then he thought about her father, and decided to think about other things to keep his mind off of Maggie's assets … such as losing John's friendship.

At the top of the stairs, she stopped and swayed a bit, causing him to grab her temporarily.

"Are you okay, baby?" he asked, not realizing that he had spoken a little pet name for her.

"You just called me baby," she giggled.

"Did I?" he asked, not realizing what he had just said. "Sorry about that. I should be shot."

"It's okay. I like it," she said as they walked closer to her bedroom. When they arrived at her door, she stopped.

"Thanks for coming to my rescue … again," she said as she swayed in the hallway. "You always seem to be there when I need you."

"It's my job. At least for tonight," he said. "I'm glad that I could help."

"You're like my knight in shining armor." she said as she looked longingly into his eyes. Her gaze was so powerful that it made him feel uncomfortably stimulated.

She put her arms around his neck and kissed him again slowly and sensuously, pressing her body against his. Then afterwards, she leaned her head on his chest and hugged him. She could feel his heart beating rapidly underneath her ear.

"Maggie, you shouldn't kiss me like that," he said nervously, thinking of self-preservation.

"Why not? I like kissing you like that."

"That's not the way that you kiss a family member. I'm like your uncle."

"You're not my uncle," she corrected him. "Besides, you are so handsome. I can't help myself," she said as she picked up her head, looked at him and stroked his face.

He did not reply, but rather, he was silently praying for strength. He was afraid to find out what else she had in her little bag of tricks.

"Good night, sweet knight," she said with a smile. Then, thankfully, she turned around, walked into her bedroom and closed the door behind her.

He watched her walk into the room, than after she closed the door, he stood there staring at the door. If that were any other woman, he would have followed her in there. But, that was Maggie and it was not going to happen. Instead, he tried to snap out of it.

"Get your mind out of the gutter," he told himself. He shook his head to try shake the kisses off his lips. The feeling of them remained, however, and he escaped downstairs to try to forget what just happened.

While still trying to get the image of Maggie out of his head, Mike decided to sit on the bed, take out his laptop and do some work. His mind kept drifting back to the kisses, and then the image of her body in the bathing suit on the beach popped into his head.

"Oh no, you don't. Don't go there," he said aloud to his mind.

He shook his head and tried to concentrate on his work. Nothing like working on a divorce case to get your mind off sex, he thought. After about a half hour, he was so involved in what he was doing that he did not notice that Maggie had appeared in his bedroom.

As if he felt her presence, he looked up into the dimly lit room and saw her standing there dressed in a pink satin half robe. He was speechless, and immediately felt something stir inside him. His chivalrous attitude immediately went out the window, and nothing could not get his mind off her now. His heart practically stopped as he watched her slide the robe off her shoulders, revealing a pink ruffled teddy. She was gorgeous.

"Oh God ... Maggie ..." was all that he could mumble as she walked toward the bed. He was in a frozen state ... in more ways than one.

"Do you like it?" she asked as she walked closer, then sat down next to him, "I bought it just for you."

She stroked his bare chest as he kept his laptop strategically placed on his lap.

"You look beautiful, Maggie," he admitted. There was no denying that she looked like an angel.

She leaned in and kissed him, and even though his head told him to stop, the rest of his body told him otherwise. This moment was a culmination of two months of inhibited desire ever since he was attracted to her on the beach. He did not stop her as she straddled his legs and kissed his neck.

He did not stop himself as he explored her upper body. In this moment of passion he forgot who he was. He didn't care about who she was. He just wanted her. His long repressed carnal instincts had taken over.

As he spun her onto her back to take control of the situation, he looked at her face. He noticed a glimmer of doubt in her eyes. Suddenly, he snapped out of and recognized what he was doing. This was not just another one of his many conquests. This was Maggie. He started to question his sanity.

She realized that he had begun to retreat from the passion, and she did not want to lose him. She could tell that he hungered for her, as she could feel the heat emanating from his body, and his heart pounding out of his chest. She knew that she was this close to having him.

"What the hell am I doing?" he scolded himself in a low voice, as he suddenly stopped.

"No, no, no, no, no ... Don't stop. Make love to me Michael," she implored.

"I'm sorry, Maggie ... I have to stop!" he said.

He moved off of her and into a kneeling position. He could see her disappointment.

"This ... is a big mistake."

"Why? I don't think it is a mistake. I know exactly what I am doing."

"You don't know what you're talking about," he reasoned.

"I know exactly what I am talking about, Mike. I want you to be the first."

He grabbed the sides of his head as if to rip the lusty feelings out of his head. It was not easy. She was still sitting there, making herself available to him, and not taking no for an answer. It usually would have been the answer to his dreams, but not tonight.

"I can't do it, Maggie, please try to understand," he said.

"But you want me ... I can tell."

"Wanting you ... is not the problem ... That part is easy."

"Then, what is the problem?"

"It's everything else. Your father, for one. What would I say? ... John, thank you for trusting me to look after your daughter. By the way, you're going to be a grandfather."

"You're very cute, you know," she said, thinking that the last comment was amusing. She still did not see the gravity of the situation.

"It's not funny, Maggie. I'm very serious."

She moved a little closer again, and reached out to put her hand on his cheek.

"I love you," she confessed, hoping that it would stir amorous feelings inside of him. It had the opposite effect.

New Beginnings

"Don't say that, Maggie," he said as he stood up and backed away from the bed. He stood up so quickly that it was like he was on fire.

"It's true!" she insisted as she lifted herself into a kneeling position.

"Maggie, do you even know what you are saying?" he asked, treating her as if she were just another teenager with a crush.

"I know exactly what I am saying, Michael, I am in love with you," she persisted, as she stood up off the bed and walked towards him, causing him to back off a bit more.

"You can't be in love with me."

"Why not?"

"You hardly know me. We've only known each other for three months."

"So? Are you trying to tell me that I don't know when I'm in love?"

"Well, it's probably just some kind of crush."

"I can't believe you just said that," she said softly, as tears suddenly started to well up in her eyes, and she sat back on the edge of the bed. "Do you think that I would go this far for a crush?"

"Maggie ... I'm sorry. I had no idea that you felt this way. Why did you think that I would say yes?"

"I could tell that you are attracted to me. Am I wrong?"

"No, you're not wrong."

"And then the kiss at the party. You kissed me back. Upstairs too."

"I know."

"Why did you do that if you did not want me?"

"I don't know ... I wasn't thinking straight. I should have pushed you away. And this ... this right here is definitely wrong, Maggie."

"Why is it wrong?"

"Maggie, you are a very intelligent girl. You should know why this is not the right thing to do."

"I'm not a girl!" she insisted, insulted by his patronizing tone. "I will be eighteen in April."

"That does not make you eighteen now."

"I thought that you cared about me."

"I do care about you ... why do you think that I said no?" he reasoned.

He attempted to make her understand what he was going through. But, she still would not give up. This whole experience was torture for both of them.

"I thought long and hard about this. I've waited so long for someone like you. I want to be with you. I want to take care of you. I want to have your children."

"Children? Maggie, please stop saying those things."

"But, I mean everything that I say."

"It's impossible, can't you see that?"

It took a moment for his reasoning to sink in, and she sat silently searching for something to say. How could he not see her side of it? This was unbelievable. It was so humiliating.

I can't believe that you are rejecting me!" she said with disbelief, "I spent almost one hundred dollars on this stupid negligee."

"Maggie, I'm sorry … what do you want me to say?"

"I want to say that you will make love to me, Michael. I want you to say that you love me."

"I can't do that, Maggie. I already told you why I can't."

Maggie broke down and started to cry with her head in her hands. It was probably the combination of alcohol and the embarrassment of being rejected that made her lose her composure. She could not believe that this was happening. She had spent so much time planning the trap, that she never even considered the fact that he would say no. She was mortified, and wanted to crawl under the floorboards of the house and never come out.

Mike wanted to comfort her. He wanted to take her in his arms and make her feel better, but what could he possibly say? He was the reason for all of her sorrow. At the same time, he was relieved because it seemed that she had finally accepted the fact that he was not going to give her what she wanted.

"What is wrong with me?" she wept as she slumped down onto the bed. She continued to weep uncontrollably.

When she asked that question, he could not stop himself from needing to comfort her. He sat down on the bed next to her, a bit guilty that he had been the cause of all this anguish.

"Maggie, there is absolutely nothing wrong with you."

"Then why don't you want me?"

Mike did not answer. The truth would have required more answers. He wanted her, but he could not have her. It was impossible. As she lay there suffering, he laid down next to her and stroked her hair, trying in some way to console her. Then she turned and buried her head into his chest and he held her in his arms.

Neither one of them said another word, and she nuzzled in close enough to him to feel his heart beat. It was such a warm and comforting feeling to be in his arms, and her earlier humiliation started to subside. As she thought about what he said to her, she realized that night had not been easy for him, either. She drifted off to sleep knowing that he cared for her, maybe more than he was willing to admit. He was one of the good guys, and that she was more in love with him than before their fruitless encounter began.

Some time in the early morning, Mike was awakened by a sensational dream about her. He dreamed that they had made love, and it was so vivid that once he woke up and saw her lying there, he was not sure if his experience was a dream or reality. It did not take long for him to realize that it was all a hallucination, but he knew that he had to get her out of his bed as soon as possible, however comforting her body felt against his own.

He managed to slip out of her embrace and stood up. He gazed at her sleeping in her silky dressing and he thought she looked like an angel. He hated the fact that the circumstances forced him to refuse her, and he wished that things were different. He grabbed her robe off the floor and with it draped over his arm, he lifted her up from the bed. He carried her up the stairs and to her room, and carefully placed her into her bed. He looked at her sleeping peacefully and bent down to kiss her on the face. He could not help himself.

Afterwards, returned to his room alone and in deep, tortured contemplation. What was he going to do next? Somehow, he managed to fall asleep and when he awoke the next day, a decision had been made. He would buy the condo that he had looked at earlier that week. It was in a town that was about thirty minutes away, near the mall. He needed his own place, and as soon as possible. There was no other choice.

When he awoke the next morning, he tried to think of a delicate way to let Maggie know of his verdict. He did not want her to believe that it was all her fault. He dreaded telling her, especially considering what kind of condition she might be in after a night of merriment and embarrassment. He showered, dressed and prepared himself for what could be an extremely difficult morning.

He found her in the kitchen a bit more cheery than expected. Seemingly, she was not suffering from a brutal hangover from the previous night's activities. She was luminous, and it surprised him. It was almost like she had forgotten what had happened.

"Good morning!" she said with a sunny disposition.

"Good morning," he said with surprise at her cheerfulness.

"I made a pot of coffee already. Do you like pancakes?"

"Yeah, sure," he said as he yawned and stretched. The shower may have cleaned his body, but did nothing to make his head clear. He was still working on a couple of hours sleep.

"When did you get up?" he asked, looking through squinty eyes at the clock. It was eleven.

"Well ... I got up, took a shower, went to church, now I'm back here ... I guess that I got up at around eight," she chimed, "I'm making bacon too, is that okay?"

"Sure," he replied, "you mean you've been out already?"

"I had to go to the store and get some blueberries. I'm making blueberry pancakes."

Her conversation was a little quick for him that morning. She acted as if she had already consumed three cups of coffee.

"I thought that you would be sleeping in tonight. After the party and all that."

"No ... I feel fine. I had a little headache this morning, but I took an Advil and it's gone now."

"That's good to hear. I thought that you would be in bad shape today."

"I'll survive," she said, then she wanted to change the subject. "Do you want me to bring some coffee over to you"

"No, I can get it," he said. He walked into the small area of the kitchen and past her to find the coffee pot. On the way back to the table, they almost ran into each other and found themselves face to face.

"Whoops," she said

"Sorry," he replied.

As he returned to his table, he was still stunned at her exuberance. This was the young woman who had cried herself to sleep only hours ago. The night before, she had been inconsolable. Now, it was like the memory of that night had been lifted right out of her brain. There was no noticeable pain or embarrassment about the previous night. It drove him crazy. He had to say something.

"Maggie ... about last night ... I'm really sorry," he blurted out.

"What about last night?" she asked, seemingly oblivious to the events of the night before.

"Don't you remember what happened?"

"Yes," she said with a tentative voice. "I went to the party, then you picked me up."

"So you don't know what happened after that?"

"Is this about the kiss by the car?"

"Not exactly, Maggie."

"Well after you drove me home, I went to my room ... Right?"

"Yes."

"Then, what is the problem? I think that I remember everything."

"Not everything, sweetheart."

"Then what is it?" she said, trying to scan her memory bank for the missing data.

"Oh, nothing much," he said, "but, I have to tell you that you look great in pink."

She paused and it all started to return to her memory. The pink teddy. The botched seduction. The humiliation.

"Oh my God! That wasn't a dream?" she gasped.

"No, sweetheart. It was real."

Suddenly, she felt nauseous. The hangover was back. She escaped into the downstairs bathroom to lose her breakfast. He waited for her to return, and when several minutes passed, he decided to check on her situation.

He tapped on the door, and heard her retching on the other side.

"Are you okay in there?" he asked, knowing full well what the answer was.

"No," she said pitifully.

"I've got to tell you, this is really dealing a blow to my ego. I told you what happened last night and you immediately threw up."

He heard silence, then water running as she rinsed out her mouth. The she opened the door, and he could see that she was much whiter than before.

"I've been throwing up all morning. I was starting to feel a little better, but …"

Her news was interrupted by another run to the toilet. This time, as she threw up he stood by her and rubbed her back to comfort her.

"I'm so glad that we can share these special moments, Maggie. Twisted ankles, shitty diapers … throwing up after a rough night."

"I feel like I'm going to die!" she moaned as she hugged the porcelain.

"You're not going to die. You just have a terrible hangover. I'm surprised that you even got up this morning."

"I'm never going to drink again," she promised, as she stood up from the praying position and one again rinsed out her mouth.

"I can't tell you how many times I've said that," he commented as he patted her on the back as she finally found the strength to leave the bathroom. Her stomach had finally settled, and the two walked back into the kitchen. He sat down at the kitchen table and watched her as she attempted to follow her schedule as planned. Pancakes and all.

"Maggie, forget about the pancakes for now. Sit down. We have to talk about what happened last night."

"Do we have to?" she sighed, "it's a little embarrassing."

"Why embarrassing?"

"Besides the fact that I probably made a fool of myself?"

"Maggie, that's not true."

"Yes it is. I wish that it was all a dream."

"Well, it wasn't a dream. Trust me," he said, "You said a lot of things last night that we have to sort out."

"I probably said more than I should have."

"Maybe it was because you were under the influence?"

"Not entirely."

"Meaning?"

"Well, the alcohol gave me more courage than I would have had normally."

"So, you meant everything that you said?"

"Everything that I remember." she said with a confused look, not sure of which secrets she had divulged.

"Maggie, you told me that you loved me."

"I was afraid that you'd say that."

"Did you mean it?"

She paused for a second, trying to figure out how to get out of it. She thought about lying to him, but then decided to get it all out into the open.

"Yes, Mike. I love you."

"I can't believe this. How did this happen?"

"Well … it was kind of a gradual thing."

"Was it something that I said of did? Did I give you the impression that I was interested?"

"Mike, it was everything. It started with the Christening and what Grandma Mo said."

"Good old Gram."

"Then it was the way that you would look at me … on occasion. Then we got along so well down at the shore. We seemed to enjoy each other's company. Didn't we? It wasn't just my imagination, was it?"

"No. We do get along very well. I grant you that."

"Then you came to my rescue at the soccer practice, carrying me to the car. Then later we had a fun taking care of Allie. I felt like we connected. I got the feeling that you liked me. Maybe you didn't mean to send me those signals, but that is the way that I received them."

"I do like you Maggie. Very much. But, I did not mean to send you those signals."

"Then last night, after the kiss by the car, you did not push me away. I thought that you wanted me as much as I wanted you."

"These were special circumstances, Maggie. I couldn't say yes, whether I wanted to or not."

"But did you want to say yes?"

"I'd rather keep that to myself," he said. He did not want to open that can of worms, but it gave her the impression that maybe he was not tempted.

"You can tell me. I know that I wasn't very good at it."

"Good at what?"

"Seduction."

"Oh, you were very good at it."

"Really?"

"Couldn't you tell? I was very... motivated, until I came to my senses."

"But, you were a gentleman about it."

"Eventually ... but before that I was ... well anyway, I doubt that your father would have approved of my behavior."

"He might not have, but I thought it was kind of nice," she said, with a dreamy look as she seemed to remember what happened.

"Maggie, was there ever a planned sleepover at your friend's house?"

"Not really."

"So, it was all a set up?"

"Sorry, but please don't tell my Dad."

"Maggie, you don't have to worry about that. I like my head. I don't want to lose it."

The phone suddenly rang, making the two of them jump. Maggie picked up the receiver to find that it was her father. His ears must have been burning because they were talking about something that would have hated to hear. He called to let her know that he, Wendy and the baby were leaving and would be home in two hours. He asked how everything was, and she replied that it was great. At that moment, she looked at Mike as he watched her.

As he watched her talking on the phone, his mind drifted back to the night before, and how her body looked in the negligee. It was an image that was hard to shake from his memory, and it seemed to haunt him.

From there, he started to daydream. He dreamed that after she hung up the phone, he took her in his arms and kissed her. Then he picked her up and carried her into the bedroom where suddenly she was wearing the pink teddy. Then he kissed her neck and started to slip the spaghetti strap off of her right shoulder ...

"Mike," Maggie said, interrupting his fantasy.

"Huh?" he asked, snapping out of his dream and shaking his head to get the image out of it, "what is it?"

"Where are you?" she asked.

He would have volunteered to help her make breakfast, but unfortunately his troops were at attention. Luckily, the tablecloth hid what the fantasy had done to his body.

"I'm right here."

"What's wrong?"

"Nothing's wrong. Why would you think that something's wrong?"

"It's just the look on your face ... you have that far away look."

"Do I? I can't imagine why."

"You can go in the living room. I'll let you know when breakfast is ready."

"No, I'd rather stay here," he said, trapped in his chair because of his body which had a mind of its own. "

She walked to the kitchen counter and started to make the pancakes, even though she could not eat a bite. She wanted to cook for him, at least. It would possibly be the last time she could do that for him.

He remained seated. Standing up was the last thing that he wanted to do. He tried to breathe deeply to try to calm down his excitement, and tried not to look at her assets while she was cooking the breakfast. Eventually, he thought of enough horrible things to be able to function as a regular human being. Bringing up an unpleasant subject would also help in that quest.

"You know that I have to move out, don't you?"

"I know," she sighed with disappointment. "After last night, you really have no other choice."

"It's not only because of what happened last night. I've been here too long. Wendy and your Dad were nice enough to let me stay, but I've overstayed my welcome. I need my own place. There is a place that I looked at last week that I really like, and I'm going to take it."

"I guess that you have to do what you think is right."

"So you're not disappointed?"

"Of course I'm disappointed."

"But, do you understand?"

"I understand, Michael ... you don't have to explain it," she replied. She continued to make the pancakes as she discussed when was so painful for her to hear. She did not argue, however, because she knew that he had not other choice.

When the pancakes were done, she put them on a plate and placed it in front of him. Then she returned and poured him another cup of coffee. He felt like she was treating him almost like a husband, and it was a comfortable feeling, although the circumstances were less than normal.

"Aren't you going to have any?"

"No, I couldn't eat. My stomach will not be able to handle it," she replied.

She watched as he took his first bite and she smiled. She wished that she could see him her kitchen every morning for the rest of her life.

"Maggie, these are very good."

"Thank you."

"Are these from a box?"

"No, they're from scratch. They're my mother's recipe."

"It seems like you can do anything."

"Well, not everything." she said eluding to the night before.

The comment made for an uncomfortable moment, as his latest bite went down like a lump in his throat. He was so busy enjoying his food that he had temporarily forgotten about how he had denied her the night before.

"I'm sorry," he said again.

"So am I."

"We still have to figure this thing out."

"Figure what out?"

"What happens until I move out? What are we going to do about this situation?"

"It's very simple, Mike. I love you. You might not like it, but it's true. I can't help how I feel."

"But how are we going to live in the same house?"

She walked over to where he sat in his chair, leaned down and caressed his face, and kissed him gently on the cheek.

"Don't worry, honey. I'll survive," she said.

Then she smiled, stood up and attempted to walked out of the kitchen, satisfied with a small victory.

Maggie felt fulfillment about her situation. In her opinion, she had tried the seduction route, and it failed, but he barely withstood her advances. He wanted her so much, in fact, that he was going to move to another place to avoid being tempted by her. Everything was falling into place. As far as she was concerned, she just needed to back off a bit, and let him trap himself.

However, in the next month, he barely saw her. He bought the townhouse in a town called Red Hill, and as he waited for the closing date, he spent more time at work, including weekends. He was purposely trying to keep away from her, and attempting to forget about that night.

Eventually, the time came for him to leave for good, and since he had no furniture or belongings other than his clothes, he really did not have much to move. This was not going to be a long goodbye, as all he had was a few suitcases. He wanted to say goodbye to Maggie, but she was nowhere to be found.

As he walked into his bedroom to grab his last suitcase, he looked out of the window at the backyard. There he noticed Maggie sitting on the white stone garden bench staring at her mother's tree.

"So that's where she went," he said to himself. Mystery solved.

He put the last suitcase in the car, then walked around the side of the house and into the backyard where he found her softly weeping. She didn't notice him until he was there in front of her, and she was unable to hide the fact that she had been crying. She quickly tried to dry her tears, but it was of no use.

"I was looking for you," he said.

"Were you?" she sniffed,

"I wanted to say goodbye. I should have known that you would have been here," he said walked into the colorful memorial garden, and close to the tree, facing her.

Earlier in the year, tree bloomed it's pink flowers and was surrounded by a garden of different varieties of spring and summer flowers that Maggie tended with great care. The memorial garden was one of her great passions as it was a constant reminder of the mother that she missed. After the summer, the flowers had died out, but Maggie replaced them with multi-colored chrysanthemum plants. As Michael looked around at Maggie's sanctuary, he was impressed at her talent.

"I'm never going to see you again," she sniffed dramatically as she hung her head down.

"Of course you are going to see me again," he said, knowing that it would be rarely. He was determined to break his attraction to her.

"I'm going to miss you so much," she said. "Why do you have to go?"

"You know why I have to go. Why are you so upset?"

"I can't help it. I know that I'm never going to see you again. You're going to move away, get married, have kids and I'll never see you again."

"Maggie, don't cry … Come on, sweetheart."

She stood up from the bench and rushed over to hug him, burying her head into his chest. She hugged him so tightly and with such emotion that it overwhelmed him.

"It's all my fault!"

"It's not your fault. I was always going to get my own place. You know that."

She did not reply, but still hugged him tightly, as if she would never let go.

"Maggie …" he said as he turned her face up towards him and looked down into her waterlogged eyes, then he brushed the tears from her cheek. "You know, it's not the end of the world," he tried to joke.

"It's awful. This is one of the worst days of my life." she sniffed.

"You're so silly," he said as he smiled.

He stroked the hair out of her gorgeous blue eyes that sparkled from the tears. He gazed down at her sweet face and she captivated him. She was beautiful. Instead of backing away, which was his first instinct, he could not help himself but to lean down and kiss her. The kiss was long and sensual, and she put her arms around his neck and responded wholeheartedly. When the embrace was released, she stood there without words, but she was no longer upset. She was in heaven because he had initiated the kiss.

"I've got to go," he said as he put his hand on her cheek. "I'll see you soon."

"Goodbye." she replied.

With that, his next stop was to walk into the kitchen where John and Wendy were eating lunch, unaware of the scene that had just occurred. He thanked them, said goodbye to his hosts, then walked out of the door.

Maggie walked to the side of the house and watched silently as his car pulled out of the driveway, then sped down the road. It was then that she hung her head down into her hands and the tears returned.

Chapter Twenty-Three

WHO'S TO BLAME?

Mike settled into his condominium well. It was close enough to the city, which was a necessity for work. It was also far away enough from Maggie, so that his urge to see her could not be fulfilled on a whim. He was thirty minutes away from her. Hopefully, the distance between them would cure him from The Maggie Flu.

Meanwhile, Maggie was missing Mike terribly. She also felt a bit guilty and needed to confess to somebody. The declaration of guilt came unexpectedly two weeks later in Allie's bedroom.

"Wendy, it's all my fault!" Maggie confessed as she grabbed a diaper from the cabinet and handed it to Wendy.

"What are you talking about?" Wendy said, continuing to change Allie's diaper.

"Why Michael moved out."

"Michael moved out because he was sick of the long commute, not because of anything you did."

"No … it's true. It is my fault."

"Maggie, really, there is nothing that you could have done to make him want to leave."

"Wendy, I have a confession to make."

"What is it?" Wendy said as she lifted the baby off of the changing table, placing her on her hip, and turned to face Maggie.

"I tried to seduce Michael!"

"That's ridiculous," Wendy said, trying to stamp out any unfounded guilt that Maggie had. "What could you have possibly done?"

"Well, you know when you and Dad went to your parent's house? I went to a party that night."

"Go on."

"I got a little drunk and Lizzy and I hatched this plan to have Michael … save me."

"Save you? What do you mean by that?" Wendy said as she walked over and put the Allie back into the crib."

"Well, Lizzy called him and told him that I was in trouble. You know … with a guy?"

"What happened?"

"Michael came over and found me in the room with this guy, Josh. Bottom Line, he got me out of there."

"Thank goodness for that, Maggie, that was pretty dangerous. What if he didn't come?"

"I knew that he would."

"Well, you were probably right about that."

"Then I kissed him by the car."

"You kissed him? What did he do?"

"He let it happen, but I could tell that he wasn't into it. I think he was trying not to embarrass me in front of my friends."

"I can see why you might think that you tried to seduce Mike, but that is just an innocent …"

"There's more."

"I was hoping that you not would say that."

"I didn't sleep over my friend's house after all. He brought me home and we both went to separate bedrooms. Then there was phase two of the plan."

"Phase two? Maggie, do I want to hear this?"

"Probably not."

Wendy braced for the rest of the mea culpa.

"I walked into his bedroom in a negligee and told him that I wanted him to make love to me."

"Oh my God …" Wendy said in complete disbelief. Then she was frightened to hear the rest of the story. Situations that she did not want to think about raced around in her head. She did not want to hear what came next, but had to ask.

"What did he do?"

"He turned me down," Maggie said with a tinge of disappointment. "He was nice about it, though. As far as I can remember."

"What do you mean, as far as you can remember?"

"I don't remember a lot of it. I thought that I dreamt it at first, but the next morning, Mike told me that it really happened."

"And he did turn you down, didn't he?"

"Yes."

"Thank God!" Wendy proclaimed. She sat down on the rocking chair as if her legs were too heavy to carry her body. The feeling of relief overwhelmed her.

"Don't tell my Dad," Maggie begged.

"Maggie, when I married your father I promised myself that I would not keep any secrets from him, but this is one of those occasions where I am going to have to break that promise. There is no way I am going to tell him about this ... Trust me."

"Thank you," Maggie sighed.

"But, you have to tell me ... how did you come up with this plan? Where did you get the negligee?"

"I was talking to my friends and they thought that it was a good idea. I bought the negligee at a party."

"Who would have a negligee party at the age of seventeen?"

"Wendy, you would be surprised."

"Do you realize that you are under age?"

"Yes ..." Maggie said in an exasperated fashion, "I have been reminded of that a lot recently. But, you don't understand. I'm like the only virgin in the Senior class."

"I'm sure that you're not the only virgin, Maggie."

"I feel like I am," Maggie sighed.

"I'm sure that that's not true. There are more virgins than you know. Besides, what's the rush? Don't you want to wait until you find the right guy and it's special?"

"Mike is the right guy," Maggie explained, "I'm in love him and I wanted him to be the first."

"Did you tell him that?"

"Yes."

"I can't believe it!" Wendy gasped.

"Wendy, he's the perfect, guy ... you know that don't you?"

"He doesn't have a perfect past. He's not exactly ..."

"Pure? I know that. You told me, remember? He told me too."

"And you still don't care?"

"I can't help the way I feel Wendy. I'm in love."

After the conversation ended, Maggie walked away, confident in her feelings for Michael. She was also relieved to pass on the horrible secret that had haunted her.

She was relieved, but Wendy was not. John's teenaged daughter had just confessed to being in love with her twenty-six year old cousin, and had attempted to seduce him. While Wendy was relieved that Mike was able to resist the temptation, she still wanted to hear his side of the story. She needed to know the real reason why he moved out so suddenly.

A couple of days later, Wendy was at Mike's door looking for some answers. She pretended that she was there so that she could help him arrange his new household. She had other motives. She waited until the baby had fallen asleep in the play yard, as Mike was relaxed on the couch before she hit him with both barrels.

"So, Maggie told me that she tried to seduce you," Wendy blurted out. That was subtle enough.

Mike was in the middle of a sip of beer and nearly spit it out. He coughed a little, stood up straight then composed himself.

"Does John know?" he asked.

"No way." Wendy replied, "and I'm not going to tell him."

"I'm sorry that you have to keep a secret like that from him."

"Well, I figure that I'm just saving him from an early heart attack."

"So she told you everything, then."

"The whole story. The party, the rescue ... the negligee ..." she explained, "then the gracious way that you let her down easy."

"She said that?" Mike replied, knowing that Maggie left out a few minor details. He was glad that she didn't tell Wendy everything.

"Yes, she said that you were very gentle about it."

"I tried to be," he said with care in his voice.

"Do you have any idea why she would try to go that far?"

"I don't know, Wendy," he insisted.

"Did you do anything to give her the impression that you were interested?"

"Wendy, I just don't know ..."

"What do you mean?"

"Well, I may have given her some signals , here and there."

"Such as ..."

"We spent a lot of time together. We enjoyed each other's company."

"So, that doesn't mean anything."

"And. then there is the other thing."

"What other thing?" Wendy was afraid to ask.

"Remember when we were on the beach when I argued with you about whether or not that a woman in the distance was Maggie?"

"I remember."

"Well, before that, I was watching her. I didn't know who that woman was, but I thought that she was so beautiful. I wanted that woman, Wendy."

"So, that's why you argued with me."

"I couldn't believe that it was Maggie. All of the sudden, I felt like an awful person for staring at her. But, I never forgot that wonderful feeling I got when I first saw her. She was perfect, Wendy. She still is…perfect."

"Oh my God."

"When you and I were teenagers … remember we used to have these long conversations, and I would tell you about the perfect girl that I would want to marry? Do you remember that?"

"Yeah …"

"Do you remember what I liked?"

"Sure … she would have had long brown hair"

"Check."

"Blue eyes."

"Check."

"A nice body."

"Big Check."

"A sense of humor."

"Check."

"A great personality … smart."

"Check, check."

"And a virgin."

"Ladies and gentlemen … We have a winner."

"Oh my God … Mike … You're telling me that Maggie's your perfect girl?" she asked.

"Unfortunately, yes. But, she's about six years too young. Not to mention that she just happens to be your husband's only daughter, so the torture is complete."

"So that night with the negligee …"

"I had to fight every natural urge I had … If she was just a little bit older, and someone else's daughter, she probably would have gotten her wish," he pointed out. "And in turn, I would have gotten my wish."

"Oh Michael, this is a problem."

"So, to answer your question…yes. I may have given her signals here and there. Not intentionally … Maybe she caught me staring at her once or twice, and she knew what I was thinking. I don't know."

"I can't believe this is happening!" she lamented.

"So now, you know why I had to leave. I could not stay in the same house as her and see her every day, and not think about her. I had to get out and get the temptation out of my head."

"Now, I understand. Is it working?"

"No."

"This is a problem."

"She's just so innocent, Wendy. She's like an angel," he said, "It drove me crazy when she tried to seduce me. I wanted her so badly, but I couldn't have her. I just felt dirty afterwards."

She thought about how he described Maggie as an angel. Maybe he was trying to deny his true feelings.

"Maybe a little time away from each other will do you both some good." she said as she walked over to pat him on the back.

"One could only hope." he replied.

During the drive home, Wendy fretted about Mike and Maggie's disappointing situation. Maggie was a beautiful and loving young woman and was exactly the type of woman that she always wished that her cousin would marry. Mike was a handsome and dependable man who would be the perfect husband for Maggie. Unfortunately, the whole idea of them as a couple seemed impossible.

Chapter Twenty-Four

TEMPTATIONS

Thanksgiving came and went, and although Mike was invited to join the family for dinner, he did not. He was still not ready to face Maggie without desiring her. The Maggie Flu had not yet been cured. Moreover, the feeling of want was more intense than ever and he tried everything to conquer it. He picked up his workout routine. He threw himself in his work. He even went to bars to try to pick up strange women. He never could bring another woman home because all he could think about was Maggie.

"You can't avoid us forever," Wendy pointed out as he tried to excuse himself from Christmas dinner. "So, I will see you on Christmas. Grandma Mo is expecting you."

Grandma Mo. She had started everything. He wasn't even sure that he was ready to see her.

Mike had run out of excuses, and not reason his way out of it. Wendy wanted him to be there, and it was time to stop running. He would finally have to face Maggie. It had been over two months since he had last seen her, but his attraction was still strong. He decided that he needed a cushion, and her name was Nancy Garten.

Nancy Garten was a colleague from work. She was a good friend, but not a romantic partner. She was just there for the free food, as he put it, when he asked her to come with him. She had nothing to lose. Her family lived across the country in California, and her boyfriend was on a business trip. She would have spent the holidays alone. Mike said that it would be a winning deal for both of them.

The invite was also a payback for a favor that she had done for him. She had saved him at the Maddock and Associates Christmas party when Mike was cornered in the cloak room by the Man-eater. He had been warned by the other men to watch out for the Man-eater at the annual Christmas party, because when she got a little drunk, she go a little aggressive and liked to break in the younger men.

However, they did not identify the woman, telling him that he would find out soon enough. He seemed amused by the warning, because he had been well experienced with women, and figured that he could handle anything that was thrown at him. It was not until he was invited into the cloakroom by a woman named Carolyn, that the trap was sprung. She was a very attractive, statuesque woman in her fifties who has had her share of improvements, head to toe. She told him that she wanted to show him something interesting, and he followed her willingly, not fully realizing what he was agreeing to do.

That interesting something, that she wanted to show him, turned out to be her newly purchased breasts. Before he knew it, his shirt was half off and the seduction was under way. A couple of more minutes in the closet, and the Man-eater would have claimed her victim. Mike was seriously considering succumbing to the temptation before Nancy walked in and threw a wrench into the fun and games.

"Thank you. She would have eaten me alive." Mike said after the rescue.

"You're welcome. I saw her bring you in there. When I didn't see you come back out, I figured that she had you caught in her web."

"It wouldn't have been a bad way to go, though."

"Are you serious?" Nancy asked with disgust on her face, "you really would have done it?"

"Well, she made it very difficult to say no. She made a lot of promises and I'm sure she would have delivered."

"You guys are all the same," she said as she rolled her eyes. "It's all fun and games, isn't it? You don't think about the consequences until the next morning when the devil asks for your soul."

"Nancy, are you comparing Carolyn to the devil?" he teased.

"She annoys me. She gives women a bad name. She's the laughing stock of the firm. Big joke."

"She's just having fun."

"Fun? Sex is about more than having fun. It should be a loving act between two people who are committed to each other."

"You sound like Maggie."

"Who's Maggie, one of your old girlfriends?"

"No, Maggie is my cousin's seventeen year old step-daughter. You know, Wendy? The one who got married earlier this year?"

"The doctor's wife?"

"Yeah. Maggie is the doctor's daughter."

"What did she say?"

"She pretty much read me the riot act about my past, told me that people should be in love when they make love."

"Sound like she has more sense than you do."

"That goes without saying."

"You should listen to us. Stop being such a male slut."

"Listen, I've been in a prolonged dry spell. I haven't had any fun for at least six months."

"Poor baby. There's more to having fun. There is respect for yourself and others. Carolyn doesn't have any of that. I would stay away from her."

The two looked over at Carolyn and noticed that she was leading another young man to the slaughter. The Man-eater would get her wish after all.

Eventually, Mike admitted that even though it was tempting, it was better that he did not complicate his life with an in office affair. Nancy saved him from that predicament, and he was truly grateful. But his little encounter with Carolyn proved to him that he still could be tempted, and for a ten minute period, he did have someone else on his mind besides Maggie Stanton.

On Christmas morning, Wendy informed Maggie that Mike was bringing a companion. Maggie was extremely disappointed because she had gotten her hopes up too high. She still could not wait to see him, though. It had been such long time since they had seen each other, and his last kiss was still on her lips.

Once she saw Nancy and Mike at the front door, she tried to be cordial. She managed to force a slightly cheerful smile. She tried her best to be the perfect hostess, and Mike did not notice that she was less than authentic.

He did notice, however, that she looked amazing. She was quite beautiful in her blue satin holiday dress, black stockings and pat and leather heeled shoes. She appeared mature, and absolutely breath-taking. It almost took his breath away. After the long absence, seeing her this way was well worth the wait.

"Maggie, I would like to introduce you to my friend Nancy."

"Nice to meet you Nancy," Maggie said, sounding very believable. Mike could not tell that Maggie wanted to rip Nancy's head off.

Maggie took their coats, and turned to hang them up in the hallway closet. Once Mike and Nancy turned towards the living room to make introductions, Maggie threw the coats onto the closet floor, and closed the door.

As Maggie mistreated Nancy's fur coat, then returned to the kitchen, Mike introduced his date to his Aunt Sarah and Uncle Joe, who were talking to Wendy. He introduced her to the other guests gathered near the Christmas tree. Everyone was friendly, except for the young woman who was stabbing cheese in the kitchen.

Wendy handed the baby over to John and then left to find Maggie in the kitchen. Wendy could tell that she was upset by the way she was treating the cheddar.

"Careful, sweetheart, that's the only cheddar that we've got. It has to look good on the table," she joked.

"He didn't even notice my dress," Maggie pouted, and began to slice the cheese. Her eyes were beginning to well up with tears, and she brushed one away. "I thought that you said that blue was his favorite color."

"Blue is his favorite color. I'm sure that he noticed how beautiful you are, Maggie. He just couldn't say it in front of his friend."

"Some friend … he's probably …"

"He said that she's just a friend from work."

"Do you really believe that?" Maggie said with a hint of sarcasm, "I don't."

Maggie lifted up the plate of cheese and crackers and started walking in the direction of the buffet table. Wendy stopped her and grabbed a tissue to blot out any running mascara around Maggie's eyes.

"Maggie, pull yourself together. Take a deep breath," she said.

She managed to convince Maggie to take a deep breath and relax. Maggie breathed in slowly and let it out.

"Are you all right?"

"I think so"

"Think about it … You've got your whole family out there. It's Christmas day. You can't walk around with a scowl on that beautiful face. You're going to ruin everyone's day."

"I don't know if I can pretend, Wendy, it's too hard."

"Sweetheart, you can do anything. You can't show him that you're upset. If you act like nothing's wrong, it will make him wonder, don't you think? Now, try to put a smile on your face, and get out there."

Wendy was not trying to coach Maggie on how to make Mike want her more, instead, she wanted Maggie to pull herself together. She didn't want her step-daughter moping in the kitchen during Christmas festivities. However, she unintentionally gave Maggie something to strive for. For the rest of the day she decided that she would play hard to get, and maybe that would change Mike's tune.

Maggie gathered up all of her strength and walked out into the area where the appetizers were all laid out. She walked towards a commotion in the living room. There she found Mike and Nancy kissing under the mistletoe, and the family gathering around with approval, with the exception of Grandma Mo, who shook her head.

"The appetizers are ready!" Maggie announced after clearing her throat, then she disappeared back into the direction of the kitchen.

Hearing Maggie's voice nearly gave Mike a coronary attack, since he knew that she must have seen the mistletoe event. He wanted to tell her that it was all a set up, and that the kiss meant nothing. He had just been inadvertently caught under the mistletoe at the same time as Nancy and Sarah noticed it, and encouraged them to kiss. She put him on the spot, which started an avalanche of "Do it's" until they finally had to do it.

There was no spark in the kiss. He felt as if it was more like kissing his sister, and Nancy felt the same way. Another dead giveaway of the mutual discomfort was the fact that after the kiss, Nancy whispered "That was awkward."

Maggie walked back with another dish and acted as cheerful as humanly possible. Even though her exterior was jolly, Maggie's insides were in turmoil. The kiss that she witnessed was a shock to her system, and it took every amount of willpower that she had to keep from escaping to the sanctuary of her bedroom. But, Maggie was a trooper, and she hung in there. Outwardly, she had holiday cheer coming out of her ears, and it did not go unnoticed by Mike.

He had expected her to be troubled, but he had misjudged her. She was not acting like the girl with the teenaged crush that tried to seduce him in September. She not only looked older, but she acted more mature, as well. He looked at her with different eyes for the first time, and he liked what he saw.

As Nancy made small talk with Mike's relatives, assuring them that she and Mike were just good friends, Mike wandered into the kitchen to try to find Maggie. Instead he found Wendy, and she punched him in the arm.

"Ow! What was that for?"

"Did you have to kiss her in front of everyone?"

"What, the mistletoe? I just did that to make your mother happy. Suddenly everybody's like … Look who is under the mistletoe … then everyone was telling us to kiss. I couldn't just leave Nancy hanging."

"So that was what happened?"

"Yes … I told you … we're just friends. I felt like I was kissing … my cousin, for instance. It was like kissing you." Mike explained, "Besides, I wouldn't worry about how it affected Maggie. It didn't seem to bother Maggie at all."

"Well maybe she has moved on," Wendy commented, trying to hide the fact that it was really killing Maggie.

"Maybe she has," Mike replied.

The he leaned in to tell her a little secret.

"God she looks good."

"Doesn't she? We shopped for the dress together."

"I could have sworn that she got blue just to tease me."

"No, we were not thinking about you at the time," she lied.

"The blue matches her eyes."

"You noticed that, huh?"

"I'm not blind, Wendy. Of course I noticed."

"I guess not."

"Well, It doesn't matter anyway. Maggie has moved on, and that's what we wanted, right?"

"Exactly."

Mike began to doubt Maggie's feelings for him. Suddenly, he was not so sure of himself, and was feeling a bit silly about all of his earlier worries. He had spent so much time afraid to see her, and he found that he was worried about nothing. She had seemingly moved on.

During dinner, he could not help but to watch her intently. She did not look at him once. It was like he did not even exist. The fact that she ignored him interested him all the more, and he was finding her irresistible.

His undivided attention towards the attractive young lady was quite noticeable to his companion for the day, and as he stood alone by Christmas tree with his eyes only on Maggie, Nancy walked over to him and asked him about it.

"Mike, is there anything going on between you and Little Miss Sunshine over there?"

"Why would you say that?" he said as he drank a little sip of beer.

"For one thing, you can't keep your eyes off of her."

"I think that you are seeing things," he said, hoping that anyone else did not notice. He wondered how obvious he had been in his attention to Maggie. If Nancy noticed it, who else did?

"I know what I saw, Mike. You've been burning a hole into that little blue dress of hers," she whispered since a few relatives walked into the room, "and she's been giving me dirty looks all afternoon."

"Now, I know you're crazy ... she's had a smile on her face all day."

"Maybe when she looks at you, my dear, but she keeps the ocular daggers for me. She looks like she would like to wring my neck."

"She's not like that. She doesn't have a vicious bone in her body."

"I think that you are in denial," she replied in a melodic fashion as she took a sip of wine.

There was a quick end to the conversation as Joe walked over and asked what the two of them had been talking about so secretly.

"Nothing secretive, Uncle Joe … just talking about the tree," Mike lied.

"Beautiful tree," Nancy agreed.

Uncle Joe started to make some small talk, and then was joined by Aunt Sarah. They both began to sing the praises of Mike, as if they were trying to set him up.

Mike excused himself from the conversation, because he had lost sight of Maggie. He wanted to find her, so walked into the kitchen. He didn't see her there, and he knew that she was not in the dining room or living room.

"She's outside," he heard a familiar voice say.

He turned around and noticed that Grandma Mo was wheeling herself into the kitchen.

"Who?" he asked.

She motioned for him to lean in to her whisper.

"Maggie … she's outside, behind the house on the deck."

"Why do you think I'm looking for Maggie?"

"I may be old, my dear, but I'm not stupid … or blind, for that matter."

"I never said you were."

"Michael, If I was a young man your age, and there was a beautiful girl outside, I wouldn't be sitting here wasting time talking to my old grandmother."

"I'm not wasting time, Gram."

"Get out there. Michael."

"Right," he agreed. He kissed her on the cheek and walked in the direction of the deck door. As she kept watch. He peeked outside, and saw her leaning against one of the deck walls. As he opened the door, she noticed who it was and she suddenly turned away.

"There you are …" he said, "I was looking for you."

"Were you," she said with a dejected sigh.

"It's a little chilly out here, sweetheart. Aren't you a little cold?"

"I'm fine," she replied. She tried to hide the fact that she had been crying silently in the dark, and discreetly wiped a tear from her eye. "Shouldn't you be with your girlfriend, and not here with me?"

Maggie tried her best not to sound spiteful, but her disgust was prevalent.

"She's not my girlfriend."

"Oh … so then she's just the woman that you are having sex with?"

"We are not having sex, sweetheart, she's just a friend from work," Mike replied.

"Whatever."

New Beginnings

"Maggie, you can believe what you want, but I am telling you the truth. She has a boyfriend who is away on business. She would have been alone today, if I didn't ask her to join us."

"Oh ..."

"So, you can stop giving her dirty looks."

"I was not giving her dirty looks," she said as she turned around to face him, trying to defend herself.

He could tell that she was fibbing, and he raised an eyebrow to show his disbelief. Finally she had to confess.

"Okay, I was. But, you have to understand how I got the wrong idea. You were kissing her in the living room in front of everyone."

"It was the mistletoe. I was on the spot. I didn't want to embarrass her in front of everybody ... you know how stuff like that happens."

"No, Mike ... I don't ... I've never been kissed by a guy under the mistletoe."

"Never?"

"No, never."

"Well, you should have been."

She was quiet, but inside she imagined herself in Nancy's situation. She wished that she was the one that he was kissing under the mistletoe.

A cold breeze whisked her dress around a little bit, enough to reveal her black stockings up to the thigh. Mike could see her shivering, and wanted to put his arms around her to keep her warm, but he did not. Instead took off his blazer, moved in closer to her and put it around her shoulders. He stayed close, since he needed the warmth of her body to keep from freezing. He was close enough to smell the scent of her intoxicating perfume. It reminded him of that night.

"Do you want to go back inside?" he asked, trying to snap out of the trance.

"In a minute," she replied as she tried to stay warm. She wanted the intimacy to last a little longer.

He looked down at her shivering in her holiday dress, and he rubbed her arms to keep them warm. She looked up at him and she was so beautiful at that moment.

"You know, you look gorgeous today," he acknowledged.

"Do you think so?" she replied, satisfied that he finally noticed her. "I was wondering if you would notice the dress."

"It's not just the dress, Maggie. You could be wearing a burka and you would still look stunning. You'd look beautiful in anything."

"Thank you for saying that."

"It's true, Maggie. You are beautiful. I can't keep my eyes off of you today."

The sudden overflow of compliments was embarrassing to her, but she welcomed the attention. She needed to hear his approval, as pleasing him had become her mission. She knew that he was attracted to her, and she wanted to feed the fire of his passion.

"So I could be wearing anything, and you would still like it?"

"Anything, as long as you are in it."

"If I was wearing a pink teddy, would you like that?" she teased suggestively.

"Especially the pink teddy," he replied tenderly.

Suddenly he was drawn to kiss her, and the feeling overwhelmed him. As if he had no control over himself, he leaned down and kissed her. The embrace was intense, but short. It was long enough, however, for the two of them to want more once the clinch had been broken.

"We better get inside," Maggie said, breathing heavily and looking around to make sure that no one was watching them.

"You're right," he replied.

The two were able to walk undetected back into the kitchen. She gave him back his blazer, checked if the coast was clear, then she kissed him quickly on the cheek as he put it back on.

He watched her as she walked, and he felt a fire inside of him that he found was hard to suppress. The embrace on the deck had left him wanting much more. It was time to think of tax audits and plane crashes once more.

He walked back into the living room and ran into his grandmother. Who was camped out waiting for a report.

"Well?"

"Well what?"

"What happened?"

"Gram, not now."

At that moment, Maggie walked over, not expecting to run into the other two. She tried to get away without being noticed, but Maureen had seen her.

"Wait a second, young lady. Come over here."

"Yes, Grandma Mo?"

"You are forgetting something. Come closer"

"What is it?"

Grandma Mo waited until the two of them were close to each other and then pointed up to the ceiling. "Mistletoe," she said with a smile.

Kissing was about to get a little tricky, especially with the whole family in the living room. Mike's heart was still beating soundly as he tried to shake the experience on the deck. Now he was faced with a Herculean task. But, with half of the family watching and egging them on, they really did not have much of a choice.

"I guess that we have to do it," Mike said to Maggie with a shrug of his shoulders.

"Guess so," she said as she looked around to see if her father was around.

"Where is your father?" he asked in a whisper.

"He's right over there."

He was there, but happily unaware that the following kiss would be a bit less than innocent. He was just smiling and laughing, enjoying the entertainment.

"I hope you don't mind, Nancy," Grandma Mo asked triumphantly, not knowing that it would not bother Nancy in the least.

"No ... not at all ... go right ahead," Nancy said with a smirk.

All systems were go as Maggie and Mike prepared to kiss, each of them thinking that it had better be a quick one or the family would know that they had done it before ... several minutes ago, as a matter of fact. They kissed quickly and it was quite anti-climactic for all those gathered.

"Oh Goodness, Michael. What kind of kiss was that?" Grandma Mo moaned as if his last kiss was an insult to the entire family.

"Well, Gram, her father is right over there. What do you want me to do?" he joked.

"John, turn around. You're scaring Michael," Grandma Mo ordered poor John. Then the rest of the group joined in telling John to turn around.

"Okay, okay," John agreed. "I don't want to see it anyway."

Once John's back was turned, Mike planted a long, soft and sensuous kiss on Maggie's lips, as he dipped her down. The gathered crowd clapped with approval, along with Nancy, who was surprised that Mike actually went through with it. Wendy walked into the living room to see what the commotion was and was shocked to see Maggie and Mike kissing in front of everyone. Only Wendy knew what this meant to the two of them.

When the kiss was over, Maggie needed to adjust her dress as she breathed out. He had blown her off her feet, and she was weak in the knees.

"How was that?" Mike asked his grandmother, as he held Maggie steady.

"Now that was much better, Michael, you're back in the family," Grandma Mo declared. "You can turn back around, John."

"Dessert is ready!" Wendy declared, trying to divert the attention of the crowd, especially John who was luckily oblivious to every little look between his Mike and his daughter.

As the crowd followed Wendy, John stopped the two of them by the Christmas tree. After a quick heart attack, they found out that he was not planning on killing either one of them. He just wanted to take a picture of them. He had been taking pictures all day, and this was not out of the ordinary on a holiday.

As he stood there with his arm around Maggie, Mike felt her slip something into his jacket pocket. After the picture was taken, and he and Maggie separated, he checked the pocket and was intrigued to find a note inside.
"My room. Twenty minutes."
He looked up quickly and searched her out, and when he saw her across the room, she was smiling at him. He thought that she had lost her mind. The house was full of relatives, and there was no way that he would be able to meet her in her room undetected. This was such a risk. What did she expect him to do?
"Are you crazy?" he mouthed silently from across the room.
All she did was smile and hold up two fingers. Ten minutes for each finger. He had twenty minutes.
Ten minutes passed, and dessert was about to be placed on the dining room table. There was so much conversation and Christmas music playing. Mike did not hear any of it. The only thing he could think of was the fact that Maggie expected him to meet her upstairs in ten minutes.
"Mike..." Nancy said.
"Huh?" he asked, breaking out of his trance.
"Yoo-hoo, where is your mind right now? I just asked you a question."
"Sorry," he said.
She repeated the question. It was something about a case they had been working on together. He answered the question and then drifted back into to his fantasies.
Five more minutes passed, and the family was eating cake and pie and drinking coffee while they conversed. Mike observed Maggie as she walked out of the dining room, and noticed that she did not return. It was then that the pace of his heartbeat quickened immensely.
"She is really going through with this!" he thought. His mind raced, and he wondered what he should do. Finally, with three minutes left, he excused himself from the table.
Maggie waited in her bedroom on her bed for five minutes, and when the twenty minute mark came and went, she was disappointed. She was not surprised, however, because she was asking for a very tall order. She had asked him to have a fling in her bedroom with her father and the entire family in the house. It was not a very smart thing to do. It was a momentary lapse of

sanity, however exciting a tryst might have been. Mike had been the more sensible one.

She looked in the mirror, checked her makeup and hair, sighed and shrugged her shoulders. She turned off the lights and turned the doorknob intent on opening the door and leaving the room behind. Yet, when she opened the door to her bedroom, she saw him standing right in front of her.

"I'm a little late," he explained.

She grabbed his arm and pulled him in. The two embraced and he pinned her against the wall, kissing her lips with a fury and then her face and neck. She closed her eyes and let the pleasure sink in and overtake her senses.

He stopped and tried to put a little sanity into the situation by stating the obvious.

"This is so risky," he said.

"I know. I don't care right now," she purred.

"I could get shot, you know."

"Shut up and kiss me, Michael." she scolded.

"Okay."

They kissed again, and their progress led him to lift and carry her onto her bed, as she brushed the pillows and stuffed animals onto the floor. They necked feverishly, breathing heavily with their hands exploring one another. Neither one of them had a further thought about where they were and how much risk there were taking. His blazer and tie were thrown in the corner, and his shirt was unbuttoned and about to be torn off his body.

Things were moving very quickly as he kissed his way down her body and he slowly lifted her dress to kiss her midsection. Then, he noticed something peculiar about her black stockings.

"What's up with your stockings?" he said, "They are like the iron curtain."

"They are control tops," she giggled.

"You're perfect. Why the hell would you need control tops?" he asked as he kissed and tickled her stomach, playfully snapping the impenetrable undergarment.

He then moved back up her body to kiss her neck, face, then lips.

"It's probably better off that you have this chastity belt down there or we could get into a lot of trouble. It is the danger zone, after all," he teased.

She giggled in reply, enjoying every moment. It was all very funny at he time until the two of them heard something that interrupted their passion.

"What's that?" he asked as he lifted his face up from her neck.

It was a little noise coming from the baby's room.

"It's the baby," she panted as silently as possible, "I think she's awake!"

"Oh no ... what are we going to do?" he said in a panic as he practically dove off the bed.

He knew that soon the baby would be howling and either Wendy or John would come upstairs in an instant to collect her. They didn't have much time.

She quickly reached over and turned on the table lamp next to her bed in order to aid Mike as he scrambled to find his lost clothing. As he scrambled, she straightened up her dress, which was a bit crooked, but still in place.

"You stay here ... I'll go into Allie's room," Maggie directed he fumbled to button his shirt. "After Wendy or Dad comes up, then you can come in like you just heard the baby cry ... Something like that."

"Are you sure that it'll work?"

"It better. Just make sure that nobody catches you in here," she said

"That's the last thing I want."

She leaned over to kiss him again. "God, I really wish that we had more time," she whispered with much disappointment.

"So do I." he agreed as she left to walk towards the door.

She was able to leave her room just ahead of the sound of footsteps coming up the stairs. She quickly picked up Allie and tried to comfort her as Wendy walked into the bedroom.

"Our little pumpkin is awake," Maggie said so innocently that it would have won her the Academy Award.

"Hello sweetheart!" Wendy said to Allie as Maggie passed the baby to her mother.

A couple of minutes later, Mike walked into the room as planned, asking how the baby was. He would have fooled Wendy with his acting prowess normally, but she noticed a missed button on his shirt and the fact that Maggie was trying to get his attention to tell him about it.

"Oh no ... you've got to be kidding me! Are the two of you crazy?" she asked with disbelief.

"What?" Mike shrugged trying to pretend that nothing was out of order.

"The button," Maggie pointed out, directing him on where the blunder was. Mike instantly fixed the error.

"Terrific," Wendy sighed sarcastically. "You are crazy."

"I'm so sorry, Wendy," Maggie begged, "don't tell Dad, please."

"Maggie, how many secrets do you expect me to keep? The whole family is right downstairs!"

"Nothing happened Wendy. We were just ..."

"Just what, Mike ... kissing? Making out? I can tell from your creative buttoning that some clothes did come off."

"Only mine, Wendy. Maggie had her dress on the whole time."

"For how long, Mike?" Wendy barked back.

"Wendy, I'm so sorry. It's my fault. Really. I asked him to come up here. He was just doing what I asked."

"Maggie, I don't blame you," she said, darting an accusatory stare at her favorite cousin. "Can you bring Allie downstairs? I need to speak to my cousin alone, please."

"Oh … okay," Maggie said.

Maggie had doubts about leaving Mike alone with Wendy when she saw the murderous look on her face. Mike motioned for her to go ahead, so she gathered Allie into her arms and finally left.

"What the hell is wrong with you?" Wendy said, sternly, "what if John had been the one to come up here?"

"I wasn't really thinking straight."

"You weren't thinking at all, Michael … at least not with your head."

"That's not fair."

"Fair? You are trying to ruin my marriage."

"I am not trying to ruin your marriage."

"Let me tell you something. If it comes down to a choice between you and him, I'm picking him."

"I haven't done … anything … we didn't do … anything."

"And what if Allie didn't start crying? How far would it have gone?"

"It wasn't going go very far … all of her relatives are downstairs … We were just making out …"

"Mike, I'd like to ask you something. Did you have a problem with the control tops?"

"What?"

"The control tops. Did they give you a problem?"

She could tell by the guilty look on his face that he knew what she was talking about.

"That was your idea?" he asked.

"Of course it was! Maggie doesn't need control top pantyhose. There is nothing to control! But at least it stopped the two of you from making a huge mistake. That was more than just making out, Michael."

"But, I would not have taken it that far, Wendy. I promise you. I even told her that it was good that she had the control tops. Ask her!"

"And what if they weren't control tops? What then?"

"I didn't want to sleep with her, Wendy. I just needed to spend some time alone with her that's all. I missed her."

"She is my husband's only daughter, Mike, not one of your latest conquests."

"I know that, Wendy."

"Why would you even risk it? She is seventeen years old ... and a virgin. Thank God for that. She has no experience with men. You've heard of them, right? Virgins? These are girls that haven't had sex. I know that you haven't had much experience with these type of girls."

"I've heard of them, yes ..." Mike said, replying to her sarcasm with his own.

"But have you ever been with one?"

"No, I haven't."

"You just can't be nonchalant about it, Mike. The first time can often be a very uncomfortable and painful experience."

"We weren't going to have sex. I swear!"

"She is in love with you. Do you understand that? She would do anything for you. If you wanted her to make love to you, she would have done it. Even with the relatives and friends downstairs ... including your friend, I might add. You are playing around with her emotions, Mike. She is going to get hurt.

"I don't want to hurt her."

"You are hurting her. You're giving her false hope. She wants more from you than you are able to give."

"How do you know that I can't give her what she needs?"

"I know you, Michael. I've seen you operate."

"Listen, she invited me up here. She gave me a note. What was I supposed to say?"

"You could have said no, Michael. You're the adult. You have free will, don't you? You say no."

"You guys are sending me mixed signals. I thought this is what everyone wanted. Grandma Mo told me to kiss her under the mistletoe. You encouraged her to buy a dress in my favorite color, and make sure that she is irresistible. What did you expect me to do?"

"We wanted you to get to know her. Treat her with respect. Maybe fall in love with her. I don't think that Grandma Mo expected that you would fool around with her in her father's house with all the relatives downstairs. We didn't think that you would treat her like your other so-called dates. Like she was just another notch on your belt."

"You know that it's not like that, Wendy."

"But, that's your track record. I don't want Maggie to be another statistic of your uncontrolled libido."

"Wendy, that's not fair! I really care about Maggie. You know I do."

"Okay ... Then, do me a favor. If you want her so badly, walk down those stairs and tell everyone in that room that you want to be with Maggie. Make a commitment to her," she suggested. "Don't hide it, Mike. Don't have secret liaisons, like a Casanova, behind everybody's back in her father's house. Just go down there and tell everyone that you love her and that she is the person that you want."

"You know I can't do that."

"Why not?"

"Because … she's…"

"Too young? That's funny," she said with sarcasm. "She's not too young to screw around with, is she?"

"Wendy, you know I care about her, but it's not that easy. I can't just make a commitment like that. You know that."

"Doesn't she deserve someone who will love her unconditionally?"

"Of course she does."

"Then don't string her along. Let her go and leave her alone. Let her find someone who can love her that way," Wendy demanded. "Or, if you feel that you are that man, tell her. Make a decision. Things cannot stay as they are, no matter how fun it is for you."

"This is not fun for me," he insisted.

"What else would you call it? It's exciting, isn't it? You have this gorgeous young woman who worships the ground you walk on. The tiniest bit of attention from you gives her a thrill. She doesn't realize that she's being used."

"It's not like that"

"I've watched you go through other girls like they are your toys, but I am not going let you use my step-daughter to add to your collection. Maggie is too special."

"I know she's special."

"Then treat her that way."

"What do you want me to do?"

"Stop encouraging her or commit to her. No more of these games."

After she left the room, her words stung his ears. He did not realize how disgusted she was about his past behavior and was surprised that she thought that he was treating Maggie in a similar fashion. It never occurred to him that he was hurting Maggie. He thought that he was making her happy, and in turn he was happy. He really did care for her, but he was unsure as to how much he cared. Did he love her? He was not sure. But, he did know that he loved to be with her.

However, as he thought about their most recent encounter, his conscience finally told him that what he had done was wrong. He should have turned her down. He should have left her alone. But, his lust took over and he could not control his actions. When it came to Maggie, it seemed like he was powerless.

He walked down the stairs and found Nancy patiently waiting on the couch. Dessert was over ... for everybody ... and several of the guests were preparing to leave, including his Aunt, Uncle and Grandmother. It seemed like a good time to take his leave. He motioned in Nancy's direction, and she nodded as if so say "Oh God, yes!" He grabbed his coat out of the closet and quickly picked up Nancy's coat before she saw it on the floor.

The family met him at the door, including Maggie, who gave him a bewildered look. She could not understand why he was suddenly leaving, and was crushed to see him go so soon. She assumed that Wendy must have read him the riot act. Maybe that was why he looked so despondent. She wanted to kiss him goodbye, but that was not going to happen.

Maggie was disappointed, but Wendy thought that it was best that Mike was leaving. As she hugged Mike, she thanked him, and whispered in his ear.

"Think about what I said."

"I will."

After that, John shook his hand firmly, and patted him on the back with the other hand. John treated him as if he was one of his most trusted friends. Mike wondered if that would be the case if he only knew...he would not be so assured. Mike could barely look into his eyes.

On the way home, Nancy had some choice words to say to her date for the afternoon. She had seen everything, and she was not happy.

"Do you have a screw loose or something?"

"What?" he asked, oblivious to why she was so confounded.

"I saw you follow her up the stairs. First she left, and then you followed a few minutes later."

"You saw that?"

"I'm a lawyer, Mike. I do pay attention to the details."

"I hope that nobody else noticed," he hoped.

"What were you thinking? It was her father's house. How did you think that you were going to get away with it?"

"Nothing happened, Nancy."

"Sure, because your cousin Wendy went upstairs. I couldn't believe it when that happened. I was just sitting downstairs waiting for the roof to cave in. How did you slither out of that one?"

"You make it sound like I'm some kind of snake."

"And your point is?"

"Nancy, that's not fair."

"Not fair? You're the one fooling around with a teenager in her bedroom. Tell me, who pushed the stuffed animals off the bed and onto the floor?"

"Very funny."

"You know that this has to end, don't you? She's underage."

"She will be eighteen in April."

"As I said, she's underage. And she's a relative, Mike. Doesn't this all seem a little icky to you?"

"She's not a blood relative, and you know that. Stop making this a backwoods type of drama."

"Okay, then lets look at it this way. She's a senior in high school. That's high school, Mike."

"I realize that."

"It's also apparent that she's in love with you. Any other woman can see that, especially after you planted that kiss on her under the mistletoe," Nancy said.

"I couldn't get out of that."

"You enjoyed every minute of it."

"What's your point?"

"What's your next move? Are you going give her your high school ring and ask her to go steady or are you going to keep stringing her along?"

After Mike dropped Nancy off at her apartment in Hoboken, he had a lot to think about during the drive back home. Once he walked in the door of his condo, his mind was made up. It all had to end.

Chapter Twenty-Five

A HORRIBLE LUNCH

On the Saturday after Christmas, Mike arrived unannounced at Maggie's place of employment. She worked in an ice cream shop called Sprinkle City that was located inside the local mall. When he saw her, she was adorably dressed in a purple apron and hat with the Sprinkle City logo. He could tell that she was extremely excited to see him. He wondered how long that would last.

She checked her appearance in a decorative mirror, made a few minor adjustments and greeted him.

"Mike, I didn't expect you."

"Hi Maggie."

"What are you doing here?"

"Do you get a lunch break here?" he asked his elated friend.

"I have around forty-five minutes at around one o'clock"

"I'll see you then." he said.

At one, he arrived and she threw off her purple apron and hat. She practically floated over the freezer case to meet him. She was so delighted to see him. She hugged him tightly as if he had given her what she had always wanted. He knew that this happiness was not going to last long. He was there to give her news that she needed, but did not want to hear.

They sat in a booth in the nearest restaurant. It was a place that was a bit noisy, full of loud music and filled with people. The noisier the better, he thought. The waitress gave them a couple of menus and Maggie ordered a soda. When the waitress left, Maggie reached across the table and grabbed his hand, as if she were expecting him to propose at any second.

"So, what's the occasion?" she asked with a big smile on her face.

He cleared his throat and started to speak.

"Maggie, we have to talk about what happened on Christmas."

"I know. That was kind of reckless. Next time we have to be more careful."

"There's not going to be a next time."

"Don't be silly, Mike. It's obvious that we are attracted to each other. Why would we deny ourselves?"

"None of it should have happened"

"What are you talking about? Is it something that I did wrong?"

"No. The blame is all mine. It's my fault that it went so far."

"I seem to remember being the one that invited you up to my room."

"I shouldn't have come up there. It was a mistake."

"It was only a mistake because we got caught."

"It wouldn't work, Maggie. We both know it."

"But, you want me ... I know you do."

"Maggie ... you are too young. Too ... inexperienced."

"Okay. So I'm inexperienced. But I can learn."

"Maggie, stop ... you don't get it, do you? I'm not talking just about sex ... It's everything."

"I don't understand" she said in disbelief, as she finally pulled her hands back.

"It's impossible, okay. I can't keep doing this. I have to put an end to it."

"But nobody has to know."

"I'll know, Maggie. Isn't that reason enough? I can't face your father ... what kind of person do you think I am?"

"Wendy put you up to this, didn't she?"

"She just wants me to make a decision, either way."

"And your decision is to what? Dump me?"

"We have to put an end to it. It's the only way."

"Put an end to what? Nothing has begun!"

"We have to stop the attraction."

"It's easy for you to say."

"This is not easy, Maggie ... far from it."

She started to become upset, and at that moment the waitress come over with her drink, asking if they were ready to order. Mike said that they were not ready, and the after seeing Maggie wipe tears from her eyes, she gave him a dirty look and walked away.

"I'm really sorry Maggie ... about everything. I wish I could give you what you want. But I can't."

"Why not? I know that you want to love me. You know it too."

"I can't be with you."

"Because you're a coward."

"Maybe you're right. But, we can't keep doing this. It's for the best."

"No matter how I feel about it?" she sobbed

"I wish it could be different."

"No, you don't. If you wished it was different, you would stand up like a man and admit that you want to be with me. You wouldn't care what anyone else thought."

"Maggie, can't you see that it is impossible? I can't have a girlfriend who is in high school. I would be the laughing stock of the firm." he said, trying the cruel approach. The words stung his lips as he said them, and he could see that they had the desired effect.

"Is that all you care about? What other people might think? What about how you feel? Even your grandmother knows what you need."

"My grandmother lives in a fantasy world. She thinks that she is doing me a favor, but she is not. I have news for you honey, she's not looking out for your best interests."

"I don't agree. I think that she knows more than you know."

"Look at you, Maggie. You have your whole life ahead of you. You should be thinking about college and a career. You shouldn't be thinking about me at all. Gram has you thinking of all this other stuff like marriage and babies. And she has you believing that we can be together. But it can't happen."

"You are such a coward! You can't see it, can you? I must be out of my mind. I must be some kind of masochist. I am getting so sick of rejection." she suddenly slid over and out of her bench chair, ready to make a dramatic exit.

"Please sit down. People are noticing you."

"I don't really give a damn, Mike, you should have thought about that before you took me here. Are you afraid that some of your important friends are here and might find out that you've been fooling around with a seventeen year old novice?"

"Sweetheart ... please." he pleaded in a low voice, "Sit down."

"I'm not going to sit down, and don't call me sweetheart if you do not mean it."

"I'm sorry."

"You are making such a huge mistake. You will never find another woman ... yes, woman ... Who will love you as much as I love you." she cried, as she wiped tears away from her eyes. "One of these days you will regret taking me for granted."

With that statement, Maggie stormed out of the restaurant, causing a little bit of a scene. He did not blame her for being so upset. This had been a horrible lunch, but Mike had achieved his goal. Maggie was appalled with him. Hopefully, she would take that disgust and move on without him.

Alone in the booth, he looked up and saw his waitress staring at him.

New Beginnings

"Are you happy now?" she asked.

"Nope. Pretty miserable, actually." he said dejectedly as he threw a twenty on the table, which was more than enough for the soda and tip. "Sorry for the disturbance."

He slid out of his seat, threw his jacket on and walked out of the door feeling like a pariah. He decided to go home and drown in his wretchedness.

Once home, he kept remembering the pain that he had caused Maggie. He was haunted about how she had started to cry in he restaurant, and how he wanted to hold and comfort her. He thought about how she told him that she he was a coward, and he knew that it was true. She tried to hurt him the way that he had devastated her. He felt that he deserved the pain and loneliness that came with his decision.

Nearly a full bottle of Merlot later, the phone rang at about eight o'clock. Wendy was on the other line.

"I heard what happened." she said, "and how you let her go"

"Are you happy now?" he asked pointedly.

"Nobody's happy," she replied. "But that was the choice that you made. It probably was the right one."

"Was it?" he asked, "I'm not so sure that it was the right one." Mike's voice slurred a bit, and she asked if he was drinking and he told her that he was.

"Are you alright?"

"I don't know. I keep asking myself if I made the right choice. Did I make the right choice?"

"Mike, I don't know. That's up to you."

"How is Maggie?" he asked.

"Maggie is devastated. She came home sick from work. Probably because she was upset."

"I know … I remember. She hates me now, you know."

"She doesn't hate you. I think that she just wanted to make you feel horrible."

"It worked," Mike lamented. "You know, I wish that she never put this idea in Maggie's head. You know, about the two of us being together."

"Who, Grandma Mo?"

"It's all her fault. If she never said anything, none of this would have happened."

"Do you really believe that?"

"She kept encouraging her."

"You can't put all the blame on Grandma Mo. She was not the only one who encouraged her, and you know that. You're not being fair."

"I just wish that she never said anything. Look at the trouble she's caused. Everything is ruined."

"Only time will tell, Mike."

"Only time will tell" Mike thought. Maybe that was true. He said goodbye and hung up the phone. He drained his last glass of wine, and put the glass into the sink. He would have loved to chuck the glass across the room. He wanted to call Maggie and take it all back, but he knew that doing that would complicate things further. He decided to leave her with her pain, and hoped that she would forget him, and finally be free.

After this latest struggle with his conscience, he walked into his solitary room. He took off his clothes, trying to detect any scent of her perfume on his shirt, since she hugged him. Finding nothing, he cursed the shirt and threw it on the floor. Once in his boxer briefs, he crawled into his cold and empty bed and eventually passed out.

Chapter Twenty-Six

SURPRISE

In mid-January, Wendy was feeling a little under the weather. It seemed that she was nauseous every morning, and at first she thought that she was coming down with the flu. After two weeks, however, reality hit her. She realized that she had felt this way before.

John walked to the entryway of the kitchen and watched Wendy feeding Allie. He smiled when he saw Allie make a funny face while eating green beans.

"You're not fond of green beans, are you Allie?" John asked his baby daughter. He watched her as she forced the food back out of her mouth.

"How can you tell?" Wendy asked.

"Just guessing," he said glibly as he kissed his green-faced daughter on the head. Then he turned back to his wife. "How are you feeling today? Do you feel any better?"

"Right now I feel good. This morning, I felt horrible."

"That's funny. Do you think that you need to go to the doctor?" as he bent over to make silly faces at Allie.

"I don't think that you're seeing the big picture, John," she said because it still was not sinking in.

"What picture is that?"

"John, it's possible that I will be sick every morning for the next two or three months."

He paused, stood up straight and let the last sentence sink into his brain, then finally realized what she meant. Bingo!

"Are you telling me what I think you're telling me?" he said, with a childlike look on his face.

"I think so. I've been late for a couple of weeks now. I bought a test, and I didn't want to take it until I told you about it," she said.

"I'm glad that you waited."

"So you are happy about this?" she asked as she stood up from her chair.

"Of course I'm happy about it," he said as he hugged her. "I'm very happy about it!"

"You don't know how relieved I am."

"Why? Didn't you think that I'd be happy?"

"Well, it's so soon after Allie."

"Sweetheart, I'm not getting any younger. I figure the quicker the better."

"Stop it, John. You're going to be forty in July. Big deal!" she laughed.

As they ate their dinner and small talked about work and other things, John could not help himself. He was so excited that he needed to talk more about what could be another blessing in his life.

"When do you think was the date of conception?" he asked, earnestly.

"I'm pretty sure that it was a couple of nights after Christmas."

"Oh yeah. That night." he said with a mischievous smile on his face. "I remember that."

"You should. We were up all night." she giggled.

"Well, it was kind of an anniversary. Remember what happened last year on that date?"

"How could I forget? It was our reunion day."

"December twenty-eighth will always be a special day for me."

"Me too."

"And if what you say is true, then that date will be even more special."

"If the test comes out positive." she said cautiously.

"I have a good feeling about this Wendy."

"John, you don't think that it's too soon?"

"Sweetheart, together we can handle anything."

After dinner, and after they put Allie to bed, the lovers escaped to the master bedroom. John waited patiently on the bed as Wendy disappeared into the bathroom to take the test. When she emerged, she had the results.

"Well?" he asked anxiously, as he stood up from the bed.

"Looks like you're going to be a father again." Wendy said with a beaming smile.

"Wendy, that's great news!" he said, then he took her into his arms and kissed her. "You have made me so happy!"

Chapter Twenty-Seven

A DAY OFF

Maggie was sick. It was St. Patrick's Day, it was one of her favorite holidays, and she was sick. She had a fever, she had the shakes and she did not want to eat. All she wanted to do was to lay in bed and wallow in her misery.

She was alone. John was at work. Wendy was out with Allie at a "play group" that they attended weekly. Wendy had met some new friends there, and she looked forward to it every week, but she offered to stay and keep Maggie company. Maggie convinced her that she would only be in bed all day, and it would not be necessary for her to miss being with her friends. Wendy left and assured her that she would be back at around two o'clock.

At around noon, she heard the doorbell ring, and she was not about to answer it, especially in her pitiful condition. The doorbell kept ringing, and Maggie covered her ears with her pillow and tried to ignore it. Then, suddenly she heard the sound of a key being slid into in the lock, and then the door was opened.

At first she thought that it would be Wendy. But why would she ring the doorbell? Plus, she did not see the van in the driveway. It wasn't her father, either. What she saw in the driveway was a black convertible that she had never seen before.

Against her better judgment, and any advice that she had ever gotten about dealing with prowlers, she decided to try to see who it was that was in her house. She threw a robe over her flannel pajamas and slipped out of her room to mount an investigation..

She heard someone in the kitchen open the refrigerator, and she searched for some kind of weapon to use to subdue this horrible food or soda thief. She looked around and could not find anything that would do the job, until she set her eyes on a Valentine's day bud vase which was on top of the entertainment center. She grabbed it and walked towards the kitchen.

Weapon in hand, she ran directly into Mike, when was on his way to the living room. The meeting startled them both.

"Mike!"

"Maggie! I didn't know you were home," he said at he noticed Maggie's strange appearance. She had this crazy look about her. Her clothes were disheveled and her hair was everywhere. Her eyes were glassy.

"What are you doing here?" she asked, as she tried to hide the vase behind her.

"I took the day off. Wendy invited me over for lunch. I think that she forgot about it. I still had a key, so I let myself in."

"Oh."

"Was that vase meant for me?" he said, as he noticed the weapon behind her.

"Well … yeah. I didn't know who was down here. I didn't recognize the car."

"The Jetta died on me. I had to get another one. By the way, I'm glad that you didn't have a gun," he joked, which made her raise her eyes and smirk. She was not in the mood for jokes.

"Very funny." she said with a bit of sarcasm.

"What are you doing home?"

"I'm sick." She said in a dejected tone as she walked past him and sat at the kitchen table and slumped forward to put her head on the table as if she were a kindergartener at naptime.

"Where's Wendy?" he asked, as he stood at the doorway and tried to stay as far away from her as possible.

"She's at a Mom and Baby play group at the church. She said that she'd be home at around two. She offered to stay, but I told her that I didn't need her to do that."

"Do you have a fever?" he asked, beginning to feel pity about her sorrowful condition. He walked over and put his hand on her head.

"I'm pretty sure of it. I have the chills, and body aches, and a slight headache."

"Can I check?"

"What are you doing to do?" she asked guardedly.

"No, not that. I have a much better way of checking," he said as he leaned in and kissed her forehead. The conclusion was clear. "You're hot."

"Thank you." She said with a smile.

"Well, at least you still have your humor." he commented with a smile as he rubbed her back. "Did you take an Advil?"

"No."

"Why not?"

"I was sleeping. I didn't want to get up."

"Did you eat?"

"No."

"Maggie, you want to be a nurse. You should know how to take care of yourself, first."

"I'm not a nurse yet." She said lazily.

"Alright, sweetheart. Are things still where they were when I lived here?"

"I don't know." She said, giving no assistance, as he walked towards the kitchen cabinets.

"It looks like we're having another one of those special moments," he commented as he walked towards the kitchen cabinets.

"You know me. I'm always willing to show you a good time."

He looked through kitchen cabinets and finally found what he was looking for, the bottle of Advil. Taking two out of the bottle, he handed them to her with a glass of cold water. She ingested them and then after that was done, he grabbed her hand.

"Lets go."

"Where are we going?"

"You're going to take a warm bath."

"We are?"

"You are."

"Do I look that bad?"

"I'm not going to answer that question," he said, pleading the fifth.

"I think that you just did."

He led her into the upstairs bathroom and turned on the water. Then he turned around to see her pitifully leaning against the sink with her eyes closed.

"Wake up, honey." he said as he tugged on her arm.

"I don't want to wake up." she said with her eyes still closed.

"This will make you feel much better. Soak in the bath for a little while, put on some clean pajamas and a robe, and I'll meet you downstairs. I'll make you some soup or something."

"Mike, I'm really not in the mood to do anything. I just want to go back to bed."

"Maggie, trust me."

"I don't want to take a bath right now."

"You're getting in there. If you don't get undressed and get in there, I'll do it for you."

"That's not much of a threat. You're supposed to threaten me with something that I don't want."

"Maggie ... come on." he laughed with a bit of amusement, "I'm trying to help you out, here."

She finally agreed and he left the bathroom to let her relax in the tub. He was right. It was a good idea. She closed her eyes and imagined the sickness washing off of her, as well as all the horrible unsanitary things. After she was done, she dried and brushed her hair, put on a clean nightgown and a warm, fuzzy robe and slippers. She walked downstairs to find Mike sitting there, watching the St. Patrick's Day parade on TV.

When he heard her walking down the stairs, he turned around to see her rejuvenated face.

"Now there's the Maggie that we all know and love," he said as she approached the couch with a smile. She seemed to be feeling better, although her eyes were still glassy, but at least the Advils must have made the fever go down. He stood up, kissed her forehead again and had better news for her.

"Well?" she asked.

"The fever is down. You're still warm, though. How do you feel?"

"A little better. Cleaner, for one."

"I found some cans of soup in the cabinet. Is chicken with wild rice, okay?"

"Yes."

He set her up in the living room in front of the television with a blanket, brought a tray over and after the soup was done, he delivered it to her, with a bowl for himself. The two ate together, and after they were done, he put the dishes into the sink and returned to the couch, where she laid covered in a blanket.

When he sat down, she laid her head on his lap as she laid on her side and watched the parade on television. She closed her eyes as he stroked her hair. She was in heaven. The feel of his touch was so relaxing that it didn't take long for her to fall asleep. She was in such a deep sleep that suddenly, she started to snore.

"Now that's cute." he said softly as he stroked her hair. Every time she snored, he giggled to himself. It was all very amusing.

About a half-hour later, Wendy walked in the door with Allie in her arms with apologies ready to be said. She had forgotten about the lunch, and halfway through the playgroup, she remembered where she was supposed to be.

"I'm so sorry," she said.

Mike put his finger over his mouth and tried to quiet his cousin since she did not know that Maggie was asleep. She walked over to the couch and saw the reason for the silence.

"Looks like she's in good hands." Wendy said with a smile as she patted his shoulder. "How is she doing?"

"She feels a lot better, but she's still under the weather," he said as he looked down at his patient.

"What is that sound?" she asked, commenting on the snoring.

"She's snoring a little bit." he chuckled quietly.

"She would be horrified if I told her about this."

"Why? It's really cute."

"I'm sure that she would not agree."

"I think it's cute," he said again.

He continued to stroke Maggie's hair, and Wendy noticed how affectionate he was to his sleeping patient. It was obvious that he still had feelings for her, and the three month separation had not changed that fact.

"We should bring her upstairs. She probably would be better off lying in bed."

"No, it's all right."

"Really Mike. She'd be better off. You'd be better off too. You're getting too attached."

"Oh, okay. You're probably right." he agreed begrudgingly.

"Should I wake her up?" Wendy asked.

"No, I've got her. She's pretty light."

"You would know?"

"As a matter of fact, I would."

"I don't need to know anything else."

With Wendy following close behind, Mike carried Maggie up the stairs. Wendy carried Allie to her bedroom and Mike brought Maggie to hers. Wendy returned to Maggie's room where she spotted Mike watching Maggie sleeping.

"I must be out of my mind." he said as watched her sleeping peacefully.

"Come on, Mike, you have to get out." Wendy suggested as she tapped him gently on the shoulder.

"Right" he replied.

They walked downstairs and into the living room, where he returned to his spot on the couch. Wendy sat next to him after balling up the blanket and tossing it onto the chair in the corner. She watched him as thoughts ran through his head, and he seemed like he was in outer space.

"Would you like to stay for dinner? Lunch was pretty much a wash."

"Sure ... okay ... sounds good." he said, his mind still somewhere in Denmark.

"What's going on?"

"What's wrong with me, Wendy?"

"How much time do you have? I have a list that is getting pretty long."

"Very funny. You know, lately the way you talk to me makes me wonder if I'm still your favorite cousin."

"Lately, I've been wanting to ring your neck."

"Touché."

"But, you're still my favorite cousin."

"But, do I deserve that title? That's the burning question."

She put her hand on his shoulder as if to say that everything was all right, but he still had a melancholic demeanor.

"Mike, what's wrong? What did you mean when you said you were out of your mind?"

"It's this whole thing with Maggie. She's a smart, lovable, beautiful woman and I told her that I didn't want her. I'm crazy, right?"

"You did what you had to at the time. You weren't ready to commit to her. So you let her go."

"But, was it the right thing to do?"

"That's not for me to decide, Mike, only you can answer that question."

"I don't know the answer. Thought I did, but now I don't know."

"What do you mean?"

"I thought I was over it, but after today, it's back to square one."

About an hour later, and after some small conversation, Wendy noticed that Mike was not mentally with her. His mind was still out in the stratosphere, Finally, he looked directly at her and informed her of a change in plans.

"Listen, Wendy, I don't think I can stay for dinner after all."

"Why not?"

"I just can't do it."

"What am I going to tell Maggie? You're not just going to leave without saying goodbye, are you? ...Are you?"

"I was kind of hoping that I could."

"Don't make me the messenger, Mike. I won't do it." Wendy said as she put her hands up to block his suggestion. "You spent two hours taking care of her, the least that you can do is say goodbye. Do you want me to come up with you?"

"No, I can do it."

He walked up the stairs and into her bedroom where she was still sleeping on her side. He crouched down and stroked her forehead, kissing it to see if she was still free of the fever, which she was. The kiss caused her to open her eyes.

"Hi sweetheart." he said.

"Hi." she replied, as she remained on her side.

"Listen, I have to get going. I just wanted to say goodbye."

"You're not going to stay?" she said weakly.

"No, I can't. I hope that you understand."

"Okay." she said, trying to be understanding, but the disappointment was written all over her face.

"I'll call you tomorrow to see how you're doing, okay?"

She nodded her head yes, and he could see that her eyes were getting a little moist and she was trying to keep a forced smile on her face.

He stood up, with his difficult task completed, and prepared to leave the room. As he turned to walk away, she spoke to stop him.

"Mike,"

"What, sweetheart?"

"Thank you for taking care of me."

"It was my pleasure." He replied as he walked back.

"You know, I never hated you."

"I know baby, " he said as he leaned down to kiss her cheek.

There was a momentary pause and glance between the two of them. Then she stared into his eyes, and it seemed to mesmerize him. She reached out and grabbed his hand.

"I know that you don't want to stay because of me, but, please stay for dinner."

"Maggie, that's not true."

"Please. It's a holiday. You should be with family. You can't disappoint Wendy. It's her first big St. Patrick's Day dinner in her home. If you're worried about me being here, I'll probably be stuck in here all night. I promise that I won't bother you."

"You never bother me, Maggie. I wouldn't be fair if you stayed up here. That's ridiculous."

"But I will stay up here, if you decide to stay for dinner."

"It's not necessary."

"So you will stay?"

"I never said that I would."

"But you know you want to stay. She cooking ham and cabbage and potatoes ... soda bread. You have to admit that it is tempting."

"Of course it's tempting."

"So you will stay?"

"Alright." he relented.

"Good." she said with a smile. Then she raised herself onto her knees and hugged him, but became a little dizzy and started to lose her balance causing her to react by saying "Woh!"

"Watch it, sweetheart." he said as he steadied her.

"I guess I'm still a little bit woozy." she said as she hugged him tightly to keep from falling.

"Well maybe you should lay back down."

"Okay." she agreed as she returned to the bed and back under the covers. He helped her cover herself and she thanked him as he stroked her head.

"You know, it's very hard to say no to you." he sighed. "It must be those blue eyes of yours."

"You don't seem to have a problem saying no to me." she pointed out.

"But it's never easy."

There was a strange silence between them, as he knew that he admitted something revealing about himself. What had started as a lighthearted remark became an insight into his heart. Every time he saw her, he had a struggle with his instincts.

He started to feel uncomfortable as the seconds of silence seemed like hours. He tried to search for something to else to say, and finally told her to rest and he'd see her at dinner. With that he walked out of the room and closed the door, and she turned over and smiled.

Mike walked down the stairs and back into the kitchen, where he found Wendy lifting the ham out of the refrigerator. It started to slip out of her hands and he was quick to help her out, and she thanked him.

"How did she take the news?" Wendy asked.

"I'm staying."

"You're kidding?"

"No, she talked me into it."

"Really?"

"She started talking about the dinner and my mouth started to water."

"She knows you pretty well."

"Too well."

John came home at five-thirty, walked directly into the kitchen to give Wendy a long, sensuous kiss. He swept her off her feet.

"Ooh, what was that for?"

"I just wanted you to know how much I missed you today." he said as he continued to kiss her neck. He whispered something naughty in her ear and she giggled.

"Johnny, if you keep that up, I might forget about dinner altogether. Then what will Mike eat?" she said as she pointed to the other person in the kitchen, who was uncomfortably involved in the private conversation. John turned around and noticed Mike sitting at the kitchen table.

"Oh Mike. I didn't see you." John said with a bit of embarrassment.

"I could tell." Mike chuckled. It was obvious that John had only one person on his mind when he walked in the door.

New Beginnings

"Sorry about that."

"No problem. It's your house. You can do whatever you want."

John walked over to Mike as he stood up to shake his hand. He was glad to see Mike. It had been several months since they had seen each other, and there was some catching up to do. They talked about work, sports and everything male bonding depends on. They also agreed to set up a golf date.

Allie woke up from her nap and Mike volunteered to retrieve her, which was a surprise to both John and Wendy. As Mike left to get Allie, John grabbed Wendy from behind, and started to flirt with her, leaning over to kiss her on the neck again, then she turned around to face him.

"What are you up to?" she asked, almost embarrassed by all the attention.

"Did I ever tell you how sexy you look in green?" he said as he gave her the magic look.

"Johnny, come on. This is really bad timing for that look."

"I've been thinking about you all day. Give me a half hour. We'll go in the downstairs bedroom. I want to get to you before you begin to get tired."

"I'm cooking dinner."

"So? It's all in a pot. Just turn it down and come with me," he said as if he were practicing hypnotism.

"John, I can't just take off in the middle of dinner. What about Allie?"

"Mike's taking care of Allie."

"That doesn't concern you?"

"Not in the least. He needs the practice." he said as he played with the buttons on her blouse. He knew that she was starting to crumble under the pressure, and was very close to giving in.

"You know he could be putting a diaper on her head, for all we know."

"Maggie is upstairs and she will help him." he said as he started to kiss her neck again. She closed her eyes as the pleasure began to work on her self control, and her body began to ache for him.

"Johnny, please. You're wearing me out. I can't hold off for long."

"Then you're exactly where I want you. Make love to me, Wendy."

"John, you know I can't say no to you." she said weakly. Her will had been broken.

"That's what I was counting on." he replied as he lifted her into his arms. After stopping to turn down the ham and cabbage, he carried her into to the downstairs bedroom for their interlude.

Meanwhile upstairs, Mike picked up Allie and noticed that she had a little package for him. It wasn't a pleasant one.

"Oh great." he said, wishing that he had not volunteered to be the good guest. He laid her on the changing table and tried to remember his lesson back in August. What was that she told him to do?

"Watch that she doesn't roll over," he heard Maggie say from the doorway. He turned and noticed her standing there, fully dressed and ready to have dinner.

"Hi Maggie. How do you feel?"

"Good enough to have dinner."

"Glad to hear it."

"How did you get stuck doing this job?" she asked with a bit of amusement as she saw the clueless look on his face, as Allie cooed and gurgled at him.

"Your father came home with that goofy look, so I decided to give them some privacy. Allie started crying, and that was my way to make a gracious exit."

"My Dad, the lover. Who would have thought it?" she said as she walked into the room and closed the door behind her.

"So, since I assumed that dinner might be postponed a bit, I decided to do my duty as the guest."

"Doo-dy being the descriptive word."

"Very descriptive. Although, I just volunteered to get her, I didn't think that I would be dealing with this horror show."

"Just a little hint, Michael, whenever Allie wakes up from a nap, someone is usually dealing with something like this."

"Point well taken," he replied. "But, thank God you're here," he sighed, thinking that she would save him from the arduous task ahead of him.

"Don't thank me, Mike. I can't do it for you."

"Why not?"

"I'm sick. Remember?"

"Well, I think I'm going to be sick."

"You'll be fine. Just don't breathe."

"What do I do, again?"

"I'll talk you through it."

She talked him through it and after Allie was all cleaned up, Mike played with her on the floor as Maggie watched until Wendy came upstairs to declare that dinner was just about ready. The four of them met John downstairs and they all enjoyed each other's company as they ate their St. Patrick's Day feast.

Chapter Twenty-Eight

REGRETS AND HEARTBREAK

Ever since the St. Patrick's Day encounter, Michael found himself thinking more and more about Maggie. Absence had not taken his mind off of her, and there were still the family gatherings that he would attend, where he found himself enthralled with her presence.

The latest family get together was on Easter. Mike found himself once again watching Maggie intently, although he tried so hard not to watch her. He thought that she looked wonderful in her yellow Easter dress, but when she disappeared upstairs and returned in a pair of tight blue jeans and red sweater, his attention was constant. The combination looked fantastic on her trim, but curvy body. He was beginning to have an infatuation with her, and it drove him crazy.

He found himself anxious around her, like he was the one with the crush as he nervously tried to make conversation. This was all very unsettling to him. He was usually the one in control. His interest in her had continued to grow.

But, as his longing for her increased, she seemed to act as if she had lost interest in him. There were no more flirty looks, or glances from across the room. She treated him more like a relative, which would have been nice in September, but was not as welcome in April. He was getting his wish, but was this what he really wanted?

Once home and asleep, Michael had a vivid dream about Maggie that made him wake up covered in sweat, and in need of a cold shower. She was in the pink teddy, sitting on his bed and asking him for her wish. He had been experiencing these dreams on a regular basis, and one was more realistic than the next. He wished that he could erase the memory of her standing in her negligee, or the feeling of her body in their last close encounter. But, then again, he never wanted to forget.

He needed to find a way to stop thinking about her. Somehow, he had to will himself out of this infatuation. In desperation, and on a Friday night on the eve of his twenty-seventh birthday, he proceeded to the nearest watering hole to drown his sorrows and put his old skills into practice.

Finding a woman who was willing to come home with him was never difficult, because Michael never had a problem in that area. Usually, he was attracted to a certain type of woman, but if looked for a woman like that, he would bring home someone who was too similar to Maggie. Instead, he found a woman who was exactly the opposite.

His choice for the night was a barfly named Delilah. She had bleached blond hair, was thin as a rail, loud, and extremely forward. He assumed, from the was that she acted, that she had been around the block a few hundred times. She was normally the type of woman that he would avoid like the plague. Tonight, however, he was just looking for a warm body to make him forget about his forbidden and tormented attraction to Maggie.

He took her home, and as he had sex with her, he tried to close his eyes and pretend that she was Maggie, but it was of no use. Nothing about Desiree could trick him into thinking that she was Maggie. After the deed was done, he did not feel any satisfaction, rather, he felt like disinfecting his entire body. He just wished that she would leave.

He also had another unexpected feeling of guilt. That never happened to him before. Sometimes he felt regret, but never guilt. That emotion came out of nowhere. He felt ashamed of himself, which was also not a feeling that he had experienced before.

"What is wrong with me?" he thought to himself.

As Delilah snuggled in a little closer to him, he wondered how many men had used her as their personal playground. It could have been hundreds, from the way she had been acting. Normally, sex was a way to blow off steam or have a little fun. This latest encounter was not worth the payoff. He was exhausted, since he had not slept very well. The remorse kept him awake, and every time he closed his eyes and started to dream, he dreamed of Maggie. This little liaison had been a worthless excursion.

He managed to act the good host and stay in his bed next to her until it was close to sunrise. At the smallest instance of light, he slithered out of bed and made his getaway into kitchen. From there, he looked out the kitchen window to see the sunrise, which made him feel worse because ever since July, sunrises always made him think about Maggie.

He made a pot of coffee and while he looked through his bare refrigerator, she came up behind him and hugged him, which startled him. He wanted to be sick, but he had to be a gentleman about it.

"Hello you," she said in a graveled voice. Not exactly the sweet sounding voice that he had heard months before, and that voice came with pancakes.

"Good morning," he said as he turned around.

She stood there, wearing his shirt, which normally would have been very appealing, but today it was not. Her face was pale, and he assumed that she must have had a brutal hangover. She looked like she needed a cup of coffee, and fast. As he handed her a coffee, she looked as if she was expecting a kiss, but somehow he was able to avoid it. He had to admit to himself that she looked a lot better in the dark, after a few shots of tequila.

As she sat there at the table grabbing her pained head, and begging for an Advil, Michael wondered how in the world he had gotten himself in situation. He felt like an idiot. Desperation had brought him down to this level, and he was ashamed that he had sunk to those depths.

"Would you like something to eat?" he asked. "There isn't much in here, but I'm sure that I can scrounge up something."

"I can't eat anything," she groaned, "otherwise, I'd be sick. All I need is a shower and a couch to lay down on."

"Terrific. This is going to be an all day affair," he thought, "what have I gotten myself into?"

Delilah took a shower, and afterwards camped out on the couch, as promised. Michael offered to drive her home, but instead she told him that she was too hung-over to go anywhere. Several hours passed, and Michael found himself a prisoner in his own home.

At around noon, the situation remained the same, and Michael found it unbearable. He wished that he could grab Delilah and throw her out onto the grass like a lawn dart, shutting the door quickly to lock her out, but he knew that it was just a fantasy. He found himself hating himself for having the urges and needs that brought him to this unbelievable misery.

He decided to take a shower. He had not taken one earlier, because he was afraid that Delilah would take off with the silverware. Considering that Delilah had not left the couch for the last few hours, he assumed that it was safe to escape into the sanctuary of a hot shower. He wanted so badly to wash this mistake from his body. He looked at himself in the mirror and saw a pitiful reflection.

"Happy Birthday, stupid ass," he said to himself, then shook his head because it was such an inauspicious beginning to the new year.

The shower was more satisfying than the liaison had been. He washed until the hot water ran out. Once he was clean, he heard the front doorbell ring. He suddenly realized that Delilah was about the answer the door.

He threw a towel around him and had a little trouble opening the bathroom door, which he locked. He finally opened it, and raced to the living room, where he saw Delilah walking back and flopping onto the couch after closing the door.

"Who was at the door?" he asked as he adjusted his towel so that it was no longer falling off of his body. He could feel the heat of Delilah's stare in the towel's general direction. "Well?" he asked, trying to divert her attention.

"It was some young woman."

"Young woman? What did she look like?"

"Long brown hair, blue eyes. She was pretty upset."

"Oh my God ... Maggie!" Michael gasped. His heart sunk into his stomach and he felt sick. "Where did she go?"

"I don't know, she just took off. She's probably still in the driveway. How should I know?"

Michael raced towards the door and didn't seem to care that he was clad in just a towel.

"You may want to throw on pants or something like that, lover boy." Delilah suggested.

"Not enough time!" he said as he hurried out the door.

He ran towards his driveway and noticed that a car was still there, thank God. When she saw him, she immediately started the car intent on leaving before he had a chance to speak. He tried the door on the passenger side, but it was locked.

"Maggie ... Let me in."

Maggie wiped a tear from her eye, shook her head no.

"Maggie, I will lay behind the car if I have to ... open the door, please," he pleaded as he rushed behind the car to stop her from pulling out.

She momentarily pondered the thought of running him over, but there was no way that she could do that. She still loved him, although she was heart-broken to find a strange woman in his home, especially one who was so ... peculiar.

Michael's pleas started getting the attention of a neighbor, who peeked from behind her window curtain to catch a glimpse of the action. He was putting on quite a show for the neighborhood.

Thankfully, Maggie turned off her car and Michael returned to the passenger side door. The door was still locked, however, and Michael pleaded again.

New Beginnings

"Maggie, please let me in ... I'm dressed in just a towel, here," he begged softly, almost wanting to get down on his knees.

Finally, Maggie felt enough pity on him to unlock the door. Michael breathed a sigh of relief, opened the door and sat down. She looked straight ahead, and tried to be strong.

As he searched his mind for his first word, he heard her speak instead.

"I'm sorry that I showed up out of nowhere," Maggie sniffed in a trembling voice, biting hard on her tongue to keep from shouting out loud. "I should have called. I don't know why I'm even here. I guess that I just wanted to say happy birthday to you in person."

"Don't apologize, Maggie. I'm just sorry that you saw what you did. I wish that I had answered the door and not ... her." He said the word her as if it made him nauseous to think about the previous night.

"You don't have to explain anything to me, Mike. I understand what goes on. I may be inexperienced, but I know that men have their needs. It just has to be the right kind of woman ... that's all."

"Maggie..." he said tenderly, wishing he could tell her how right she really was.

"I wanted to invite you to my eighteenth birthday party," she sniffed. "I should have called, but I wanted to show you my car, and give you the gift."

"It's a nice car, Maggie."

"Isn't it?" she said, half-heartedly. "My Dad came with me to pick it out."

Her voice quivered as she spoke, and he could tell that she was barely keeping it together. She searched the car for a tissue, almost frantically, as if the tissue was going to stop her from falling apart. She managed to throw in a couple of mindless statements about the car, but he knew that she was just trying to keep herself on an even keel. Finally, the pressure was too much. She had to know.

"Mike, what is wrong with me?" she asked, "why do you want her and not me?"

"Maggie ... I ..." he said in stunned reply. He had to stifle himself so that he would not reveal anything else.

"Is that woman in there what you want? Is that what you are looking for?" she interjected.

"Not at all."

"Then why is she there?"

"Because ..."

He searched his brain for a good reason, but not the truth. He knew that this one night stand was an attempt to get his mind off of Maggie, but he couldn't tell her that.

"It just happened, Maggie. Don't ask me to explain it."

"So, you would make love to her and not me."

"It wasn't love, Maggie. Far from it."

"So it was just sex? It's amazing how guys like you always say that it was just sex, and that makes it okay."

"You know how it is with guys like me," he said, with biting sarcasm.

She was starting to talk like Wendy, and it was not a good sign. He knew that she was disgusted with his actions, and although she tried to hide it at first, she was furious.

"Damn it! What the hell is wrong with you? Why do you do things like this?" she shouted. "Sometimes I get so mad at you that I want to scream!"

"You seem to be doing a pretty good job of it right now!" he said, suddenly defensive.

"This isn't funny, Mike."

"I'm not laughing. None of this is funny, Maggie. I'm sitting here in a towel, and a teenager is scolding me. I case you didn't know it, I don't need your approval about how I live my life."

She darted a hurt look in his direction, and immediately, he wanted to take it back.

"Please get out, Michael," she begged. "I really need you to get out!"

"Wait … I'm sorry. I don't want to let you drive away like this," he insisted, "you're too upset to drive."

"I'll be the judge of that!" she snapped.

"Maggie, come on. Come inside."

"Are you serious? I wouldn't be caught dead in there."

"I'll get rid of her."

"Oh, that's gallant, Mike. What are you going to do, dump her on the curb?"

It was a wonderful thought. It would have been be the answer to his problems. But, he knew that it was just a dream.

"You know what I mean," he said,

"No I really don't. What do you mean?"

"I just don't want you to leave like this. I want you to stay."

"Luckily, you have no choice in the matter," she said as she re-started the car. "So, unless you want to greet my father while dressed in a towel, I suggest you get out of my car."

He was not winning the argument, and he knew it. Nothing that he could say was going to change her mind. Reluctantly, he accepted her demands and opened the door.

"Don't bother coming to the party. I don't want you there," she said vindictively as she gave him a dirty look. "I'd rather stab out my eyes than see you there."

The tears were gone and there was confidence in the way that she spoke. He knew that was determined to leave, so he slinked out of his seat and onto the driveway, closing the door. She looked at him standing there in just a towel and completely exposed to all who could see him. She felt a little pity for him, but he had brought this on himself. It was his own damned fault.

He had never seen this side of her before. She was angry with him, and she was letting him have it. It was different than that day at the restaurant when he tried to let her down easy. She was now in control, and he had become the lovesick puppy.

She never did give him the gift, but he figured that if she had, she probably would have thrown it in his face. This birthday was getting worse by the minute. He walked back into the condo and found his sleepover slug on the couch waiting for him. She was laughing at him, in between frequent coughs.

"So how did it go, Romeo, did you catch her?" Delilah asked

"Yes."

"Are you in trouble?"

"What else is new?"

"Does she know that you love her?"

"She's only seventeen."

"So what? I thought guys like you liked fresh meat."

"You don't know anything about me. You're insane."

"That may be true, but you are in denial. You want her."

"I don't know what gave you that idea."

"You raced out of here dressed in only a towel, lover boy," she laughed, "I think that it's pretty obvious that you're in love with the little virgin!"

Once home, Maggie ran into her room and threw the gift against her wall, hearing the sound of breaking glass. She then fell upon her bed and started to cry. The cry did not last long, though, but she just had to get it out. She kept telling herself that she was so stupid. She was stupid for loving him. She was stupid for crying in front of him. Stupid, Stupid, Stupid.

She looked at the gift that she brought for him as it lay there in a mangled heap on the floor. She knew that it was destroyed from the sound that it made when it hit the wall, but she was still curious to look at it. She walked over, picked it up and tore off the wrapping paper, careful not to cut herself with the broken glass.

The gift was a framed picture of her and Michael. It was taken on Christmas. She remembered when it happened, because as it was being taken, she was slipping the twenty minute note in his pocket. She carefully took the picture out of the debris, and deposited the broken frame and wrapping into the garbage can. She looked at the picture and contemplated tearing into a million pieces. She decided, however, to take the picture and carefully put into her night table drawer.

After that, she dried her eyes, pulled herself together and decided that she would not think another thought about Michael Burke. It was over. He would never change. Somehow, she would get over him, however difficult it would be. She had to do it. There was no other option.

Chapter Twenty-Nine

A MILESTONE

Two weeks week later, Maggie had finally reached the age of eighteen. It was a little too late, as far as she was concerned, and a bit anti-climactic. Maybe if she had been this age when she first met Mike, it would have made a difference. That didn't matter now. Mike was a non-entity.

Maggie did not know why she broke down in the car. She had been so strong at every family party since that horrible lunch. She was a pillar of strength. Any woman would have been proud of her for her intestinal fortitude. She managed to survive four grueling months without flirting, teasing or tempting Mike. She had tried to move on. Then in one moment, as she was staring into the eyes of a hung-over barfly, it all fell apart. She was disappointed in herself.

She heard a knock on her bedroom door, and John was there with a package for her.

"Sweetheart, this came in the mail for you."

"Thanks Daddy," she replied. She always called him Daddy when she felt vulnerable. She kissed John and he gave her the package.

"I think that it's from Mike. Is that his address?"

"Yes," she replied, knowing full well of his address. At that moment, Wendy appeared at the door.

"Did she open it yet?" Wendy asked John.

"She's just about to."

At that moment, Allie started crying in her bedroom.

"I got it," John volunteered, then he kissed his wife.

Maggie opened the package and inside it was a leather box meant for jewelry. When she opened the box, inside she found a gold pendant heart with an angel inside that was holding a small diamond. The heart hung from a gold chain that hung just below her neckline, when Wendy helped her put it on.

"Oh Maggie … It's beautiful!" Wendy gasped.

"Yes it is," Maggie agreed.

"Is there a note?"

Maggie found the note, and read it aloud to Wendy.

"Happy Birthday to a true angel. Sorry that I won't be there to help you celebrate. With love, Michael."

"Wow …" Wendy remarked.

Wendy remembered the conversation that she had with Mike back in October, when he called her an angel. Now, he gave her an angel as a gift. Wendy started to think that Mike's feelings Maggie might have grown into love.

"With love … what does he mean by that?"

"I don't know, Maggie. You'll have to ask him."

"Wendy, how can I not love him?" she sighed as she leaned back onto the bed. "I'm never going to get over him."

"He is making it very difficult, especially when he does things like this." Wendy agreed.

"I wish that I didn't tell him to stay away today. I want to see him so badly."

"In your condition, I'm glad that he is not here. I would have to barricade your bedroom door."

"You're hilarious!" Maggie commented as the two women shared a laugh.

John came in, carrying little Allie after changing her diaper and putting on her clothes for the day that Wendy had laid out.

"What did I miss?"

The two women looked at each other and laughed again.

Midday, the small party was on. Robert and Anne Channing were there, as they were for all of the family occasions. Wendy's parents did not travel the two hours to be there, which was understood, but they sent Maggie their very best, and had sent her a package in the mail. Maggie also received a package from John's mother in Florida. In her card, they told her that she missed her, but promised to see her in June for her high school graduation. Scott could not be there either, since he was still in college, but he sent a gift certificate instead.

Maggie had also invited a few girlfriends from school, including Lizzy and her parents. They had news that Darlene had John's previous house up for sale. The news was surprising, but not unexpected. They also had other, more revealing news about why Darlene was moving out of town.

"It seems that you ex-wife had a secret of her own." Vickie Mendenhall divulged, bursting with gossip that she was dying to tell.

"What is it?" John asked, not too interested, but he would find out anyway.

"Well, my dear, your ex-wife was having in affair for the past three years … with George Cooper."

"Three years? Are you sure?"

"Positive. Patty Cooper has filed for divorce. She's planning on taking everything he owns."

This little tidbit of information was fun to Vickie Mendenhall, but it was a slap in the face to John. Even though he knew that Darlene and George were having an affair, and he kept it a secret to secure his own divorce, he did not know was how long it had been going on. For a year and a half he had dealt with the guilt that came with cheating on his wife and ending his marriage. Even though he was deliriously happy with Wendy, there was often the thought that his second marriage ended because of his lack of restraint.

But, this revelation gave him some closure. The fact that she was having an affair way before he met Wendy explained why his second marriage went into freefall. It was not his fault after all. The destruction of the marriage had begun with her actions. He just did not know it at the time.

As John stood there in shock, Wendy embraced him.

"John, I'm sorry," she said.

"There's nothing to be sorry about. I'm just glad that I know about it," he said, "I do feel pretty foolish, though. I guess that I was walking around with blinders on."

"You should get that house back," Sam Mendenhall insisted, "she got it under false pretenses."

"It's okay, Sam. I don't need the house. I have everything that I want."

Later, Wendy found John lying in the bed and in deep contemplation. When she came a little closer, he turned and smiled at her.

"Hi beautiful," he said.

"Are you all right?" she asked, as she crawled next to him, lying on her side, facing him. She put her hand on his chest and stroked it lovingly. Then kissed his arm.

"Yeah, I'm fine," he said as he put his arm around her body and pulled her closer so that her head was on his chest.

"That was quite a shocker, huh?"

"About Darlene?"

"Yeah."

"I knew about the affair, Wendy."

"You what?"

"It wasn't until after we filed for divorce, though. I caught them together."

"Why didn't you say something?"

"I kept it a secret because I used it to get a quick divorce," he said, "but, I didn't know that the affair started so long ago. That, I didn't see coming."

"So, she's the reason that your marriage fell apart."

"All those late nights. She was probably with him. I always wondered what happened to make her so distant."

"Now you know."

"She did me a favor, Wendy."

"Why do you say that?"

"If it wasn't for the affair and the way she treated me, I would have never pursued you. We wouldn't have Allie, and this little one on the way," he said, as he put his hand on her abdomen. "I was never really happy with her. Maybe in the beginning, I thought I was, but that didn't last very long. I thought that I would never be content again. I'm so lucky to have another chance at happiness."

"So am I."

"I love you so much, Wendy. I'm a very lucky man."

All the gifts that Maggie received that day were wonderful, but they were not as beautiful as the angel heart that she received from Mike. It wasn't until later on, after the guests were gone, that Maggie received something even more beautiful from her father and Wendy. It was a diamond tennis bracelet.

Once Maggie was back in her room, she laid on her bed and held the angel heart pendant in her hand, inspecting it carefully. She didn't notice until that moment that there was an inscription on the back.

"For my angel. With love, M"

After reading that small inscription, her love for Michael returned like a flood. She wondered what he meant by the inscription. My angel. With love. The whole situation drove her crazy and she was more confused than ever.

Chapter Thirty

UNEXPECTED NEWS

It was a beautiful Saturday morning in late April. The women of the house had a plan in mind. It was going to be a day of shopping for a prom dress, lunch, and gossip. John stayed behind to take care of Allie, but he was still an essential part of the fun since Wendy made sure that he handed over his credit card.

"Take good care of it," he said to Wendy as she slipped the card from his fingers.

"Oh, I will give it plenty of attention," Wendy teased.

Wendy teased John, but she wasn't the type to shop and spend mindlessly. She had not planned to go overboard. She just needed some new maternity clothing, and a prom dress, shoes and a bag for Maggie.

"Are you sure that you're feeling well enough to be out there so long? You've been a little under the weather, especially in the morning."

"I think that I'm coming out of it. I've been feeling better lately. I'm actually feeling a little frisky for a change."

"Frisky, huh?"

"Very frisky," she said as she walked her fingers across his chest.

"So, can I pencil you in? I have an opening for tonight in my appointment book."

"Oh, I think that it's an appointment that I can keep."

"Then, I will see you later," he said. He put his arm around her and kissed her, and as he did so, he slid his hand down and grabbed her behind. He whispered a suggestive thought her ear, and she giggled.

"Okay you two. That's enough. Not in front of the children," Maggie joked as she rolled her eyes.

This was a scene that had been quite normal for the past year. Her father was now an extremely satisfied man in every area. She was happy for him, but sometimes all this wedded bliss could be nauseating. Maggie was extremely jealous and wished that she could find the same contentment in her own life. It seemed awfully hard to come by.

"See you later, handsome." Wendy flirted as she walked towards the door where Maggie waited. John watched her intently, wishing to he could postpone the shopping for at least another hour.

The first order of business was the prom dress, which was the most important search of the day. Maggie tried on several dresses, of all different colors, but nothing seemed to fit right or look right. They had just about given up but they decided to go to another shop. It was there that they found it the perfect dress.

When Maggie walked out of the dressing room, Wendy was floored.

"Oh Maggie … that's it"
"You think so?"
"Definitely."

When Maggie saw her reflection in the mirror, she had to agree. It was glamorous turquoise blue taffeta gown that had a straight bust line and spaghetti strings. It had had an open back with ruching at the bottom, and a small train. It was perfect, and the search was over. They were even able to buy the shoes and handbag in the same store. The trip was quite successful.

They were also able to find maternity clothes for Wendy. Wendy was very quick about it. She just grabbed a few shirts and pants that were made to expand as she grew. Everything was running like clockwork. When they walked into the restaurant with bags in had, the two were very satisfied. It had been a very productive day.

As they sat down, Maggie reminisced about the restaurant.

"You know, this is the place that Mike lowered the boom on me."

"Excuse me?" Wendy asked.

"This is where he took me when he told me that it wouldn't work. He met me for lunch, took me to this place, and then lowered the boom."

"I'm sorry Maggie, I didn't realize that he brought you here. We could go somewhere else if you would like."

"No, it's okay."

The phone rang in Wendy's pocketbook and she checked the number.

"It's your father," she said with a smile.

"Tell him that we're a success" she said as she raised both her hands in triumph.

"I will," she said as she opened the phone. "Hello handsome."

"Hi sweetheart," he said, with a hint of sadness in his voice. She could immediately tell that something was wrong.

"John, what's wrong?" she asked
"I really don't want to tell you on the phone."
"Just tell me John, whatever it is."
"It's your grandmother."

Grandma Mo died unexpectedly in her sleep early that morning. She had been feeling a little under the weather recently, but Wendy's mother explained that no one would have been able to guess that when she went to sleep the night before, she would not wake up the next day. The death was listed as natural causes, and the family was happy that she was finally with her husband, and she had left this world peacefully and in her own bed.

Burkes came in from every corner of the country to their original home in Upland, NY. Since Maureen Burke had eight children, there were plenty of them. All Maureen's children were there with their spouses to say final good-byes to their beloved mother. Starting with the oldest, Katherine, there were also Mary Kate, James, Patrick, Ronald, Meagan, Thomas and Joseph, who was Wendy's father. Many of Wendy's cousins were there as well, but not all of them could make the trip. It was a family reunion. They were all there to celebrate the life of Maureen Sullivan Burke.

After the initial shock of seeing Grandma Mo's lifeless body lying there with flower arrangements all around her, the family comforted each other with conversation about the great lady. Stories were being passed around, and there were plenty to tell. Wendy also had the added job of introducing her new husband to those who did not know him. As she introduced him to the family, she searched the crowd for Maggie, and did not see her.

Meanwhile, Mike arrived a little bit late, since he drove straight from work. He needed to tie up a few things on a busy Monday and had told the family that he would be late for the early showing. By the time that she walked in, everyone else had gotten over the initial shock of seeing Grandma Mo lying in state. He walked in at around two-thirty, hugged and kissed his parents Thomas and Jeanette, and hugged his sister Tara, and shook his brother in law Daniel's hand.

Then he took a deep breath and walked towards the casket to say goodbye to his biggest fan. As he kneeled in front of her coffin, he touched her hand and felt no warmth, and she was a shell of herself. He was unprepared for the moment, and almost broke down, but he managed to keep it together. Determined to be the strong one, as usual, he turned around to comfort those he loved, then after making the rounds, he found a quiet corner in which to sit.

Wendy walked into the hallway and found John, who was talking to Robert, Anne and Scott. The Channings had just arrived after the two hour drive from New Jersey.

"Thank you so much for coming," she whispered with red eyes as she hugged Robert and Anne. "I really appreciate you driving all the way out here."

"Oh, we loved Maureen ... she was a pip," Anne exclaimed.

"Wonderful lady," Robert added.

"Have any of you seen Maggie? I wanted to introduce her to the rest of my family."

"I just saw her walk into the other room," John said as he stroked her arm. "How are you doing, sweetheart?"

"I'm fine," she sniffed, while clutching a tissue in her hand. She hugged John again and excused herself. She walked to the entrance of the grieving room and found Maggie. She was walking towards Mike, and then stood in front of him.

Mike looked up to see Maggie's sympathetic face, and suddenly he felt very vulnerable. His emotions started to flare up inside of him, and he felt shaky as if he were about to break down.

"Are you all right?" she asked, noticing his discomfort.

"I'm fine, Maggie," he lied.

Suddenly, his face was flushed, and he looked very uncomfortable. He started to feel claustrophobic, and breathing became a little difficult.

"It feels so stuffy in here ... don't you feel hot?" He said as he adjusted his tie back and forth. He was in a panic. She had never seen him in this kind of helpless condition. It was un-chartered territory for both of them.

"Michael, you feel a little warm," she said as she touched his cheek, "Maybe you should go outside for a few minutes and get some air."

"Do you think so?" he asked.

"Yes honey, I think that it would be a good idea. You've been on the road for two hours, and just walked in the door. You could use a few moments to pull yourself together."

"Maybe you're right."

"Come on," she said as she grabbed his hand and led him to the exit. The two of them walked outside so that he could have some space.

Once outside, he took a deep breath of cool April air. He loosened his tie further, and took off his jacket. He felt his body temperature cooling down, and his breathing became normal again.

"Do you feel better?" she asked as she rubbed his back. She was so loving, and just what the doctor ordered.

"Much better," he said.

"Good."

"I think that it was the flowers. There were so many of them."

"She was well loved."

They walked around to the back of the building and into a little shady area where they could talk without being interrupted. He sat on a stone wall that surrounded a small flower garden as she stood across from him, and they and continued to talk.

"I can't believe she's gone." he said. "I was mad at her. I didn't want to see her. Now she's gone."

"Nobody knew that she was going to die," she reasoned.

"Still, I should have seen her."

"Mike, you are being too hard on yourself. She was two hours away. It wasn't exactly around the corner."

"You don't understand, Maggie. It didn't have anything to do with how far away she was. I didn't even call her."

"Honey, you can't do anything about it now. She knows that you loved her."

Mike hung his head then uncharacteristically started to softly cry. Then, he suddenly fell apart as he leaned his head into the midsection of her black dress. She cradled and kissed the top of his head as he sobbed, and rubbed his back until he was able to compose himself.

"I'm sorry," he said, a bit embarrassed by his lack of strength.

"Don't be."

"I'm usually not like this. Always cool under pressure," he said as he wiped the tears from his eyes.

"You needed to let go, Mike. It's not good to hold it in."

"God, I'm going to miss her."

"I know," he said as she continued to caress him.

"You know, she really cared for you," he said.

"I loved her too. She was my favorite of all your relatives."

"She's the one that gave me the idea for the necklace ... you know ... the angel?" he explained, "She once told me that you reminded her of an angel."

"Really?"

"Yes, really."

"It's a beautiful necklace, Michael. I wanted to tell you that I loved it, but ..."

"You were still hurt. I know. It was a stupid mistake. I knew that before I even saw you that day."

"Don't think about it now, sweetie," she said as she stroked his forehead, kissed it, then moved the hair from in front of his eyes. "Don't worry about it. If you want forgiveness, you've got it ... Okay?"

"I don't deserve it."

"Yes, you do."

"Maggie, what do you see in me? I'm such a train wreck."

"I see the man that I love," she said.

"So you still love me after everything I've done?"

"Call me crazy."

"You are crazy," he said with a smile.

"Do you feel a little better?" she said as she put her hand on his cheek.

"You always make me feel better."

"I do my best."

"Thank you," he said, "I don't know what I would have done without you."

He stood up and kissed her tenderly. The kiss was followed by a long, much needed hug.

"I guess that we better go back inside," he said as he put his jacket back on, then straightened his tie. "How do I look?"

"Irresistible," she replied.

He then grabbed her hand in his and kissed it, and the two walked back towards the building. Once inside, she sat with him in the great room and held his hand.

Wendy walked back into the grieving room and was approached by her cousins Tara, and Darcy.

"Wendy, who is that young woman sitting with Michael?" Mike's sister Tara asked in a subtle voice. "She's not his normal kind of date."

Wendy looked over and saw Maggie sitting next to Mike, stroking his shoulder lovingly to comfort him.

"That ... is my husband's daughter, Maggie."

"Oh, Maggie ... Isn't she's the one with ..."

"The breasts that would feed an army? One and the same."

"When my mother told me that, I almost dropped the phone. I can't believe that Grandma Mo said that!" Tara gasped.

"Well, you know Grandma Mo. She was liable to say anything ... at any time," Wendy whispered.

"Still ... it had to be embarrassing. How did Maggie handle it?" Darcy asked.

"She was incredibly gracious, although I know that she must have been mortified. Who wouldn't be?"

The three women watched as Maggie cared for their loved one, holding his hand and talking to him softly.

"She's a very beautiful girl ..."

"I know," Wendy agreed.

"How old is she?"

"She just turned eighteen."

"She looks like she cares for him a lot," Darcy pointed out.

"She's madly in love with him," Wendy replied.

"Really?" Tara asked with great interest.

"Absolutely."

"What about him?" Darcy asked.

"Well ... I think that he feels the exact same way but he can't go the extra mile and admit it."

"Sounds like my brother., Tara said. "He never could make the right decision when it came to women."

"They do look good together," Darcy said.

"They will make beautiful babies," Tara said, mimicking Grandma Mo. The three women snickered, all part of the joke.

"She said that too," Wendy giggled.

"I know!" Tara laughed. "I heard that she pulled out all the stops that day ... the hips too."

"It was brutal," Wendy agreed. "We were all sitting there with our mouths wide open."

"By the way, I notice that you have been pretty busy lately. One baby in the carriage and another one on the way," Darcy remarked

"Well, I have to make good use of these child bearing hips."

The three women laughed as silently as they could, but still made a commotion in the room, and it caused Maggie to look up. They decided to continue their conversation into the hall.

As the women discussed the situation, Maggie walked out into the hallway and into the gathering.

"There she is," Wendy said aloud. "Maggie, I want you to meet my cousins, Darcy and Tara.

"Nice to meet you," Maggie said, shaking Tara's hand first, then Darcy's.

"So, Maggie, I see you are taking care Michael," Darcy commented.

"He's very upset," Maggie said. They could see the look of concern in her eyes.

"This one isn't easy for him," Tara commented.

"He was very fond of Grandma Mo," Darcy pointed out, "We all were."

"So, where is my little brother?" Tara asked. "Wasn't he outside with you?"

"We just went for a walk. He needed a little air. It was the flowers. I think that it was a little overwhelming for him. I think that he's back in the big room now. Would you like for me to go and retrieve him?"

"It's not necessary,"

"It's no trouble ... I'll can go get him," she said as she went to find him. As they watched her leave, Wendy turned to her cousins.

"See what I mean?"

At four o'clock, the first wake session was over. Scott left to return to college after giving everyone his final hug goodbye. Everyone else returned to the household of Joseph and Sarah Burke to relax and eat before the second session started at seven.

While in the house, Maggie found out that Mike had planned to drive back to his home that night and return in the morning for the funeral. Obviously, he was not thinking straight and she called him on it.

"You're not making any sense, Michael," she insisted," It's a two hour drive from your condo to here.

"I'll be fine, Maggie. Don't make a big deal about it."

"I won't let you leave. Not in your condition."

"I've heard that one before."

"Well ... I was upset. It was different circumstances. You are already tired, and it's too far to go."

"I appreciate your concern, sweetheart, but you can't stop me from leaving."

"I will sit on you, if I have to," she threatened.

"Well, that's the best offer I have had all week," he joked, which made her smile.

"Seriously. Mike ... you should stay in town. It does not make any sense to go home and come back. Can't you see that?"

At that moment, Wendy came into the picture and Maggie called her over.

"Wendy, Mike said that he's going to drive all the way back to his home tonight, and then return tomorrow."

"Well, that doesn't make any sense, Mike, why would you do that?"

"Wendy, I'm not prepared to stay over. I did not get a hotel room, I don't know why. I guess that I wasn't thinking clearly, but now, everywhere is booked. There is no other place to stay."

"Of course you have a place to stay. Don't be ridiculous. We have a couch in the living room. You can stay on a couch, can't you?

"I guess I could do that."

"Then it's settled."

Mike realized that he was outnumbered, and did not argue any longer. He knew that he had an overnight bag in his car for the occasions that he needed to stay overnight in the city because of work, so he didn't have a good excuse to leave. The bag had a dress shirt, underwear and socks, and toiletries. He also had a gym bag in the car with clothes that he could use to sleep in. It wasn't exactly stocked, but it was all that he needed for the next day.

When it was time to leave for the seven o'clock session, The family returned to the funeral home for the final chapter of their exhausting day. Maggie stayed behind to take care of Allie, so that John could be in the funeral home with his wife. Maggie wished that she could be there to help Michael, but realized that it was more important to take care of her sister, as promised.

After the second wake session was over, it was nine o'clock and the Burke family returned to their respective homes for the night. John, Wendy and Michael returned to Wendy's parent's home, while the rest of the family was scattered in different motels in town. Luckily every Burke had a home for the night.

Halfway through the night, Maggie could not sleep and decided walked down to the kitchen. She was not exactly hungry or thirsty, but more curious to see how Mike was doing. She walked down the stairs and past the couch. When she did not find Mike there, she looked around the house, and did not find him. Eventually, she found herself looking out the front window, but his car was still there, and she was happy to see it.

She grabbed a glass from the cabinet, turned on the cold water and held her hand underneath the running water until it was the right temperature. As she filled the glass, she looked out the back window to see if he was in the backyard. It was then that heard a voice from behind her, and almost dropped the glass onto the floor.

"Looking for someone?" Mike asked as he leaned against the entrance to the kitchen. She was startled and turned to face him, and her heart skipped a beat as she saw him standing there dressed in sweatpants with no shirt.

"You frightened me."

"Sorry about that."

"Where were you?"

"I couldn't sleep, so I went for a little walk outside."

"What's the matter?'

"I don't know ... I just can't sleep. Too much going on, I guess."

She walked over to where he was standing and inspected him closely. He looked exhausted. She gently placed her right hand on the side of his face, and stroked his cheek.

"You look tired," she said, then she gave him two slight taps on the cheek.

"Maggie, I'm worn out. But, I just can't sleep."

"Working a lot?"

"I've been practically living at the firm lately. I've got several cases that I'm working on. Well, I don't want to bore you with the details, but I'm lucky that I was able to get away for the wake and funeral."

"I have an idea."

"Uh oh … The last time you had an idea you got me in a lot of trouble with my cousin." he said.

"It's nothing like that Michael." Maggie scolded. "Just come with me."
she held his hand and led him towards the living room.

"Is this when you sit on me?" he teased.

"Not exactly"

"That's a shame."

"Listen. I owe you one. You took care of me a month ago, and it's my time to return the favor."

"Maggie, if you bring me upstairs to your bed, that will guarantee that I will not get any sleep. Plus, the family is up there," he joked.

"We're not going upstairs, silly."

"Are you sure? Afterwards, I would probably sleep like a baby."

"Michael … Don't tease me."

"Sorry," he said with a impish smile.

She led him back to the couch and sat down, then directed him to lay down beside her and rest his head on her lap. She stroked his head for a few moments, intending that it would make him relax and eventually drift off to sleep. For a few minutes, he was able to relax and become a little bit sleepy. He felt very comfortable receiving her care. He closed his eyes and felt himself drifting off to sleep.

But eventually, it drove him crazy to be so close to her, and her tenderness had the opposite affect. He shifted his position, when he shifted it accidentally opened her robe, then suddenly he could feel her bare legs underneath his head and passionate thoughts ran through his brain. His heart started to beat rapidly as her fragrance overtook him. He tried to ignore it, but eventually he could not take it anymore.

"Oh God … I have to sit up," he said as he opened his eyes and sat up suddenly.

"What's wrong?"

"I just can't lay here like this. It's too much. I can't do it."

"Mike, we're not doing anything. I was just stroking your head."

"That's enough, Maggie. Trust Me," he said.

"I just wanted to help you relax."

"I'm not relaxed. Far from it. I was too close to the danger zone," He said as he slid over to the farthest edge of the couch.

"Oh," She said with a timid smile, enjoying his suffering just a little bit.

He started to practice some deep breathing exercises, as she waited patiently. When he finally calmed down a bit, he broke the silence.

"You're not making it easy, you know."

"I know. You said that in December," she sighed glumly, expecting to hear the same words that she heard then. "Mike, seriously, I don't know what I'm doing wrong. I wasn't trying to tease you. I swear. I was just trying to help."

He realized that she was blaming herself for their current uncomfortable situation, and he had to laugh to himself. If she only knew how much he wanted to make love to her at that moment, she would know that she wasn't to blame.

"Maggie … stop," he said more emphatically as he moved closer to her and put his fingers over her mouth to stop her from talking. He then brushed her hair back with his hand. "I'm not blaming you at all. It's all me."

"All you?"

"Yes. You are not doing anything wrong. You're doing everything right without even trying. Just your presence here is turning me on. Right now, I want you more than I've ever wanted anything."

"Oh," She said, with a bit of surprise. "Really?"

"Yes, really," he laughed. "Right now, you're irresistible."

"Well … what do you know about that?" she said, a little surprised at his admission. "You do realize that this is horrible timing."

"Sweetheart, lately that has been the story of my life."

It was not exactly the proclamation of love that she yearned for, but she was still satisfied. She was finally getting to him. He put his arm around her and kissed her head, as she rested against him, with her head and hand on his chest, feeling the warmth of his body. They held each other silently until they inexplicably drifted off to sleep.

"Maggie, wake up," Wendy said, as she shook the young woman's arm. Wendy had come down to the kitchen to get an early bottle for Allie, and found Mike and Maggie laying together on the couch. Somehow, she was sleeping next to him, with his arm around her.

"Come on, Maggie … wake up!" she pleaded.

Maggie opened her eyes, realized where she was and sat up, shaking her head to get all her marbles together.

"Oh God! I must have fallen asleep!" Maggie panicked.
"You've got to get upstairs before someone else sees you."

Maggie quickly slid out of Mike's grasp, stirring him a bit, but not waking him. Once again, Wendy had saved Maggie from disaster, and Maggie was extremely grateful.

Chapter Thirty-One

AFTERMATH

The next morning, the family gathered for Maureen's funeral. The services were held at Holy Trinity Church, which was where Maureen christened all her children and where her children were married before moving to other locations. This is also the place where Wendy and John exchanged their vows more than a year before.

The service was both beautiful and sorrowful. Afterwards, the funeral procession led then to Holy Trinity Cemetery, where she was laid to rest in a plot next to that of her husband, Michael. After a final toast, the family left the cemetery and returned to Joe and Sarah's home for the repast.

Once inside, the family mingled and talked, catching up with each other's lives. Everyone was leaving later on in the day and returning to their homes, some earlier than later, but for the moment everyone acted as though it were a long awaited homecoming. The last time most of Maureen's children had been home was fifteen years ago for the funeral of their father. They were telling stories, mostly about Grandma Mo. It was a true celebration of her life. She would have loved to have been there.

In the kitchen, Wendy was catching up on all the family gossip with her cousins Tara and Darcy as they served the food onto the buffet table. The three women laughed about the past, and thoroughly enjoyed each other's company.

"I wish it didn't take events like this to get us all together," Wendy commented, and the two other women agreed. Unfortunately, it was easier said than done. Both Darcy and Tara lived four hours away from Wendy's home in New Jersey.

"Look at my brother over there," Tara pointed out. "What do you think?"

The three women's attention turned to Mike and Maggie who sat on the couch talking to each other. They could tell that Mike and Maggie shared a close connection, as he leaned in to whisper something into her ear and she smiled.

"I wonder what he just said to her," Darcy mused.

"Whatever it is, it's none of our business," Wendy stated.

"I hope that he's not giving her the usual lines," Tara said as she rolled her eyes.

"Tara, I really doubt it. I think that he really cares about her," Wendy replied.

"My goodness, could my brother actually be in love?" Tara said is a mocking tone.

"Shh ... Tara. Not so loud. They'll hear you," Darcy scolded.

"I just want him to grow up already. He's twenty-seven years old. This Peter Pan thing is getting a little pitiful," Tara reasoned.

They all agreed that she was a sweet and beautiful young girl who would be the perfect match for their only remaining single cousin, and since this pairing was Grandma Mo's last wish, they all wanted it to happen. Wendy explained that it was easier said than done, and she begged them not to talk too loudly since John was not in on the plot to marry off his daughter.

"John still considers her his little girl. I don't know how he would feel about it," Wendy explained, "But, you can tell that Mike is very attached to her, can't you? He once thought that she was untouchable. Lately, I don't know if that is necessarily true."

"What do you mean lately?" Darcy asked.

Wendy pulled over her two cousins until they were out of hearing range of anyone else, especially John. Then she told them every detail of the tale of Mike and Maggie. She told them about the trap and rescue, and of her attempt at seduction. She informed them of the Christmas romp, and how afterwards he made the decision to let her go. Then she told them about the one night stand with the girl from the bar and how Maggie found out about it.

"What a jerk," Tara said, disgusted with her younger brother.

Then Wendy told them about the angel necklace and note, which seemed to redeem Mike in both of their eyes.

"Then ... there was last night."

"What happened last night?"

"I came downstairs to get a bottle for Allison and I found the two of them laying on the couch together, asleep."

"They weren't ..."

"No, they were dressed. They looked kind of cute, actually. I don't think that John would have agreed, though."

"What do you think happened?"

"I really don't think anything happened, but I'm just glad that John didn't see the two of them. Luckily, I was able to wake her up and rush her into her room before anyone else was any wiser."

"Maybe Mike doesn't think that she's so untouchable, after all." Tara joked.

"Tara ... stop." Wendy scolded with a smile.

"Maybe Grandma Mo is getting her wish," Darcy said. The three women nodded and looked up to the ceiling.

"Maybe so," Wendy agreed.

Later on in the day, most of the relatives said goodbye and left. Some of them left to take a plane, others had a long drive ahead of them. John, Wendy and family remained to help clean up the mess that was left behind, along with Mike and his parents. Tara, Darcy and their husbands and children were also there, as were Darcy's parents, Meagan and Harry Peale. Tara and Darcy lived about two hours further away, upstate in NY.

Thomas Burke was trying to have a conversation with his son, Mike when he realized that it was not going anywhere. Mike was quite distracted. It was obvious that he had other things on his mind as he kept his attention set on Maggie. Tom adjusted and finally changed the subject from work to a far more interesting subject for his son.

"She's very attractive, isn't she?" he asked.

"Yes, she is ... I mean ... who?" Mike said breaking out of his daze.

"John's daughter."

"Sure ... I guess that you can say that she's attractive," he said, trying to pretend that he hadn't been staring at every inch of her body.

"Michael, stop. I'm your father. Do you think that I haven't noticed that you have been watching that young woman?"

"Is it that noticeable?"

"Well ... yes."

"Do you think that John noticed it?"

"I don't know."

"I hope not."

Finally, Mike decided to open up to his father. He needed an opinion that he trusted and his father was the best man for the job.

"Dad, I don't know what to do," Mike said, opening up his heart to his father.

"What's going on?"

"Can we speak in private, outside?"

"Of course we can," said Tom.

The two men walked out the back door and outside into the small yard where there was a round picnic table and benches for them to sit and talk. Mike seemed nervous, and that worried Tom.

"So, Michael. What is the problem?" Tom asked.

He secretly hoped that Mike had nothing earth shattering to tell him. He knew that Mike had some questionable relations with other women in the past, and he hoped to God that his skirt chasing son had shown some restraint with John's attractive daughter.

Finally, Mike took a deep breath and started to spill the beans.

"Dad, I can't get her out of my head. I think about her all the time. I dream about her. When I see her I can't keep my eyes off of her. I don't know what to do."

"Please don't tell me that you've been playing around with John's daughter."

"No, Dad. It's not like that. Well, we have kissed, but I really care about her. We have a connection."

"How does she feel about you?"

"She loves me, Dad."

"What is the problem?"

"Well, she's John's daughter, for one."

"Does John have a problem with you?"

"No, we get along great. We play golf together on occasion."

"Again, what's the problem?"

"Dad, don't you think that she's a little young?"

"Do you think that she's too young?"

"I used to. But, now I'm not so sure. What do you think?"

"She's young, but she's smart, and beautiful, and based on the way she took care of you yesterday, I believe that she's very affectionate towards you."

"I know."

"What are you afraid of?"

"I don't know."

"This is what happens when you're in love, Michael. You doubt yourself. You wonder if you're doing the right thing."

"I don't know if I'm in love, Dad. I've never been in love before."

"I think you are, Michael." Tom said.

"That's what Desiree said."

"Who is Desiree?"

"Dad, you don't want to know. Call it a momentary lapse of sanity."

"I've heard that you've had a few of those. Tell me, I spent all this money on Catholic school. What happened?"

"College ruined me," Mike joked.

Mike thought that he was a funny line, but his father gave him a stern look. Then the conversation got serious.

"Michael, you know this all has end don't you? You can't play around forever. There's nothing wrong with a little purity and goodness in your life. You need something that is real. You have to grow up."

"I know."

"And if you are seriously thinking about becoming involved with that young woman in there, you better be sure before you take that next step. I wouldn't want her to get hurt."

"That's the last thing I want, Dad."

Later, the older women of the group wanted to know more about the beautiful girl who gave so much special attention to Mike. They asked her about herself and her future plans. They also managed to, in a roundabout way, ask her about she wanted to have children sometime in the future.

"Of course. If I find the right guy," she said, gazing over at Mike who had returned from his meeting with his father and was sitting across the room. He had not heard any of the conversation. As if by design, he glanced in her direction, then they both quickly looked away.

"So I hear that you have your prom coming up," Darcy asked, walking into the conversation, changing the subject.

"Yeah ... Wendy helped me pick out a beautiful dress a couple of days ago. It's turquoise blue, with spaghetti straps, goes down to the floor and has a small train in the back."

"She really looks gorgeous in it ... I'll send you some pictures," Wendy said.

As she spoke, Mike watched and his interest was peaked. He walked close enough to hear more of the details, but not obvious to give away his position.

"So, do you have a date?" Jeanette asked.

"I'm going with a friend from school. His name is Josh."

"What?" a voice said with utter shock. The ladies turned to where the voice was coming from and saw Mike standing there with a shocked look on his face, as he waited for an explanation.

"I'm going with Josh."

"Josh from the party?"

"Yes, Josh from the party. What about it?"

"You can't go with him."

"Why not?"

"You know why not." he said with all seriousness.

The women looked back and forth at either of them as if they were watching a tennis match. Mike realized that the argument was of great interest to all of the women in attendance, and wanted a little privacy.

"Can I speak to you outside, please?" Mike requested.

"Mike, there is really nothing to discuss."

"Maggie ... I need to talk to you outside," he said with a forced smile, and more determination as he tipped his head and motioned in the direction of the front door. In order to prevent any further awkwardness, Maggie apologized and excused herself to follow him outside.

"Uh oh," Wendy said.

"What's going on?" Jeanette inquired.

"I think that your son is about to get himself in trouble," Tara said in a melodic voice.

"I've got to hear this!" Darcy said playfully as she listened by the door.

"Darcy, don't do that," Jeanette said, but then watched as Darcy and Tara put their ears against the door. Wendy tried to restrain herself, but found herself listening to the play by play. The more mature ladies restrained themselves from the surveillance.

Once Mike and Maggie were outside and thought that they were out of earshot, the heated discussion began.

"Mike, why are you embarrassing me like this?" Maggie said with much uneasiness.

"Maggie, I won't allow you to go with that guy," Mike stated.

"You won't what?" she said with astonishment.

"I mean, I wish you wouldn't go with him," he said, noticing that he had been too forceful. "I don't trust him."

"Josh? Josh is harmless."

"Josh is not harmless. He wasn't harmless seven months ago, and he is not harmless now."

"Mike, you don't understand. We're just friends," she tried to explain.

"You may think that, Maggie, but I looked into his eyes that night."

"He's my friend. I can't just dump him."

"Honey, if you don't listen to what I am saying, I will have to warn your father about this guy."

"You're joking, right?"

"No, I'm not."

"Really, you would tell him what happened that night? Everything? You wouldn't care how it made me look?"

"I'm just trying to protect you, Maggie. I don't want you to go with him."

"So, what do you want me to do? Call him up and tell him that I'm not going?"

"I don't trust that guy. If I have to tell your father, I will."

She could not believe what she was hearing. How dare he threaten her like this! Who did he think he is?

"Michael, let remind you of something. You have seen and felt more of my body than Josh could ever dream of doing. If my father should be worried about anyone, it should be you."

Inside, the women strained to hear what was going on, and Darcy managed to hear the last sentence, which made her feel a bit guilty for eavesdropping.

"Oh boy," she said.

"What is it?" Wendy asked.

"I really shouldn't be listening to this."

"Why?"

"Something has been going on," she whispered softly to Wendy and Tara.

"No, no ... stop ... I don't want to hear it," Wendy gasped, trying to shut down her ears.

At that moment, John saw the gathering by the door and walked over to see what the commotion was all about. Wendy told him that it was nothing, then found some task for him so do to get him out of the area. The rest of the women decided that their continued stakeout was not the right thing to do, and they no longer listened to the private conversation outside.

As the women released their ears from the door, the conversation outside became more heated.

"Maggie, You're not being fair. I'm just looking out for you, that's all. I just don't want him to take advantage of you."

"Well, that's the pot calling the kettle back."

"I can't believe you just said that!"

"You heard me."

"It's not the same thing. You know that I care about you."

"Do I? I can't tell. Which is it today? You care ... you don't care ... It's like a rollercoaster ride." Maggie argued. "What gives you the right to think that you can tell me what to do? Who do you think you are?"

"Maybe I know what's best for you," he argued. Once he said that, he instantly wanted to take it back, but it was too late. He could see her blood boil, and her eyes became icy.

"Because I'm so young and gullible?" she said as she walked towards him with rage in her eyes.

"That's not what I meant," he said, backing away a bit. He really did it this time.

"You really crack me up! I'm not a child you know."

"I know that, baby."

"Don't call me baby!" She demanded.

She was suddenly taking offense of the pet name that she had liked so much the night before. It was just the wrong time for him to use that particular nickname. He was pressing all the wrong buttons. He could not do anything right.

"I'm sorry ... okay?" he pleaded, "I just don't want you to get hurt."

"I am getting hurt. Can't you see that? Josh has nothing to do with it."

"Maggie ..."

"Josh is my friend. That's all. Not that I have to justify it ... to you. I don't even know why I am doing this! I don't owe you an explanation and I don't need your permission!"

"But, I thought that after last night ..."

"Last night? What did you say to me that I didn't already know?" she asked, almost mocking him. "You want me. You said that seven months ago. It's nothing new. You still can't think that you can tell me what to do."

"I can't help it. I don't trust him."

"It doesn't matter what you think!"

"Doesn't it?"

"Should it?" she asked with a sarcastic laugh, wondering what kind of explanation he would come up with next.

He backed away and took a long pause. His head was spinning, and he had no answer to give her at that moment. She rolled her eyes and started to walk away. She assumed that the excuses would follow, and she did not want to hear them.

"Michael, I'm really getting sick of this," she said in an exhausted tone, "You know how I feel. I haven't exactly been shy about it. Why can't you just tell me how you feel ... for once?"

"Maggie, What do you want me to say? It's not that easy."

"Sure it's easy. Maggie, I love you. See? What's so hard about that?"

Again, he did not say anything, and she had just about had enough.

"I'm going inside," she said as she walked towards the house in disgust.

"Maggie, don't be mad," He begged as he gently held her arm to try and stop her from going inside the house. She looked at him sharply and he let go.

"Why do you care about what I do, Michael?" she asked with a weak sigh. "Do you even know? Maybe you should ask yourself that question and get back to me."

With that said, Maggie stormed off towards the house. She walked into the house, and the women in the living room pretended not to know what had happened. She needed a place to get away from everyone. She was mad enough to cry, but she did not dare do it. She didn't want to give Mike the satisfaction. She wanted to scream. How dare he think that he could tell her what to do? He had not earned that right. She did not talk to Mike again, other than to say a cold "Goodbye."

Soon afterwards, Maggie was in the back seat of her father's car, on the way home. She looked out the window and noticed that the sun was setting. The symbolism of that moment made her cry. The sun was setting on her dreams.

Once they left, a shell shocked Mike turned to his father who had a beleaguered look on his face.

"What happened?" Tom asked.

"What always happens, Dad? I screwed up," Mike replied, then walked away.

There was nothing left to be done. As he prepared to take the miserable drive home, he was approached by his mother. She had something to give him. It was a small, antique white box.

"What is it?"

"Your grandmother's engagement ring. She wanted you to have it."

"Why me?"

"She said that you would know. She also gave me this letter for you that goes with it."

She handed both items to her son, and hugged him.

"Everything is going to be alright, sweetheart."

"I wish that I had your confidence."

"I've always had faith in you, Michael. I still do."

"Mom, I don't know what I am doing. I'm completely lost."

"You'll find your way."

"I hope that you're right."

"Are you going to be okay?"

"Yeah Mom. I'll be fine."

On the way home, he kept replaying the argument in his head. He felt like he had been sideswiped. He did not understand why Maggie would want to go to the prom with Josh and he was surprised that she had taken such a strong stand against him. He was stunned.

Although he did not trust Josh, he was not going to tell John about the incident in September. It was just a bluff. He did not want to hurt her and his aim was only to protect her. He would have to take care of that problem himself, no matter how much she would hate his interference, or how it would affect their relationship.

Once in his condo, the first thing he did was walk into the kitchen and grab a bottle of beer. It had been a long and upsetting day, and the ride home seemed longer than usual. He needed to kick off his shoes, take a deep breath and analyze the situation.

He sat on the couch and emptied his jacket pocket and held white ring box and letter in his hands. He opened the box and stared at the ring, dreading the letter that came with it. He knew that it would be the last letter that he would ever read in his grandmother's handwriting, and it was a torturous moment for him, because he already missed her so much.

He took another deep breath, and finally had the courage to open the letter. Emotions started to overwhelm him as he saw that it was her personal stationary. He ran his fingers over the embossed heading, and throughout her writing. Her handwriting had always been so perfect, almost like you would find in a penmanship textbook. Even though the writing was a little frail, it still was like he remembered.

"Dear Michael,

If you are reading this letter, it means that I have gone to meet with my late husband, which is a reunion that I have long awaited. I cannot tell you how much I have missed him, and how happy I am that I will be able to see him again. I hope that you will be happy for me as he and I are united in heaven.

Unfortunately, this means that I will not be able to be there to give you this ring. I have saved it for you to give to your future bride. I hope that the woman that you choose is all that you desire in your heart, and that you have picked a woman who you believe is your soul mate. It is also my wish that you believe that this woman will be a wonderful mother to your future children.

I am sorry that I will not be there to see you start your family, as it is what I always wanted for you. But, I will always be with you as your guardian angel. You are very special to me, and I wish you all the best for your future. I will miss you, my Michael.

Love always,

Your Grandmother Maureen

New Beginnings

P.S. We both know who your soul mate is. She is not too young. Do not let her marry some little twit. She is your perfect match."

Mike laughed in between tears when he read her postscript. She still had to get the final word. He realized that she was right all along. Maggie was his soul mate.

"So what do I do now?" he said as he looked to the heavens. He wished he had Grandma Mo there so that he could ask her for advice.

After deep contemplation, he knew that things could not remain the same. He realized that he was no different than Josh in some ways, because at times he had taken advantage of her love for him. She was right about how their relationship had been a rollercoaster ride, and it was all his fault.

He had to make some kind of choice about what steps he needed to take in order for their relationship to move forward ... or backward. She deserved someone who loved her without conditions, or reservations. He had to decide if he was ready to be that man.

As for Josh, Mike planned on taking care of that matter in his own way.

Chapter Thirty-Two

HE WAS RIGHT

On the Saturday before the Prom, the doorbell rang at the Stanton house, and John opened the door to find Josh standing there impatiently.

"Hello Doctor Stanton, I am here to pick up Maggie," said Josh, who did not look him directly in the eyes.

"So I hear, come on in," John said, trying out his best stern father routine. It was not hard to be suspicious, since Josh had this look about him that was hard to trust. At that moment, Maggie walked down the stairs to greet Josh.

"Hey Josh."

"Hey Maggie. We better hurry up or we'll be late for the movie," he insisted, as he glanced quickly at John, who was still watching him skeptically. Josh gave all the signals that he wanted to leave as soon as possible.

"Goodbye, Dad," Maggie said as she gave him a kiss and a look as if to say, "Don't worry, Dad."

John watched the young couple walk out of the door, then enter Josh's car and drive off down the road. Once that was over, he found Wendy in Allie's room and told her of his reservations.

"Wendy, have you ever met Josh?"

"Yes, I've seen him once or twice, I think."

"What is your impression of him?"

"I don't know him well enough to make an informed opinion. Why? What are you thinking about?"

"I don't think that I like him. He rubs me the wrong way. I don't feel like I can trust him with my daughter. I have this funny feeling up my spine."

"Mike doesn't like him either," Wendy said, not realizing that she opened the door to a whole other subject.

"Mike? What do you mean?"

"He doesn't like Josh."

"How does Mike know him?"

"I'm not really sure," Wendy fibbed, "but, I do know that he was not happy when he found out that she was going to the prom with Josh. They even had an argument about it."

"When?"

"At the repast after Grandma Mo's funeral."

"Where was I? I didn't see them fighting."

"It wasn't a huge explosion, John. Just a small argument."

"Is that why she was so upset on the way home?"

"You noticed that?"

"She is my daughter, Wendy. I do pick up her downhearted moods once in a while. I've also learned not to ask any questions."

"Mike suggested that she tell Josh to get lost, and in turn she told Mike to get lost. She was extremely aggravated at him."

"Why?"

"She thought that he was trying to tell her what to do."

"And nobody tells Maggie what to do," John said with recognition of the fact.

"Exactly."

"Why would he even try?"

"Well, he's fond of her. They got along very well in those three months that he lived here. They are still very good friends."

"Sure. He's like another big brother. That's probably why he was being so protective. Don't you think?'

"Yeah, sure ... You're probably right."

Maggie and Josh had planned to go to a movie at the mall, but she was a little surprised when Josh drove to the new drive-in for the movie. He did not mention that the plan had changed, and it was news to her.

"I thought that we were going to the Mega-plex at the mall."

"Did you? I could have sworn that I told you that we were going to the new drive-in," he lied, knowing full well that he never mentioned the word drive-in. "It doesn't make a difference, does it? I mean, if you want to leave ..."

"No, we don't have to leave," Maggie said, ignoring her inner voice that was screaming at her. She decided to use this situation to make a point. She wanted to prove to Mike that he was wrong about Josh.

Josh, on the other hand, had different plans. Fifteen minutes into the movie, Josh shifted his position and leaned in to grab and kiss her. For some reason, she did not push him away, and that was her first mistake. She was thinking that it would be payback for what Mike had done with Desiree.

Soon, she was in over her head. What began as an experimental kiss became a little more heated. Nothing felt right. He did not kiss like Mike, and was not as gentle when he touched her. He was also much more forceful than he was back in September, as he groped at her body. This foolish experiment had gone horribly wrong, and she needed to bring to an end what had become a very uncomfortable dilemma.

"Josh, stop. That's enough!" she said.

Josh did not stop, but seemed to work a little faster, trying to undress her as quickly as possible. His hands were very busy, and his ears ignored her pleas.

"Stop Josh!" she demanded, then when he once again ignored her, she made sure that he understood that she meant business. This statement was made with her knee.

As Josh writhed in a jackknife position, Maggie shoved him aside, then started to put herself back together.

"What the hell did you do that for? What kind of psycho are you?" Josh said as he gasped for air.

"I told you no, Josh. You were not listening to me," she reasoned, "Now did you get the message?"

"Oh, I got the message, you bitch. Loud and clear."

"I can't believe that you attacked me like that. What were you thinking?"

"I was thinking that I wanted to get laid, Maggie, what do you think?"

"What made you think that you could get away with assaulting me?"

"I thought that you wanted it. You kissed me back."

"I kissed you. That was it. I didn't expect you to attack me."

"You really are a virgin, aren't you? You're a tease, too."

"Mike was right about you," she admitted, which was not easy for her to do.

"Who is Mike? That guy, your uncle?"

"He's not my uncle," she said defensively.

"Then, what is he? Your bodyguard? Your guardian angel? What did the asshole say to you?" Josh asked, still trying to recover pain emanating from his ruptured body parts. Where was an ice pack when you needed it?

"He told me not to trust you."

Maggie insisted that Josh drive her home immediately, and from that moment on, the date was over. The drive-in was a half and hour away from her home, and close to the mall, which in turn was close to someone else's residence. Instead of spending another half hour traveling with Josh in the same car, she asked him to drop her off at Mike's condo. From there, she would figure out what to do. She planned to ask Mike to give her a ride home or call her Dad or Wendy to pick her up. She did make sure that Mike's car was there, before she told Josh to leave.

Once left alone on Mike's doorstep, she broke down a little bit because of her intimidating experience. Something like that had never happened to her before, and she felt so vulnerable. She needed the comfort of someone that she loved, and the first person that she thought about was Mike.

Then, suddenly had this horrible feeling of despair. "What if he has company?" she thought, dreading another face to face with one of his take home floozies. There was also the prospect that he might be unhappy with her. She did say some terrible things to him on his aunt's lawn, and they hadn't spoken since. But, she had not other choice. She had to knock on the door, or she would be forced to walk home.

She rang the doorbell, and there was no response. It wasn't until she rang the doorbell again that the music was turned down and she heard someone approach.

When he opened the door, she noticed that he looked a little disheveled and scruffy from a missed morning shave, which made him a bit more attractive in her eyes, if that was possible. He was dressed in a dark blue half buttoned down casual shirt which draped out over his blue jeans. He was not the usual clean shaven, lawyerly Mike that she was used to seeing.

"Maggie!" he said, obviously stunned to see her standing there at his doorstep. Immediately, he felt his heart pounding in his chest as he saw her face. She looked exhausted and a little bit vulnerable, and her eyes were wet from the tears. She was adorable.

"I'm sorry to bother you Mike, do you have company?" she asked, hoping that he was alone, but given his appearance, that chance was fifty-fifty.

"No, sweetheart, I'm alone."

"Good." she sighed with relief.

She walked into the door, looked into his eyes, then suddenly fell apart and hugged him, burying her head into his chest. As she hugged him, he struggled to kick the front door closed behind her with his bare feet.

"Maggie, what's wrong?" he asked as she cried in his arms.

She squeezed him so tightly that it scared him. She was almost breaking his ribs. He wondered if something had happened to a family member and he delicately asked what was wrong. He was relieved to find out that no one had died or had a terminal disease. He kissed her forehead and she let go, then he lead her into the living room, where he turned down the volume on the stereo further and they sat next to each other on the couch.

"Tell me. What is it?" he said as he put his hand on her clenched hands.

She took a deep breath, as he wiped a tear from her eye with the other hand, and she prepared herself for the mea culpa.

"You were right about him," she confessed as she looked directly into his eyes.

"Right about who?"

"Josh."

"Oh God, what did he do?" Mike asked as he closed his eyes. A sudden fear of what she had to say started to run through him.

"He took me to the drive in," she sniffed.

"Uh oh …"

"And he got a little … aggressive … and wouldn't take no for an answer. I kept saying no and he wouldn't stop."

"I'm going to kill the little shit!" he said, feeling the rage grow inside of him. He suddenly stood up and started to pace.

"Mike, you don't have to. I took care of it."

"What did you do?"

"I punted his walnuts into next week." she said, and for the first time she cracked a little smile.

"Good girl. Couldn't have happened to a nicer guy," Mike said with a sigh of relief as he sat back down. He tried not to imagine the pain that Josh had experienced, but he also felt a sick kind of satisfaction at the same time.

"Then I told him to drive me home, but I was so close to here. I wanted to get away from him as soon as I could. I just wanted to come here, and re-group before I go home. I'm sorry."

"Don't be. I'm glad that you came here," he insisted.

"I had to talk to you. You're the only one I could tell about this. I wanted to tell you that I was wrong."

"There's no need, sweetheart."

"I can call my Dad to pick me up."

"No, I'll drive you home. Don't worry about that. I'm just glad that you're all right. You are all right, aren't you?"

"Yes … no … I don't really know. I just can't believe that I was so stupid. I thought that we were going to a regular movie theater. When he pulled up to the drive-in, I should have told him that I was against it. But I said that it didn't matter. Why did I do that, Mike?"

"You trusted him, Maggie."

"But you told me not to trust him."

"Since when did I know everything? I've got a long history of making stupid mistakes. Maybe you wanted to prove that I was wrong."

"I should have trusted your judgment. You were right."

"I'm sorry that I was right. Believe me, I take no pleasure in being right about this. This is one of those cases that I wish that I was wrong."

"I was scared, Mike."

"I know, baby," he said as he reached out and held her tightly, "I'm just glad you're okay."

At the first opportunity, he asked her if she wanted a soda, and she nodded her head yes. When he opened the door, all he could find were beer bottles and Gatorade in his bachelor refrigerator. Finally, after arranging a mental search party, he was able to find a bottle of Pepsi.

He walked over and handed her the soda and he opened a beer for himself. He chugged half of the bottle immediately, as he tried to get the image of Josh with his hands on Maggie out of his head. How dare that snake put his hands on her! He wanted to ring Josh's neck. He wanted to put his fist through the wall. but, he did not outwardly show the rage that he felt.

He sat down and put his arm around her to comfort her some more, and she leaned into him, as he rubbed her back. Then, she looked up and inspected his appearance, reaching up to feel the beard stubble on his face.

"I've never seen you like this. You're usually so perfect. Even when we painted that day, and you had paint all over you, you still shaved."

"I didn't expect to see anyone today. I could shave, if you want."

"No, don't. I like it. You look rugged. Rough face, messy hair ... bare feet. You look very sexy."

"Do I?"

"Absolutely."

"Well, don't expect me to keep it. I do have to go to work on Monday."

"Why not? You could start a new trend over at Maddock and Associates."

"I'm sure that they'd appreciate it," he laughed.

She continued to gaze up at him and caress his stubbly face, and she smiled at him admiringly. Her stare gave him this sudden urge to lean down and kiss her, but at that moment, the doorbell rang an stopped his advance.

"That ... must be the pizza," he said with a little disappointment as he excused himself.

Maggie exhaled slowly, and she cursed the doorbell. She returned to drinking soda on the couch with her feet up on the coffee table, waiting for him to return, wondering what would happen next.

He brought the pizza into the living room and asked her if she had eaten, which she had. She thought that it was funny that it was almost eight-thirty, and he was having such a late dinner.

"So this is how bachelor's live?" she asked. "Beer and Pizza?"

"Pretty much. I'm not much of a cook if you don't count the Ramen noodles."

"So this is all you eat?"

"I do go out to dinner from time to time. With my important lawyer friends," he joked.

"Don't you ever get a home cooked meal?"

"Not unless Wendy or my Mom are cooking ... or you. You're a very good cook, you know."

"Thank you."

"You could always come over here and cook for me if you don't think that I'm eating right."

"I may take you up on that offer."

"Please do."

"Alright. I will," she promised. This was a promise that she intended to keep.

He opened the box and breathed in the steamy aroma of the pizza.

"Are you sure you don't want any? It's good. Pepperoni and sausage!" he tempted in a singing voice while using a slice of pizza as his tool.

She watched as the pizza slice danced in front of her eyes, and the temptation was too much to resist.

"I really shouldn't. I already ate."

"Maggie, don't try to impress me by denying yourself. You know that I already think that you are perfect. One slice is not going to kill you."

"Okay, I guess that I'll have just one," she relented.

"That's my girl," he said.

She grabbed a slice and a paper plate that was supplied by the restaurant, and took a bite. He was right. It was delicious. He turned on the television, and the two relaxed and watched a game while eating their pizza. They were very comfortable with the situation and enjoying each other's company. There was a compatibility between them that seemed very natural, almost like it was second nature. For her, this disastrous night was turning into a date to remember.

Then her thoughts traveled back to the drive-in and her horrible experience, and she was once again kicking herself for being such an idiot. She had placed her trust in the wrong person.

"He said that I was a tease," she blurted out, which threw a wrench into the comfort zone.

"He doesn't know what the hell he's taking about," Mike replied.

"Maybe he's right. Maybe I sent him the signals. I didn't mean to. I never wanted to be with him. I just wanted to go out."

"Don't blame yourself, Maggie. He's just an idiot."

"An idiot that I still have to go to the prom with."

"Do you have to go?"

"Mike, it's only a week away. I've got the dress, and the shoes and everything else. He rented a tux and we have a limousine to take us there. It's too late to back out now."

"So you're stuck."

"Yes, I'm stuck. I'm going to the prom with the last person that I want to spend the evening with. I'd rather spend Friday night, eating pizza here with you."

"Sounds good to me, at least I wouldn't have to worry about you."

"You would worry about me?"

"Are you kidding me? After what you just told me? I'm probably going to be a basket case."

"Really?" she asked.

"Really. Even after you neutered him at the drive-in."

The couple laughed, and he was happy to see her enjoying herself.

"Do you feel better now?" he asked.

"I'm always better when I'm with you."

"I'm glad to hear you say that." he replied.

"I don't deserve it, you know. I can't believe that you're even speaking to me after all those horrible things I said to you at Joe and Sarah's house."

"You were telling me what I needed to hear, Maggie," he reasoned.

"But, you were right."

"It doesn't matter if I was right or not. I had no right to tell you what to do. It's your life. I can't tell you how to live it. Like you said, I haven't earned that right."

"I can't believe that I said that."

"It's true, though. We both know it.

"Anyway … I'm sorry."

"So am I."

She was happy to know that he forgave her for jumping down his throat after his grandmother's funeral. At least that matter was settled, as it had been a burden on her shoulders ever since she realized that he was right.

"Tell me something Mike," she said, thoughtfully.

"What is it?"

"Am I wasting my time?" she asked.

"What do you mean, exactly?" he said as he took another gulp of beer.

"The two of us. I know that you care about me, but is it just some stupid fantasy of mine? Do you think that you could ever love me the way that I love you?"

He paused as if his heart stopped, but his heart was beating quite rapidly. As he searched in his mind for something to say, the truth kept popping to the top of his brain. He tried to keep his feelings from being exposed, but it had been such a long hard journey on this road of denial that he desperately needed to take another course.

"You can tell me the truth. I can take it," she said uncomfortably, sensing his apprehension and dreading his answer.

"Maggie, I already do love you."

"But, as a friend, right? Part of the family?"

"It's so much more than that."

"What do you mean by that?" she asked as she shifted her position and gazed into his eyes.

He knew that this was the moment that she had been hoping for. From this moment on, things would change between them if he only admitted the truth. For some reason, he finally decided not to hold back any longer. Suddenly, he finally felt the courage to tell her how he really felt.

"I can't deny it anymore. Especially after what happened to you today."

"Deny what?"

"How I feel, sweetheart," he said, then paused, about to reveal his secret, "Maggie…I'm in love with you."

"You love me," she said as a statement, almost in disbelief.

"With all my heart."

"Like a lover? That kind of love?"

"Yes."

"How did this happen?"

"You wore me down, I guess."

"You actually love me?"

"I adore you, Maggie," he admitted, "I think about you all the time. I even dream about you. You were right. You knew it all along."

She sat there for a second, with her hand over her mouth, and was stunned by his declaration. It was almost like she was dreaming, and hoped that she would not wake up. But, this was real. She wanted to scream with delight, but a sudden calmness came over her, and she knew what she wanted.

"Are you happy, now?" he said, exhausted from finally letting the secret out. He felt such a tremendous relief, like a weight had been lifted off his shoulders.

"I'm very happy," she said. "How long have you felt like this?"

"I've been fighting it so long, Maggie, I don't even know. I'm sorry it took me so long to admit it. But I can't live another day without you. I'm done pretending."

"And you don't care what anyone else thinks?"

"I don't care. Let them say what they want."

"So … no more Desirees?"

"Never again. And no more Josh for you, Missy."

"Definitely not, except for the prom, of course. But, I'd rather be with my boyfriend, eating pizza and doing other things."

"Boyfriend. I like that. I like that other things part too."
"So do I."

She stood up and then sat on his lap. Immediately, his mental exhaustion turned into stimulation.

"Tell me something," she said as she played with the hair that was in his eyes, then stroked his stubbly face.

"What would you like to know?"

"When you dreamed about me, what was I wearing?" she asked as she carefully started to unbutton the rest of his shirt.

"Oh, I don't think that I want to go there."

"Tell me."

"Most of the time, you are wearing the pink teddy. Other times, you are wearing a bathing suit or nothing at all."

"Nothing at all? How would you know that?"

"My imagination can do wonderful things, sometimes," he said weakly as she opened his shirt, completely exposing his chest, and she brushed her hand across it, caressing him gently. Her intimacy made him plead for mercy.

"Now you're not being fair."

"What?" she asked innocently.

"You can't expect me to keep my hands to myself if you keep doing things like this. I am a man, after all. I can't keep telling myself no."

"Then don't." she said as she shifted, straddled his legs and kissed his neck.

His body was ready to respond to her, but his brain kept trying to resist. His brain was losing. He closed his eyes and tried to concentrate on anything else but her, but it was not working. She was all that he could think about.

Finally, he could not take it anymore and met her kiss with his own, flipping her onto her back. He kissed her lips, her cheek and as he kissed her neck, then she whispered his name and had a request.

"Make love to me," she said, seductively.

"Maggie, There is nothing in this world that I want more."

"Then, what's stopping you?"

"Are you sure that's what you want?" he said as he looked for any doubt in her eyes. "Especially after what happened earlier?"

"I didn't want him, Michael. I always wanted you, and only you. And I want you now. Please don't say no this time."

"It isn't possible to say no this time."

"Then don't."

They began to kiss more passionately, and as they kissed, he started to unbutton her top, kissing her neck. Then suddenly, he stopped.

"Wait, wait. Hold on a second," he said, then kissed her quickly. He abruptly stood up and held out his hand.

"What are you doing?" she asked, afraid that he was rejecting her again.

"Maggie, I don't want your first time to be on a couch." he said.

She smiled, then placed her hand into his as he helped her stand up from the couch, and then he lifted her into his arms. He brought her into the bedroom and laid her down on his bed. They embraced again, this time more passionate and more active in many ways. He kissed and caressed her entire body and the result was a feeling of ecstasy that she had never experienced before.

He pulled away again, still upon her, and cradled her head. He looked directly in her eyes as he asked the questions again.

"Now, you are sure this is what you want?" he asked.

She smiled softly, and the look on her face told him that she had no reservations. The feeling of his bare body against hers was warm and natural, and she knew that the next step was the right one.

"Yes, I love you, Michael. This is what I want," she assured him.

With that, there were no more questions or doubts. They embraced and she finally got her wish.

After they made love, she laid on her back, and he was on his side stroking her lovingly and gazing at her.

"You're so beautiful," he said. "I love you so much."

"I love you too, Michael." she replied.

"How are you doing? Are you okay?" he asked her.

"I'm extremely satisfied," she assured him, a bit worn out by the lovemaking.

"I hope so. I tried to ... well, you know ... since it was your first time. I was a little intimidated."

"I couldn't tell. You had total control over the situation."

"I knew what to do to please you, Maggie, but after that...I became very nervous."

"Why is that?" she giggled in disbelief.

"You waited your whole life and I was the first one. It's a lot of pressure."

"What were you worried about?"

"I was thinking about what Wendy told me. She said that the first time is not always ... pleasant."

"I think that she was trying to scare you off. Protecting my purity."

"Probably, but I knew that it was the truth."

"You must have been the first for other girls. What did you do then?"

"I was never the first for anyone before you."

"All those women, and you never slept with a virgin?"

"No, baby. You were the first ..." he said as he leaned in and kissed her, "and you will be the last."

He returned to his place upon her, and the two exchanged a mutual kiss. Then he kissed one side of her face, than the other, causing her to smile. He cradled her head, resting on his elbows on either side of her.

"So what happens now?" she asked.

"Well, now I give you my high school ring and ask you to go steady," he teased as he kissed her neck.

"Seriously, Mike," she said, not knowing the inside joke.

"Now I tell the world that you're my girl, starting with your father and Wendy."

"I still can't believe that you're in love with me," she said.

"I can't believe you love me. What are you thinking?" he joked.

"I'm thinking that I'm a very fortunate girl."

"I still don't know what did I did right."

"You didn't have to do much, Michael. All you had to do was walk into the church at the christening. I was yours from that point on."

"For me, it was the first time I saw you on the beach. You took my breath away," he said. "It was an image that I've tried so hard to forget."

"Why did you try to forget?"

"I was afraid."

"Afraid of what?"

"Afraid of being in love. It scared me. I was never in love before," he said. "But, it was easy to love you. The hard part was trying to forget you."

"Now, you're not afraid?"

"After what happened today, I realized that I could lose you, and the fear went away. I didn't want to waste any more time. I love you too much, Maggie, and I want us to be together."

"You would have never lost me," she said. "I always believed that all roads led here."

At around ten-thirty, he drove her home. He offered to walk her to the door, but she didn't want to try to explain the circumstances of her new form of transportation. Josh's treachery would be a secret between Mike and Maggie, as would the change in their relationship. Even though Mike was now eager to tell all the world of his love for Maggie, she convinced him to wait until after the prom until they revealed their secret.

While in the driveway, they checked the windows for curious onlookers, and when there were none, they kissed goodnight. As she opened the door and said goodnight again, he asked her about the color of her prom dress.

"It's turquoise blue," she replied with a knowing smile.

"Blue, huh? I'm beginning to think that this was all a conspiracy."

"Obviously," she replied.

"What were you trying to do to me?"

I was trying to make you fall in love with me, of course," she said with a sly smile.

"Mission Accomplished," he said. "I adore you, Maggie."

"I love you too, Mike."

She blew him a kiss, then she closed the door and walked to the to the front door of her home. He watched her go in, then sighed and smiled to himself. He paused for a second to recall their night before he put the car in reverse to start his journey home.

Chapter Thirty-Three

THE SECRET

On the night of the prom, Maggie dressed in her gown, and was ready for Lizzy, Josh and Lizzy's date, Samuel to show. They had planned to take pictures in the backyard. She was hoping that John would be there to see her before she left. He had planned to cut out early to be there, but a late emergency with one of his patients kept him at the office.

"I hope that Daddy gets here before I have to leave."

"He'll be here," Wendy assured her, although her assurance was more a hope than a certainty.

The doorbell rang, and Maggie could not wait to see Lizzy, although she was earlier than expected. She also thought that it might be her father. Maybe he forgot his key. The person who was at the door was someone she did not expect.

When Maggie opened the door, Mike looked at her with amazement. She was breathtaking. As he stood there with his mouth open, she was the first to speak.

"Mike!" she said with astonishment, "this is a surprise! When we talked on the phone last night, you didn't tell me that you were going to be here."

"I wanted to see you on your special day," he said, "But, I didn't know that I could cut out early until earlier today. I wanted to surprise you."

"I'm very happy that you are here," she said as he walked inside the house and she closed the door. She wished that she could hug and kiss him, but was afraid that they would be discovered by Wendy and their cover would be blown.

"I like to make you happy," he assured her. "You're my girl."

"I love to hear you say that," she said.

"I love saying it."

He moved in a little closer and noticed that she was wearing the angel pendant.

"I see that you're wearing the necklace," he said as he reached over and lifted the charm into his hand, then let it softly down into it's place.

"I told you that I loved the necklace. It's gorgeous."

"Sweetheart, you are more beautiful than anything that I've ever seen," he said affectionately. "You're just overwhelming."

"Do you like the dress?" she said as she twirled in front of him.

He grabbed her hand, leaned into her and whispered softly into her ear.

"I love the dress, and you look breathless in it, but I have to admit you were more beautiful on Saturday," he said as he gently put his hand around her waist and pulled her close. "We can get that pizza and go back to my place. You just say the word."

"Careful, Mike. Wendy is right in the kitchen," she whispered with a giggle.

"I can't help it. I want you all to myself," he explained.

He lifted her right hand to his mouth and kissed the inside of her palm, which made her shudder. They looked at each other, hungry to kiss, but then they heard footsteps and quickly separated.

Wendy walked into the room, since she had heard the doorbell ring. She had expected to see Lizzy as well, and was surprised to see Mike standing there. She gave him a wary look.

"This is unexpected."

"I aim to please," he replied with an impish glance at Maggie, which made her blush.

"Aren't you supposed to be at work?"

"I got out early."

"Are you going to control yourself today?"

"I am not here to make any trouble. I promise."

"Because it's a very special day for her."

"I know," he said, assuring both women that he had planned to be a good boy. With that guarantee, Wendy returned to the kitchen.

The doorbell rang, and Maggie turned to Mike with a word of caution.

"Don't kill him, okay?" she whispered in his ear.

"Who me?" he replied. "What makes you think that I want to kill him?"

"Experience," she replied. "Really, Mike. I'm serious."

"I'll be a saint. I promise."

"You better be a good boy," she directed in a playful way.

"I'm always a good boy," he teased, "but, I'm going to expect a reward."

That comment made her slap him playfully on the arm.

Maggie opened the front door and saw that the three other prom attendants were there. Josh took one look at Mike, and almost turned around. He remembered the last time the two were together, and it was not a pleasant experience.

As Mike kissed Lizzy on the cheek, he stared at Josh, and with one look, Josh knew that Maggie had spilled the beans about that previous Saturday. Mike played nice, through clenched teeth, and when he was re-introduced to Josh, he was extremely courteous. Josh, however, noticed that the handshake was a little too firm and the stare was a little too lethal.

He offered to retrieve some soda from the kitchen, when only the young men wanted. He walked into the kitchen, passing Wendy, who returned to the living room where the prom attendants were waiting. Suddenly, the door burst open and John ran into the home.

"I'm so sorry Maggie. I hope that I'm not too late," he said apologetically. He kissed Wendy first, then gazed at his daughter.

"Maggie, you look absolutely beautiful," he said as he kissed her cheek.

"Thanks Daddy."

"Lizzy, nice to see you again. You look wonderful."

"Thanks, Dr. Stanton."

"Dad, you know Josh, and this is Lizzy's date, Samuel."

John shook both of the young men's hands, then noticed that Mike came out from the kitchen, carrying two cans of soda.

"Mike ... I didn't expect to see you here."

"I came to see her off," Mike explained.

John seemed to accept the story, mainly because he was more worried about being late for the pictures that he was about to take. The group walked outside as John, Wendy and Maggie were occupied with finding the best place to take the pictures. Mike finally had an opportunity to have a little chat with Josh. He did so while keeping an eye on Maggie, to make sure that she did not catch him misbehaving.

"I want you to know that if you lay a finger on her tonight, I will cut off your balls and shove them down your throat," he warned in a low, menacing voice.

"Man, I don't want any trouble," Josh said, backing off.

"No trouble. As long as you keep your hands to yourself."

"I guess she told you about Saturday."

"I wouldn't bring that up if I were you. It's taking all the willpower I have to keep me from kicking your ass."

"I'm sorry, okay?"

"I'm not the one you should apologize to."

"I will ... I promise."

"So, I am clear?"

"Crystal clear." Josh replied in a weak tone.

After pictures Josh ran into John, who had planned to give Josh the obligatory warning of his own.

"Listen Josh, I would like to speak to you for a moment."

"Dr. Stanton. I know what you are going to say. I got the message from Rambo over there already."

"Rambo?" he asked, as he turned and his attention was directed at Mike.

"Yeah. He already took care of it. Very convincing. I will be a perfect gentleman. Don't worry."

"You better be," John warned, a little surprised that Mike had already threatened the date. "That's my job," John thought to himself as Josh walked away. Then he watched as Wendy took a picture of Mike and a positively beaming Maggie.

"What is going on over here?" John asked himself in a low voice.

The prom attendants finally left in the limousine, and Michael had planned to leave at that moment, but he could not bring himself to leave. He could not relax until he saw Maggie back home and safe. He spent the rest of the evening at John and Wendy's house, waiting for her to come home. Wendy knew of his intentions, but Mike tried not to make it obvious to John. But now, even John could tell that something was fishy. Maybe it was the fact that Mike watched the window every time a car passed.

At eleven o'clock, Mike even started to pace a little bit. He was not wearing a hole in the floor, but it was quite obvious that he was nervous about something. It was enough to make John wonder what going on.

"Wendy ... what is he doing?" John asked when Mike was out of earshot.

"I think that he's worried about something." Wendy said, trying to be vague.

"Why is he still here?"

"I told him that he could stay in the guest room tonight."

"Why? He lives only thirty minutes away."

"I think that he wants to make sure that Maggie gets home all right." Wendy said, but didn't explain any further.

John nodded his head, but her answer left John more confused than before. Then, as if he had just had a moment of epiphany, John suddenly wondered why Mike had such a keen interest in his daughter. He knew that they were friends, but this looked suspicious. Why was he so protective, anyway?

"Wendy, are you sure that this is just a big brother thing?" he asked as he started to stare in Michael's direction. It was obvious enough to make Wendy try to divert his attention.

"Hon, would you like to come upstairs with me?" she whispered alluringly, trying to change the subject.

"Hmm?" he asked, still looking at Mike with suspicion and not hearing her seductive tone.

"Johnny ... I'm trying to seduce you. Please try to pay attention."

He heard the word seduce and that got his attention.

"What, sweetie?" he asked as he finally looked away from Michael and into his wife's loving eyes.

"I asked you if you would like to come upstairs with me."

"Now?"

"Yes, now," she said, "stop giving Mike suspicious looks and come upstairs."

"I was not giving Mike suspicious looks," John said, trying to defend himself and be as convincing as possible.

"Yes you were, my darling," she scolded, lightly. "Now, leave him alone and follow me. I have something to show you."

"Wait ... I just want to ask ..."

"John, the baby is asleep and someone is already keeping vigil waiting for Maggie to come home. We don't get these opportunities very often."

"But why is he keeping vigil? That's what I want to know."

"That can wait until tomorrow. I need you now," she insisted.

It was at that moment that John got the hint. His wife wanted him to give her that special attention that only a husband could give, and she was not going to take no for an answer. All of a sudden, he could not think of anything other than making love to his beautiful wife. The questions for Mike would have to wait until the next day. There were going to be many questions.

"Mike ... see you tomorrow," John announced as he took Wendy's hand and she led him off the couch and in the direction of the stairs.

"Goodnight Mike," Wendy said as she walked with her lover.

"Goodnight," he replied as he watched them walk up the stairs and disappear into the upper hallway.

About an hour later, John and Wendy lounged together after making love, and she noticed that his mind was elsewhere.

"John, what are you thinking about?"

"It's about what happened before. I have this feeling that I can't shake."

"What do you mean?"

"Wendy, what is going on between Maggie and Mike?"

"What do you mean?"

"He was acting like someone who is in love. Am I seeing things?"

Wendy decided to just come out with it and not beat around the bush. Wendy could sense that something was happening and John needed to be prepared.

"He loves her."

"Mike loves Maggie?"

"Yes."

"Does she know?"

"I don't know."

"Does she love him?"

"Oh God, yes."

"How did I know that you were going to say that?"

"It's kind of obvious. John. She's been after him for about a year. She's got the …"

"Hearts in the Eyes? How did I miss that?"

"You weren't looking," she replied.

"And you're sure that he loves her?"

"You saw him, John, you yourself said that you thought that he was in love."

"I saw it," he sighed. "I know what it looks like."

"It has finally happened to him."

"But, did he tell you that he loves her?"

"Not in so many words. I think that he's afraid to admit it. He's been fighting it tooth and nail for a year."

"How did this all happen?"

"Well, it all started with my grandmother."

Wendy told the story of Mike and Maggie as best as she could, but she kept out all of the parts that he might not want to hear, such as the attempted seduction and the interrupted tryst in Maggie's bedroom. John did not need to hear those details. What Wendy did say was that Maggie had loved him from the start, and that Mike had tried in vain to resist her.

John wasn't really surprised. He had seen the way that they looked at one another earlier that night while taking pictures and the smile on his daughter's face. He noticed how Mike acted that night, and how he would not leave until he saw that she came home safely. That was not just concern for a family member. Mike had been genuinely worried about her.

"I've got to talk to him," John said with determination.

"I'm sure that you can talk to him tomorrow."

"I can't believe that I didn't notice it. It was right in front of my face for months. I knew that he had a fondness for her, but I didn't think that he loved her. I thought it was more of a connection between friends."

"He hid it well, John. But, he was in a constant struggle with his feelings."

"But, why?"

"Think about it, John. When he met her, she was seventeen years old with a doting father who just happened to be his cousin's new husband. He is worried about everything but his own happiness."

"He didn't think that I would approve? I don't get it."

"Why do you think? He probably thought that you were going to wring his neck."

"Wendy, why would he think that I would disapprove? I like Mike. I know that he cares for Maggie, and would be good to her. That's what any father wants for his daughter."

"But, the fact that she was your daughter made him resistant because she was special and he did care for her. He was not going to just jump in, like he has with so many others. He did not want to run the risk of hurting her."

"So now things have changed?" John sighed.

"I don't know. Something was different tonight. He was more comfortable, somehow. Maybe he's going to tell her tonight. Maybe he's told her already. God knows he's waited long enough."

At around midnight, Mike was still continuing his vigil. He was a bit tired, however, and his eyes were making his quest impossible. He decided to sit on the couch, and then rested with his feet up. Before he knew it, he had fallen asleep.

She walked in the door after her long night, carrying a bag that contained her dress. After she hung the dress up into the hall closet, she noticed that Mike was asleep on he couch. She had been surprised to see that his car was still in the driveway, and smiled when she saw him asleep on the couch. He looked so adorable. She walked over, crouched down in front of him and kissed him on the head, stroking it gently. The feeling of her touch awakened him and he opened his eyes to see her glowing face.

"Hello sweetheart," he said with a smile.

"Hi."

"When did you get back?"

"Just now."

"What time is it?"

"Around one."

He yawned and sat up, and she sat on his lap, put her arms around him and kissed him.

"Did you have a good time?"

"Yeah. The prom was nice. But, the rest if the night could have been better. Afterwards, we went to a party, and some kids got really drunk and were acting ridiculous. They got kicked out, though," she said.

"Was your boyfriend one of those guys?"

"Who, Josh? He's not my boyfriend. My boyfriend is tall, dark and handsome."

"Is he?" he said.

"Yes he is," she teased.

"I've got to meet this guy," he said, and his statement was met by a giggle and a kiss.

"Oh, by the way, Josh was a perfect gentleman."

"Good for him, and his jewels."

"It was almost like he was afraid to touch me."

"I would have broken all of his fingers."

"I know what you said to him. Balls down his throat. Nice touch."

"The rat," he sighed. He knew that was going to happen. "Are you mad at me?"

"Why should I be mad at you?"

"For interfering."

"Well, now that you're my boyfriend, I'm glad that you interfered."

"My instinct told me to follow the follow the limousine and sit in the parking lot until you were returned safely into my arms."

"I am surprised that you're still here."

"I wanted to make sure that you got home all right."

"You didn't have to wait up."

"I wanted to. I didn't exactly make it, but."

"It's the thought that counts. I'm glad you're here. I missed you."

"I missed you too."

They looked at each other, and then kissed again, a bit more passionately than before. Then, knowing where they were, she decided to call it a night.

"I better get to bed. I have a long day tomorrow," she said. "Lizzy is picking me up at seven."

"Seven o' clock? You have barely enough time to sleep."

"We want to get an early start. We're only there for one night, and coming home on Sunday in time for the big soirée."

"Oh yeah, Allie's party. I almost forgot. I've had so many other things to think about."

"Wonderful things," she agreed.

She stood up from his lap, and held his hand as he followed her towards the stairs, and close to his room.

"There's room for two in there," he said, hinting at the room. "You can go in your room, break out that pink teddy that I've been dreaming about, come back here, and we can get reacquainted."

"You know that I wish that I could join you, but that is not the best way to let my father know that we are a couple."

"Oh, you don't think that he would like it if we both came out of the guest room tomorrow morning exhausted from a night of lovemaking?"

"No, I don't think that he would, oddly enough," she said with a laugh.

"He'll know about us soon enough, Maggie. I'm going to talk to him tomorrow."

"Tomorrow? I'll be down the shore tomorrow."

"I know."

"Why do you want to talk to him while I'm not around?"

"It's been a week since we got together. I don't want to wait any longer. I want to talk to him man to man and get it all out in the open before Allie's party on Sunday. I want everyone to know about us."

"You don't fool around, do you?"

"No, Maggie. Once I have made a decision, I go all out."

"But, my Dad."

"Don't worry. Wendy will protect me. She's small, but she packs a good punch," he laughed.

His joke made her roll her eyes a bit, since the thought of him talking to her father alone made her nervous.

"I don't know about this."

"He likes me, remember?"

"That was before you became my lover."

"It'll be fine. I'll just tell him that I'm madly in love with you."

"That might work."

"And I want your body."

"Now, I'm worried."

"No, really. I'll be good. I promise," he said, "Just go down there tomorrow and have a good time with your friends. But, do me a favor, be careful. It gets crazy down there on prom weekend."

"So I've heard. I'll be careful. I promise."

"I wouldn't want anything to happen to you," he said. "You're the most important person in my life."

"Keep saying things like that and I will join you in the guest room, forget about the consequences."

"I mean it."

"So do I.".

He looked down at her and brushed her hair off her shoulder, and cupped his hand on her right cheek. He leaned down again and they exchanged another kiss.

"Goodnight Maggie," he said, "I will miss you."

"Goodnight."

Chapter Thirty-Four

LIKE A DREAM

The next morning, John had planned to have a long talk with Mike, but was called away to the office. John usually did not go in on Saturday, but this morning he received a call from a frantic mother who had a screaming child. In these instances, he was always on call. He met the mother at the office, and little Frank Cooper felt much better. He had a ear infection, and John was able to give him ear drops to deaden the pain, then he wrote out a prescription to cure the infection.

Patricia Cooper and Frankie had not been in his office for nearly a year, since John's divorce from Darlene. Patricia had been good friends with Darlene and did not approve of the way that John and Darlene parted ways. He lost a few other customers that way, but he still had plenty of patients to keep him in kids and diapers throughout the week.

After the revelations of Darlene's affair with George Cooper surfaced, he did get some of the patients back, but Patricia Cooper did not return. Any thought about Patricia Cooper had not crossed his mind since, until her frantic phone call that morning. Her new pediatrician was away, poor Frankie was in distress, and John Stanton was her only option. He was surprised to receive a genuine thank you from her for going out of his way to help out her and her eight year old son.

When Mike awoke the next morning, he walked into the kitchen and found Wendy there. She was making scrambled eggs and bacon, and he could not wait to feed his hungry stomach.

"So what happened last night?" Wendy asked as she spooned some eggs onto his plate.

"What do you mean?"

"About Maggie, you big dope," she said as she shook her head. "I saw her this morning, and from the look on her face, you can tell that something is up."

"I don't know what you're talking about," he said, feigning ignorance.

"Actually, she's had this dreamy look on her face ever since that date with Josh."

Mike started to chuckle under his breath because he knew that Josh had nothing to do with it. He tried to hide the smile on his face, but he could not disguise his happiness.

"I knew that it wasn't Josh," she stated.

"It could be. You never know," he laughed.

"Mike, cut it out."

"What?"

"Tell me what you know or I will hit you with this spatula."

"Okay, okay," he said with his hands up in front of his face to block any strike from her lethal weapon.

"Maggie and I are together. We are a couple."

"You're kidding! So you did tell her that you love her?"

"Yes."

"How did it happen?"

"It just came out. I couldn't stand it anymore, Wendy, I love her so much. I had to tell her."

"So, what are you going to do?"

"I'm going to talk to John today."

"I can't believe it!" she said with astonishment.

"I finally came to my senses."

"Wow … this is moving fast," she commented.

"Faster than you think," he said as he dug into the pocket of his blue jeans and pulled out a small white box and put it on the kitchen table.

"Michael! Is that what I think it is?" she gasped as she put her hands over her mouth.

John returned home at about noon, with a bouquet of flowers for his blushing bride. He could not believe that it was more than a year since their wedding. The year had gone so quickly, and it was a happy one. "All years should be as good as this one" he thought.

He walked into the living room and found Wendy on the floor playing with Allison. Wendy was trying to teach her how to walk, but Allison would just stand, wobble and land back on her behind. He leaned against the doorway and smiled as he watched two of his girls. He was so contented. It was a wonderful feeling.

Wendy felt his presence and turned around, noticing the flowers in his hand.

"What's the occasion?" she asked

"I'm hoping to get lucky tonight."

"You got lucky last night," she teased, "Besides, you don't need flowers for that."

"Well, then it's a thank you for last night," he said as the two met in the middle of the room and kissed. After kissing, she thanked him for the bouquet and took it into the kitchen to put in a vase. As she left temporarily, he lifted his baby daughter.

"Hello, Allie!" he said as he kissed and cuddled her. She giggled at his attention. He brought Allie into the kitchen to watch Wendy put the flowers into the vase.

"So, I saw that Mike's car is still in the driveway. Where is he?"

"I think that he went outside. He's waiting to talk to you," she said. "He told me that he loved her, John. He finally admitted it to me."

"So this is it, huh?"

"John, you have to prepare yourself. There's more."

"What do you mean?" he asked.

As if Mike's ears were burning, he walked back into the kitchen. When John saw him, the conversation was halted. Wendy never was able to prepare him.

"John, can I talk to you a second?" Mike asked.

"Sure," John replied.

After Wendy took Allie from John, he invited Mike to sit down in the living room so that the two men could have their heart to heart. John awaited the news that he thought that he was well prepared to hear.

Mike looked at John and took a deep breath. He was a bit more nervous than he expected, but he no longer wanted to keep the secret.

"John ... I'm in love with Maggie," Mike said.

"I know. Wendy told me," John said, confidently.

"I know that Wendy explained some things to you already."

"Actually, Wendy thinks that you were in love with her from the beginning. Is that true?"

"Probably. But, I tried not to think about her in that way because she was your daughter. I didn't know how it would work out. She was very young. She's still ... young."

"I know."

"But John, I can't help myself. I love her. I can't live without her," he explained, "I know that there is a nine year difference between us ..."

"Mike, I'm not one to talk. There is a thirteen year difference between Wendy and I ... but she was a bit older than Maggie is now."

"I know."

"And she's never had a boyfriend before."

"I know."

"So, I need to know, what are your intentions towards my daughter?"

"John, the reason that it took me so long to make this decision is the fact that she is your daughter. I wanted to be sure about my feelings for her, before I took the next step. I want you to know that I am not taking this lightly, and I've thought long and hard about this before I made this decision."

"What decision is that?"

"I want to ask her to marry me."

John suddenly felt a little faint. He did not expect to hear those words. He would have been prepared for anything else. The news hit him like a brick to the temple.

"That ... I wasn't prepared for," he said, while almost needing a paper bag to breathe into. This was all so unbelievable. "Wendy didn't tell me."

"Wendy didn't know until this morning. She probably didn't get a chance to tell you."

"Isn't this a little quick?" John asked, feeling a little faint. He was prepared for the declaration of love, but not this. Now he knew why Wendy said that he had to prepare himself.

"John, It may seem sudden to you, but it's been forever for me. In a way, it's almost like we've been courting for the past year. We have this connection... you know? My affection for her has been building month by month. I've been in love with her for months and I just had to finally admit it to myself, and let the truth take over."

"Mike, I know that you care about her, but marriage?"

"John, I love her. She's a beautiful, intelligent, loving woman who loves me. There is no one else on this earth that I would rather spend the rest of my life with. I want to build a life with her, have a family ... all of it."

"You do know that Maggie wants to go to college to be a nurse."

"Yes, I know. Nothing is going to change that. The marriage doesn't have to happen right away. I just want her to know that I am serious about our future together. I want to show her that I am committed to her, and the best way to do that is to ask her to marry me."

John contemplated Mike's words, and the feeling behind them. He knew that he had a deep affection for Maggie that could not be denied.

"So you love her that much?"

"I love her more than anything else in my life, John. I want to marry her. I don't care how long it takes, five days or five years."

"Are you sure that she feels the same?"

"I know she loves me, John. We make each other happy."

"Then that's all I can ask for."

"So I have your blessing?"

"You're a good man, Mike, and you're a good friend. I know that you have great affection for her and I can see that you are in love with her. I trust you. I'm glad that it's you."

"Thank you John, I will love her for the rest of my life."

"I'm counting on it." John replied as he stood up to shake his future son-in-law's hand. Then the two men hugged.

As Mike left, after hugging Wendy and kissing little Allie, John felt a little wistful. Soon, Maggie would be engaged and then eventually married. Mike was now the man who would be responsible for her future happiness.

"I can't believe this is happening. I feel like I just got hit by a truck."

"Mike is a great guy. I couldn't have picked a better husband for her."

"I know he is. He couldn't have a better woman."

"They are the perfect match ... just like us." she assured him as she reached out to hold his hand. "He will make her very happy."

"He better," he said, sounding as if it were a joke, but inside he was serious.

Earlier that day, Maggie and Lizzy drove down to the Jersey Shore and checked into a beachfront motel that John had reserved for her. He wanted to make sure that the motel was a good one, so he paid for everything. He did, however, make them promise not to have a party in the room, and that warning was more or less for Lizzy since Maggie was normally not the type.

As Maggie and her friends sat on the beach, roasting and checking out the guys, her thoughts were at home. She was worried about how her father would react to the big secret, and wished that she was there to help Mike break the news. After lunch, she tried to call Mike on his cell phone, but she could not get in touch with him.

The entire day passed without any contact with her new lover. She started to worry, and Lizzy noticed that she looked like she was not having a good time.

"Maggie, what's going on?" Lizzy asked.

"It's nothing," Maggie replied.

Usually when Maggie needed to think, she wanted to be alone. Unfortunately, she was supposed to be having a good time. Finally, she could not take it anymore and she excused herself from the group. She walked to the nearest pier and look out onto the horizon. Once there, she finally felt the peace that she was looking to find as she gazed out into the waves.

She called Lizzy to tell her where she was, so that he friends would not worry about her when they returned to the motel to find that she was not there. She just explained that needed some time alone to think, and she would return to join them just after sunset. She just wanted to see the sunset for some odd reason.

When Lizzy hung up the phone, she explained to the other friends that Maggie needed some time alone. It was at that moment that another of the girls pointed out that someone interesting was walking towards them.

"Ladies, I've got dibs on that guy! That guy is gorgeous!" the young woman said with enthusiasm.

Lizzy's rolled her eyes, but turned her attention to the object of the girl's affection. It was then that she recognized the man who was walking towards them.

"Oh my God!" she said.

Maggie relaxed on a bench on a dock that overlooked the crashing of the waves onto the rocks below. Alone in her tranquility, she tried to collect her thoughts and think about what direction she would now take with her life. She breathed in the salty air and closed her eyes, thinking about what had happened that morning and how she wished that she was there.

She was so transfixed with her thoughts and the ambiance around her, that she did not hear someone approach from behind her bench.

"So, I heard that you're going to watch the sunset."

Maggie could not believe her ears. She recognized the voice immediately. It was Michael! It was the answer to her prayers.

She leapt up from the bench and hugged him, and the two exchanged a long, sensuous kiss. Once separated, she told him that she was happy to see him.

"I can't believe you're here!" she said, as the two of them returned to sit on the bench. "How did it go?"

"Pretty well, incredibly."

"Was he surprised?"

"Very. I think that he's a little shell-shocked. I told him that we loved each other, which he was pretty prepared for. But, when I told him the other thing, I think that is what threw him for a loop."

"What other thing?"

"You're not going to believe it."

"Try me. I'll believe anything."

Mike paused and prepared to stun the love of his life.

"Maggie, I love you with all my heart. I want to be your first and only lover. I want to wake up and see you every morning. I want the last person I see every night to be you. I want to spend the rest of my life with you. I want to be the father of your children. I want all of it."

"Are you saying what I think that you are saying?" she asked as her heart nearly stopped.

"That I want you to be my wife?"

"If that's what you mean."

He pulled a white ring box out of his pocket and opened it. To her astonishment, it was a diamond engagement ring. He knelt down in front of her, and held her hand. Her dream was about to be fulfilled.

"I love you Maggie. I can't live without you. Will you marry me?"

"Please don't tell me that this is a joke."

"It's no joke, baby. I love you more than anything."

"Michael! I don't believe it! Are you sure about this?"

"I've never been more sure about anything. How do you feel about it?"

"It's all that I've ever wanted. I want to be your wife."

"So it's yes?"

"With all my heart, yes!" she said with a tear rolling down her cheek.

The couple hugged and embraced, kissing each other passionately. Once the clinch was released, he opened the box, and showed her the ring.

"Oh Mike, it's beautiful! When did you get it?"

"This is my grandmother's ring."

"It is?"

"She left it to me in the will. When my mother gave it to me, she also gave me a note from Grandma Mo."

"What did it say?"

"The note said that I should give the ring to my soul mate, and that she knew who it was."

"Good old Grandma Mo."

He placed the ring on her finger, and it fit perfectly. They looked at each other in amazement.

"I guess that it was meant to be," he said, as he wiped the tears from her eyes and kissed them softly.

"I'm so happy!" She wept, "I just can't stop crying!"

They talked together and held hands while waiting until the sunset. When it happened, it was more beautiful than any she had ever seen.

"You do like babies, don't you?" she asked.

"I'm definitely pro-baby. Especially if they might look like you."

"Or you."

"I'm definitely into the family thing."

"I don't mean right away. There is college. I still want to go to college."

"I understand."
"But, I really want to have your children, Mike."
"Well, you wouldn't want to waste those child bearing hips."
"No, I wouldn't want to do that," she laughed.
"Or the ..."
"Don't you say another word."

The next day, Maggie was already home from the shore before noon, with plenty of time to spare until the guests came over at one. When she walked in the door, she was greeted by Wendy with a big, congratulatory hug, and happy tidings. Then, her father walked over. John was a bit guarded, but smiled when he saw his daughter's beaming face. Wendy excused herself to give father and daughter some time alone. They walked over and sat on the couch to have a heart to heart.

"Are you happy, Maggie?" he asked. "Did I do the right thing?"
"I'm very happy, Daddy. Thank you so much for your blessing. It means so much to me. I love him so very much."
"So I've heard. You know, it's all been such a shock. Two days ago, I find out that you love him, and he loves you, and then all of the sudden he wants to marry you. It's all very fast."
"He's a good man, Daddy."
"I know, Maggie, and I know that he will take care of you. I trust him with your future. That's why I said yes. I want you to be happy, Maggie."
"I'm so lucky." she said.
"Are you kidding? He's the lucky one," he said as he reached out and hugged her. He held her tightly, almost wishing that he could shrink her back to size so that she would be six again. It was very hard to let go of his first girl.

An hour later, Mike was the first to arrive, and was greeted with a hug by his fiancée. Soon, the guests started to arrive, and since Mike had called his parents with the big news on the previous night, the word of mouth spread so quickly that everyone knew of the wonderful news and wanted to see the ring on her finger and congratulate the happy couple.

As John watched his daughter's face beam with joy as she showed her friends and family the ring, he turned to look at the picture of Jenny on the wall and smiled. He wondered how she would feel at that moment.

"She would be very happy for her," Wendy assured him, as she walked over to hug him from behind. He turned around to face her, putting his arms around her as well.

"Do you think so?"

New Beginnings

"Yeah. Just look at Maggie's face. She's ecstatic," Wendy pointed out as they watched Mike and Maggie celebrate their love.

"She is happy, isn't she?"

"You've done a great job, John. She's a wonderful woman."

"I know. She is great isn't she? Scott is a great guy too. I guess that I did do a good job after all."

"Yes, John. Jenny would be proud."

Made in the USA